Worldly Goods is Michael Korda's first novel, but his previous bestsellers include *Charmed Lives* and *Success!* He was born in London in 1933 and educated in America, Switzerland and, after serving in the R.A.F., at Oxford. He has also written regularly for the *New York Times*, *Vogue* and *Playboy*. He is editor-in-chief of the New York publishers, Simon & Schuster.

"Michael Korda has fashioned an intriguing tale around a world of wealth and power – a world he knows better than anyone else."

ROBERT LUDLUM

"A first novel that reads like anything but."

KIRKUS REVIEWS

"A high gloss of readability."

LONDON REVIEW OF BOOKS

"The most fascinating novel I've read this year."

NANCY FRIDAY

"*Wordly Goods* has the sweep of *Kane and Abel*, the glamour of *Celebrity*, plus an ending that is guaranteed to keep you up very late indeed."

PAUL ERDMAN, author of *The Last Days of America*

Worldly Goods

Michael Korda

CORGI BOOKS

The author wishes to express his thanks for research material in the following documents:

Raul Hillberg, *The Destruction of the European Jews*

Eugene Levai, *The Black Book on the Martyrdom of Hungarian Jewry*

Alex Weissberg, *Desperate Mission*

– and also the memoirs of Admiral Horthy and Prime Minister Kallay, as well as the transcript of the proceedings of the Nuremberg War Crimes Tribunal in the case against Admiral Horthy.

WORLDLY GOODS

A CORGI BOOK 0 552 12255 6

Originally published in Great Britain by The Bodley Head Ltd.

PRINTING HISTORY

Bodley Head edition published 1982
Corgi edition published 1983
Corgi edition reissued 1983

This book is set in 9½/10 Mallard

Corgi Books are published by
Transworld Publishers Ltd.,
Century House, 61–63 Uxbridge Road,
Ealing, London W5 5SA

Made and printed in Great Britain by
Cox & Wyman Ltd., Reading, Berks.

For Margaret, as always, with love
And for Dick and Joni, in friendship

What though the spicy breezes
Blow soft o'er Ceylon's isle;
Though every prospect pleases,
And only man is vile. . . .

– BISHOP REGINALD HEBER

Part One

Capital Gains

1

The day Paul Foster's corporation was listed on the Big Board of the New York Stock Exchange in 1958, a reporter who managed to break through the secrecy surrounding him asked for the key to his success. 'The first billion dollars is hard,' Foster replied. 'After that, it's easier.'

But, Foster reflected, as he stood in his office and looked down at the lights of Fifth Avenue twenty years later, it was never easy.

He turned away from the windows and went back to his desk with a sigh. When he had arrived in New York, he didn't have so much as a telephone — he walked around with his pockets full of small change and made his deals from telephone booths. A telephone booth was still all he needed, even today, he told himself. He might even be better off.

For years Foster had resisted the temptation to build an organization around himself, but this was America — display was an asset like any other. Grudgingly, he had consented to a building, to a company cafeteria, a reflecting pool in the lobby, the private dining room next to his office.

What did it matter to him, after all? Foster seldom left his own office, which was designed around the paneling of a Grinling Gibbons library, a masterpiece for which Foster had outbid the Metropolitan Museum of Art. The priceless library shelves now contained rows of identical gold-embossed red morocco-leather file boxes, one for each year since the founding of the corporation. Every box cost over $500 to make — Foster kept one of the most distinguished leather craftsmen in America busy on his behalf — and all of them were empty. Foster didn't believe in keeping records, particularly where other people could get at them.

The boxes were for show. The only safe place for information was in his head. He trusted nobody. Trust was for amateurs.

Foster despised amateurs, and feared weakness — particularly his own. In his youth, he had learned the hard way that only the strong survive. Those who lacked discipline died, to be disposed of with brutal, sordid efficiency.

Foster had survived. He exercised daily and kept his weight down. Hardship as a young man had given him the blessing of a small appetite. Food did not concern him. He preferred to eat at irregular hours, an apple, a couple of poached eggs, a yogurt, which made it difficult for him to bear the social occasions he had to attend from time to time. Several times a year he was compelled to mingle with his executives, but he seldom succeeded in putting them at ease — in fact, he invariably seemed out of place and uncomfortable among them.

Even Foster's fellow tycoons were nervous with him — not so much because of his reputation for cunning and ruthlessness, which they envied, but because on the rare occasions when he spoke in public or gave interviews, he sounded like a European social democrat rather than an American capitalist. Among the chairmen and presidents of other *Fortune* 500 corporations, Foster was regarded as a dangerous liberal, suspected even of being an intellectual. He read books, talked about Ricardo, Marx, Keynes, Sartre, spoke several languages fluently and once startled the financial editor of the New York *Times* by suggesting that the country needed a Hegelian Secretary of the Treasury.

It might have surprised the man from the *Times* that Foster sometimes woke up screaming in the middle of the night. When it happened, Foster put on the light, took five milligrams of Valium, washed down the pill with a sip of ice water from the thermos flask by his bed, glanced at the enameled clock that stood on his night table along with a plate of fresh fruit, several books, a note pad and a gold pencil, and tried to calm his nerves by looking at his paintings.

These terrible dreams were like the visible fragments of past horrors that lay deep below the surface. Because

12

of them, Foster preferred to sleep alone. He usually took a woman to the master bedroom, which he never used when he was alone, then withdrew to his own smaller room later, when she was asleep. Often he contrived to send her home in the middle of the night with the chauffeur, with the excuse that he had work to do.

During his one brief marriage — to Dawn Safire, the movie star — he had been unable at first to persuade her to use her own room, but after a few nights in Foster's bed she moved into it gratefully. 'I need my beauty sleep, darling,' she said, 'and besides, your nightmares give me the creeps.'

Dawn hadn't considered what married life would be like with a man who never went to bed before one o'clock in the morning, who often woke at three and invariably rose at five to telephone Europe for the London, Paris and Zurich opening prices. Foster acquired a movie studio to further her career, bought houses in Malibu, Cuernavaca and Beverly Hills, entertained lavishly wherever they went — but his heart wasn't in it. Even at his own dinner parties, he usually spent most of the evening on the telephone. Dawn complained that she was tired of Foster's black telephone spoiling her carefully arranged table. When she came down one evening to find a white one in its place among the flowers, she decided the marriage was over.

There was no difficulty about alimony. Foster pyramided Dawn's assets, put her into shopping malls and marinas, wrote her in as a silent partner in a couple of mining deals. He made her rich, and though she left him for a Mexican millionaire, he let her have the houses in Malibu and Cuernavaca, selling the property in Beverly Hills to a Lebanese arms merchant for twice what he had paid for all three, so that he lost nothing by his generosity. 'It's nothing personal,' Dawn told him the day they signed the papers. 'I just don't seem to be able to make you happy, so what's the point?'

The answer to that question, if there was one, eluded Foster as it had Dawn. He had a taste for good living, but no great capacity for enjoyment. The past still haunted him, no matter how many companies he controlled (and he had long since lost count).

A light glowed on Foster's desk — he hated bells and

buzzers — and he turned on his Speakerphone.

'What is it?' he asked.

'Lord Meyerman is phoning from London.'

'Put him on.'

Foster had a reputation for brusqueness with his staff, but in fact he was merely shy, and found it difficult to handle the normal amenities of life. His mania for privacy was notorious. Other powerful men hired PR firms to get their names in the papers. Foster paid a fortune to keep his name *out* of them. A private elevator took him directly to his office so that he wouldn't have to cope with people saying good morning, or struggle to remember their names. There was nothing absent-minded about Foster — he simply liked to concentrate on one thing at a time. Whenever he was involved with a woman, his secretary put a card by Foster's telephone with the lady's name typed on it, in case he forgot.

There was a click, and a guttural voice said, 'How are you, dear boy?'

Lord Meyerman's accent was hard to place. The layers of assimilation covered one another so that he spoke upper-class English in an accent that embraced Budapest, Vienna and Berlin, with an occasional, unmistakable trace of Yiddish.

'I hear you did Biedermeyer out of Wyoming Oil Shale,' Meyerman continued. 'A nice acquisition.'

'It's not settled yet.'

Meyerman chuckled in his oily, knowing way. Foster could see him in his mind's eye: the predatory nose, deceptively softened by flesh; the hard black eyes, which so many people mistakenly assumed were soulful or sad, to their subsequent cost; the double chin. Doubtless he was smoking a cigar, the fat fingers holding it with surprising delicacy.

'I didn't telephone to pry into your secrets, Paul. Though, *entre nous*, I would try not to provoke Biedermeyer *too* often. He looks like a buffoon, but he's a bad man to have for an enemy.'

'One already has so many enemies. The only way *not* to have them is to fail.'

'Quite. But some are more dangerous than others. Actually, dear boy, that's why I'm calling you. I heard an alarming piece of news.'

14

'Alarming for whom?'

'For your old friends the Greenwoods. But also for you, and possibly even for *me*. Irving Kane is writing a book about your family.'

'That's not possible!' Foster said, his voice rising. 'What could he *know*?'

'He's an investigative reporter. A question here, a question there . . . I don't suppose there's any way he could find out *everything* — still, if he goes through the testimony from the Nuremberg trials and pays a visit to Budapest, he could put two and two together, I suppose. He's no fool.'

There was a brief silence while Foster considered this news. He was not a man who reacted quickly to things. He preferred to think them over, to weigh the options. Experience had taught him, along with much else, that it was wiser to let the other person do the talking — even Meyerman, who knew more about Foster's affairs than most people. That Kane was no fool Foster already knew. He felt a slight spasm of tension somewhere in the pit of his stomach and willed himself to suppress it.

'Are you still there, dear boy?'

'Of course,' Foster replied, with an effort at calm that, he knew, was unlikely to convince Meyerman. It was more a question of pride. 'How did you find out?'

'I sat opposite his publisher at dinner last night. David Star. Do you know him?'

'I've met him.'

'He was full of enthusiasm. A big best seller! He's convinced of it.'

'That's all we need, my God!'

'Well, it's worse for the Greenwoods, dear boy. Not too many people will want to do business with the man who tried to sell the Nazis the atomic bomb!'

Foster sighed. There were things it was wiser not to talk about over the telephone. Meyerman should know better, he thought to himself. He wondered if there was some way to take advantage of Kane's inconvenient interest in the affairs of the Greenwood family, but could find none on the spur of the moment. One always had to allow for the unexpected in making one's plans, but a scandal about the Greenwoods now, at this delicate moment, would be premature. Once Kane started to dig into the Greenwood story, who knew where it might lead him?'

'Can he be bought?' Foster asked.

'I wouldn't think so. It might even be dangerous to try.'

'Most people can be bought.'

'You can only buy journalists by giving them a better story. I don't think you'd want to do *that*, Paul. The first thing to do is to find out how much Kane knows. Perhaps you could meet him casually, at a party . . . Pump him a little. Sound him out.'

'Possibly . . .' Foster did not sound enthusiastic about the prospect. It was all very well for Meyerman, whose appetite for parties was insatiable and who had never spent an evening at home in thirty unless he was giving a party himself, but Foster seldom went anywhere.

'Star told me that Diana Beaumont is giving a party for Kane in a couple of days, as a matter of fact. A perfect opportunity. Kane drinks like a fish, so you should have no trouble finding out what he knows. It might do you good, you know . . . You should go out more often, dear boy.'

Foster gave a grunt of annoyance. He disliked advice, and besides, he had suddenly remembered who Diana Beaumont was. 'I can't go there,' he said sharply. 'She's Nicholas Greenwood's mistress.'

A soft noise came over the Speakerphone — Meyerman puffing on his cigar, weighing his words, playing for time.

'I think she's about to become his *ex*-mistress, dear boy,' he said with the enthusiasm of a man who loves gossip. 'I've heard rumours that the old man wants Nicholas to settle down and get married. A *serious* marriage, you understand. Diana wouldn't be at all what the old man has in mind.'

'Nicholas is already married.'

'Only in the eyes of the Church, dear boy. A source of mine in the Vatican says there's been some negotiation there about an annulment . . . Well, you can imagine, it wouldn't be difficult with the Greenwoods' influence. Nicholas' poor little wife has been in a private institution for years. A lovely place near Montreux — all that good Swiss air! They say there's an attendant for every patient, a French chef, a ski instructor . . . Of course, I don't suppose it matters much to her, since she's in a strait jacket most of the time.'

16

'Does this Diana know she's about to be dropped?'

'Dear boy, women always know when a man no longer loves them. They have *Fingerspitzengefühl*, a sixth sense, for betrayal. Diana may not know she knows it, but she knows it.'

'Spare me the philosophy!'

'It's not philosophy, it's experience. If you had listened to me before you married Dawn ... well, never mind *that*! More important, there's another piece of news, something almost nobody knows *du coté de la famille Greenwood*.'

'So far, all this is not news, it's gossip.'

'Never underrate gossip, Paul. Because something is frivolous does not mean it's unimportant. Your lack of frivolity is a weakness, not a strength, though it runs in the family, I suppose ... Anyway, it seems Nicholas and Diana had a child.'

Paul reacted silently. In any situation, you had to search for the other person's soft spots, weaknesses, the little secrets precariously concealed. He wondered if this was Nicholas' soft spot, but doubted that it was. 'An heir to the Greenwood fortune?' he asked quietly.

'No. The child is illegitimate. He was born ten years ago, when Nicholas and Diana were first living together. The old man was furious. After all, he was in a very *delicate* position himself at the time, and the last thing he wanted was a scandal. So he descended on the young lovers with his checkbook and his lawyers, and had the child placed in a foster home.'

'Nicholas didn't object?'

'He always does what his father tells him to. *You* know that. It must have been painful for Diana, but she was very much in love, and I don't suppose she had much choice. Also, she thought Nicholas would marry her. A woman will put up with anything as long as there's a prospect of marriage. So now she still isn't married, and Nicholas is playing around very publicly with other women ... You should by all means go to her party, I think. It might be even more useful to talk to her than to Kane. And certainly more stimulating.'

'How much does she know about the Greenwoods?'

'Ah,' Meyerman said with pleasure, 'I was wondering when you'd ask that ... Not as much as you and I do. Be

17

careful, though, Paul.'

'Of what?'

'She's an intelligent woman.'

'There's nothing wrong with that.'

'No indeed. But so often men underestimate a woman's intelligence when she's beautiful. Even you. You'll keep in touch?'

'Naturally.'

'It's always important not to forget one's real friends, isn't it? That was old Greenwood's first sin, after all . . . *Auf Wiederhören*, dear boy.'

Foster leaned back in his chair and sighed. Meyerman knew everything and everyone. Despite his ungainly appearance, he cultivated women like a connoisseur, with astonishing success. Foster had shared a flat with Meyerman in London when they were both young and poor — my God, how poor! — and even then Meyerman's success with beautiful women was phenomenal. Meyerman was convinced that most women secretly preferred ugly men. Women liked to have a monopoly on beauty, and felt there was less at stake with an ugly man. Perhaps Meyerman was right, Foster reflected. Certainly he had been envious of Meyerman's conquests then, and resented the many evenings he spent walking the wet streets of Fulham in his thin, cracked shoes while Meyerman monopolized the flat with a girl. Foster had had only one girl in London, and it was not a subject he cared to dwell on.

Once a week, on Sundays, Foster had pressed his one good suit with an old steam iron, polished his shoes to a high gloss and gone off by himself for a couple of hours. Meyerman assumed his roommate had a girl friend and kept asking Foster who she was, but after some hesitation Foster answered that he merely went to the Ritz Hotel in Piccadilly and stood in the lobby.

'Whatever for?' Meyerman asked.

'I watch the rich people coming in for tea. When I can afford to, I want to do it right,' Foster replied. When he became rich, he had done just that, though he no longer had the time to enjoy it, which was really rather sad, he thought, and typical of life.

Foster pushed the button on his intercom and said,

'Savage.' The desk in front of him was empty. Foster seldom dealt in paperwork — it was the function of people like Burton ('Bud') Savage to look after the details. Savage was an able administrator who believed in numbers the way some people believe in God: they explained everything, they justified everything, in the end they *were* everything.

'Savage.' The harsh voice boomed metallically from the speaker. Foster winced and turned down the volume.

'What do you know about David Star's company?' he asked.

'Book publishing. Twenty, twenty-five mil a year, tops. Star inherited it from his father, has most of the stock. He's shopped for a buyer a couple of times, but he doesn't really want to sell — unless some *shmuck* offers him twice what the company's worth. Funny you should ask. There's a rumor in the street that Nick Greenwood is making Star an offer. I think it's probably bullshit.'

'Why?' Foster drummed his fingers soundlessly on the desk top. It never failed to annoy him that Savage, a Connecticut WASP and a Yale man, used Yiddish words to convey his toughness, or what he liked to call his 'street smarts.' Foster seldom swore in any of the languages he spoke, and on the whole disliked people who did.

'What's Nick going to do with a book-publishing company, Paul, for Chrissake? You'd get a better return on investment putting the fucking money in a savings bank.'

Foster stared at the Speakerphone. Savage was probably right — where numbers were concerned, he was hard to fault — but he didn't know all the facts. The Greenwoods might well think it was worth buying a publishing company just to know what was in Irving Kane's book. And possibly to suppress it. Nicholas might not be thinking that way, but it would certainly have occurred to the old man, as it had already occurred to Foster.

'Put out a few feelers,' Foster said.

There was a pause at the other end while Savage turned this over in his mind. He cleared his throat noisily, then expressed his disapproval. 'You want my advice, Paul,' he said, 'walk away. What the hell do we need a book-publishing company for? It's not a business you want to be in.'

'I like books.'

'So join the Book-of-the-Month Club. Listen, Paul, I know how you feel about Nick Greenwood, but we can't spend the company's money just to stop him every time he wants to acquire some cockamamie thing. What have you got against Nick, anyway? It doesn't make business sense to spend millions of dollars just to spit in his soup!'

Foster did not seem to have heard Savage's objections. 'Talk to Star,' he said.

'For real? If we're not careful, we could end up owning a fucking publishing company.'

'That's all right.'

Savage sighed. 'You're the boss,' he said glumly. 'I just hope he doesn't want cash instead of stock.'

'Even cash. At any rate, you can *suggest* cash. Once we have him on the hook, we can always find a way to make him take our stock.'

'I hope you know what you're doing, Paul. Speaking of which, do you want me to keep on shorting silver?'

'Until I tell you to stop.' Foster turned off the Speakphone and pushed the signal button for his secretary. 'Do we have a file on a Diana Beaumont?' he asked.

There was a moment's pause. 'She's cross-referenced under Nicholas Greenwood, Mr. Foster.'

'Anything recent?'

'We received an invitation from her a few days ago. A publishing party, I believe. Your name was probably on somebody's PR list.'

'What did we do?'

'We declined.'

'Now we accept. Send something over, with a note that I've changed my mind.'

'Flowers?'

'I don't think so. Everybody sends flowers. Perhaps caviar.'

'How much, Mr. Foster? A pound?'

'Certainly not. Two kilos, at least. Bring me the file and a pot of tea.'

Foster paced back and forth in his office until his secretary, one of three motherly women who were used to his long hours and irregular habits, silently placed a silver tray and a leather folder on his desk.

Foster waited until he was alone, poured his tea and opened the file in front of him. He was not a man who read

20

the gossip columns, so most of the information in the file was new to him, and largely irrelevant. He already knew almost everything there was to know about the Green-woods and spent a fortune to keep up to date on their business affairs, but Niki Greenwood's private life was of little interest to him. Foster knew Niki had a mistress, but the fact was neither remarkable nor had it until now figured in any of Foster's calculations.

He quickly read through the one-page synopsis of Diana's life. Some of it was vaguely familiar to him. She owned a small public relations business, which specialized in best-selling authors and movie people. Foster nodded approvingly. He admired women who were independent. After all, Nicholas was rich and generous, so this Beaumont woman didn't have to work . . .

She had been a famous model fifteen years ago. Foster nodded again. It was hardly to be expected that Nicholas would choose a woman who wasn't a great beauty. There was a brief mention of the fact that she had been married to the young Earl of Windermere for two years. Foster closed his eyes. He remembered that there had been a scandal. The earl had been involved in drugs, orgies, gambling . . . Foster couldn't remember the details, but Meyerman would surely know.

He shuffled through a bunch of press clippings, then picked up a recent W photograph and examined it carefully. For one heart-stopping moment he thought the picture had been misfiled, that it was not Diana Beaumont, but someone else. Had somebody played a joke on him? he wondered — but the idea was absurd and unthinkable. He closed his eyes and saw a face exactly like Diana's, then opened them again and examined her picture more carefully. The eyes were the same, the mouth — even the shape of the face. It was uncanny, and upsetting. Foster sipped his tea glumly and fought down a host of memories. Sentimentality is a weakness, he told himself firmly, then picked up the photograph again.

Diana Beaumont had been caught leaning casually forward at a formal dinner party. She was laughing, her long blond hair framing an almost perfect face. She had high cheekbones, her breasts were partly exposed by the cut of a daring evening gown. The way she wore her hair was different, he told himself hopefully, but in every other respect he had to admit the resemblance was startling, despite the deep tan and the dramatic make-up. He was hoping that her voice would at least be different. If it were the same, it would be too much to bear.

At the edge of the photograph a man was whispering in her ear, his face partially cropped off. From what Foster could see of the eye and the nose, it looked like Nicholas Greenwood. He did not seem happy.

Foster looked at Greenwood's eye at the edge of the photograph. Greenwood was a playboy — nothing like as tough as his father. Old Matthew Greenwood was a killer; Nicholas for all his wealth, was still an amateur. Foster understood Niki's weakness — he had found it years ago, and it nearly cost him his own life. One day he would pay Niki back for that, but not yet. The timing had to be right. In the end, timing was everything.

He bent over and examined the photograph of Diana Beaumont again. She had the firm look of an athlete, the clear eyes of someone who took care of her health. He searched for flaws and found none. What, he wondered, was her weakness? With men it was usually vanity or greed; with women, it was often more complicated.

He put the photographs and clippings back in the folder neatly — Foster hated disorder — then finished his tea. It was surprising how much trouble a little thing like a book could cause, even at this late date . . . It would make a good story, Foster thought — good enough to make it worth $20 million or $30 million of old Greenwood's money — or his shareholders', anyway — to ensure it was never published!

He pushed the signal button again and spoke to his secretary. 'Get me the Paris office,' he said.

'It's very late there, Mr. Foster.'

'Get Rosenthal at home then. There's somebody I want him to find for me. We have a confidential file on him — Günther Manfred von Rademacher. Send it out to Paris by pouch tonight.'

But even as Foster mentioned the name, he felt an unfamiliar flush of anxiety. Rademacher was someone he had hoped to forget for the rest of his life. Foster closed his eyes briefly. High above Fifth Avenue, in his air-conditioned office, surrounded by antique paneling so beautiful that Hoving of the Met had actually wept when

Foster outbid him for it, Paul Foster could suddenly smell the smoke, the ashes, the filth of the concentration camp. Scenes of terror and betrayal flashed in his mind, and despite the carefully regulated temperature, he felt himself perspiring.

Then he forced himself to think logically. The Greenwoods had more to fear that he did.

He opened his eyes, breathed deeply, and resumed his study of Diana Beaumont's file. One shouldn't go into a situation without doing one's homework, he told himself. Only amateurs do that.

2

'Who else is coming to the party?' Nicholas Greenwood asked as he paced restlessly around Diana Beaumont's bedroom.

'Nobody much,' she called out from the bathroom. 'It's for Irving Kane's new book. Aaron Diamond, his agent, will be here. David Star, the publisher, you know. A lot of press people, writers, movie producers, that sort of thing. Not your kind of evening at all.'

'I may stay for a few minutes.' Greenwood sounded like a man who hopes to be persuaded he doesn't have to. 'My God,' he said, glancing at the New York *Times* on the bed, 'silver is still going up.'

'Suit yourself, darling.' Diana emerged from the bathroom brushing her long blond hair, wearing bikinis hardly larger than a G-string and a man's silk shirt with the initials. 'NG' over her left breast. Greenwood lit a cigarette and stared at her with admiration. She was one of those women who made every commonplace act — brushing her hair, leaning over to examine her toenails, fastening her bra — into an erotic gesture. There was something about Diana's cool, calm, matter-of-fact acceptance of her beauty that attracted and infuriated him at the same time, as if her looks were an asset equal to his wealth.

It was not just that Diana was beautiful — the world was full of beautiful women. She was also strong-minded, intelligent and independent. Other women in Diana's position might have been content to live luxuriously as the mistress of a wealthy man, but Diana worked as hard as Nicholas — harder, in fact, since Nicholas was still given to fits of laziness and self-indulgence, and lacked the *Sitzfleisch* to stay at his desk ten or twelve hours a day, the way American businessmen do. Left to himself, Nicholas would have been content to be a playboy, but his father

24

would never have permitted it, and Diana had never encouraged him in that direction. She had a taste for luxury, but she enjoyed working too. She was, as she once remarked to Nicholas, not cut out for life as an odalisque, despite a figure and a sensual nature that would have qualified her for the role.

Her ancestors had bequeathed her not only an enviable bone structure but also a strong streak of Yankee common sense and caution. Nicholas had been shocked to discover, years ago, that when he gave Diana a check, she invested the money instead of going out on a spending spree. She also carefully squeezed toothpaste from the bottom of the tube, used soap until it was a thin sliver and shopped for bargains. She had more underwear than any other woman Nicholas had ever known, but she washed it herself, and even repaired it, sitting cross-legged and naked on the bed with a needle and thread, totally absorbed in the task. He tried to persuade Diana that it was easier to throw things away when they showed even the slightest sign of wear, but in this, as in so many other things, he was unable to change her. She was the first person he had met, except for his father, who refused to give in to him.

All his life Nicholas had been used to getting his way, easily, even automatically. He was rich, charming, handsome, daring. Women adored him. Few of them noticed or cared that he was also childish, impetuous and terrified of his father.

Diana had noticed, and cared. It was not enough, in her eyes, to be a rich young man with a string of polo ponies and an *équipe* of racing cars. She expected Nicholas to be a man, and because of her, he had finally confronted his father, turned himself into a businessman, taken control of the family's American interests. He owed Diana a great deal, but at the same time he resented her, and for a long time had consoled himself with other women who had no expectations of him.

Diana had been the only real love of his life, but he was no longer comfortable with her. She knew his weaknesses and understood him all too well. Besides, there were pressures on him now to make what his father referred to as a 'serious' marriage, and whatever Diana's qualities might be, they did not include a fortune.

25

Yet he was still attracted to her, and against his better judgment, he took the hairbrush out of her hand and leaned over to kiss her. Despite the deterioration of their relationship, despite the knowledge that he was going to betray her, despite his numerous infidelities, Nicholas was still moved by Diana's sexuality. It was a habit he found hard to give up, and his inability to give it up confused and angered him, making the need for sex even more urgent. Like many men, he slept with other women to prove his independence, and he rationalized this by comparing it to Diana's need for self-sufficiency. She had to have a business of her own to prove to herself that she wasn't dependent on his money. It was important to her psyche. Was it so very different that he had to prove he wasn't dependent on her for sex?

The argument had never convinced Diana, and in fact did not even convince Nicholas, but he clung to it because he needed some justification for his behavior. The worst of it was that sex with other women was never as good as it had been with Diana at its best, and he toyed with the notion that if just once they could recapture the sexual ecstasy they had felt for each other, he might change his mind and stay with her, but of course that ecstasy could not be recaptured and he knew it, just as she did, and at times he was saddened by the loss.

No doubt Diana was even sadder about it, but she was too proud to show it. She was also too proud to give him a nice, easy fuck as a way of avoiding the problem, though, in fact, a nice, easy fuck was just what she wanted, had it been presented as a peace offering instead of a last-minute demand. A half-hour earlier she might have put her arms around Nicholas and tried to recapture the old days, but he had waited until the party was about to begin, as if he wanted to prove that he came first, that he could always get what he wanted from her.

'Not now,' she said with a frown, 'I've just done my face.'

'Well, then I won't touch your face.' He opened her shirt and put one arm around her waist, sliding his hand under her pants.

'Stay for the party,' Diana said, 'then you can spend the night. I have to get dressed now.'

'What is this nonsense? I remember the days when you

26

used to meet me at the airport and we fucked in the back of the limousine.'

'So do I, but there weren't half a dozen other women in your life then. You didn't turn up at the door for a quick fuck on your way somewhere else.'

'You're the only woman I've ever loved, and you know it.'

'The sad thing is that it's probably true. Now give me back my hairbrush, please.'

'Take it if you can,' Nicholas said, holding it just out of Diana's reach. As she jumped up to grab it he put both arms around her, picked her up — she was a tall woman, but Nicholas Greenwood was over six feet, with an athlete's body — and threw her on the bed, holding her with one arm as he unfastened his trousers with the other.

Nicholas waited for her to laugh. This was a game they had played before, but Diana's gold-flecked emerald-green eyes looked back at him coldly, and he felt a certain loss of dignity, with his trousers down around his knees and his erect penis caught up in his undershorts.

'I'm not going to fight you,' she said. 'You go right ahead and fuck me. Only no bruises, please, and leave my make-up alone. I have a party to give. And if I were you, I'd take those trousers off.'

Nicholas felt his erection subside, got up off the bed, pulled up his trousers and zipped them. 'I'm sorry,' he said. 'I had underestimated your capacity for bitchiness.'

'No. You thought I was good for a quick lay, that's all. A nice, healthy fuck between appointments, along with a drink and a change of shirt. Never mind, for somebody as rich and attractive as you, that can't be hard to find. It's just not a service I render.'

'I apologize.'

She shrugged. Nicholas' ego, she knew, was such that an apology was a major concession on his part — he offered it as if it were a necklace of inestimable value.

Calmly, she examined her make-up in the mirror, smoothed her hair, straightened her bikini pants and pulled on a diaphanous black silk shirt. Diana was not one of those women who take a long time to dress. She required very little embellishment, and though Nicholas had often taken her to the Paris showings, she had never taken much interest in them. '*Haute couture* is for when

27

I'm old enough to need it,' Diana told him, and she showed no signs of having reached that age.

'We should have married,' Nicholas reflected sadly.

Diana sighed. It was a source of constant amazement to her that she still loved Nicholas, despite his betrayals. It was exactly the kind of weakness that feminists were always complaining about in women, and Diana, though she was no feminist, despised it in herself. Loving Nicholas had once been a challenge, a pleasure, an adventure. Now it was merely a burden, but one she seemed unable to rid herself of. She missed him when he was away, as he now was most of the time, but when he appeared there was a tension between them that inevitably erupted into a quarrel. They fought over the past because it was clear to both of them there was no longer a future, and at times she hated herself for not having the strength to break off the relationship once and for all.

She stepped into a long tight skirt, slit up to the thigh on one side, and bent over to put on her high-heeled sandals. 'You can't say you didn't have the chance,' she said.

Nicholas shrugged. 'It's never too late,' he said without much conviction.

'Yes, it is. I've got a career, and made a life for myself. And you have your freedom. It's what you always said you wanted, isn't it? Besides, what about the Church and your father?'

'Laura has been in that damn Swiss asylum for years — there would be no problem in getting an annulment now. And my father is very old.'

'He's still alive.'

Diana stared at Nicholas for a moment, waiting for a reaction, but he was silent. She knew all too well that he still lived in the formidable shadow of Matthew Greenwood, that he always would. Nicholas took every risk a wealthy sportsman could find, but at night a telephone call from his father would bring sweat to his brow and a slight tremble to his powerful hands. On those occasions he spoke in a language Diana did not understand, but his fear needed no words of explanation, and after putting down the receiver, he always poured himself a large brandy and went to bed without making love again.

Old Greenwood brooded over his vast empire from a

wheelchair and a hospital bed in the Villa Azur at Cap d'Antibes, where a male nurse looked after his remaining needs, and a male secretary kept him informed and in touch. In the mornings, before the breeze came up, he was wheeled back and forth on the terrace while his secretary walked beside the wheelchair, reading to him from the newspapers. It was important, Nicholas explained, to keep the old man interested in the present. When he thought about the past he became depressed and fearful, as if there were still shards of it that could emerge and hurt him, even at the end of a long life and surrounded by high walls.

'Yes,' Nicholas said in a somber voice, 'he's still alive. All the same, at this late date, matters could be arranged. We could even bring the child to live with us.'

Diana turned towards him in a cold fury. 'You bastard,' she said, 'don't you ever do that to me again. I've burned all that out of my mind. You and your goddamn father did that to me, and I've never forgiven either of you. If you ever bring it up again, so help me God I'll kill you!'

Nicholas looked at her and sighed. 'Do you know,' he said after a pause, 'I believe you would.'

'You can bet on it, Niki. I'm a woman of my word. Now, are you going to stay for this party or not? I have things to do.'

Greenwood sighed, acknowledging defeat. 'Perhaps I'll stay a few minutes. I don't expect you to believe me, but I do have a business appointment.'

'Dinner with a starlet?'

Nicholas looked furious, but held his temper in check. He was determined not to put himself in the wrong again.

'Not at all,' he said, lighting a cigarette to control himself. 'I'm going to Washington. Just between the two of us — we have developed a nuclear power plant that is small, efficient and absolutely safe. An entirely new process. We're talking about billions of dollars.'

'Will the stock go up?'

'It will take off. Of course, the government has to approve the process, and fund a pilot program in a few places. I see no problems there, but one has to be careful. There's lot at stake. Come, let's have a drink.'

'Why not? It's going to be a long evening,' Diana said.

Nicholas put on his jacket and followed her down the

corridor to the big living room overlooking Central Park, where Frank, Diana's hired butler, was putting the finishing touches to the buffet table.

'The usual, Mr. Greenwood?' Frank said, reaching for a bottle of Russian vodka.

Greenwood nodded, watching Diana as she made a quick tour of the room to see that everything was in place and that a copy of Irving Kane's new book was prominently displayed.

'Always the professional,' Nicholas said. 'Business must be improving.'

'What makes you think so?'

'Caviar. In fact, a vulgar amount of it.'

Diana turned to look at the buffet table, in the center of which sat a life-size swan carved in ice. Its back was hollowed out to hold a large can of fresh Beluga Malossol, and a small card dangled from its beak.

'Ain't it something?' asked Frank. 'It arrived a few minutes ago. Took two men to carry it up.'

'Very nice,' Nicholas said, with a hard edge to his voice. 'A gift from a wealthy admirer, no doubt.'

Diana ignored his tone. Nicholas had nothing to be jealous about, to her regret, and for that matter, not much right to be jealous. The swan intrigued her, but she could think of nobody who was likely to have sent it; indeed, when she first saw it as they entered the room, it ocurred to her that Nicholas might have ordered it as a romantic gesture, and she was therefore all the more annoyed that it was about to become an issue between them.

'I can't imagine who sent it,' she said. 'Certainly not Irving Kane. It's hardly his style, and anyway, he's always broke, what with alimony and back taxes.'

'It's a princely gesture, my dear. Even I would think twice about it. You must be very busy while I'm away to attract this kind of present. Why don't you look at the card?'

Diana picked up the card and unfastened the ribbon that held it to the swan's dripping beak. 'How odd,' she said. 'It reads: "I look forward to being there. Paul Foster." '

Nicholas glared at her, his fingers tightening around his glass. 'Have you been seeing Paul Foster?' he asked. 'Are you trying to make a fool of me? You know perfectly well

30

that Foster's got some kind of crazy vendetta against me! He did us out of that uranium-mine acquisition last year — the moment we express interest in a company he bids against us and drives the price up. He even tried to buy up enough of our stock to get a seat on our board of directors! It cost me a fortune to stop him. The man's a maniac. Everybody knows he hates me — and you're playing with him behind my back?'

'I'm doing no such thing. Control yourself.'

Nicholas' face turned red beneath his sportsman's tan. 'Don't tell me to control myself!' he shouted. 'We have an adult relationship, yes, I don't expect you to live like a nun — by God, I know you better than that! But *Foster*? A man who's after my blood?'

'Niki, I don't even *know* the man.'

'Bullshit! Foster doesn't need public relations. He's spent a lifetime hiding from the press. There's only one reason why he'd be sending you a swan full of caviar, and it's between your legs!'

'Get out!'

'I wouldn't stay if you paid me. You tell your friend Foster not to meddle in my business. And enjoy yourself. I hear that he hired call girls at five hundred dollars a night to come up to his apartment and give him a golden shower. I suppose he finds it cheaper to pay you for several sessions with caviar.'

Diana stared at Greenwood for a moment, then threw her drink carefully and precisely into his face.

Greenwood picked a silk handkerchief out of his breast pocket, wiped his face, smiled politely and slapped her with the flat of his hand so hard that she fell back against the sofa. He inclined his head gravely toward Frank, who was standing rigidly to attention, his eyes fixed on the ceiling, then turned on his heel and walked out.

Frank cleared his throat. 'Can I get you something, Miss Beaumont?' he asked.

Diana fought back her tears. 'A vodka.'

'He sure took a dislike to the swan.'

'He did that.'

'Are you okay, ma'am?'

'I'm fine, Frank. I just have to do my face again.'

'He packs a punch. You *sure* you okay?'

'Never better. Mr Greenwood has just freed me from

31

ten years of romantic illusions.'

'Can I give you some caviar?'

'Yes. And Frank: when you go tonight, take Mr. Green-wood's things with you. Anything that fits, you can keep.'

When Diana re-entered the room, after repairing her make-up, it seemed to her, in the glow of aftershock, that her first guests were visitors from another planet. Irving Kane, the guest of honor, stood shuffling and weaving in the middle of the floor, his face a mottled red and his shirt unbuttoned from neck to belly. On one side he was sup-ported by his agent, Aaron Diamond, and on the other by his publisher, David Star, a tall nervous man running to fat, with glasses as thick as the bottom of Coke bottles. Star's pale eyes seemed to swim behind the lenses as he attempted to focus on her.

'Congratulations,' Diana said to Kane, but he merely stifled a belch, then said in a pleading whisper, 'I got to piss.'

Diana pointed to the door and signaled Frank to show Kane the way, but he brushed off the butler's arm. 'Don't need no help,' he mumbled as he staggered out of the room, crashing into several pieces of furniture.

'I'm not sure he's right about that,' Diana said.

Aaron Diamond gave her a kiss. 'I apologize,' he said, wiping his lips with a handkerchief — he had a morbid fear of germs and always carried a pocketful of Kleenex and a small bottle of disinfectant spray in case he was obliged to make use of a strange toilet. 'Irving was a little high when we picked him up at the hotel, but I hadn't figured on getting a limo with a bar in the back. With traffic the way it is, he picked up a real buzz on the way over. Meet my date.'

He waved toward a statuesque young woman in a cling-ing metallic silver shift, who said a few words in a guttural language.

'She don't speak English,' Diamond said unnecessarily. 'She's a Finn or something. Big star over there, not that anybody gives a fuck here.'

Diana glanced at the young woman, who towered at least a foot and a half above Diamond in her high heels and with her hair piled up. 'Isn't she awfully tall for you, Aaron?' she asked.

Diamond studied his date carefully, as if he had just noticed, then shrugged. 'Ah, what the hell, Diana,' he said, 'you know how it is. On their knees, they're all the same height.'

'You wouldn't get an argument about that from Niki Greenwood.'

'I saw Nick leaving as we came in. He looked mad as hell, frankly. I was going to pitch him a package, but it didn't look like the right moment. I hear he's after your company, Star.'

Star nodded lugubriously and accepted a glass of champagne from Frank. 'I think it's the old man who wants it, actually,' he said. 'Nick himself couldn't care less.'

'You want, I'll make the deal for you,' Diamond said. 'I've done plenty of business with Greenwood since he bought the network and the studio. I knew his old man, too, though he's a vegetable now, from what I hear. I met him a few times in Antibes, way back. He had a cabaña at Eden Roc, big yacht, lots of girls.'

'What was he like?'

'Big guy. Bigger than Nick. Heavy accent, like Bela Lugosi.'

Star blinked. 'Kane says there's a wonderful story there. You know that for years he's been trying to write a book about the very rich Jewish families and the deals they made with the Germans? He wants to call it *The Golden Traitors* . . . Anyway, he's come up with some sensational stuff on Greenwood. In fact, he's thinking now he might build the whole book around him, like a novel.'

'I didn't know Greenwood was Jewish.'

'Everybody who matters is Jewish,' Star said. 'Kane showed me some interesting background on Greenwood. He turned up in Lisbon during the war, you know, with a lot of money. When the war ended, he was off and running. Real estate, resorts, banking, uranium when it was the fast game, you name it.'

'I remember when he bought the casino in Cannes,' Diamond said. 'They had a wheel fixed so whenever he played there, he won. He hated losing.'

'Who doesn't?' Star asked.

'Sure, but Greenwood was nuts on the subject. He was winning his own money! I wouldn't think he'd give a shit about books.'

33

'Neither would I, frankly,' Star said, 'but Nick made it perfectly clear it was his father who suggested the acquisition. He seemed a little surprised himself.'

'It doesn't figure. Guys like that buy movie studios so they can fly out to the Coast and get laid. What's in publishing for a guy like Greenwood? It's small potatoes.'

Star looked pained, though he basically agreed with Diamond's analysis. For a moment he seemed ready to defend his profession, but instead he merely shrugged. 'All I can tell you, Aaron, is that he's interested.'

'He probably wants to read Kane's manuscript,' Diamond said.

Star frowned. 'It's funny you should mention that. Nick Greenwood phoned me today, after Irving talked about his plans on the *Today* show. You know who else has called me? One of Paul Foster's heavies. *He* wanted to know if the company was for sale too. Quite a coincidence, isn't it?'

'Foster! He's one tough cookie! I've done business with him, too. You know, when Foster was married to Dawn Safire, she persuaded him to take a cruise, just to relax. He was going crazy, sitting there on a ship with nothing to do except *shtup* Dawn. Then he finds out there's a satellite and he can make telephone calls worldwide at three dollars a minute. "The hell with that," he told the captain, "I want to rent the satellite for the whole cruise."

'And he *did*. It cost him thirty-four thousand dollars. The British couldn't believe it. They asked for a certified check in advance, and one of Foster's people turned up in London with it in an hour. Foster spent the whole cruise in his stateroom making calls, happy as a clam.

'Dawn told me that he was hoarse by the time they docked back in New York, and the first thing he did when he got into his car was to place a call to Abu Dhabi. I got to say he's not a bad guy, for someone who took his name from a shoestore.'

Diana laughed.

'No, I'm not joking,' Diamond said. 'He was a refugee in London after the war, and he decided to change his name. The story is he was saving up to buy a good pair of shoes, and he sees this pair he likes at Foster's, on Jermyn Street, so he decided to name himself after the fucking store. Meyerman told me that. I go to the same place myself,' he added, pointing down at his navy-blue crocodile-skin chukka boots.

'Paul Foster may be coming tonight,' Diana said. 'He sent the caviar.'

Diamond raised an eyebrow. 'Tell you the truth, I'm surprised. He's invited everywhere, but he never shows up. You know him?'

'No. Nobody knows him. He was on the list. He declined, then he sent the caviar, with a note.'

'He's got class, no doubt about that.'

'And money,' Star added.

'Next best thing,' Diamond said.

Diana gave a good party, and she knew it. She liked people, which was rare, and knew how to make them comfortable. In the days when she had been the Countess of Windermere, before the earl had taken the dreadful slide that ended in gambling debts, sexual scandals and an ignominious flight to Australia under an assumed name, Diana's parties had been the talk of London.

When she found herself stranded in England with no assets but a title and her looks, it was Meyer Meyerman who suggested that she put her talents to use on his behalf. He was already rich and famous, and there were those who supposed his social ambitions had been fulfilled by a knighthood, but Sir Meyer was not content to take his place with the likes of Sir Jimmy Goldsmith and Sir Charlie Clore.

Meyerman aspired to better things and hired Diana for what one observer called 'a run at the peerage.' She arranged his parties, drew up the guest lists, saw to it that the right journalists and politicians were invited, and managed to get Meyerman out of the world of rich businessmen and into the *beau monde*. Stars, best-selling authors, politicians came to his parties and invited him to theirs, and eventually aristocrats, prime ministers and even royals followed. Meyerman straddled the worlds of finance, politics, the arts, the 'jet set' (as it came to be called) and the palace — a pudgy Central European Colossus with a cigar. He had shrewdly chosen Diana for her beauty, her connections and her energy, knowing that an American ex-countess and a Hungarian knight would be forgiven any excesses. 'The English,' he told her, '*love a* social climber, provided he's a foreigner. It's the native climbers they can't stand.'

The day he received his peerage from the Queen and left St. James's Palace as Baron Meyerman of Battersea, he sent Diana an envelope that contained a flimsy piece of paper. It was a deposit slip for 500,000 Swiss francs, held in her name by a discreet little private bank on the Bahnhofstrasse in Zurich. Attached to it was a card that read, 'Noblesse oblige,' followed by a sprawling 'M'.

Many people supposed that Diana had been Lord Meyerman's mistress — ugly as he was, he was reputed to have a sexual organ so large that many women went to bed with him out of sheer curiosity — but in fact Diana was already living secretly then with young Nicholas Greenwood, and her relationship with Meyerman was and remained one of friendship and mutual respect. Neither of them was the kind of person to mix business with pleasure.

When she moved back to New York to be closer to Greenwood, Diana decided to go into business for herself, though Nicholas would have been perfectly happy to support her in style. He respected the decision and understood her need for independence — though it soon became well known in certain circles that if you wanted to do business with Nick Greenwood, or Meyerman, it didn't hurt to have Diana Beaumont look after your PR account.

Diana was not ambitious herself, though she enjoyed success. She had no great desire to make a fortune or build up a large company. Her sense of humor and her enjoyment of life were too great to allow for any single-minded, compulsive drive to dominate her, and she had no feminist need to succeed for its own sake. She simply liked to keep busy, and to be independent. The Duchess of Windsor had once said to her, as she told many people, that a woman can never be too rich or too thin, but Diana thought the Duchess was not only wrong, but a poor advertisement for her own advice. Diana herself had a full, voluptuous figure and as much money as she needed. She worked because she wanted to and because it was more interesting than sitting at home waiting for Nicholas or any other man.

She would have been the first to admit that her 'relationship' — a word she hated, but what else could you call it? — with Nicholas, like her friendship with Meyerman, had brought her many clients and opened many doors. Diana was a realist — a woman in business needed all the help she could get. She consoled herself with the fact that she gave value for money. Her clients were invited to the appropriate parties, interviewed for the big talk shows, carefully rehearsed on closed-circuit television before appearing with Carson or Donahue, and introduced to the right journalists in the soothing atmosphere and flattering light of the Four Seasons, over lunch or drinks.

Irving Kane was a particularly difficult client. He had spent the first years of his career as a gifted investigative reporter, and had emerged from Vietnam as something of a folk hero. His report on Operation Phoenix made his name almost synonymous with the First Amendment in the eyes of many people, and it shot to the top of the best-seller list, which was hardly surprising, since he had a gift for turning factual reporting into what was soon to become known as 'nonfiction novels.' Kane won the Pulitzer Prize, appeared constantly on television, fought two rounds with Norman Mailer, and was swiftly corrupted by his own success. Once his discoveries had made news; now he merely sought headlines and a spot on *Merv Griffin*.

Kane drank, Kane fought, Kane made a public spectacle of himself. He was a boy from a middle-class Chicago family who had made it to Harvard and become a tough reporter, and somewhere along the way he had settled for money and fame. His reputation as a trouble-maker was so well founded that Diana would have turned him down as a client, except that she liked Aaron Diamond and David Star.

Diamond had been a friend in the old days, when she had still been married to poor Windermere, with his unfortunate taste for orgies with *au pair* girls and for baccarat, while Star, in his own quiet, shy way, worshiped her from afar — though in all the years she had known him he had never made a pass at her, except for one drunken moment in a taxi after a National Book Award party, for which he instantly apologized.

Once or twice a month Star invited Diana to dinner at Lutèce, where he gravely flirted with her, happy to be in the company of a beautiful and intelligent woman who shared his interest in food. 'If you ever decide to get married again,' he once told her over a glass of chilled *framboise*, 'I want an option.'

'You have a wife already,' Diana said gently.

'I could buy out of that contract,' he offered gallantly, but both of them knew he couldn't. He was too much of a gentleman.

As the room filled up, Diana gravitated naturally toward Star, who was industriously helping himself to caviar.

'Good crowd,' he said.

'The usual. There are no surprises in PR.'

Star brushed a stray egg of caviar off his lips and laughed, his eyes spinning behind the thick lenses. 'By the way, I hope I'm not paying for all this caviar?' he asked.

'No. It's a present from Paul Foster.'

'Ah. Meyerman's partner in crime.'

'Is he?'

'So Kane says. After all, there was poor Meyerman, teaching Commercial German at a business school off the Fulham Road in 1946, a Jewish displaced person with no prospects, and by 1950 he was already well on his way to fame, fortune, knighthood, and a life peerage. Of course you know all about that, I forgot.'

'Yes, but Meyerman was never forthcoming about the past. He did once say that behind every fortune lies a crime, but he was talking about someone else.'

'And *quoting* someone else. Foster was his partner, you know. Then he split up with Meyerman, and surfaced here in 1948. It would be interesting to know how Foster and Meyerman made their first stake.'

'Meyer never said.'

'I suppose not. What's the line in *Die Dreigroschenoper? Und der Haifisch, der hat Zähne* ...' Star exuberantly hummed the opening bars of *The Threepenny Opera*, a villainous expression on his face. 'Mackie Messer, Mack the Knife, that's Foster all right; but who he stabbed nobody knows ... Except Meyerman, I suppose. Look out for your china!'

'Why?'

'Here comes Irving.'

'Oh, God. Hi, Irving. Feeling better?'

Kane *did* seem to be feeling better, having obviously held his head under a cold tap. His spiky gray hair stood on end, and his shirtfront was soaked, but he was back in business again. He accepted a glass of champagne from Frank, despite a warning glance from Star.

'They treatin' you okay, man?' Kane asked Frank. As a civil rights advocate of the sixties, Kane considered it his duty to subvert other people's servants.

'Just fine,' Frank replied rapidly, retreating behind his bar. A Mason and a Methodist lay preacher, he had nothing but contempt for Kane, who was now helping himself to caviar cheerfully, spooning it out of the can like Jell-O, with the fierce hunger of a man determined to kill a hangover before it got started.

'Christ, Star,' he said between mouthfuls, 'I'm going to ask Aaron to get me a higher royalty rate next time round. You're giving parties like you were the fucking Czar. You been speculating on silver?'

'Paul Foster sent it,' Diana explained.

'*That* son of a bitch? You know, he tried to talk me into writing a book on what he's doing in Guatemala. It's one of his pet projects. He flew to LA to see me. I had to drive out to the airport and meet him on his plane. When we'd talked, he took right off and flew back to New York! He reminded me of Kurtz in *Heart of Darkness*. I kept looking around the cabin for skulls.'

'How did it go?' Diana asked.

'No good. He wanted to talk about literature, I wanted to talk about money.'

'Speak of the devil,' Star said, nodding toward the door.

Diana looked up to see a tall, simply dressed figure standing in the doorway. Behind Foster a large beefy man, wearing aviator sun-glasses, surveyed the room with professional care.

Foster did not seem to Diana, at first sight, at all the kind of person she had imagined him to be. About six feet tall, he had a slim, almost boyish figure. He was dressed as he always was, in a manner appropriate for an elegant funeral, and from a distance even his face was set in the lines of a professional mourner, or possibly an undertaker who took his work seriously.

Foster always wore a dark-blue, almost black suit, black shoes, a white shirt and a black silk tie. Even in a tropical climate or at one of the resort hotels he owned, he wore the same somber clothes. Early on in his life he had acquired a first-class London tailor, bootmaker and shirt-maker. His valet ordered a new suit or a dozen shirts for Foster whenever it seemed necessary, always of exactly the same cut, style and material. He never wore a watch, cuff links, a tie clasp or any other jewelry, and his suits were so impeccably fitted that it was obvious he never carried a wallet, money, loose change, keys or any of the ordinary things most men have in their pockets. When Foster wanted to remember something, other people made a note of it. In the unlikely event that he might need money, someone would be at his elbow to provide it. Body-guards, chauffeurs and administrative assistants waited to unlock doors for him, or tell him the time.

He dismissed the bodyguard and made his way across the room in Diana's direction, apparently unconscious of the fact that his entrance had stopped all conversation. None of the guests said hello to him. Since Foster disliked being photographed, he was seldom recognized, and the few people who knew or suspected who he was had never met him and therefore didn't know what to say.

When he was a few steps away from Diana, Foster paused for a moment and scrutinized her. There was something rather alarming, Diana thought, about the intensity of his gaze, as if he was trying to fix her in his memory. He looked, for one instant, faintly troubled, then he seemed to remember his manners. He took two more steps toward her, gracefully took her hand, touched it with his lips in the Continental gesture and brought his heels together without an audible click.

'Delightful,' Foster said in a low, hushed voice — though whether he was referring to the party or her-self, Diana found hard to judge. She had to strain to hear him.

Since he was leaning over her hand, all she could see of Foster close up was his short, silvery-blond hair. When he looked up, raising his head, she was surprised to find that the pale-blue eyes were not at all those of a ruthless cor-porate raider. In fact, they seemed warm and sympa-thetic. There was something conspiratorial in the way he kissed her hand, a suggestion of intimacy that somehow managed to convey the impression that she and Foster knew something nobody else in the room did.

Diana recognized Foster's instinctive gamesmanship even as she took in, for the first time, his face. The nose was strong but crooked, obviously badly broken at some time in the past. There were other traces of Foster's past on his face — the faint suggestion of old scars, thin white lines that were almost concealed by his rich man's tan, and no doubt by artful cosmetic surgery.

It was, Diana thought, a strikingly handsome face, despite signs of hard wear and extensive damage. She wondered what Foster had looked like before whatever it was had happened — probably quite different, except for the eyes, of course. For a moment she wondered if he had had a face-lift, but Foster did not seem the kind of man for that. It was instead the face of a man who was motivated by deeper, more powerful needs than vanity, one that managed to suggest cruelty and humor at the same time, a combination that Diana found intriguing, if a little chilling. There was a strong hint of sensuality in the lips, she thought; then she realized he was waiting for her to say something. Clearly he had not come there to mingle with the other guests — he had walked straight over to Diana as if the room were empty, to present her with his undivided attention.

'I'm so pleased you could come,' she said. 'And thank you for the caviar.'

'It's nothing.' Foster dismissed it with a wave of his hand.

'Do you know everyone?'

Foster seemed puzzled by the question. His eyes flicked quickly back and forth, taking in Aaron Diamond, David Star and Irving Kane, and he nodded. 'I know *some* people here, yes,' he admitted without pleasure. 'Your pictures don't do you justice.'

'Why, that's very kind of you . . . What pictures?'

'It doesn't matter. From a photograph one can only tell so much. The shape of the face. The eyes. The face is there, but the person is not.'

'Is that why you're never photographed?'

'No, no, that's for quite a different reason,' Foster said, though he did not seem inclined to explain what it was. 'I must apologize for staring at you when I came in. You must have thought me rude.'

41

'Not at all. No woman is ever unhappy to be noticed. You *did* seem a little surprised.'

'Surprised? No. The truth is that you reminded me of someone I used to know. I told myself, "Well, she'll say something and the voice will be different," but the voice is the same too. I felt this a little bit when I saw your photograph. I expected to be disappointed, and I wasn't disappointed at all.'

'Who is it that I remind you of?'

'It does not matter,' Foster said, his accent slipping, though it clearly *did* matter to him.

For a moment he seemed to have lost his grasp of English, along with his legendary self-control, and Diana momentarily wondered if Foster was drunk. However, he recovered, took a breath and said, 'I'm so glad to be here,' as if he had just learned the phrase from a guidebook.

'Where did you see my photograph?'

Foster evaded the question. 'I expected you to be more of a woman of the world,' he said. 'Glamorous, but a little *hard*. Not that I have anything against *les femmes du monde*, you understand. Without them there would be no couturiers, no jewelers, no interesting gossip and nobody to teach young men about sex. But I see that this is not at all what you are.'

Diana laughed. To her surprise, she *liked* Paul Foster. Not only was he charming, but he seemed to have come to the party for the sole purpose of meeting her, which was intriguing in itself. He had obviously been caught off-guard by something and exposed more of himself than he had intended to, but now that he had overcome his initial embarrassment, his expression was more wary. She doubted that a man like Foster went anywhere without a purpose, and she was curious to find out what it was.

'Strangely enough,' she said, 'I've always nurtured a secret desire to be a *femme du monde*. Frankly, I thought I *was* one. Other people seem to think so.'

He stuck out his lower lip and shook his head. 'No, they're quite wrong. For women of the world, beauty is a serious business. They don't ever let you forget that. You, I think, *enjoy* being beautiful. Well, why not? One should enjoy what one has, no? Money, beauty, health, whatever . . . Am I not right?'

'You're absolutely right. And you flatter me.'

'I hope so. Though I'm out of practice, alas. How did you hurt your face?'

Diana reached up to her cheek in surprise and stared at Foster. 'Does it show?' she asked.

'Only a little. You needn't worry. Most people wouldn't notice, but I have an eye for details, and besides, I know a bruise when I see one. You will say it's none of my business, and you will be right, but I would put just a touch more make-up there when you get a chance. Who hit you?'

'What makes you think someone hit me?'

'Because a woman seldom walks into a door with her cheek. The nose or the forehead, just possibly. I hope you hit him back?'

Diana laughed. 'No,' she said. 'I never got the chance. Besides, he's a lot bigger than I am.'

Foster nodded, as if he had witnessed the whole scene. 'Was it Nicholas?' he asked softly. 'Such a temperamental man . . . So much energy, but no control, as if that terrible father of his had never allowed him to grow up.'

'Look, I didn't say it was Niki. I'd really rather not discuss it, if you don't mind.'

Foster took her hands in his — grabbed them, in fact — and assumed a mournful expression. For a moment Diana thought he was about to cry, but he merely said, 'Forgive me,' in a low, husky voice. 'It's what comes of living alone so much of the time,' he went on to explain. 'I ask too many questions when I finally meet someone I like. One gets so tired of talking about money.'

'The rich men I know never tire of talking about it.'

Foster shrugged. 'It's just another commodity.'

'It can't buy you happiness?' Diana asked with a laugh.

Foster looked puzzled, as if the cliché were unfamiliar to him. There were gaps in his knowledge of English, though he concealed them well most of the time. 'Happiness?' Foster asked. 'But only boring people are happy. It's a second-rate ambition . . . Listen, I want to talk to you some more — but I'm keeping you from your other guests.'

Indeed, Diana realized, her guests were staring at the two of them, while Kane, Diamond and Star, who stood in a small circle about six feet away, looked like people who had been invited to meet the Queen Mother and then been turned away at the door.

Hastily she led Paul Foster over to them, signaled Frank to bring him a glass of champagne, and made the introductions, which were entirely superfluous, since all three knew Foster. Indeed, Kane's hostility was so evident that he reminded Diana of a horse about to put its ears back and throw its rider, not that Foster seemed to notice or care. He greeted each of them with distant courtesy and a rather formal handshake, though in Star's case Foster actually clasped the publisher's hand in both of his for a moment, to indicate his respect for a man who owned his own company, however small.

'We were talking about Guatemala,' Kane said with a menacing leer.

'Ah yes? My pet project.' Foster did not seem to be on the defensive, indeed he gave impression of being at once distracted and amused. 'I still think you ought to write a book about it.'

'The answer is still no. You're trying to buy a country in the name of progress. Do you realize what's going on in the jungle? There's a whole tribal society going down the drain there. Indians in blue jeans!'

'I prefer them in feathers and monkey skins too, my dear fellow, but they want to wear blue jeans like everybody else. Besides, I am more worried about what will happen to us, when we run out of paper, oil, minerals, fertilizers. We spent nearly one billion dollars to build a plant for processing wood pulp there. The whole installation was shipped from Mobile, Alabama, on a barge — the largest man-made object ever floated! The trees are turned into a liquid, which is pumped through pipelines to the dockside, then brought here in tankers.'

'Is it profitable?' Star asked.

'Not yet. In fact, it's been hard to attract capital so far. People read about Guatemala and all they think about is juntas and coups. But every government is terrible, each in its own way. One achieves what one can despite them, no?'

'I'm on the side of the Indians,' Kane said.

'So am I,' Foster replied firmly. 'I built them a hospital. And a soccer stadium.'

Foster became more animated when he talked about his work. His hands, which he normally kept to his side as if by an effort of will, rose and he began to gesticulate. He

44

pointed, opened them wide at shoulder level to indicate the size of his undertaking, waved them to express his chagrin over Kane's short-sighted criticism, held them together, as if in prayer, to signify his affection for the Indians. However perfect his accent (and even that slipped a notch or two in his torrent of enthusiasm, taking on the rhythm of some other, more emotional and glottal language), his hands betrayed his European background. Like Meyerman, he had been unable to conceal in his new identity the ancient body language of commerce, the indispensable hand signals of the bazaar, the souk and the marketplace.

Foster apparently noticed this flash of alien enthusiasm. He seemed, Diana thought, like a man who lived uncomfortably with the image he had created for himself, as if simply *being* Paul Foster was an exercise in self-control. She wondered briefly what lay beneath the surface, as he put his hands to work spooning caviar precisely onto a piece of toast and squeezing a drop of lemon juice onto it.

'I hear caviar is getting scarce too,' Star said.

Foster nodded. 'Another diminishing natural resource, yes,' he said, 'I'm exploring the possibility of breeding sturgeon here on a commercial scale. The United States must become energy-sufficient, of course, but why not caviar-sufficient, too?' Diana was about to laugh, but he seemed perfectly serious.

'Is it a practical proposition?'

'Certainly. Only one has to keep the water at exactly the right temperature or the sturgeons don't mate. They're fussy that way.'

'Aren't we all?' Diana asked, with a sigh.

'Indeed,' Foster said, lifting his champagne glass in a toast, and giving her a frankly admiring stare over the rim.

'Don't you find the language a problem?' Star asked.

Foster looked puzzled, as if he was afraid Star was making fun of him. Jokes sometimes took him by surprise, English being an acquired language. Besides, few of the people around him made jokes in the normal course of the day.

'With sturgeons?'

'No, no, with Guatemala.'

'Ah,' Foster said with relief. 'Not at all. I speak a little Spanish. Also German, of course. Much of the business class there is of German descent.'

Star nodded, 'You're lucky,' he said. 'It's a great pity nobody learns foreign languages any more in this country. You must have an ear for languages yourself?

Foster smiled modestly. 'I learned German, English and French as a child.'

'And Hungarian?' Kane asked suddenly.

Foster's face turned blank, and his eyes lost their warmth. He was not used to people prying into his secrets. His origins were carefully unpublicized, and his accent failed to offer any meaningful clue. Clearly, however, Kane had struck a nerve.

'Naturally, I know a little Hungarian, too,' Foster said blandly, dismissing the accomplishment with a wave of his champagne glass. 'French is the language of diplomacy; Hungarian is the language of survivors.'

'Which one is your native language?' Kane asked, boring in.

Foster lifted an eyebrow. '*All* of them,' he said.

Kane drained his glass, crunching the ice cubes between his teeth. It was a noise that Foster particularly hated, and his tight-lipped smile showed it.

'I guess old Greenwood was pretty good with languages too,' Kane said.

Foster shrugged, expressing a mixture of polite boredom and indifference, although his eyes were alert. 'Possibly,' he said. 'I wouldn't know.'

'No kidding? I would have thought you knew him.'

'Not at all.'

'He's an interesting guy, Foster. I'm thinking of writing a book about him — about that period, anyway.'

Foster stared at the wall above Kane's head. 'I don't think it's a wise decision,' he said. 'Go to Guatemala instead. I'd be happy to pay the expenses, even to finance the book. I'm sure I could work out a deal for you with Aaron and Star.'

Kane shook his head. 'I'm on to a good story,' he said.

'Have you already started to write it?'

'Sure. I need more material, but I've already got some great stuff. Somebody told me Nick Greenwood's father flew to Lisbon in 1944 in Hitler's own airplane. He had a

46

suitcase full of jewelry so heavy it took two men to carry it through customs.'

Foster smiled coldly. 'That wasn't Greenwood,' he said. 'It was Manfred Weiss. Baroness Weiss had a great sentimental attachment to her jewelry. She wouldn't leave without it. Or her dogs. *They* came out on the Führer's airplane, too.'

'I heard Greenwood was involved in the German atomic-bomb project.'

'Do you think so? He wasn't Einstein, you know. He was just a businessman.'

'Atomic bombs are business, just like everything else. I don't need to tell you that, Foster. Matthew Greenwood was apparently selling the Krauts uranium by the goddamn carload. He had a brother who was involved in it too, but I don't know what happened to him. There's a guy called Rademacher who knew the whole story. He was a big buddy of Greenwood's, one of Hermann Göring's bright boys.'

Foster feigned indifference. 'It was a long time ago. Most of those people are dead.'

'This one isn't. I've got a lead on him. He's living in the South of France. He's got files, documents, letters — a fucking gold mine! Ever heard of him?'

'Never. The name is totally unfamiliar to me. I must say it all sounds interesting. I'd like to read the manuscript.'

'Nobody reads my manuscripts except my publisher, but how about an interview?'

'No, no, I never give interviews. Besides, this is a sensitive area.'

'Sensitive? It was thirty years ago, for Chrissake. It's just history now.'

'What could be more sensitive than history, my dear fellow?' Foster waved his champagne glass. 'Now you must forgive me, gentlemen, but I promised our lovely hostess a few minutes of my time.'

He gave a perfunctory bow and took Diana by the arm in a grasp that was at once a firm indication that he had had enough of the conversation and a gesture of intimacy, in what proportions it was hard to tell.

'Are you still thinking about selling your company, Star?' Foster asked as he turned away.

Star fingered his tie nervously as if he was trying to

47

make sure it was still there. 'I'm thinking it over,' he said.

'I hear Nicholas Greenwood is interested.'

Star nodded. He was perspiring heavily, and his glasses had fogged up. 'Nick seems interested, yes,' Star admitted.

'Has he made an offer?'

'I don't feel I can talk about that . . .'

'Of course,' Foster said smoothly, 'but don't accept anything without coming back to me. I can do better, I promise you. Besides, it's the old man who wants your company, not Nicholas. The moment his father dies, Nicholas will sell you off like a side of bacon. Do you want Matthew Greenwood telling you what to publish — or his son, for that matter? If you're going to sell, sell to me. I like books.'

'What have you read lately?' Kane asked, narrowing his eyes aggressively in preparation for an argument.

'Spengler,' Foster said. 'A disreputable philosopher, but by no means uninteresting. He predicted the decline of culture and intelligence in the twentieth century. People accused him of pessimism, but how right he was!' He gave Kane a brief smile, with the air of a man who has just had the last word.

Foster gently moved Diana away from them in the direction of the fireplace, sat down on the sofa beside her and signaled Frank to refill their glasses. He seemed in remarkably good spirits, despite an occasional nervous glance at the crowd of strangers around him.

Foster turned his back toward the room and moved closer to Diana, one arm over the back of the sofa protectively so that his hand was near her shoulder. It was, she thought, by no means an unpleasant feeling.

'I owe you an apology,' she said. 'I had no idea Irving Kane would be so aggressive.'

'That's all right. Journalists aren't paid to be polite. In fact, it is I who should apologize to you.'

'For what?'

'I came here under somewhat false pretenses. I wanted to talk with Irving Kane, and it seemed a good opportunity. I hadn't expected a dividend in meeting someone as charming as you.'

Diana looked at him closely, but he seemed quite sincere. There was, in fact, something appealing about Foster. He seemed genuinely interested in what other people

48

had to say, even when he disagreed with them, unlike most men. People like Augustus Biedermeyer, the beer millionaire, behaved at parties as if they had hired the entire guest list as paid listeners, and did not even seem to *hear* interruptions or disagreement. Even Nicholas, whose vanity was sexual rather than financial, felt that wealth gave him the right to pontificate on any subject from politics to modern art, and he dominated every conversation by simply not listening to anyone else. Foster *listened*, his head bent slightly to one side, his lips set in a slight, polite smile that betrayed a certain irony and a natural capacity for malicious amusement. Only the eyes were cautious and skeptical, occasionally reflecting the arrogance and ruthlessness of the inner man.

Or perhaps she was overestimating him? Diana wondered. Because Foster was secretive, it was easy to assume he had something to hide, even if it was only himself. On the surface he seemed content to be courtly, in a manner that was almost a parody of Middle European charm. It occurred to her that Foster might in fact be putting on an act, for his own amusement.

He seemed to feel this himself, for he leaned forward and said, 'I'm out of practice at this sort of thing.'

'What sort of thing did you have in mind?'

'Parties. Social talk. Conversation.'

'You have a certain reputation for being a recluse.'

Foster laughed. 'A recluse? Like poor Howard Hughes? No, no, my dear, I can't see myself sitting in a motel room growing my fingernails. My problem is that I'm easily bored.'

For a moment Diana wondered if Foster was criticizing her, or perhaps merely her abilities as a hostess, but he touched her hand lightly and said, 'I'd forgotten how pleasant it can be to talk to someone.'

'You must talk to people all day long.'

'Yes, yes. But that too is mostly boring.' Foster took a sip of champagne. He seemed momentarily glum, as if his exuberance had worn off. 'Do you enjoy your work?' he asked.

'Yes. Do you?'

'Not so much anymore. The beginning was an adventure. Now it's very big, but not so interesting. I'm hoping for a new adventure.'

'Guatemala?'

49

'No, something altogether more exciting.'

Diana was about to ask him what it was, but Foster's words were spoken with a force and note of tension that were entirely different from the relaxed charm he had so far displayed. For the first time there was some hint of the legendary Foster, whose corporate raids and financial manipulations had shocked and fascinated the press for years. She found that aspect of him curiously exciting. She had, she knew, a weakness for decisive, powerful men, and had turned Niki into one, with partial success. Foster, like Meyerman, seemed to need no help. He had a natural strength and hardness, which, like Meyerman, he went to some pains to conceal.

She changed the subject, since his tone indicated that he didn't wish to pursue it further, conscious that she was giving him a small, conversational victory, which he would be subtle enough to appreciate. 'Why are you so interested in Irving Kane's project?' she asked.

'Idle curiosity. Nothing more.'

'That doesn't sound plausible. Does it have to do with Niki?'

'Perhaps a little, yes.'

'The two of you seem to hate each other, yet you've never met. Why is that? In fact, when Niki saw the caviar you sent, he stormed out in a rage.'

'Ah? Frankly I hadn't anticipated *that*. That's when he hit you?'

'Yes.'

'So childish . . .' Foster put his hand on Diana's and sighed deeply. 'Is he still so bitter about me?'

'Apparently. What have you done to him?'

Foster smiled. 'Nothing,' he protested. 'What could I do to a man like Nicholas Greenwood, with his father behind him? They're giants! Six billion dollars a year, worldwide. I don't do more than the half of that, yet.'

'He seems to feel there's something personal between you.'

'No, no. It's only business, I assure you. We compete. It's the American way. Of course, *some* people think Nicholas is overextended, that he lacks the old man's genius. That often happens in the second generation. He's put a lot of money into nuclear technology. A family obsession, by the way . . . If it works, the stock will go up

50

like a rocket, but if it doesn't . . .' Foster moved his hand down to show the parabola of a falling rocket.

'I thought all that was secret.'

'There is no such thing as a secret, not when there's big money involved.'

'You don't think Niki's new toy will work?'

Foster shrugged. 'I know very little about nuclear reactors — though of course I have people to advise me. Advanced technology is always risky. Look what happened to RCA when it went into the computer business! Even if it works, there are problems of production, a huge capital investment, the possibility of accidents. I prefer to deal with things I can feel or touch myself. There's always a market for a good movie, or a hotel room, or a million tons of aluminum. Let someone else go to the moon. I am just a trader at heart.'

'You're also a romantic.'

'Nobody has told me that for a long time. What makes you think so?'

'The way you talked about Guatemala. And the fact that you're holding my hand. An unromantic man would have put his hand on my thigh.'

Foster stared at his hand, as if it belonged to someone else. 'You're right on both counts,' he said.

'Is that why you lead a life of secrecy?'

'It's not so secret. It's simply dull. Money starts as a game and ends as a burden. Do you still ride?'

'Not much anymore. How did you know I like horses?'

Foster smiled evasively. 'It's my business to know things. I saw a photograph of you riding with the Black and Tan in Ireland — a perfect seat. And it's not hunting country for amateurs.'

'You *are* well informed.'

'Nicholas is also quite the horseman, I think. Polo, hunting, steeplechasing . . . Of course, it would be the danger that interests him. He's not happy unless there's a chance to hurt himself — or someone else. It's not surprising women find him attractive.'

'Oh, he's attractive all right. But perhaps I'm getting a little too old for that kind of attraction. And tired of being hurt. Surely you can't have come here to ask me all these questions?'

'Not at all. Though, in fact, you are the one who is asking

51

questions . . . However, I would very much like to see you again. Is it possible?'

The question seemed to Diana oddly old-fashioned, or maybe the translation of something more appropriate in a foreign language. Perhaps, she reflected, in his strange polite way Foster was merely asking whether her relationship with Nicholas permitted her to see him. 'It's *possible*,' she said with a smile.

For a moment, as she said it, she thought Foster might think she was making fun of him, but he merely nodded. 'If you're worried about Niki,' she continued, 'please don't be. I think that ended tonight. Perhaps we could have lunch?'

Foster patted her hand gently and appeared to give the suggestion serious consideration. 'I am untypical,' he said. 'I don't usually bother with lunch. I have a yogurt, perhaps an apple, at my desk. Americans eat too much. Though I must admit my own people are worse.'

'Which people?'

Foster smiled, as if he had almost been found out. 'Why, Europeans of course!' he exclaimed, showing his teeth and giving every indication of good humor. 'I can see we are going to be friends. It's a long time since anybody has made me laugh — or since an attractive woman has smiled at me.'

'Surely a man in your position — '

Foster waved his free hand. 'Sex one can buy,' he said, 'though it's a boring transaction. Attachments, friendship, a nice chat, those are not for sale. I'll telephone you. Perhaps you'll come and see my farm. You'd find it interesting. I think. We'll have a good chat.'

'Is it far?'

'Not far. An hour. I must go now. Say goodbye to Star and Kane for me. And Aaron, of course.'

'Can't you stay? The party is just beginning.'

'I wish I could. Nothing could give me greater pleasure, but in the first place, I am monopolizing your company, and in the second place, I have an appointment in Paris. My plane is waiting.'

Foster rose, helping Diana to her feet with old-world courtesy. He kissed her hand, relinquishing it unwillingly, then looked at her closely. 'You are a very beautiful woman,' he said. 'Nicholas is a fool.'

52

He slipped away quietly through the crowd without speaking to anyone. At the doorway, the bodyguard waited with Foster's overcoat at the ready, as if alerted by some magic sign. Then it occurred to Diana that there was no magic about it; Foster must simply have fixed a time with his bodyguard beforehand and been watching for his signal. He was clearly a man who had a reason for everything he did, and a precise schedule. Like a playwright, he went out of his way to contrive surprises for the audience. She would not have been surprised if he had vanished in a puff of smoke once he put his coat on, but instead he walked off without looking back.

After all, Diana thought, why should he? But for the first time since the dreadful beginning of this evening, she felt happy. Whatever Foster was, he was not the monster that Niki had so often described to her. She felt a certain curiosity to know what lay beneath that carefully arranged surface, and realized with surprise that she was impatient for his call.

'Great party,' a rasping voice said at her elbow.

Diana looked down to find Aaron Diamond standing beside her, surveying the crowded, noisy room through a thick monocle, held delicately between thumb and forefinger.

'I'm glad you enjoyed it, Aaron. How's your client?'

'Kane? Sloshed. Don't worry, Star and I will take him back to the hotel before he breaks anything. Listen — I saw you talking to Foster. Watch yourself.'

'I'm a big girl, Aaron.'

'I'm not saying you're not. And Foster can be a pretty nice guy, for a billionaire. But he doesn't do anything without a reason. Nick can be a real bastard, but Foster is in a different league.'

'I'll be careful. In the meantime, I'm going to have some more of his caviar.'

'Never say no to the good things of life,' Aaron said with a laugh, 'whoever they come from. Foster is a great guy for gestures. You know, when he was after Dawn Safire he sent her a can of caviar — he knew she was nuts about the stuff — and she's eating it with a spoon when she feels something hard in her mouth. Dawn picks it out, and guess what it is? A goddamn diamond! Foster had it put in the caviar as a surprise for her. She broke

53

her goddamn tooth!'

'I'll eat carefully, Aaron.'

'You do that. I'll tell you another story. When Foster had a piece of Ted Krieger's company, he gave Krieger a big party at the Bistro, everybody in LA was there, there were bowls of caviar all over the place. The next morning Foster voted his stock against Krieger. He had enough support on the board to force Ted's resignation. Krieger couldn't believe what had happened to him. He sat there at the head of the board-room table in his four-hundred-dollar brushed blue-jean suit and *cried*. "How could you give me a party with caviar, then do this to me behind my back?" he asked, and Foster said, "Ted, the caviar was last night; today is business." '

'What happened to Krieger?'

'He cut his wrists in his own Jacuzzi. He was an old guy and he wasn't used to losing.'

'I'll be careful, Aaron, I promise. I'd be very interested to know just why it is that Foster and Niki hate each other. It's more than business.'

'I'm not so sure. Krieger thought there was something more than business, and look what happened to him. I'll tell you one thing, *bubi* — if you find out, don't tell me. There's things it don't pay to know.'

Part Two

Gifts from the devil 1935

Hungary is a country abounding in scenery of the most exotic character, where many places will be visited with admiration, like Szeged and Debrecen, lying just in the middle of the great Hungarian plain, where the amazing peculiarities of Magyar life may be contemplated on the very spot.

— JOSEPH KAHN
An Illustrated Guide of Budapest

3

Baron Matthew de Grünwald put down his gun and surveyed the scene before him with a certain pride. He was a big man, nearly six feet tall, wearing a London-tailored suit of plus fours, an impressive figure with a hawklike nose, hooded eyes and a massive chin that was only just beginning to be softened by flesh.

To his left he could see the women and children of the family watching the hunt from carriages. To his right his brother Steven, elegant as always, and as always taking no interest in the sport, was lighting a cigarette. Farther down the line of the *battue* were Prince Hamilcar Hatványi, Matthew de Grünwald's maternal grandfather; Prince Béla Bardossy, Steven de Grünwald's father-in-law; and finally the guest of honor, all of them obscured in smoke.

There were not a dozen men in Europe who could afford to put on a hunt like this, Matthew de Grünwald reflected with satisfaction, and it was therefore all the more irritating that Steven was displaying his lack of enthusiasm, both for the sport and for the guest of honor. Matthew flicked an empty cartridge case toward his brother's blind and made an upward gesture with both hands. Steven nodded, picked up his rifle and fired into the middle distance, without taking aim.

Behind Matthew the head gamekeeper clucked disapprovingly. 'One shot where it counts is worth five where it doesn't,' he said glumly, staring in Steven's direction, but one glance from the baron shut him up. Whatever Matthew thought about his brother, he was a Grünwald, and not to be criticized by servants, however venerable.

In any event, the important thing was that the guest of honor was having a good time. That, after all, was the purpose of the whole day. It made good business sense;

even Steven agreed with that, though in other respects he was not overjoyed to see this particular guest shooting from the blind where King Edward VII, the Kaiser, the Emperor, the Prince of Wales and His Serene Highness the Regent of Hungary, Admiral Miklós Horthy, had stood at various times.

Matthew's grandfather, Baron Hirsch de Grünwald, had despised hunting himself, but as a Hungarian banker and an industrialist, he knew what was expected of him. Nobody, not even a king, could resist an invitation to a good day in the field, and if killing animals brought in customers, then the animals would have to do their duty and be killed, though Hirsch himself merely watched the slaughter from his carriage, a blanket wrapped around his frail legs. He was not a sentimentalist, about animals or anything else.

Nor was Matthew, though he suspected Steven of a certain sentimental streak, an unwelcome and inconvenient genetic gift, no doubt from the maternal side of the family. Matthew believed in business. He had devoted his life to it, with appropriate pauses for the pleasures of the flesh and the table. For the sake of business, he had made a strategic marriage with Cosima von Schiller, whose courtier father, *Hofrat* Baron Anton von Schiller, held a controlling interest in two of Austria's largest banks. It was a marriage that had brought Matthew no happiness — not that his happiness had been a consideration. It was a matter of business, and in business it was frequently necessary to make a sacrifice. One day, Matthew thought, his son Nicholas would thank him for what he had done, as Matthew had thanked *his* father, and his father had thanked old Hirsch — though not a day passed that Matthew didn't wish he had married a woman like Steven's Betsy, or indeed Betsy herself, who surely didn't lie in bed with her eyes shut and her legs closed.

In the meantime one had to be practical, about marriage, unfortunately, and more important, about business, despite Steven's misgivings. All over Europe — in fact, all over the world — banks were going under, great fortunes crumbling, industrial empires collapsing, in the wake of the Great Depression. The Grünwalds, however, continued to prosper, to the envy and rage of their competitors.

From his main office in Budapest, Matthew de Grünwald controlled a vast and complex international business — banks and mines in Hungary, chemical plants and factories in Bohemia, coal mines in Austria, oil fields in Rumania, not to speak of companies all over the world in which the Grünwald Bank, either directly or through a Swiss subsidiary, held a controlling or a minority share.

If it was necessary to make compromises to keep the Grünwald fortune intact, so be it, Matthew told himself. Doing business with the Germans made sense, after all. They were uncouth and led by a mad-man, but what could you do? A nation of ninety million could hardly be expected to wallow in its own defeat forever, whatever the Allies had decided at Versailles. At least Hitler was an anti-Communist, even if he did look like 'a dishonest valet,' as Prince Hatványi had remarked on more than one embarrassing occasion.

Matthew de Grünwald had nothing to fear from the Germans, and saw no reason not to do business with them. He was a Catholic, married to a Catholic, as was Steven, and as was normal in Hungary. True, old Hirsch de Grünwald's race and ancestry were a little more doubtful — even very doubtful, in the eyes of some people — but that was two generations ago, and Matthew's position in Hungarian society and business put him beyond criticism. He had shrewdly loaned money to the Nazis before they came to power, just as his father had loaned money to finance the coup that brought Horthy to power, and the result was a great deal of satisfying new business.

Matthew had even been invited to meet the Führer, and he had frankly been surprised to find the Reich Chancellor in an ill-fitting brown suit with black patent-leather shoes — was there nobody in Germany to advise him on such matters? Still, Matthew came away with a generally good impression of the man.

Hitler had spoken of the need for friendly ties between the Hungarian people and the new Germany, though admittedly at tedious length and with many stupefying and inaccurate excursions into the early history of the Hungarian *Volk*. He analyzed in detail the unique position of Magyar as the only non-Indo-European language of Europe, speculated on its relationship to Finnish and

Turkish, suggested that the Magyars might represent an early, pure Aryan stock despite their regrettably dark appearance, and expressed his admiration for the Regent Horthy, about whom he waxed both lyrical and hysterical.

On the subject of trade between Hungary and Germany, the Führer was more down-to-earth. Fate had placed the Hungarian people at the crossroads between Asiatic Bolshevism and European civilization. Germany needed Hungarian grain and, above all, minerals. He foresaw a day when a great motor road — one might almost call it an *Autobahn* — would link the ancient imperial cities of Berlin, Vienna and Budapest, much as the Danube had formed the spine of the Austro-Hungarian Empire in the days of its historic greatness. In the meantime, there was an opportunity for trade, industrial cooperation, financial credits. The future, the Führer predicted — his eyes glittering, his soft, damp hands closed over Matthew's in a gesture of enthusiasm and friendship — was without question rosy. The possibilities for men of vision and good will were nothing short of colossal.

'*Kolossal!*' he repeated with emphasis, staring into space in rapture as he dismissed Matthew while his entourage obediently contemplated the ceiling in imitation of their leader, as if the rosy future had appeared there in living color for all to see.

The spectacle of a dozen Germans standing in an over-furnished, pompously decorated *salon* in a state of mass hypnosis, their hands modestly clasped in front of their genitals, did nothing to diminish Matthew de Grünwald's enthusiasm for business ties with the new Germany, which did not, in any case, seem to him significantly more crazy than the old. The Kaiser had been just as mad, and with a crippled arm to boot.

Matthew's visit to the Reichskanzlei had been arranged by his friend and hunting companion, Hermann Göring, who fairly bubbled with enthusiasm as they walked down the steps past the Chancellor's guard to the Horch touring car that Göring used in those days.

'I could tell the Führer likes you,' Göring said as they settled in the back seat, the big car dipping noticeably under his weight. 'Take it from me, he doesn't often touch people with his own hands. It's something to do with electrical flow, I think. Some quack told him that the body discharges energy whenever you touch someone.' He chuckled and leaned over to pat Matthew on the knee. 'Of course, you and I discharge energy in a more conventional way.' He leered and winked in a gross parody of masculine bonhomie made all the more grotesque by the layer of rouge on his cheeks and the strong scent of perfume. '*That* side of the Führer's life is something of an enigma, even to me. Never mind, that's the first step. I'm going to outflank those stuck-up reactionary bastards in the army and the navy. They won't allocate me the resources I need. Fine! I'll go elsewhere!'

'That will cost money, Excellency.'

Göring laughed, a great, booming, Wagnerian roar of laughter, unlike the high-pitched, nervous giggle he affected in the Führer's presence. 'You people think of nothing but money,' he said amiably, punching Matthew in the stomach with a bejeweled fist. 'Money is no problem. The Luftwaffe needs guns, factory space, raw materials, and I'm not being given my fair share. You produce what we need and I'll raise the money. In the meantime, damn it, you're banker. You'll lend us enough to get things started. Don't argue. I can see by your face that you can already smell a nice profit in it.'

'There's the question of guarantees, Excellency.'

Göring laughed. 'Your guarantee is in my somewhat corpulent person, Grünwald. You couldn't ask for anything more solid than that. Work things out with my people.'

'With pleasure, *Herr General*. But there may still be problems . . .'

Göring frowned. 'Problems? With whom? You can handle any difficulties with your government. Rich men always know how to arrange these things. Oh, I daresay you'll have to give a few handouts here and there. That's — what do you people call it? — part of the over-head. At this end, things will go fine. Don't worry, my dear Grünwald, in Germany it is I who will decide who is Jewish and who is not.'

'He has a certain vulgar charm,' said Steven de Grünwald's wife Betsy.

'I can't see it,' her sister-in-law Cosima said. 'He reeks of eau de Cologne, and I think his cheeks are rouged.

Anyway, his costume is ridiculous.'

The two women were seated in a landau, Betsy blond and luxuriant, Cosima thin and pale, her gray eyes and straight mouth reflecting disapproval. In front of them the Hatványi groom stared into space, holding the pair of matched bay Trakheners quiet with his hands. The horses were used to the noise of shooting, but the smell of blood always upset them.

Like all the Hatványi servants, the groom wore clean white gloves, a leftover from the time when the lower classes didn't wash and it was necessary to protect the gentry from the sight and touch of their filthy hands. Not that Tibor probably washed all that much even now, Betsy thought. Time stood still on the Hungarian *puszta*, at least in matters of hygiene.

Both women wore tailored loden capes, rakish felt hats decorated with pheasant plumes, long skirts and short jackets with gold buttons in the Hatványi hunting colors of dark green piped in scarlet, and carried binoculars.

Behind them stood a second open carriage for the children and the two English nannies, though in fact the boys had long since run off to stand with the gamekeepers in the butts, and even Louise had managed by means of tears and protests to join them there, leaving the nannies to their own devices.

Close-by, the head butler was busy supervising the last-minute touches of the luncheon table. Nearly twenty feet long, it had been brought from the house in pieces by oxcart, and set up *à la russe*, in buffet style. In the center a stag's head with gilded antlers rose from a bed of flowers, ferns and evergreen branches, and to each side of this rustic centerpiece stretched the gleaming rows of Prince Hatványi's silver hunting service, laden with country hams, game pies, galantines, fresh foie gras with truffles from Fauchon's in Paris, so many different kinds of sausages from Hungary and Germany that one could hardly even count them, let alone taste all of them, salads, aspics, vegetables in mayonnaise, eggs à la Romanoff (sprinkled with caviar), *fraises des bois* brought in from France overnight in the Hungarian embassy's diplomatic pouch, whole pineapples cut open and filled with strawberries from the Hatványi hothouses, crystal bowls of iced fruit salad in kirsch, cakes, tarts, strudel, pies, meringues, mousses and cold soufflés.

A row of pink-cheeked maids in green uniforms stood under the trees while the servants placed chairs and folding tables in spots that were known to have a particular picturesque view and the butler busied himself testing the temperature of the wines.

'Picnics are always nice, I think,' Betsy said. 'It's such a change to live simply . . .'

'I suppose so, but what a lot of noise.'

At the far end of the cleared field, near the edge of the rolling forest, a long waist-high barrier of bracken and branches had been constructed. Behind it, their backs to the ladies, the hunters stood, each with his own gun-bearer and gamekeeper.

Betsy could see Steven, elegant in his English tweed suit, perched on a shooting stick. He was smoking a cigarette, his Mannlicher carbine balanced over his knees, either from boredom or distaste. Matthew, old Prince Hatványi and Betsy's father, Prince Bardossy, were standing in postures of keen anticipation, the gunbearers leaning forward beside them, ready to hand over a loaded rifle in exchange for an empty one whenever necessary, while the gamekeepers in their long cloaks discussed each shot like theologians debating a point, keeping their eyes open for the slightest sign of movement from the tree line.

On the far right, in the position of honor, loomed the bulky figure of General Göring, dressed in a fur-lined, knee-length leather jerkin, worn over a suede tunic. His stout legs — the general's thighs were as thick around as a normal man's waist — were squeezed into high boots of soft leather, and around his enormous waist he wore a wide medieval belt, decorated with heavy silver studs and a jeweled buckle, from which hung a fringed leather pouch, a silver-mounted dagger and a gold hunting horn. He was accompanied by an aide-de-camp in uniform, a servant carrying an extra rifle, and a bodyguard in a belted raincoat and a bowler hat.

'He looks like Lauritz Melchior as Siegfried,' Betsy said.

'Even Melchior is not so fat. They say he's a morphine addict.'

'The children thought he was rather jolly. He *does* look like something out of a children's story.'

'Grimm's Tales perhaps. He's not the kind of general we

used to see at home. *They* were gentlemen.'

'Cosima, he was a hero in the war. He led the Richthofen squadron and was awarded the Pour le Mérite. At least give him credit for that.'

Cosima sniffed. 'Field Marshal von Konrad,' she said, 'always used to tell my father, "Aviators are the *nouveaux riches* of warfare." Besides, most heroes are vulgar. This one is no exception.'

Betsy started to sigh, then stifled the impulse. Cosima had a typically Austrian sense of propriety. Despite their reputation for frivolity — perhaps *because* of it — Austrians expected all the conventions of society to be observed in public.

'At least the men are having a good time,' she said, though she was reasonably sure that Steven was hating every minute of it.

'Men always have a good time. Myself, I think boar hunting is barbarous. A stag hunt is altogether more elegant. There's a certain dignity about it. Where is the sport in slaughtering wild pigs?'

Besty could have replied that the boar were preserved with much difficulty and at great inconvenience to the local peasantry for the sole purpose of being slaughtered by the gentry from time to time, but secretly she agreed with Cosima. It was more like war than a sport, and though the animals were large and potentially dangerous, the hunters were protected from them by a thick barrier. The only people who risked danger were the beaters and the gamekeepers as they thrashed through the woods and the undergrowth with their sticks and dogs, driving the animals toward the guns. She could hear them in the distance, giving out the traditional blood-curdling cries of the hunt while the dogs barked with excitement and fear.

At the firing line the odor of blood and gunpowder lay heavy in the damp autumn air. In front of each hunter was a row of dead wild boar, heavy, muscular creatures, their sharply curved, yellowing tusks bared in a last, defiant snarl. The boar were ill-tempered, surly animals, with bloodshot, malicious eyes, quick to charge and hard to kill. At close quarters they could slice through a man's Achilles tendons; if you were knocked to the ground, you stood a good chance of being disemboweled with one quick, slashing thrust.

Even from a distance, Göring's pile of corpses was bigger than anybody else's — the Hatványi gamekeepers were under strict orders to drive as many of the animals as possible toward the general, whose feet were surrounded by spent cartridges.

'They're coming up,' Betsy said.

The firing ceased, the gamekeepers appeared out of the trees, waving their round green hats pinned with a single long feather, the dogs barking and leaping beside them. The general strode forward to examine his kill, his hands, in soft red gauntlets with gold studs on the knuckles, placed on his ample hips. He put one foot on the back of the largest boar, drew the horn from his belt and blew a long triumphant victory blast, the melancholy sound echoing across the valley, drowning out the cries of the children as they raced one another up the slope toward the carriages, Paul in the lead, Nicholas just behind him, Louise — whose tomboy ways so infuriated Nanny — doing her best to catch up with her brother and her cousin.

'It's not fair, Mama,' Nicholas shouted, out of breath, as the three children reached the carriage, 'Pali started ahead of me.'

'He didn't,' Louise said. 'I saw.'

Cosima looked at her son impatiently. 'Don't quarrel with your cousins,' she said. 'More important, straighten your clothes, please. The three of you look like gypsies.'

In fact, the children in no way resembled gypsies. Louise wore a middy blouse and a long dark blue skirt; her blond hair was tied with a ribbon in the Hatványi colors of red and green. To Betsy's distress, the girl had her father's looks, which would have been altogether satisfactory in a boy but seemed harsh and angular in a girl. It could not be said that Louise was plain, thank God, but her face promised to be dramatic, almost *belle-laide*, rather than conventionally heart-shaped and beautiful like her mother's.

Both boys wore sailor suits, from Rowes of Bond Street, sent by the Grünwald London office, which also made regular shipments of Typhoo tea from Harrods for the nannies, and Trumper's Eucris hair lotion for Steven.

Paul de Grünwald at eight was tall for his age, with his mother's fair hair and his father's pale, intelligent eyes.

65

His cousin Nicholas a year older, was darker, more robustly built, with something of his father's ruthless energy and will to win already showing in his young face.

Nicholas and Paul were rivals, bound up in a never-ending competition which neither one seemed able to win. Nicholas had learned to ride before Paul, and Paul was determined to catch up. Paul was the faster runner, but Nicholas was the stronger of the two and could easily outwrestle his cousin. Both boys were clever at their studies — as Matthew said with pride, there had never been a stupid Grünwald — but like his father's, Paul's intelligence was deeper, he had a stronger streak of intellectual curiosity.

It was recognized throughout the family that Louise was probably smarter than either of them, but nobody, including Betsy, thought this an advantage in a girl, and there was great relief when she was discovered to have a natural talent for riding. After all, the Empress Elisabeth had been the greatest horsewoman of Europe; riding was a perfectly correct pastime for a young woman, and besides, wonderful for the figure and the posture, which you couldn't dismiss at all as side benefits for a girl who would one day have to marry.

'Louise,' Betsy said, 'stop fussing over the carriage horses and comb your hair. Here's Nanny now.'

And indeed both nannies appeared, carrying combs and hairbrushes, to tidy their respective charges. The children lined up obediently — experience had taught them that in the end Nanny always won — watching their elders as they strolled up the wide field, radiating the self-satisfaction of men who have had a good morning's sport.

Göring strode in the lead, his face red with excitement and exertion. He paused by the children, gave them a broad wink, reached into his hunting pouch and handed each of them a boiled sweet wrapped in cellophane. 'Glucose,' he explained. 'We're developing it in Germany to issue to the troops, for extra energy. Not that you rascals need it.' He leaned against the side of the landau to greet the ladies, removing his gauntlets and folding them into his belt.

'Baroness,' he said to Cosima, 'my respects. Madame, likewise. What a wonderful day! You know, the Führer is fanatically opposed to hunting. He's always telling me, "Göring, how can you look at a beautiful, innocent deer, with those lovely limpid eyes, and then shoot the poor creature?" He simply doesn't understand all this, he's a humanitarian. Whenever I am with him, I feel I am in the presence of a superior being, but we poor mortals have to take our pleasure as we find it.'

'Speaking of pleasure, a glass of champagne, Excellency?' Betsy asked.

Göring mopped his face with a large bandanna. 'Delighted,' he said, accepting a glass from the silver tray in the butler's hands. 'Your health!' He drained the glass and took another, sipping it more slowly. 'Excellent stuff! Is it local?'

Betsy shook her head. 'Not at all,' she said, 'it's French. Hungarian wines are in general very good, but the champagne is too sweet.'

'Well, you can't beat the French at certain things. Champagne, needless to say — ladies' underwear, perfume. The Führer has often told me that his greatest ambition is to see Paris with his own eyes. Of course, he's thinking of the museums, you understand, not lingerie and champagne.'

'No doubt an opportunity for a state visit will come up,' Cosima suggested coldly.

Göring laughed. 'I don't think a state visit is exactly what the Führer has in mind, dear lady. Which of these beautiful children is yours?'

'The boy on the left, Niki.'

The general waddled over and shook Nicholas by the hand, then picked him up, threw him in the air, wrestled with the boy and put him down again, with a great bull-like roar of boisterous good humor.

Nicholas stood dazed, not sure whether to run or cry. He was terrified momentarily by the sudden assault — like most children he was never sure whether adults were playing or intended serious injury — but out of some deep instinct for human nature, he held his ground and tried not to cry.

'He's a strong one,' Göring said to Cosima; 'a real trooper. What about you, dear child, what's your name?'

'Paul, Excellency.'

'And can you wrestle too?'

'Yes, Excellency. But I think I'm small enough to deserve a handicap.'

The general paused for a moment, threw back his head and roared with laughter, tears running down his fat cheeks. 'Oh my,' he said, choking slightly, 'this one is going to be a bright one, you mark my words, a lawyer or a financier, he'll buy and sell us all. Who are the two old witches?'

Betsy looked at the nannies, who luckily had no German, and were staring at Göring with undisguised hostility and disapproval. 'They're the children's nurses, Excellency, Nanny Crum and Nanny Bell.'

'They're English?'

'Yes, of course.'

'I don't understand why throughout Europe, even in Germany, the upper classes have English nannies for their children. One can't trust the English. Perfidious Albion — a clever, dangerous people. Perhaps we ought to form a corps of German nannies, then we would rule the world like the British. Or the nursery, at any rate! Come, let me help you ladies down, and we'll go to lunch. I am starving. There's nothing like a good morning's killing to give a man an appetite!'

'Disgraceful,' Nanny Bell said with an emphatic sniff. 'He might have hurt the poor tyke. A grown man like that throwing a small child around. And him a general, at that.'

'He's not like any general I ever saw,' said Nanny Crum. 'Dresed up like a costermonger. He smelled of perfume, too.'

'A Hun. Well, they can't help the way they are, you know. But it's not right, exposing the children to all this. I don't mind my children watching the grownups shoot a few pheasants, and of course they will hunt sooner or later, but then they're tired and whiny and run a fever afterward, from all the excitement.'

'And there's accidents.'

'There's always accidents where there's hounds and horses, then it's "Nanny, it hurts," and too late then, isn't it? But I don't call this proper sport.'

'Not proper sport at all.'

'Ah well, when in Rome, do as the Romans do, they say.

But you wouldn't think a general would behave like that, would you now?'

'Foreigners,' Nanny Crum said darkly. 'They just don't have the same standards we do.'

Prince Béla Bardossy, Betsy's father, also hated foreigners. He watched with disapproval as the Grünwalds escorted the general to the luncheon table. He liked to think of himself as a man without prejudice, but he believed in breeding, and when you mixed bloodlines you bought trouble, in the long run.

He loved his grandchildren, Louise and Paul, as much as any grandfather in the kingdom, doted on them in fact, but the sins of the fathers were vested upon the children — it was surely in the damn Bible somewhere, he thought to himself. In the end the Grünwald blood would cause them problems and unhappiness, and it would be *his* fault because he had consented to Betsy's marriage.

The prince looked at Göring, busily loading his plate like a fat German hog, and felt a mixture of disgust and shame. He had nothing against the Germans, they were good soldiers, God knows they had fought better than the Austrians, but they were *parvenus*, pushy, arrogant and given to hysteria in moments of crisis, like the bloody French they hated so much. The Kaiser had been bad enough — the Hohenzollern family had hardly any breeding at all — but this one was worse, dressed up like a Wagnerian tenor for a boar hunt, a damn foreigner whom the Grünwalds had no business bringing here. But in a way that was the trouble with the Grünwalds. They were foreigners too.

Prince Bardossy moodily sipped peach brandy from a flask as he looked over the Hatványi countryside. In the end only the land mattered. You couldn't imagine Hungary without her aristocracy, and without land there was no meaning to being an aristocrat. The sin of the Jews, when all was said and done, was not that they had killed Christ. It was simply that they believed in money, not land.

Not that Bardossy hated the Jews *personally*. Had he not allowed his daughter to marry a half-Jew? True, there were too many Jews in Hungary, but where were there *not* too many? People complained that when a Jew took over the village store, he lowered his prices to drive the Magyar shopkeepers out of business, then brought in his cousins to take over the bankrupt shops, until you woke up one morning to find the Jews had all the local trade and money in their hands. What could you do? They were a people who stuck together — and who understood money. The Magyar gentry could hardly be expected to enter trade themselves, and as for the people, it was in nobody's interests that they learn to read and count.

Bardossy offered his flask to Prince Hatványi, who had been thanking his gamekeepers for the morning's sport. The two men stood silent for a moment, both of them lean, tall and deeply tanned, with the fierce high cheekbones and narrow black eyes of the true Magyar.

Old Hatványi had very nearly been expelled from the English Club when his daughter married Matthew de Grünwald's father. Twenty-five years later, Putzi de Fekete had called Bardossy 'a Judas on horseback' when he gave his blessing to Betsy's marriage to Steven. Nothing changed in Hungary. Hatványi and Bardossy were proud men, but they shared the aristocrat's sense of priorities — a marriage that preserved one's estates for another generation or two was a marriage worth making, even at the price of a little Jewish blood.

They still had *their* land, free and clear of debt, while Putzi de Fekete, for all his nationalistic talk, lived in an apartment in Budapest, without a hectare of land to his name, a miserable creature whose title was only good for engraving on calling cards to impress the *nouveaux riches*.

'A good day's shooting,' Bardossy said.

'Not bad. Forty-eight boar. Hardly like the old days, when we shot them by the hundreds. Also, I think they're smaller now. Before the war we always lost a gamekeeper or a beater, but the damn animals don't seem to have the same spirit they used to.'

'That's what comes of putting out food for them in the winter, Prince. They grow fat and lazy.'

'Like our friend down there?'

Bardossy stared at Göring, who was busy handing out mementos to the gamekeepers. He traveled everywhere with a large trunk of souvenirs and gifts. The case, which his aide-de-camp had fetched from the limousine, was fitted with carefully labeled drawers, each containing a different grade of gifts appropriate to every occasion and recipient. The gamekeepers, doffing their hats, were receiving small bronze medals, with Göring's likeness minted on the face, and on the obverse a stag with a swastika in his antlers, surmounted by the motto 'The hunt of the animal develops the courage of the man.'

Bardossy shook his head. 'I think our people would rather have a tip so they can go out and get drunk. But no, I don't think the general is fat and lazy. He's fat and *dangerous*. If I were Grünwald, I would take care.'

Hatványi nodded. 'I've known three generations of Grünwalds,' he said, 'four if you count the children. They're shrewd.'

'They're shrewd, yes. Possibly *too* shrewd. It's in the blood, I'm afraid.'

'Give me a kiss,' Betsy de Grünwald whispered to Steven, 'you smell like a hero — leather, sweat and gunpowder.'

Steven put his arm around her and kissed her cheek.

'Not the cheek, please. The mouth. Nobody is looking. They're all too busy watching General Göring hand out party favors. That's better, *mon amour*.'

'You're looking beautiful,' Steven said as Prince Hatványi's Gypsy trio emerged from the woods and began to play for the guests.

'Yes. Can we sneak away to the castle?'

'Alas, not. The serious gift-giving is about to start. Believe me, everybody wants to get away as soon as possible. All this food will be left for the gamekeepers and the beaters, and they can't start eating it until we leave.'

Steven drew her over to the family circle, where Göring stood, surrounded by the two princes, Matthew, Cosima, some of the gentry from neighboring estates, most of whom were related to either the Hatványis or the Bardossys or both, and the children, still staring at the general with what looked very much to Betsy like vulgar curiosity.

Göring's aide-de-camp had produced a Leica and was snapping away at the scene, to the irritation of Hatványi, who believed that photographs were middle-class — gentlemen had themselves painted.

Betsy noticed that the expression on the general's face

was that of a greedy child in a state of frenzied anticipation. Though Göring was extravagantly generous, it was well known that he expected his generosity to be reciprocated and, if possible, exceeded.

Often the general's aides specified in advance exactly what present would please their master. When Göring had paid a visit to Baron von Thyssen, it had been tactfully but firmly suggested to the baron that the general had always wanted to own a Holbein sketch. Thyssen had balked at this, since the sketch in question was a prized part of his collection. He made the counter-offer of a superb Dürer engraving, but word was then passed back to him that certain valuable orders for alloy steels would be placed with Krupp instead of Thyssen, so the baron reluctantly surrendered his Holbein to Göring, who accepted it with such boyish excitement and pleasure that one might almost have thought the gift came as a surprise to him.

Matthew whispered a few words in Göring's ear, the general's pudgy fingers trembled with tension and the Gypsies stopped playing. For once Göring had been kept in suspense, since his staff had not yet had an opportunity to study the catalog of the Hatványi-Grünwald collections to pick out the suitable present for the general.

Matthew clapped his hands, and three Hatványi servants appeared from behind one of the cars. The first one carried a dark-green velvet pillow, on which lay a magnificent gold-inlayed hunting dagger, engraved in the Turkish manner of the sixteenth century, its hilt set with uncut rubies. The second carried a matching curved sword, its sheath carved with hunting scenes. The third carried a long Turkish hunting spear, the shaft covered in gold and precious stones, the damascened, curved blade inlaid with scenes of lion hunting in gold.

'A token of our joy at your visit, Excellency,' Matthew said, waving toward the small procession like a conjurer. 'There is not a museum in the world that has a finer set of sixteenth-century hunting weapons than this.'

Tears of joy ran down Göring's cheeks. He embraced Matthew de Grünwald, his weight almost knocking Matthew to the ground, and, speechless with delight, he shook hands with the two princes, kissed Cosima, threw his arms around Betsy in an exuberant bear hug, then gave Steven's cheek a friendly pinch.

'Bring them here,' he shouted, 'give them to me, quickly, *quickly!*' He ran his hands over the blades, fondled the precious stones, exclaimed in admiration at the workmanship, held each piece high above his head so that everybody could admire his new possessions, then stood silent for a moment, contemplating them in exhaustion, like a man suffering from postcoital sadness. He accepted a glass of champagne and raised it in a toast. Now that he had his gifts, he seemed calmer and more genial, eager to begin presenting his own.

With surprising speed he handed out trinkets from the traveling case, calling out to the harried aide-de-camp the appropriate item for each person as he moved among the guests. '*Rittmeister*,' he shouted, 'a compact for the baroness, not that one, idiot, one of those with diamonds, a cigarette case for Prince Bardossy, a signed photograph for the two English spies . . .'

Each of the children received a present, a firm Germanic handshake and a pinch on the cheek that brought tears to their eyes. Paul received a Hitler Youth pocketknife; Nicholas a rather more elaborate sheath knife, with a portrait of the Führer engraved on the hilt; poor Louise, rather disappointingly, a silver medal of the Bund Deutscher Mädel on a red-white-and-black ribbon.

For Steven, the general produced a Luger 7.65mm carbine, the same long-barreled pistol with a wooden stock that the Kaiser had used for deer hunting, since he found it difficult to hold a full-sized rifle because of his withered left arm. A small silver escutcheon was set into the stock, engraved with the general's monogram and the *Parteiabzeichen*, an eagle holding a swastika and staring into space.

Such ceremony as Göring was willing to summon up he reserved for Matthew de Grünwald. The general took a large box wrapped in ordinary butcher's paper from his aide, borrowed Paul's pocket knife to cut the string, ripped open the cardboard with his big fingers and presented to Matthew a striking bronze bust of himself, executed in loving, if somewhat flattering, detail.

Göring contemplated his own likeness with satisfaction. 'It's nice work, don't you think?' he asked.

Matthew nodded, holding the heavy bronze in his arms

and wondering where he could put it down.

'I'm glad you like it. Tell me, is everything working out well?'

'Yes. Of course, it all takes time.'

'That's understood. It's the organization that matters. If I had to wait my turn until the army gets all the tanks it wants and the navy has enough submarines, I'd be failing in my duty to the Führer. If we can subcontract for my anti-aircraft guns say, here or in Czechoslovakia, then so much the better, so long as we get fast delivery, a quality product and decent financing. It's good busines for everybody.'

'True. We've found no difficulty so far in placing orders. My brother Steven has managed to place several orders for heavy machinery and instruments in England. Of course, the transactions go through a third party, but the English have only to look at the blueprints and specifications to know who the real customer is.'

'And they don't care, eh? "Business is business," that's England's motto! Eventually they'll build the bombsights for us that we'll use on them! Not that there'll be a war. The Führer believes in diplomacy, but a diplomacy based on strength.'

'In Hungary we are obliged to have a diplomacy based on weakness. That explains the Hungarian national character. Speaking of strength, has Your Excellency been made aware of the work the English are doing in science?'

Göring shrugged massively. 'Let them do what they like,' he said, 'we'll still beat the shit out of them.'

'Of course. They have a government of old women. Totally contemptible! Still, if they should one day have a real leader, it might be a different story. In any case, my brother Steven was there on business last week and came back with an interesting rumor. The British are trying to buy uranium.'

'What?'

'Uranium, Excellency. It's a rare earth.'

'What's it for?'

'There's speculation that it could be a source of energy. Electricity for a thousand years from a lump of ore. That sort of thing.'

Göring laughed without mirth. 'Fairly tales,' he said.

'There's also talk in certain circles of using it for

74

weapons. Death rays, and so forth . . .'

'Death rays? It's all nonsense.'

'Probably. I gather that they're thinking more in terms of a colossal bomb rather than death rays.'

'They haven't even got *rifles*,' Göring snorted contemptuously. 'The British generals still believe in the horse! Not that most of our own are any better.'

'I wasn't talking about the generals, Excellency. The interest in nuclear physics is still confined to the elite. My brother had dinner with H.G. Wells. Professor Lindemann was there too, from Oxford. Wells is convinced there will one day be a bomb the size of a grapefruit that can destroy London.'

'Wells is a novelist. Lindemann is a Jew.'

'They're both well-connected. Wells talks to Keynes, to Eden, to Ramsay MacDonald . . . Lindemann is a close friend of Churchill's.'

'Churchill is *kaputt*. A prophet without honor. Ribbentrop says he's drunk half the time. Not that one can trust Ribbentrop, of course . . . Still, if the British are really interested, I suppose we ought to look into it. Though in the end it will be bombers that matter.'

'No doubt. Oddly enough, there's a man in Budapest who knows a lot about it — a professor of physics called Meyerman.'

Göring spat. 'Meyerman! Lindemann! Einstein! Always Jews!'

'They're good at the sciences, General.'

'Also at business, they tell me,' Göring said unpleasantly, staring hard into Matthew de Grünwald's eyes.

'That, too. In any event, this Meyerman showed me some very interesting papers, one from the British journal *Nature*, the other from *Wissenschaft*, in Germany. Steven, who understands these things better than I do, was most impressed. Of course, with scientific progress, there is always risk —'

'Yes, yes. Let me tell you a story about progress,' Göring interrupted lugubriously. 'Only the other day Dr. Messerschmitt showed me his new fighter plane. I told him to take off the glass canopy. How can a man fight if he can't stick his head out in the wind to see what's going on?'

'A good point.'

'No. It seems that the damn thing is so fast you *can't* stick your head out! So Messerschmitt had his way, damn him! I don't like things I can't understand.'

'Who does? Still, one can't ignore progress. I assure Your Excellency there's *great* interest in uranium. Not just from the British, either. Meyerman told me he had a visitor from Herr Himmler's staff recently — a nice young man with a degree in physics. Very knowledgeable. He just happened to be in Budapest on a sightseeing tour and dropped in for a chat — I gather he hopes to see Oxford as well.'

Göring's heavy face seemed to harden. His eyes narrowed, the corners of his mouth turned down brutally, all the geniality was drained out of him. '*Scheiss!*' he exclaimed. 'Himmler — that's a more serious matter! This visitor was interested in — what the hell is it called?'

'Uranium. Yes.'

'Bombs are my business, not Himmler's, the swine. If you only knew, Herr Grünwald, the jealousy, the backbiting that goes on . . . I'm a simple man who only wants to do his duty to the Führer. I have tremendous responsibilities! The Luftwaffe, the Office of the Four-Year Plan, number two man in the Reich — it's a terrible burden, my dear fellow, with no possibility of personal gain. Or very little, anyway. Much less than people think. Still, what are personal sacrifices in comparison to the welfare of *das deutsche Volk*?' Göring stared into space for a moment, fingering the massive ruby in the hilt of his dagger and pulling in his stomach.

'Just so, Excellency. The Führer appreciates it. And the ordinary people. One only has to listen to them talk about you — '

'Yes, yes, they adore me, there's no doubt about *that*. I tell you, it's deeply moving to see their faces, Grünwald. Particularly the children! Where exactly do we find uranium?'

'By a coincidence, Excellency, here in Hungary.'

Göring looked at Matthew thoughtfully and raised one eyebrow. '*Na*,' he said, 'I should have guessed. Well, if that damn chicken farmer Himmler wants it, I'll take it before he does. I want an exclusive option, you understand. None of it goes to him, or to the bloody British.'

'That's understood. As for the details . . .'

'Price I don't discuss. I'm not a Jew. I'll send a man to see you. His name is Rademacher. Now let's go back. I want a bath and a nice cup of English tea before dinner.'

As Matthew shepherded the general back toward the carriages, he passed Steven and Betsy, and gave Steven a wink. 'He's bought it!' he whispered while Göring stopped for a moment to chat with the two princes, standing with his feet apart and his hands on his hips, in what was instantly recognizable as his Mussolini pose.

'Bought *what*?' Betsy asked, when Matthew and his guest were out of earshot.

'For years,' Steven said, 'we've been sitting on these mines full of uranium. It has no commercial value — they use it in laboratory experiments, but only in very small quantities. Well, now it seems we've found a use for it. We're going to sell it to the Germans.'

'What will they do with it?'

'Nothing, in all probability.'

'Did you think of it?'

Steven shrugged modestly. 'I must confess I did. I met old Professor Meyerman, from the university, and he was boring me to death. Suddenly I heard the word "uranium," and I put two and two together.'

'Clever puss! When will all this be over?'

'Soon. I'm sure the general wants a nap before he starts eating again.'

'I can't wait.'

'Family gatherings like this are impossibly boring,' Steven said.

'That's because you Grünwalds only gather for a purpose. It's not a family, it's a business.'

Steven rolled his eyes. This was an old argument — one of the few he had with Betsy. 'Matthew and I are very close, you know that.'

'Close, yes, but over the years I've come to the conclusion that you're not all that *fond* of each other. Is it because Matthew is the head of the family now?'

'Not at all. I don't always agree with his policies, but I wouldn't dispute his right to make them. Grandfather arranged the family interests so that the eldest son would always have control. He was afraid everything would be divided up otherwise. Besides, Matthew has a better head for it than I do, let's face it.'

'You're too modest. That's only because he's always known he would have control.'

'Possibly. But it's also a question of temperament. In any case, since we all have plenty of money, there isn't a problem. Our strength in business comes from the fact that we've kept everything in the family. No outsiders — we all share a common bond and a common interest.'

'All right, I admit your grandfather had his reasons for what he did — but look at the effect it has on the children! At some point the power should be shared. It's simply not fair that Niki will get control of the whole thing one day. At least you and Matthew are brothers, you have worked out a *modus vivendi* — but the boys are only cousins and they don't even *like* each other!'

'Of course they do. That's nonsense, *mon amour*.'

'You only see what you want to. Niki is like a crown prince; he knows perfectly well he's going to inherit his father's position. And Pali resents it, one can see that.'

'I can't.'

'You're not a mother . . .'

'You're being overdramatic, Betsy. They have a healthy rivalry, like all boys that age. Nothing more.'

'You think so? Just look at them.'

And indeed, the two boys were already looking at each other's knives with unconcealed envy, as they stood close to the grownups, waiting for the party to break up. They were at the edge of the cleared field, near enough to their parents so as not to be told to come closer, but just far enough away to avoid lectures, warnings and adult conversation. The excitement of the morning's shooting had worn off, and the children were restless, tired of the ceremonies, 'enervated' as the nannies would have said, though they had retreated to the carriage in anticipation of teatime, when they could have the children to themselves again and restore discipline and cleanliness.

Nicholas and Paul were running from an old tree stump, on which Louise stood, to the edge of the forest and back, a race that Paul won every time, to Nicholas' annoyance, particularly since Louise was cheering her brother on. Nicholas had won three times in a row at arm wrestling, and cursed himself for having agreed to a footrace, at which Paul usually beat him handily. They had agreed to a dozen laps, but afterwards Nicholas was determined to wrestle with Paul, then he would show him who was best, who was boss, and Paul would have to squeal for mercy in front of his own sister.

His heart pounding, his breath coming in gasps, he trailed after Paul toward the dark, shadowy edge of the forest, when he saw something moving among the low pine branches, moving with astonishing speed for its bulk, moving directly toward his cousin, who had clearly not noticed it.

Nicholas stopped in his tracks, opened his mouth to scream a warning, but instead, as if an invisible hand had been clasped over his open mouth, he remained silent. One part of him wanted to warn Paul while there was still time for a runner of his speed to turn and seek safety in the open grass of the field, but some other, darker part of him paralyzed his will. It was as if he were suddenly two people, one of them desperately trying to save Paul, the other determined not to, and the stronger instinct prevailed, leaving him the mute witness to a tragedy. He longed to shout, but he could not, and in the single instant that his eyes took in the scene, he suffered all the guilt of betrayal and cowardice, the fear of retribution, the terror of knowing that he had repressed the most basic of human instincts. 'I have murdered my cousin,' he told himself, and screamed at his own terrible silence, now that it was too late to serve as a warning.

For out of the low bushes, the boar was already bearing down on Paul. Irritated by the noise of the shooting and the pursuit of the dogs, angered by the smell of the blood, perhaps simply enraged at having its routine disturbed, the boar was determined to assert its right to peace and quiet. It was of a size and ferocity to please even Prince Hatványi — a huge, heavy, scarred, mean-eyed old survivor of countless battles whose long, yellowing tusks had cut down dogs and rivals by the dozens. It weighed three times as much as Paul, but in short bursts it could outrun an Olympic athlete and still have strength left to open him from groin to chest with one quick slash.

Paul was too surprised to scream. For one terrifying, endless moment he stopped in his tracks. The hesitation saved his life, for the boar, which was momentarily dazzled by its charge from the dark undergrowth into the open field, had been anticipating that Paul would continue running. The big animal, whose eyesight was weak to begin with, swerved for a moment, then charged into the boy from the side, knocking him clear.

With an angry grunt of bewilderment the boar charged on, skidded to a halt and turned around slowly with snuffling suspicion to search for its victim, who was lying in the long grass below the boar's line of sight. The boar waited for a noise to tell it which way to charge. Instinct and experience taught it that most creatures made a noise when they had been knocked down in the first charge — dogs whined and yelped for mercy, other boars grunted in fear or challenge. But there was only silence, and the odors of blood, gunpowder and human scent confused its sense of smell. Then a high-pitched scream from the distance attracted its attention, confusing it still further because the sound was too far away to be from the person it had knocked down. This was followed by another scream, even more high-pitched (as Louise realized what had happened), then by confused shouting from the distance.

The boar shuffled back and forth for a moment, trying to decide whether to charge across the field toward all the noise or retreat back into the forest, when a voice close-by whispered 'Mama'. The boar turned its head with a low grunt of satisfaction. Everything was in order. It had found its victim's position and prepared to charge.

Nicholas' anguished scream had frozen the members of the shooting party. Louise's scream, a moment later, galvanized them into action.

The gamekeepers were too far away to be of any use and had already packed the guns away in their scabbards and cases. Prince Hatványi crossed himself. Prince Bardossy dropped his glass and ran toward the noise as fast as he could, but at his age he could hardly be expected to outrun the children's parents, who dashed across the field in time to find Louise standing rigid in horror on the tree stump, pointing toward the edge of the forest where Paul lay face down in the long grass. About ten yards from him, on the left, was the boar, pawing the ground with its sharp, cloven feet and weaving its massive head from side to side; halfway between Louise and Paul stood Nicholas, his hands covering his face, shaking with sobs.

Steven had dropped the Luger — it was unloaded and therefore useless — and for a brief moment as he ran down the slope toward his son he realized that there was no way to save the boy, if indeed he was still alive, except by throwing himself in front of the boar, and he surrendered to the demands of his heart and his lungs, every instinct driving him forward faster than he had ever dreamed he could run.

He did not see Matthew dash forward to pick up Nicholas in his arms, he did not hear Cosima and Betsy crying behind him, he did not see a bulky figure, moving with unaccustomed speed directly toward the boar, or hear the animal's own heavy breathing. He closed the distance and dropped flat on top of the boy, then raised his head to watch the boar charging at him, wondering for one instant what it would feel like when the tusks sliced into him and where they would hit.

To his astonishment the boar changed course, turning uphill to confront its pursuers. Across the green stubble of the field the boar charged directly toward Göring, who was running as fast as he could in the boar's direction. For a man of his size he was moving fast, his face scarlet with effort, his expression one of rage. It occurred to Steven that the man and the beast resembled each other, and even the boar seemed surprised by the size and ferocity of its opponent.

For one fatal fraction of a second it hesitated, turning just enough to expose its flank to the general, who gave a bellow of triumph and with the full power of his two-handed thrust raised the ornate gold hunting spear into the air and plunged it down behind the boar's heavy neck, deep into the shoulder, the general's weight and the boar's own charge driving the point through the thick layers of muscle into the heart itself. The beast stood for a moment in shock and pain, its eyes glazed; then it trembled, as if acknowledging defeat, gave a low moan, a last feeble slash with its tusks, and fell to its side, blood pouring from its mouth.

Steven could hear his son breathing softly. He picked up the unconscious boy in his arms and walked across the

81

field, where Göring, one foot on the boar's bloody shoulder, pulled the spear from the animal, held it above his head and gave out a roar of triumph that echoed over the fields and woods, a fierce, rising 'Ha-la-li' out of the primitive Germanic past, a cry from the times of Wotan, a sound that had brought terror to the hearts of Roman legionaries when they had faced the Teutonic tribes. Then he planted the priceless spear in the ground, wiped his hands on his gauntlets and walked forward to examine Paul.

'The child is alive?' he asked.

'The child is bruised but alive, Exellency,' Steven said. 'We owe you an eternal debt.'

'That's true,' the general said happily. 'A debt of blood. This is the boy who was so smart, right? It seems he's not only smart, but *lucky* — a formidable combination, He will go far. My dear,' he said to Betsy, who had just kissed him on the cheek, 'I'd kill a boar every day for a kiss from a beauty like you. You shall sit next to me at dinner.' He turned toward the gamekeepers and shouted, 'I'll have the tusks as a trophy! And clean off that spear — the damn thing is worth a fortune!'

'Poor Niki,' Matthew de Grünwald said, as he watched the children being taken back to the nannies. 'He's trembling like a leaf. One can see what a shock it was for him. The boys are very close, you know.'

Göring nodded. 'A little slow off the mark to shout, though. He won't make a fighter pilot, that one. Still, he'll be fine. Kids have a natural strength — it's education that turns them into cowards and weaklings, except in countries likes ours, of course. By tonight, they'll all be laughing about it, you'll see.'

But that night, when Paul woke up in the nursery, bruised and stiff, he simply stared at Nicholas, then closed his eyes. And Nicholas saw from his expression that Paul knew, or had guessed, what had happened, and that the knowledge of it would always lie between them. And he cried through the night, as if he was aware that some part of his innocence had been lost forever and that a childhood rival had become, in that fraction of a second, an implacable enemy.

Part Three

Personal Assets

4

Diana was a busy woman and not usually given to
brooding. The day after her party she was not surprised
that Niki Greenwood failed to telephone or even inquire
after his personal effects. Apologies were not in his
nature, and what were a few suits and cuff links to a man
whose father owned a three-hundred-foot yacht?

At the office, she took the trouble to look up Paul
Foster's biography in *Who's Who in American Business*.
It merely confirmed his reputation for secrecy, or possibly
sly humor. The entry read: '*Naturalized citizen, 1950;
founded corporation, 1951, chairman of the board since
1952; clubs, hobbies and professional associations, none;
awards, none; address, office.*'

When she returned home in the late afternoon, the living room of her apartment seemed to have been turned
into a florist's shop. There were flowers everywhere —
the maid had used every bowl and jug and vase in the
house. On the coffee table was one of Foster's business
cards. She turned it over, but there was no message.

It was amazing how good it felt to be pursued, Diana
thought — assuming that Foster's flowers represented a
form of pursuit. In the last few years she had seldom been
seriously pursued by anyone. Diana was known to be
Nicholas Greenwood's mistress, and few men wanted to
risk crossing Nicholas, not when there were plenty of
attractive women around whom one could chase without
any risk at all. Niki was wealthy, powerful, jealous, hot-
tempered and given to violent fits of rage. Even when it
was common knowledge that he was sleeping with other
women and that his relationship with Diana was
declining, she still remained his property in the eyes of
most men, and in her own.

Apparently Foster didn't care, either because he

guessed her relationship with Niki was finally over, or because he simply wasn't afraid of anyone. It was remarkable, she thought, as she gave herself the pleasure of removing Niki's photograph from its silver frame and tearing it up, how much the two men resembled each other physically. Niki was heavier and taller; he was a handsome man and he knew it. Foster, on the other hand, seemed unaware of his looks, or perhaps merely indifferent to them. When he was talking to you, he had the priceless gift of making you feel you were the most important person in the world to him, and while Diana recognized that it was a trick or a habit, or simply part of his strategy for dealing with people, it still fascinated her, if only because for a long time now Niki had not even bothered to try.

She looked at her watch, a thin gold wafer with her name spelled out in diamonds in place of numbers, a present from Nicholas during the first, passionate month of their affair, and saw that it was seven o'clock. It was at moments like these, she thought, that you could understand why people took to drink. Here she was, successful, beautiful, intelligent and alone. It had always been her misfortune to be a one-man woman; casual affairs and one-night stands held very little appeal for her. Nicholas had been well aware of that. As he drifted away from her, he made a great show of giving Diana her freedom, knowing full well she wouldn't use it, *couldn't*, so long as a part of him remained in her life. She was faithful even when there was nothing left to be faithful to.

In moments of depression Diana retreated to the bathroom, as if the upkeep of her beauty was a kind of spiritual exercise. She was interested in her body, much as she would have been in any other valuable and irreplaceable possession. Caring for it gave her a certain peaceful satisfaction. She examined her skin, pleased to find no unexpected blemishes or flaws, then showered and washed her hair. Other women she knew went to more elaborate lengths in pursuit of beauty, but she was lucky — she didn't need to. Diana believed in exercise, hot baths and the simple life. It seemed to work for her, as her friends noted with considerable jealousy.

The longer Diana took to prepare for the evening, the easier it was to forget that she had nothing to do. Her desk and mantelpiece were littered with invitations, screening notices, preview tickets and cards to gallery openings, but she had no real desire to go anywhere alone and was unable to summon up enough energy to co-opt a last-minute partner.

For a brief moment, Diana found herself missing Nicholas, then experienced a spasm of self-disgust at her own weakness. Iris Star, poor David Star's wife, had once said, apropos of Niki, in fact, 'A bad man is better than none,' but Diana hadn't agreed then and was ashamed to admit that she felt so now. Diana treasured her independence — made a fetish of it, in the view of her friends — but even so, much of her social life had revolved for years around Niki, and most of her emotions.

Had he been there, he would have taken over her evening, gone through the clutter of invitations with an impatient snort, picked out the ones that interested him, swept her off to buy a painting, go to a party or walk out of a movie screening halfway through because he was bored and wanted to go over to '21' and drink with his cronies. At his worst, he was at least decisive. He loved action — loved it too much in the eyes of most people — and approached the prospect of a quiet evening at home in the spirit of a man condemned to death.

It was all very well to pretend that it was a relief to escape from all that, to spend a few peaceful hours watching television and catching up on the New York *Times*, but no woman is ever truly happy alone, and Diana was no exception. She stood in front of the mirrored wall in the bedroom and started her exercises, her long blond hair tied up behind her with one of Nicholas' silk handkerchiefs. She stretched, bent over gracefully and jumped, noting with pleasure that her breasts were as firm as ever, and wondering just why it was that Nicholas, after all these years of love and pain, found it necessary to look for pleasure elsewhere, in other bodies, and how long it would be before she would be able to do the same.

She got down on the floor to do her push-ups, enjoying the strain in her arms and her stomach muscles, forcing herself to do ten more than the usual number. For all that he could be hateful, despite the things that had happened between them, Diana could not see herself in the mirror without thinking of Nicholas, in the days when they had both been passionately in love, and he would suddenly take her, throw her to the floor, strip off her clothes and his own, often in so much of a hurry that he left her boots or her blouse on, or his own shirt.

Diana tried to discipline her mind, to turn it away from the insistent image, felt herself growing warm with a warmth that had nothing to do with exercise, and was relieved rather than annoyed when the telephone rang next to her bed.

She picked up the receiver and heard with puzzlement a series of faint clicks followed by a loud burst of static, then silence. A magnified and distorted voice, like a message from outer space, suddenly announced in a West Virginia hillbilly drawl, 'Stand by, please. Call for Diana Beaumont. Is she there?'

Diana indicated that she was. There was a pause, and Paul Foster's voice, surprisingly clear after all the preliminary atmospherics, came on the line. 'Do you remember we talked about going to the country?' he asked.

'Of course I do.'

'Are you free Thursday? I have a break in my schedule.'

She had meetings planned for that day, but she said, 'That would be lovely. Where is your place?'

Foster's reply was lost in static, though Diana caught the words 'an hour away.' There was a noise like water running out of a bath, then Foster's voice came back on the line. 'If Thursday is convenient,' he was saying, 'I'll have a car pick you up early in the morning. Say at eight? Then we can have lunch together in the country.'

Another sharp burst of static interrupted their conversation. 'Are you still there?' Diana asked. 'Where are you calling from?'

The static ceased. Foster's voice came back, rather less clear now. 'I'm on my way to Switzerland,' he said. 'I have to see a man there about something I didn't want to discuss on the telephone. Until next week, then.'

With that, the line seemed to go dead for a few seconds, then there was a series of high-pitched beeps, though for a moment Diana thought she heard faintly the tinny echo of a familiar voice saying, 'Hello, Paul, this is Meyer . . .'

At thirty thousand feet, the mountains were invisible beneath a thick layer of clouds. Foster had never liked

Switzerland. If he had spent the war years there, like Niki, perhaps he'd consider the Swiss less smug and hostile. Thirty-five years ago Switzerland had been the Promised Land, tantalizingly close, yet unattainable. Safety had been just the other side of the mountains, but there was no way to cross them. When other people thought of Switzerland, they thought of chocolate, of Heidi, of watches. When Foster thought of Switzerland, he thought of Matthew Grünwald in the bank vault of the Bahnhofstrasse, holding in his hands the bearer bonds that controlled the Grünwald fortune. Had he thought about his nephew Paul when he made his decision? Probably not, Foster reflected. Matthew's mind must have been racing, weighing the risks, the consequences, the benefits. Not every man has to face his own conscience in a bank vault, locked in an elegantly furnished private room with a safe-deposit box on the table in front of him and a buzzer to summon the attendant.

'Hello, Paul, do you hear me?' he heard Meyerman say, the voice echoing in the cabin from the loudspeaker set in the panel above Foster's head.

'Yes.'

'So? Did you get anything out of Kane?'

'He knows about the Wotan Project.'

'That's not too bad. In fact, that's nothing.'

'He knows about Rademacher. Kane's looking for him.'

'That's not so good. Where *is* Rademacher?'

'In France. I don't know exactly where he's living, but I'll find out.'

'*Scheiss!* Why didn't he die in 1945? Matthew should have taken care of him.'

'He had too much on Matthew. Rademacher always knew how to look out for number one. Matthew bought him off, I expect. We can do the same.'

'How much will it cost?'

'Money may not be necessary. There are other things, for a man with his . . . history . . .'

'You talked to Diana, too, I assume.'

Foster examined the altimeter on the bulkhead in front of him. They were descending. He felt cold and lonely. Was the need for companionship a weakness? he wondered. Of course it was. 'She's charming,' he said. 'And very beautiful.'

'I know *that*. Did she say anything about Nicholas' plans?'

'No. She reminds me of that girl in London . . .'

Meyerman's voice betrayed a certain alarm. 'Paul,' he said, 'this we don't need. Things are complicated enough without one of your little romances. Besides, it's always a mistake to look for the same girl over and over again. Do you know what Bernie Baruch told me when I asked him what he had learned about life at the age of ninety?'

'No.'

'Baruch thought for a moment and said, "There are millions of beautiful women in the world — fuck as many of them as you can!" '

Paul looked out at the clouds — they must be on the approach pattern to Zurich already, he thought. 'I'll do my best,' he said to Meyerman, but his mind was on Diana.

Thursday, Diana rose early, in some doubt about what to wear, and chose a well-washed pair of blue jeans, butter-soft suede cowboy boots, a sweater and an old tweed hacking jacket. Just in case she'd be offered to ride a horse, she stuffed an old pair of schooling chaps in her canvas bag, together with a hairbrush, and tied an Hermès scarf over her hair, in the horsy style made famous by the Queen of England. It occurred to Diana that the only time she had ever been presented to Her Majesty during her brief experience as a countess, her husband the earl had disgraced himself by lighting up a joint in the Steward's Enclosure at the Derby, and had been asked to resign from the Jockey Club in consequence, the first in a long series of humiliating disgraces.

She wondered why the men in her life seemed to have so little self-control: Nicholas with his fierce anger and sudden brutality; Robin Wynchcombe, the twelfth and now almost certainly the last Earl of Windermere, who pursued ruin through gambling, drugs and drinking with a passion that might better have been invested in his marriage or his lands . . .

As she washed her coffee cup she wondered briefly just where Foster's country place was. She imagined that it was probably in Westchester or Dutchess County, but none of the reference books on her shelves listed a residence for Foster. As usual he had created a mystery, but it

90

was precisely his mysteries that made him interesting — that and his obvious determination to get his own way, which was always attractive in a man.

Diana had long since learned that most men obsessed with success (and what other kind was there in New York?) made bad companions and poor lovers. Nicholas did not fit into that category, of course; he was a playboy-prince, so rich by birth that small successes and even social prestige were almost meaningless to him, but most of the men she knew were so busy hacking their way to the top of whatever tree they had chosen that they had no time or emotional energy left for anything else, and even sex merely became a question of winning another man's wife, scoring another point, basking in the prestige of a new conquest. In the end, all they wanted was a woman who could make other men envious of them — somebody to show off at parties as living proof that they were still in the game, winners in bed as well as in business.

Foster did not seem to be that kind of man. Diana found herself wondering what his private life was like. Foster hardly seemed the type for celibacy, but he had no known liaisons. Even Aaron Diamond, who knew the latest gossip about everyone, as well as the vintage stuff, had heard little of interest about Foster. Since the break-up of his much-publicized marriage to Dawn Safire, he had lived out of the limelight, unless you counted the financial press, though Aaron *had* heard that several people had grown rich supplying Foster with attractive young women who were well paid for their discretion. 'He's a busy man,' Aaron said. 'He pays to get laid, nothing wrong with that.'

She found herself wondering what Foster was like in bed and firmly directed her mind elsewhere. For years she had been a one-man woman. If nothing else, Nicholas had made her aware of her own strong sexual needs. Sex was a serious part of his life, and it had become a serious part of hers. In the last two years he had begun to deprive her of that, and at times she hated him for having aroused such deep feelings in her, only to walk away from them. On the few occasions when she had spent the night with other men, she had been unsatisfied. It was not their fault, she knew, but hers. She was used to Nicholas. How much *simpler* it must be, she thought, to be a man. But then, men had their problems too, as she knew very well.

What were Foster's problems? Why was he so secretive? He appeared to have no desire for recognition, or envy, or even approval. He pursued his goals, whatever they were, out of some deeper, private need. What exactly was it, she wondered, that drove him? And what was it that he was so anxious to hide?

Waiting at the curb in front of her building was a Mercedes limousine, with the rear windows blacked out. The radiator ornament had been removed and the chrome painted black, giving the car a faintly sinister look.

The chauffeur opened the door and helped her in so quickly that he was gone by the time she realized she was alone. Diana examined her surroundings with curiosity. In front of her was a color television set, a car phone with two lines and a hold button, a separate red telephone, presumably some kind of emergency hot line of Foster's, a well-stocked bar, a small vanity compartment with a make-up mirror, a high-intensity lamp and a stock of perfume, and a magazine rack with the latest issues of *Times, Newsweek, Business Week, Barron's*, the New York *Times*, the *Financial Times*, the *Wall Street Journal, Die Welt, Die Neue Zürcher Zeitung, Le Figaro, Le Journal des Bourses de Paris* and, presumably in deference to her, *Vogue, Harper's Bazaar, L'Officiel, WWD, Glamour, Mademoiselle and People*. Diana saw from the headlines in the financial papers that the price of silver had taken another jump. A Texas millionaire who had been playing the bear market in silver had shot himself in his Dallas mansion.

Behind her were two small reading lamps and a box containing Kleenex, Handiwipes and antiseptic throat lozenges. Did Foster, like Aaron Diamond, have a passion for cleanliness? Mounted in a small bracket on one side of the passenger compartment was a crystal bud vase with a single rose.

As the car swung up the West Side Drive, Diana searched for a button to lower the glass between herself and the driver. Unable to find it, she got up out of her seat, moved forward and tapped on the glass, since the back of the car was so large that the separation could not be reached from a sitting position. A muffled voice with a heavy accent materialized from a loudspeaker overhead, saying, 'It's not necessary, madame. If you push the ivory button on the console to your right, you can talk to me over the intercom. There is coffee in the bar.'

Diana opened the mahogany cabinet, where she found a thermos jug, a pitcher of cream, a bowl of sugar and a bowl of Sweet 'N Low, a beautiful porcelain cup and saucer that looked to her very much like Sèvres, and an antique silver spoon. By the time she had finished her coffee and glanced at the *Times*, she looked up and realized they were speeding down a commercial strip. On either side of her were gas stations, diners, discount stores, lawnmower repair shops, wholesale shoe outlets, junkyards and all the industrial flotsam and jetsam of northeastern New Jersey.

Before she could inquire about her whereabouts, the big car swung through a gateway in a wire fence, swept past two uniformed guards, who sprang to attention and saluted, passed between what appeared to be two large warehouses and suddenly emerged out onto the tarmac of Teterboro Airport, to draw to a stop beneath the wing of a gleaming white Grumman Gulfstream 2. The driver leapt out, ran around to open the door, and handed her over to a tall, heavyset middle-aged man in a trench coat and a battered hat, the same bodyguard who had accompanied Foster to the party.

'Mr. Foster is expecting you,' he said, and led her to the folding steps at the front of the airplane. She stepped into the warm, dark interior while the bodyguard hung her coat and the chaps in a closet, descended and gave a signal to the pilot. The stairs retracted into the fuselage with a low whine as the cabin door closed with a thump and locked itself shut.

'Good morning,' she heard Foster say as the engines started, scarcely audible inside the dimly lit soundproof cabin.

She pushed aside the curtain and saw him sitting behind an elegant breakfast table at the far end of the cabin. Foster stood up, seemed to hesitate between kissing Diana's cheek or hand, chose the cheek, then helped her into a chair.

'You look very beautiful,' he said.

'Thank you for the flowers.'

He gave a shy smile and shrugged.

'You travel in style. Who lays all this out?'

'The steward. He sits up front with the pilots so I can be alone.'

'And the bodyguard?'

'Luther? I didn't think we'd need him.'

'Where exactly are we going?'

'To the farm. It's in Middleburg. Virginia.'

'I hadn't counted on such a long trip. It's like being kidnapped.'

'Nothing would give me greater pleasure than to kidnap you, my dear, but it's actually less than an hour to Dulles. You'll have a look around, perhaps a ride, and we'll eat lunch.'

'You seem to have thought of everything.'

'It's my speciality in life.'

Foster, Diana noticed, was wearing his usual dark suit. He did not seem to have country clothes. She felt the airplane gather speed as it taxied down the runway, and took note of the fact that Foster did not have to wait his turn for takeoff.

'Airborne, Mr. Foster,' the pilot's voice announced over the loudspeaker, in a familiar Southern accent.

'Thank you,' Foster said.

'Do you want to take any calls?'

'No. Please tell anyone who calls that I don't want to be disturbed.'

Diana spread butter and marmalade on a croissant. 'How was Zurich?' she asked.

'A meeting with a lawyer. Just business.'

'Are your trips always like that?'

Foster nodded. 'Most of them.'

'It sounds a dull life. No surprises.'

'Oh, life always provides surprises, even for the rich.'

'Don't you get bored with making money?'

Foster took a sip of coffee and thought for a moment. 'No,' he said. 'But money isn't the *object*. I don't like being controlled by other people. To be free, you need a lot of money — and power. Of course, one pays a price. One doesn't have the time to do the ordinary things that most people enjoy.'

'So to be free, you give up freedom?'

'Perhaps. But I have been powerless. It's an uncomfortable experience.'

She handed Foster a croissant, which he waved away.

'Surely you're not on a diet?'

'Not at all. I eat very little, though. Food is a distraction. There is no middle ground, you see. Either one eats simply and doesn't think about it all, or one has to think about it all the time and eat superbly. I enjoy good food, actually, but I would find it strange to sit down to a good dinner by myself, and dinner parties bore me.'

'I love good food myself. I can't cook, but I like to eat.'

Foster smiled. 'I'm so glad,' he said. 'Most women usually say they're good cooks, but very few of them are. Besides, why should a beautiful woman cook? One can *hire* a perfectly good cook. For somebody who likes to eat, you have a wonderful figure.'

'I hold myself back with a will of iron. And I exercise a lot.'

'So do I. I have a gymnasium, with all the latest Swedish machines, an Exercycle, the running treadmill, a sauna, and so on. If I'm travelling, I have an exercise program I carry out every morning.'

'You're a very disciplined man.'

'No, no. You know better than that. We don't exercise because we're disciplined. We exercise because we're *vain*. But, yes, in other ways I *am* disciplined. I have tried to break myself of it, but it's no good. Discipline kept me alive at one time in my life, when I was younger. Possibly that gives me an exaggerated respect for it still.'

'Were you brought up very strictly?'

'No, no. The discipline I learned later.'

'Did you grow up in the country? I did, and even after all this time, I still miss it.'

'Partly,' Foster answered with reluctance, shifting uneasily in his seat. He obviously disliked questions. Most people had long since learned not to ask them. *He* preferred to ask the questions, searching for new information, new ideas, weaknesses, anything that might prove useful. 'My grandparents had an estate,' he added as a concession to Diana's curiosity.

'Do you still go there.'

Foster laughed harshly, without humor, his eyes suddenly remote. 'No,' he said abruptly. 'All of that is gone. After the war, in England, I sometimes used to go to the country, but it wasn't the same.'

'What were you doing in England?'

'I was a refugee. What they used to call a "displaced person." I got a job eventually as a messenger boy for the *Financial Times*. I knew English, you see, so it was not so hard. I learned about money, and I made a great discovery: those who *have* money are always looking for someone who will show them what to do with it. Nobody will give you a penny to keep you from starving to death, but everybody will give you the money to invest for them, if you can persuade them they'll make a profit. All you have to do is promise them a better return than the savings banks — or more excitement.'

'It sounds simple.'

'It is. The whole of business is merely using other people's money. The rest is window dressing.'

'Did it take you long to learn?'

'No. I learned it in one day. Afterward it was just a question of putting it to use. Your friend Nicholas used to be quite good at it, but I'm not sure he isn't losing his touch.'

'He still seems pretty good at it to most people.'

'Probably,' Foster said, shrugging to indicate that he wasn't interested in what most people thought. 'Of course, his father was in a class by himself, a real heavyweight. You met him, didn't you?'

'It's too nice a day to talk about all that, if you don't mind,' Diana said.

Foster took her hand. 'Forgive me,' he said with a small, apologetic squeeze. 'Later we have much to talk about. For the moment, let's enjoy ourselves. Listen: the pilot is throttling back. We're starting our descent.'

Diana felt the increased pressure in her ears as the plane lost altitude. She looked out the window at the Virginia countryside — so much like Gloucestershire on a mild autumn day — as the pilot circled slowly to join the pattern; then the seat-belt signs came on and a small Oriental in a white starched jacket and black trousers appeared from the forward cabin to remove the breakfast things.

'Thank you so much,' Diana said to him, but the steward merely smiled broadly and went on with his work. 'He speaks no English,' Foster explained. 'He's Annamese. He knows a little French, but that's all.'

'Merci,' Diana said.

The steward hissed a sound that might very well have been French, though it was hard to tell, bowed deeply and retreated through the bulkhead door to the galley, which he closed quietly behind him.

Diana heard the wheels lock down. The pitch of the engines increased and the aircraft touched down with a gentle bump. The pilot reversed thrust, and as the speed dropped quickly, swung the plane hard over to taxi toward the far side of the airport, well away from the main terminal. The plane halted. Foster helped her up. The steward moved forward to hand Foster a dark over-coat, a black silk scarf and a pair of pigskin gloves. Then he helped Diana into her jacket and pushed a button by the cabin door, which swung up silently. She walked down the steps, followed by Foster, who guided her by the arm under the wing of the airplane and across the tarmac to a dark-blue-and-white helicopter, whose rotor was already beginning to turn slowly above them in the crisp Virginia countryside.

Once inside, Foster removed a pair of dark glasses from the pocket of his jacket and put them on against the glare in the helicopter's sunny cabin. His expression, Diana thought, was always ambiguous and hard to read, but without being able to see his pale-blue eyes, she found it impenetrable.

'Is it far?'

'Not by helicopter. Perhaps twenty minutes.'

Before long the helicopter swooped low, flying over what was clearly a large estate — farm buildings, plowed fields, small houses, a lake, wooded copses. The rolling hills flattened out, and suddenly a full-size race-course appeared, complete in every detail except that there was no grandstand. Close-by were three rows of stone stables, built around a central courtyard with a fountain in the center. Diana could see several horses being hot-walked around the yard, but before she could say anything the helicopter rose slightly to clear a low wooded hill, and before her she saw a magnificent eigh-teenth-century brick house, rather like photographs of Jefferson's Monticello, surrounded by formal gardens, barren at this time of year, and an intricate box-wood maze.

'Is that your house?' she asked.

'It's called Eglinton,' Foster said, as usual avoiding a direct answer.

'It's beautiful!'

'Yes,' he said simply. 'The original house was in poor repair. It was taken to pieces, every brick and beam, and reassembled. Actually, a new, modern, concrete, air-conditioned building was built on the site, then the old house was put back together around it. Outside, it is Eglinton, just the way it was in the eighteenth century, perfectly restored. Inside, there's a modern, fireproof structure; then, inside that, the original interior, totally restored.'

'What a lot of trouble to go to,' Diana said. 'Whatever for?'

'My paintings,' Foster said. 'I thought it would be a good idea to have them in one place.'

'As a museum?'

'No. Eglinton is never open to the public. There is a curator, a restorer, a staff. They catalog the collection, add books to the library, buy up pieces that go well with the interior of the house. Perhaps someday it will be a museum, I don't know ... I have a good collection of Stubbs — better, I think, than the Queen has at Windsor, maybe even better than Paul Mellon's.'

Foster's face did not reflect any great amount of pleasure in his collection. In fact, he was so detached from the magnificent house below them, and whatever treasures it contained, that on a momentary impulse Diana smiled at him, patted his hand and said, 'I had no idea you were a collector, Paul.'

Foster raised his sunglasses and gave her a startled look, though it was difficult to tell whether or not he was pleased that she had at last addressed him by his first name.

'It's a prudent investment,' he said, as if he were justifying the cost, adding, after a slight pause, 'Diana.'

'Do you come here often?'

'Very, very seldom. In fact, nobody knows I have an interest in it, you see. It's in Louise de Rochefaucon's name.'

Before Diana could ask who Louise was, or why Paul had seen fit to create a country estate for her, the helicopter dropped gently to the lawn in front of the big house.

A Land-Rover waited for them. Standing beside it was a dignified, elderly black man, whose freshly laundered work clothes gave off a faint aroma of horses — a smell that was at once familiar and intoxicating to Diana. As she stepped into the car she noticed that the door was decorated with a small gold monogram; the letters 'LdR,' in Gothic script, were surmounted with a ducal coronet.

It occurred to Diana that the bearer of these aristocratic initials might be Foster's ex-mistress. Perhaps she was *still* his mistress; perhaps Diana had misinterpreted his signals and confused a polite invitation with something more intimate. She was out of practice, she knew, but surely not to *that* degree? Paul himself showed no symptoms of anxiety as the car bumped down a grassy track toward the stable; in fact, he took her hand in his and gave every indication that he was pleased by his outing and her company.

'That's the stables,' he said with a certain degree of pride. They were the most extraordinary buildings of their kind that Diana had every seen, of a design and size foreign to the Virginia countryside, and more appropriate to an earlier century than the twentieth. The three long wings of the stable enclosed a sanded courtyard, turning it into something very much like the town square of a European city, with a huge carved fountain in the middle, on which life-size bronze horses pranced among stone dolphins, mermaids and allegorical figures.

'My God,' Diana exclaimed, 'even the Windermeres didn't have anything like this!'

Paul beamed as he helped her out of the car. 'The fountain is not bad, is it?' he asked, waving toward it as if he had just conjured it up out of thin air. 'It's pure seventeenth century, made for the papal stables. If you examine it closely, you'll see that it's actually a watering trough. In the summer, when it's turned on, it has sprays, fountains, waterfalls, spouts in the dolphins' mouths . . .'

'How did it all get there?'

'Ah, that's quite a story. William Randolph Hearst bought it. As with everything else he acquired in Europe, he had the whole thing taken apart, every stone numbered and shipped in crates to San Simeon. Then he began to lose money, or perhaps Marion Davies didn't like it, but in any case, the crates were left sitting under awnings somewhere on the San Simeon estate. I had a few talks with the present Hearst family about some properties I wanted to buy, and during the course of the conversations they mentioned the stables. So I failed to buy a chain of newspapers, but ended up with stables.'

The interior of the stable was as ornate and cavernous as that of a cathedral, the ceiling rising in a series of high, intertwined Gothic arches, the windows cut into the stone like those of a church. The floor was dark-red clay, clean, fresh and free of any odor, the surface neatly swept in zigzag patterns, like a Japanese Zen garden. The horses wore dark-blue sheets, with gold silk borders, a small gold coronet and the initials 'LdR' embroidered on them. The leg wrapping, saddle pads, blankets, even the grooms' sweaters were in the same colors, all marked with the same initials and the ducal crown.

'Paul,' Diana said, squeezing his hand, 'you'll forgive me for asking, but just *who* is Louise de Rochefaucon? Did you build all this for her?'

He took off his dark glasses and looked at her. His expression was wary, but with a hint of amusement, as if he had been wondering how long it would take Diana to ask the question, or perhaps merely enjoying his secret.

His expression turned more serious; he put his hands on her shoulders and looked at her for a moment. 'You must understand,' he said, 'that you're the first person I've ever brought down here. Giving flowers, or even diamonds, is easy, especially when you're rich. Giving away secrets is much harder.'

'That surely depends on the secret.'

'No, it depends on one's *nature*. To a secretive person, every secret is important. I must admit that I came to your party out of curiosity. But when I saw you I was very much *attracted* — is that the right word? And when we talked a bit, I realized we had a great deal in common. More than you might think. *So . . .*'

In a confessional mood, talking about his feelings, Paul seemed to lose his command of English. Not only his accent but his grammar became slightly foreign — not unlike Niki's when he was angry, Diana thought, wondering just what bombshell Foster had been saving up for her.

'Nobody knows this,' Paul continued, giving her a dramatic stare, 'but I wouldn't want you to have the wrong impression about my relationship with Louise de Rochefaucon —'

'I don't want to pry into your secrets,' Diana interrupted.

'No, no. First of all, that's not true. I can see from your face that you're *dying* to pry into them — you wouldn't be a woman if you weren't. In any case, I don't want there to be any misunderstandings between us. Louise is — my sister.'

There was a pause while Diana digested this piece of information. Around her she could hear the gentle sounds of horses as they snorted, played with their hay or shifted position with a heavy, almost human sigh. 'I don't see why that should be a secret,' she said.

Paul shrugged. 'There are reasons,' he said. 'It's better that our relationship is not generally known. Better for her. *Much* better for me. But you see, I trust you. I don't trust many people, but I have a certain instinct about these things. That's why I brought you here.'

'I'm flattered, Paul. But what on earth is so terrible about having a duchess for a sister? Or a millionaire for a brother?'

'Louise and I are both hiding from the past. There are still people alive who could make a great deal of trouble for us. And poor Louise has had enough trouble in her life —'

'What people?'

'Ah, the groom is bringing your horse . . . Why, the same people who made trouble for *you*. *A bientôt chérie.*'

It was a long time since Diana had ridden, but the pleasure of being on a horse — a good horse, at that — was so great that she managed to put Paul's enigmatic statement, or warning, out of her mind. Horses were in her blood, they excited and calmed her simultaneously. At times, during the days when Nicholas still hunted, played polo and steeple-chased, it had occurred to Diana that their whole life together was built around horses. Certainly, after they moved to New York so that Niki could play the businessman, things were never the same between them. Diana had been born in the country — Dutchess County, New York, as it happened, where her father hunted, failed at law and drank himself to

101

death — and while she had no illusions about farm life, something in her still responded to the sight of open fields and the smell of horses. She felt relaxed as she had not done in a long time. There was a pleasure to riding that was almost, but not quite, sensual, and she vaguely wished that Paul had accompanied her.

The groom rode beside her, obviously under orders to see that she came to no harm, and no doubt also under orders to make sure she did no harm to the horse. Whatever else there was to say about Louise de Rochefaucon (and Paul had left a lot unsaid), she was a good judge of horseflesh. The horses Diana and the groom rode were both big, flashy thoroughbred geldings, handsome and docile, the kind of animals that any foxhunter would pay a fortune to own, and the horses in the paddocks they rode past were even more valuable, first-class breeding stock of the very best bloodlines.

At first Diana felt stiff and awkward, as one always does when one hasn't ridden for a long time, but she was incapable of looking clumsy or graceless in the saddle — her father would never have allowed it. Silent and watchful, the groom led the way, trying her out in an easy trot, then gravely indicating that he intended to canter, or take a small jump. He himself rode with the short stirrups of a retired jockey, which he undoubtedly was, but like the rest of Foster's staff, if indeed he worked for Foster, he was as taciturn as a deaf-mute.

The groom pointed to the left, and she followed him at the canter up a hill and out into an open clearing. Pulling up, Diana looked back at the view. In the far distance, from one of the windows of the house, a flash of light caught her attention. She shielded her eyes and saw in the far distance that Paul Foster had his binoculars trained on her.

He was waiting for her when she returned and dismounted, his overcoat thrown over his shoulders.

'Very pretty,' he said as they stepped into the car. 'If Louise were here, she'd probably find something to criticize, but to me you seemed to ride — nicely.'

'She's an expert?'

'She's *the* expert. *Haute école,* dressage — she lives for riding. And racing. And breeding.'

'You don't ride yourself?'

'I used to. When I grew up, it was considered a necessary accomplishment, like shooting, dancing, speaking French . . . Ah, here we are.'

Paul took a small key from his pocket, inserted it in the lock, placed the palm of his hand against a plastic panel beside the door, held it there until a small green light flashed, then turned the key and withdrew it. The door swung open silently and closed behind them with the heavy thud of a bank vault as they stepped into an elegant eighteenth-century hallway, in which two identical staircases curved gracefully down on either side.

'This is a great curiosity,' he explained, taking Diana's coat. 'The house was built for a couple who were no longer on speaking terms. There are two identical wings, each with its own staircase, but only one front door. I suppose they didn't want to spoil the façade, or perhaps they didn't want their neighbors talking. They lived here for thirty years without speaking to each other. Three times a day they met for meals, in absolute silence, since there's only one kitchen and dining room.'

'What was the reason?'

'Nobody knows. Perhaps even they had forgotten. It's often that way, isn't it? People who live together find it hard to distinguish between hatred and love. In any case, they were buried side by side in the garden, and they took their secret to the grave — whatever it was. In their own way, they must have loved each other, or they couldn't have held a grudge for a lifetime!'

Diana shivered. There was something chilling about the story; and the house itself, with its paneled walls and museum furniture, was strangely lifeless and empty.

'It's cold here,' he said, misinterpreting her shiver. 'The temperature is kept to fifty-five degrees year round because of the paintings.' He put one arm around her shoulder and guided her into the dining room, their progress followed by small television cameras mounted on the walls which swiveled soundlessly to keep them in focus.

'You certainly have enough security here.'

'The insurance company insists on it. Besides, I once toyed with the idea of living here, after my divorce from Dawn. That was a difficult period for me. One of my executives fled to Costa Rica, beyond extradition with several boxes of my private papers . . .'

'What happened to him?'

'Somebody cut his throat in his hotel room. There's a lot of crime down there,' Paul said with a sigh of regret.

Some unseen hand had lit a fire in the grate, and there was a cocktail table with every imaginable kind of liquor, each bottle unopened, as if Paul's staff threw away anything that was opened, replacing it with a new one.

On a folding butler's table stood a thermos of coffee, a thermos of hot water and a teapot, a bowl of ice and a bottle of champagne in a silver ice bucket. The table itself was set for two people, with silver chafing dishes, an iced bowl of caviar, plates of smoked salmon and cold chicken, and bowls of fruit. Next to the fruit and flowers a telephone had been placed, its red message light flashing. Against the wall, on an ornate marble table, a computer console hummed.

Paul offered Diana champagne, which she declined, then poured her a cup of coffee. He made himself a cup of tea and glanced at the telephone.

'Will you forgive me an instant?' he asked, and before Diana had finished nodding, he picked up the receiver, dialed a number and closed his eyes in concentration. He did not announce himself or give a greeting — clearly his call was expected. He merely listened for a few moments, drumming his fingers on the table,then he interrupted. 'Just *do* it,' he said. 'I don't want to know your problems. Tell Archfang that our man in Washington needs more money. He'll know how to take care of it . . . So put *more* pressure on him! Remind him that we're not running a girl's school. We did some favors for him, now he can give us a little help with the SEC . . . Well, if it comes to that, Luther dug up some pretty good stuff on him. If you have to use it, go ahead. I can't talk about it over the phone . . . Anything else?'

He seemed in his element, the telephone receiver cradled between his ear and his shoulder. He hummed quietly while he listened. 'Of course I know what I'm doing,' he said impatiently. 'World consumption of silver is five hundred million ounces a year, and growing fast. Production is less than three hundred million ounces. How can the price *not* go up? I know all about Love Potter, I'll take care of him ... So spread a story that we're developing a new battery using silver oxide. Eventually a car that goes two hundred miles if you plug it into your household circuit for a few hours every night ... That ought to give the price of silver a push in the right direction ... Just do what I tell you.'

Paul hung up and touched a button on the computer console before him and watched the screen. Rows of numbers flashed in green, pulsated briefly and settled down to a steady, sickly glow.

'What on earth are those?' Diana asked.

He looked up. 'The day's silver transactions. But I can have what I want — gold prices, the Wall Street closings, the currency market, our own corporate figures ... They come off our main computer and we then transmit them by microwave relay. Eventually there'll be one of these in the first-class section of airplanes, on the Metroliner, even in your car if you want one. I prefer investing in all this kind of thing to the big-scale, all-or-nothing venture. I leave that to Nicholas.'

'Are you *always* in touch with your business?' Diana asked, ignoring the reference to Niki. She had no desire to become part of the competitive game Foster and Nicholas played with each other by proxy, and briefly wondered if Foster merely wanted the pleasure of seducing Niki's mistress. But no — she was, after all, Niki's ex-mistress. There would be no victory for Paul Foster in that accomplishment. On the contrary, Niki would doubtless feel *he* had gained a point when he heard about it. He would boast about Paul Foster picking up his castoffs, knowing Niki.

'I try to keep in touch,' Paul said. 'I don't want them to discover they don't need me. Besides, at a certain level, there are things only I can decide. What they don't know, they don't have to lie about.'

'Do you have a great deal to lie about, Paul?'

He paused for a moment, slightly taken aback. The question was obviously personal, but he chose to answer it like a businessman. 'There is always something to lie about,' he said. 'If one does well, one has to conceal it from the government; if one does badly, one has to conceal it from the stockholders. It's all nonsense, of course. Nobody expects businessmen to tell the truth. If they did, the

economy would collapse in twenty-four hours . . . Come.
Let's sit down. I apologize for talking business in front of
you. It's always boring for an outsider.'

'Not at all. I'm used to it.'

'Of course. It's the disadvantage of knowing rich men.
Nicholas must have talked about his business often.'

'No, he didn't have your passion for business at all.
Nicholas was like a schoolboy. He wanted to escape from
work. I was one way of escaping — not the most important, as it turned out.' Diana was suddenly conscious that
she was referring to Niki in the past tense. 'I'd rather not
talk about Nicholas, if you don't mind,' she said.

Paul nodded sympathetically. 'Have a quail's egg,' he
said. 'Personally, I prefer plover's eggs, but one can only
get them in England, and then only for a very brief season
. . . but of course, you would know that.'

Diana dipped her egg in celery salt. It was sometimes
hard to tell whether Foster was being ironic or not. Often
he seemed to be joking when he was at his most serious.
He sipped his tea while she ate, apparently content with
this elaborate imitation of domesticity. Artificiality as
such did not seem to bother him. Like so many refugees, he
was able to make himself comfortable in any surroundings, but never at home anywhere.

Diana finished her quail's egg and stared at him. Foster's last remark, though spoken with his usual ironic
charm, had the undertones of a challenge. Was he trying
to suggest that she had lived among the very rich as Niki's
mistress but didn't belong there? It was possible, she
thought. Most self-made men had a certain contempt,
more or less well concealed, for their guests, wives, mistresses, even their children.

Even when they were generous, they wanted you to
remember who paid the bills. They were quite capable of
serving plover's eggs and at the same time despising you
for eating them. Foster had not seemed to her to suffer
from this kind of rich man's Puritanism, but perhaps it
was something that developed in a man automatically
after he had made a billion dollars or so. It was more likely
that he was simply showing his dislike of the fact that she
had once lived with Niki, and been a part of that social
world Foster avoided and despised. Foster was determined to show that he was a more serious businessman

than Niki, but it was not a display Diana was about to accept.

'If we're to get along, Paul, you must stop playing games with me. I lived with Niki for ten years. I've sat at dinner parties with some of the richest men in the world. Some of them were interesting and amusing. Most of them weren't. I grew to hate the smell of cigars. I used to smell it in my hair, in my clothes. I could hardly wait to get upstairs and have a bath and a shampoo. I know a lot about business. And about plover's eggs, too.'

'*Touché*. I apologize.'

'Don't. I don't mind your talking about business. Why should I? It's your life. At least you do it because it *inter-ests* you. Most rich men talk about business to impress women. They think it's an aphrodisiac. It doesn't work with me. I'm not impressed by numbers.'

'Nor am I.'

'No, I don't believe you are. But if you want to compete with Nicholas, do it in the board room, not with me. I used to love him. Perhaps I still do. But I'm not one of his companies for you to take over, and I'm not going to hand you a prize for being smarter than he is, or a better business-man. If you can't talk to me without bringing up the sub-ject of Nicholas, then take me home.'

Foster looked embarrassed. He placed both hands on his knees and closed his eyes for a moment, like somebody at a funeral. Then he opened his eyes and shook his head.

'I'm an idiot,' he said quietly. 'It's what comes of living alone so much. I suppose I've been showing off for you. I can't deny it. Eglinton, the stable, the business . . . it's a vulgar thing to do. The fact is that I'm a very simple man. My life is complicated, but I'm not. I liked you when I first saw you. I like you more now that you've put me in my place. I should have been asking *you* questions. Instead, like a schoolboy, I've been putting on a show for you, trying to impress. Do you think you could learn to like me, all the same? I warn you: it's a serious question.'

'I like you, Paul. I'm not sure I *understand* you. And I've been hurt quite enough recently. I don't need another kick.'

'That's a serious answer. I promise not to kick you. I may flatter you a little, but that's my nature . . .'

Diana laughed. There was something comic, but at the same time appealing, about Paul's apology. It was impossible to tell whether or not he was sincere, but he seemed to be genuinely upset with himself. She leaned forward and touched his hand. 'Flattery makes me happy,' she said. 'You needn't worry about *that!*'

'My dear, flattery makes *everyone* happy. I will tell you something. Ever since we met, I've wanted to go to bed with you.'

Diana looked at him and laughed. 'But, Paul,' she said, 'I *knew* that!'

A brief look of annoyance crossed his face, though he kept smiling. 'I had hoped to be less transparent than that,' he said.

'You're not transparent at all. That kind of thing is simply hard to hide from a woman. But I have to tell you something. I wouldn't have accepted your invitation if I hadn't decided I was going to bed with you. If you asked, of course.'

Paul kissed her gently on the mouth. He took her by the hand and led her to the doorway, then paused, went back and picked up the champagne in its bucket and two glasses. 'You never know,' he said. 'We might want it later.'

She awoke with a start to find Paul staring at the ceiling. Apparently he hadn't slept — he seemed, in fact, to be his usual alert self, and Diana wondered whether he was already anxious to return to his telephones. If so, he managed to restrain himself, which was more than she could say for Niki, who had once made love to her while closing a deal on the Speakerphone.

There was something odd about waking up in a room that was not only strange but arranged like a display in a museum. Diana half expected to find the big four-poster encircled by a velvet rope, with curious visitors staring at her, catalogs in their hands.

How often sex with a man is a disappointment the first time, Diana reflected — not for the reasons *they* think, though that is sometimes the case too, but because the anticipation is usually more exciting than the reality. Paul was anything but a disappointment. His rigid regime of exercise and diet had kept him in shape, and while he was not young, his body was hard and firmly muscled. As for the rest, he approached sex with just the same intensity and curiosity that he approached everything else. He sought out her needs, her preferences, her desires, and then, at the crucial moment, imposed his own. Somewhere along the way he had learned that in the act of love women want everything to take place at their own rhythm and in their own way until they are close to orgasm, at which point they want to be dominated.

'You're a very good lover,' she said. 'Do you often bring people here?'

'No. In fact, I've never used this room, even to stay here by myself.'

Diana looked around, and guessed that he was probably telling the truth. There were no signs of occupancy — no telephone, no television set, no personal belongings. The only object that seemed out of place was a photograph on the bed table next to her, in an ornate silver frame with Louise de Rochefaucon's ubiquitous crest.

It was a small family group, a sepia print, badly faded and torn at the edges: two couples in Tyrolean outfits, one on either side of a gray-haired old man; in the foreground were three children, two boys in lederhosen and a girl in a dirndl skirt, her hair in braids, holding a bunch of wild flowers. In the distance it was possible to make out a panorama of mountains. It seemed to Diana that a figure on the right, a large muscular man standing slightly apart from the group, his feet planted solidly apart, was vaguely familiar with his hawklike nose, thin mustache and cigar. He did not look as if he was enjoying himself.

'What's this?' she asked, picking up the photograph.

Paul glanced at it and sighed. 'Louise puts these family souvenirs everywhere,' he said with an edge of irritation, or perhaps boredom, to his voice.

'This is your family? Where was it taken? Which one is you?'

Paul examined it more closely, as if he had forgotten its existence. 'Ah,' he said, after a pause, 'that was taken on the Königssee. That's Berchtesgaden in the background . . . Such pretty walks there! Once I was hiking in the woods with my father, and we met Hitler coming the other way, dressed in lederhosen, arm in arm with Eva Braun. Naturally, there were a couple of security guards walking behind.'

'What did Hitler say?'

'He said, "*Grüss' Gott*," of course. He patted me on the cheek and Eva Braun gave me a piece of chocolate. Actually, the poor Führer looked embarrassed, because no outsider was supposed to know Eva Braun existed in those days. Of course, my father knew Hitler, so he was obliged to stop and say hello to us. My father said he looked like the guilty party in a divorce case.'

Diana laughed. Foster was a different person away from his role as the mysterious tycoon. He was relaxed, warm, funny, not at all the cold fish he was rumored to be. Diana was happy to be there, lying in bed with him, the framed photograph propped on her stomach.

Paul leaned over to kiss her, his hand on the picture, but she raised it and took a closer look.

'What a *beautiful* woman!' she exclaimed.

Paul squinted at the photograph, his expression turning wary. Diana realized suddenly that he had kissed her in order to distract her from it. All the same, she could see no harm in her curiosity.

'Who is she?' Diana asked pointing at the woman with her fingernail. Foster paused. Either he was nerving himself to answer the question or trying to fabricate a hasty lie. Diana rather wished she had never seen the photograph, but it was too late now.

Paul shrugged. One way or the other, he had clearly reached a decision. 'That's my mother,' he said.

'She's got a wonderful face.'

'Yes,' Paul said simply. 'In many ways she looked very much like you. Of course, you can't tell in an old photograph like this. And she wore her hair quite differently . . .'

Diana kept looking at the photograph while Foster tried, very gently but insistently, to pull it out of her hands. She could see little or no resemblance between herself and the woman in a summer dress and straw hat, but Foster obviously did, and it perhaps explained the way he had stared at her when they first met.

She pointed to the two boys in the photograph, realizing that both of them were also strikingly familiar. One of them was slightly taller than the other, with a self-confident, devilish smile on his face; the other boy might almost have been his twin, but his expression was more withdrawn. 'Is this one you?' she asked.

Paul nodded wearily. 'Yes,' he said. 'It's a long time ago.'

'And the taller boy?'

He took the photograph away from her and put it down on the night table. 'You would have found out sooner or later,' he said. 'It's Nicholas, of course.'

5

Diana sat up in the unfamiliar bed, staring at Paul. She felt a certain curiosity, mixed with dismay, even fear. She had made love with a comparative stranger — a dangerous thing to do. She knew nothing of Paul's motives, his past, his intensions toward her, and she felt at once cheated and used. She was not really angry, not yet at any rate, but she was both eager and reluctant to hear the inevitable explanations.

'The man with the cigar,' she said, 'that's Matthew Greenwood, isn't it?'

Paul looked somber. He gazed briefly at the dim figure in a Tyrolean costume. 'He wasn't called Greenwood then,' he said.

'Perhaps not, but it's him. He was older when I met him, and angry, but it's not a face I'd forget.'

'No.' His voice was neutral. 'He was a ruthless man. He still is.'

'Is he your father? Are you and Nicholas —'

'Brothers? No. My father is the thinner man, there . . . Nicholas and I are merely cousins. What did Tolstoy write? *"Cousinage, dangereux voisinage."* He was thinking of a different context, of course, but bad blood between cousins is common.'

'Niki never mentioned it.'

'There would be no reason for him even to *think* of me as his long-lost cousin. At the beginning of the war he went to school in Switzerland. I stayed on. So far as anybody knows, I died in a camp, along with my father. Nicholas was luckier. One can't blame him for that.'

'But you *do* blame him for that — or something.'

'No, he's innocent — which is not to say that I've ever liked him much. When we were children there was bad blood between us. However, it's his *father* I blame.'

112

'What did the old man do?'

'He left *my* father to die. And Louise, my mother, myself.'

'What for?'

'Greed, of course. What else? Listen, you're angry with me . . . No, no, I can tell. And you're right to be. I went to your party because I thought we had something in common. The old man did a terrible thing to you. He did far worse things to me and to my parents. But when I saw you that night, I felt something I haven't known for a long time. Not just sexual curiosity — that's easy — but a real desire, a *need* . . . I'm not a man who likes to admit to needing anyone. I've always thought it a weakness. But now we've gone to bed together, and I have to tell you the truth, which isn't very pretty, and may even be dangerous. Do you love me?'

'I don't know. That's a big question, and a little early to say. I thought I was beginning to. Now I'm not so sure.'

'I think I'm in love with you. It's been such a long time since I've felt that, or even said it, that I can't be sure either. But it's a definite possibility. It makes everything more complicated. At my age, love is a risky business.'

'You're not old.'

'I'm old enough to be afraid of being foolish. And still young enough to be careful. I've spent a lot of time sitting on all my secrets, putting as much distance as I could between myself and the past . . . A few people know a little bit of the truth, but not many, and not much.'

'Meyerman?'

'Meyerman knows — a lot. Not all, however. He warned me that you were not only beautiful but intelligent, by the way. He was right.'

'Dear Meyer! My ex-husband used to say that Meyer had raised flattery to an art form. Still, it was sweet of him to say that. And I'm glad you think he's not wrong.'

'Strange. I think of Nicholas as your ex-husband. I had quite forgotten about *le pauvre* Windermere. Were you happy together?'

'Shall we settle on not asking questions about each other's past? Not yet, anyway. Marrying Robin was a daring move in the wrong direction. I wasn't cut out to be a member of the British aristocracy. No more was poor Robin, as it turned out. Tell me about Matthew

Greenwood. What did he *do*? Was he a collaborator?'

'It was more complicated than that. Oh, he *collaborated*, all right, but that's meaningless. Hungary and Germany were allies, so I'm not even sure "collaboration" is the right word. His relationship with the Nazis was at the very highest level. If he hadn't been Jewish, he'd have been tried at Nuremberg, along with Horthy and people like Krupp, Flick, and so on.'

'Why wasn't he?'

'He was shrewd enough to change sides. And he had information the Allies were desperate for . . . Have you ever heard of the Wotan Project?'

Diana shook her head.

Paul rubbed his hands over his face, as if trying to summon up an old memory. 'Wotan was the code name of the German atomic-bomb program,' he explained. 'Matthew Greenwood was deeply involved. He was even responsible for the decision to go ahead with it at the very beginning — though I have to confess my father knew more about the details than Matthew did.'

'I don't see why that's a threat to you. You must have been a child then.'

'I was. So was Nicholas. It's as if the damn atom were the family curse. The old man made a fortune selling uranium to the Nazis. Now Nicholas is committing billions of dollars to nuclear energy . . . Somehow, they — damn it, *we* — can't leave it alone. As for a threat, you have to understand: someone in my position walks a tightrope all the time. One doesn't want to fall off. There's no safety net for people like me. One has so many enemies —' Foster held up both hands, to indicate an imaginary host.

'I should think the Greenwoods were more likely to fall off than you, from the sound of it.'

Paul smiled enigmatically. Clearly, he had told Diana as much as he planned to for the moment — possibly more than he'd intended. 'I don't *want* them falling off,' he said. 'That's the whole point. I want to *push* them off, at the right time. I am owed that pleasure, at least. And a good deal more.'

She looked at him, but he seemed perfectly unemotional, as if his intention was devoid of passion or feeling and made perfect sense. Whatever rage had fueled him had burned out long ago. He might have discussed buying a new suit in exactly the same tone of voice.

'Matthew Greenwood is a very old man,' Diana said.

'Yes. That's why I'm now in a hurry. If I wait any longer, he'll escape.'

'He'll be dead.'

'Death is a kind of escape — from debts, from pain, from guilt. I'm not a believer. I don't trust God to do the job.'

Paul poured more champagne and sighed. 'There are times,' he said, 'when one longs for a cigarette. It's the small weaknesses of life that are the hardest to resist . . . What was Greenwood like when you met him?'

'You must know him better than I do.'

'I haven't seen him since 1944.'

'He was in a rage. Niki and I were living together in London, and he arrived unexpectedly one evening in a Rolls-Royce. He wouldn't speak to me at first. He was too busy shouting at Niki. I couldn't understand what they were saying — they were speaking Hungarian. He slapped Niki.'

Paul nodded. 'And Niki slapped you. They both have a streak of violence. But the old man's is more dangerous.'

'I couldn't understand what he was so angry about.'

Paul gave a shrug of disagreement. 'One has to think about his circumstances. He had everything to fear from a scandal. He'd become respectable. He had a lot to hide. There he was, building up his new empire, borrowing millions, going public . . . He couldn't afford too many questions, so he flew to London to straighten Nicholas out. No doubt he thought if he shouted hard enough, Nicholas would give you up. Frankly, I'm surprised he didn't. Nicholas was always terrified of his father.'

'He almost did. But he loved me, you know. And I think he also wanted to defy his father, just once. So he ended up making a bargain instead.'

'The old man is a hard bargainer. Nicholas is not in the same league. No marriage, no baby, a discreet role as Niki's mistress . . . What made you settle for that?'

'I loved Niki. It was that or nothing.'

'Yes, it's often the way. People go into a deal arguing about the numbers, then make up their minds because of something else entirely — jealousy, hatred, love . . . If you'd asked for a million dollars, Nicholas's father would

115

probably have given it to you.'

'I didn't want a million dollars. I wanted Niki.'

'Exactly. The imponderable element! What a surprise it must have been for Matthew! Since he couldn't bully you, I suppose he bullied Nicholas instead.'

'More or less. No divorce for Niki, no marriage for us — and a low profile for all concerned.'

'And the child?'

'I refused to have an abortion. It was too late for one, anyway, and Niki wouldn't hear of it either. I went to a discreet private nursing home in Switzerland to have the baby.'

'Of course. Greenwood would have been concerned about the future. All that money! He wouldn't let it go to an illegitimate child. He wanted a dynasty he could control, so he gave Nicholas the business interests in England and America in exchange for a little discretion on the domestic front. A good bargain for Nicholas, but not much for you.'

'I wasn't bargaining. I just wanted to get him out of our lives.' Diana was beginning to cry at the memory of her humiliation at the hands of Matthew Greenwood.

Paul stroked her hair and leaned over close to her, one arm around her shoulders. 'All this is painful,' he said, 'but there are certain things I have to say. First of all, you shouldn't feel guilty. You loved Nicholas; you took him on the only terms you could. As to what happened to the child, you can't feel guilty about that, either. Children get sick in Switzerland the same as everywhere else. Not even Matthew was responsible for *that*'.

'You know about it?'

Paul shrugged. He looked sheepish. 'I try to find out everything I can about the Greenwoods. I wasn't prying into your affairs, you understand.'

'Just business?'

'Just business.' He closed his eyes. The corners of his mounth turned down, and he suddenly looked much older, a man weighed down by how much he knew about other people's secrets. The scars on his face were more visible when he wasn't smiling.

'How did you find out about it?'

'I heard a few rumors. I had them tracked down. It's just a question of patience and money. When I put someone on it, I didn't think —'

'— we'd be in bed together like this?'

He nodded. 'Quite so. This was not part of the plan.'

'I'd hate to think it was.'

'Please don't. The plan — that one, anyway — is out the window. Do you believe me? It's very important to me that you should.'

Diana thought for a moment. She ran her fingers over his face, feeling the bump of his broken nose, and wondering why he hadn't gone to the trouble to have it reset. She did believe him, if only because it was in character. Foster was not the kind of man who would make a move of any kind before he had informed himself. She suspected that he knew a great deal more about her than he was telling, and she didn't mind. All the same, she thought, it remained to be seen if he could really tell the difference between business and his personal life. In a pinch, what would he do if he had to choose between his business interests and his emotions? Diana looked at him and hoped it would not come to that, for him, or for her.

Paul opened his eyes and turned toward her. In the shadows his scars receded, and the broken nose was less obvious.

'It was a terrible experience for you,' he said, touching her hand. 'Above all, you mustn't blame yourself . . .'

'I did for a long time.'

'That's natural. But you were very young. At that age we all make mistakes. Even Nicholas and his father probably thought they were doing the best thing in the circumstances. Well, and perhaps they were . . . Nobody could have foreseen the boy would get polio — in Switzerland of all places! Is he all right now?'

'I haven't seen him in a long time. He loves his foster parents. It seems unfair to complicate his life.'

'That must be very difficult for you — to stay away. And a courageous decision. You have nothing to be ashamed of. Still, even though one cannot go back and change the past, one can make a new beginning. It's not too late.'

Diana held his hand. His voice was low, soothing, deeply serious. Perhaps the subject of children was important to him in some way — he seemed genuinely troubled and concerned. Was it because he had no

117

children of his own? None, at any rate, that Diana or the rest of the world knew about. Or was it because of his own childhood, which had obviously been painful and difficult? 'Too late?' she asked. 'For what?'

'For justice. He has rights. Why shouldn't he have a share of the Greenwood fortune? Not that money solves anything, you understand, but it allows one to make choices.'

'I can't see Greenwood — or Niki, at this point — giving anything to my son.'

'No, neither can I. But if I — or we — play the cards right, they won't have a choice. If Matthew is going to pay for what he did to me, why shouldn't he pay a little extra for what he did to you? What's the boy's name?'

'Steven. Niki had chosen it if the baby was a boy, before his father arrived and made us give the child up.'

Paul gave a grim, ghostly smile. 'Steven,' he repeated. 'How very appropriate.'

There was a long pause. Paul seemed lost in his own thoughts. Diana reflected uncomfortably on the way Paul Foster not only had swept her into *his* life, which was at once secretive and bleak, but had forced her to think of those parts of her own life she had tried to forget. For years, Diana had suffered agonies of guilt about the child she had abandoned, or been forced to abandon, if you took a more charitable point of view. It had gradually eroded her relationship with Niki. She blamed herself for giving in to him, and she blamed him for his cowardly surrender to Matthew. In the end she had given to Niki the love she might have given the child — a double ration, as it were — and it was more love than he was able to bear.

Diana had tried to think of the child only at those unavoidable, three-in-the-morning moments when she couldn't sleep. It was a missing fragment of herself that she had been unable to restore, and Paul, with his usual precision, had instantly understood her feelings. No doubt he was ruthless and manipulative, but he had the instinctive understanding of a man who had suffered himself and knew all there was to know about grief and guilt.

'What are you after?' she asked him.

The question took him by surprise. Whatever he was after, he had been thinking about it for so long that it was now a part of him, like his fingernails or his eyes. 'I have an account to settle with Matthew. A debt, if you like.'

'What does he owe you?'

'Two lives. At least. And perhaps a few hundred million dollars.'

'What are you going to *do* to him?'

'You'll see. I've given it a lot of thought.'

'And Niki? I'm not a vindictive woman, Paul. Niki's behaved badly toward me, but that wasn't always the case . . .'

'I'm afraid there's one piece of news you haven't heard, then. Believe me, it gives me no pleasure to tell you, but perhaps better from me than from a newspaper . . . Nicholas is getting married.'

Diana gave a small, involuntary gasp of surprise. 'Married? To whom? He never even hinted at it!'

'I suppose not. It seems Nicholas intends to marry Augustus Biedermeyer's daughter — Angelica, I think her name is — the one who was on the cover of *Vogue* last month. He's been negotiating it for a long time. A connection between two dynasties like that isn't made in a day, and, of course, for Nicholas it's a lifesaver. Biedermeyer has banks, insurance companies, the breweries, a healthy cash flow. And the Biedermeyer women are said to be one hundred percent reliable about producing sons, which is important to old Greenwood. Not exactly a marriage made in heaven — more like a marriage made at Lazard Frères. It should give Greenwood's stock a shot in the arm.'

Diana wiped her eyes with a corner of the sheet. 'I should have known,' she said. 'I suppose everybody else did.'

'No. It's been kept very quiet. There's a lot involved — financially, I mean.'

'There was a time in my life when all I ever wanted was to marry Niki, but he refused to get a divorce.'

'That's been taken care of. Old Cardinal de Montenuovo pulled some strings in the Vatican. There'll be a nice quiet annulment. Why not? The Church owes Matthew Greenwood a few favors for past services. He's waited a long time to collect the debt, but as long as Montenuovo is alive, he knows it would be honored. They have long memories in Rome.'

'Niki must have been planning all this while he was

still sleeping with me.'

'Well, he wouldn't want to make the break before all his pieces were in place. He's not his father's son for nothing. Please stop crying. You're on the other side now.'

'Which side is that?'

'Mine.'

Diana lay for a long time in Paul's arms, trying not to cry. She wanted to be angry, but instead she was merely sad, recognizing at last that a whole part of her life and her feelings had been thrown on the junk heap, disposed of neatly as if it were of no value, a sacrifice to the larger needs of Niki and his father. Paul was silent, perhaps because he knew silence was the best comfort, but after she had dozed for a while, he woke her up gently, kissed her and began to swing out of bed.

'You need to eat,' he said.

'I couldn't.'

'Yes, you could. Bad news always makes one hungry. When they told the Kaiser that he'd been dethroned, he said, "Let's have tea, and everything will look better afterward." He was quite right. Come, put your clothes on. We'll go somewhere and have a good meal and cheer each other up.'

Diana resigned herself to Paul's plans with a sense of relief. 'All right,' she said. 'Where?'

'Paris,' he said firmly. 'I have something to do in France. Something you can help me with.'

'I can't go to Paris, Paul. That's ridiculous. I have appointments, work . . .'

'It's almost Friday, then comes the weekend. We can be in Paris tomorrow in time for lunch. You'll be back at work on Monday. The change will do you good. You'll sleep on the plane.'

'You're impossible. Anyway, I don't even have a passport with me, let alone anything else.'

'There's no problem. You have a driver's license?'

Diana nodded, fascinated despite herself at the ease with which Paul took control.

'I'll cable my man in Paris to have the DST arrange for your entry as my special assistant. He'll have a *permis de séjour* waiting when we land. You'll need your passport to get back into the United States, but Luther can pick it up from your apartment and send it across by courier.'

'How will he get in without keys?'

'He'll find a way in. It's in your desk drawer?'

'Yes, but how did you know?'

'That's where everybody keeps a passport.'

'What about my work? You aren't serious about flying to Paris tonight, are you?'

'I'm always serious when I'm making plans, Diana. Telephone your secretary from the airplane.'

'No, let me call her now. She'll have a hell of a lot of rescheduling to do.'

'Fine. I must get up and make a few calls myself. The pilot will have to file a flight plan . . . Always these tiresome details.'

Paul stood up and reached for his shirt, and as Diana turned over to look at him, she gasped. From his shoulders to his buttocks his back was a mass of long, deep scars. The hard, livid, rigid welts were like a roadmap of pain, standing out in hideous contrast to Foster's sleek, well-cared-for body.

'What on earth are those scars,' Diana whispered, '— a war wound?'

'In a way. Not the ordinary kind of war. They're from a whip.'

'A whip? What kind of whip would do that?'

'A bull whip,' he said. 'I'm sure you've seen them on farms. About two or three meters long, made of rawhide. You can kill a man with such a whip. I've seen it done. It will cut through muscle and lay bare bone. I was lucky. I received twenty strokes. Thirty was a death sentence.'

'My dear,' Diana said, stroking him. 'How did it happen? Who did it? Why?'

Paul leaned over and kissed her. 'It was a gift from Matthew,' he said. 'A family legacy . . .'

Part Four

Mass for an unbeliever 1936–1938

The most singular mingling of races occurs in Hungary, though the German element is more or less present in all the Hungarian towns, and is now becoming rapidly assimilated.

— BAEDEKER'S
Austria-Hungary, 1930

6

The three men sat in the dark study of Matthew de Grünwald's Budapest mansion. Above them hung a big, lugubrious portrait of the late Emperor Franz Josef, one neatly shod foot resting on the neck of a dead stag, the expression of the animal and the Emperor reflecting an identical and typical Austrian *Weltschmerz*. In the background, the Grünwald family of the time had been painted in with laborious attention to detail, staring stiffly at the back of the Emperor's neck, as if they too had been shot and carefully arranged by the gamekeeper. There were other, far more valuable paintings on the walls, but the Emperor himself had presented this one to old Hirsch de Grünwald, and it remained in the place of honour, above the fireplace.

Matthew sat on the right of his visitor; Stephen to the left. The visitor himself was a tall thin young man, dressed in an elegant *smoking*, with the face of an expensive divorce lawyer, at once discreet and greedy. All three men were drinking whiskey-soda. Matthew was smoking a cigar; Stephen, as always, a cigarette in an amber holder. Baron Günther Manfred von Rademacher had refused both. He was there on business.

'You are enjoying Budapest, *Herr Baron*?' Matthew asked.

Rademacher shrugged politely. 'I haven't had much of a chance,' he said.

'You must allow us to show you the sights, the night life. It would be a pleasure.'

'Unfortunately, I have to be back in Berlin tomorrow. If we have concluded our business, that is.'

'A pity. Another time. There's a Gypsy *Nachtlokal* . . . Incredible dancing and quite beautiful women. If you like the type, of course.'

Rademacher raised one eyebrow. He pointedly declined to explain what type of woman he liked, if any.

Matthew gave him a man-to-man smile. 'I think so far as our business is concerned, everything is in order. The price per carload, the terms of payment, the rate of delivery . . . Have we left anything out?' He closed his eyes, waiting for the inevitable.

Rademacher sat silent, leaving the question hanging in the air. He flashed Matthew an incandescent smile — the phrase 'boyish charm' might have been invented for him, had it not been for his eyes. 'There's just one small matter,' he said softly. 'The commission.'

Matthew feigned amazement, though he felt none. 'What commission?' he asked. 'You're the buyer, we're the sellers.'

Rademacher chuckled amiably. 'True,' he said, 'but since there's no immediate need for this stuff — in fact, let's be frank, if the general's interest in uranium hadn't been aroused by you, you couldn't give it away — I feel we should receive a small piece of your profits. After all, without us, you don't have a market.'

Matthew glanced at Steven and shook his head slightly. His dark eyes were sorrowful. 'My dear *Herr Baron*,' he said, 'I would never have believed such a thing. If we were dealing with the French, of course, or the Turks — well, that's another matter . . . A commission is normal with them, but surely not in Germany? I can't believe the general wants a kickback?'

He carefully knocked off some of the ash, examined his cigar and took a puff to restore its glow. In matters like this, a kickback was not unexpected. It was just a question of how much. One built a little extra into the price to cover just such a contingency, so in the end Rademacher and his master would be paying themselves for their 'commission.' He blew a smoke ring in a happy frame of mind.

' "Kickback" is not the phrase I would haver used,' Rademacher said. 'After all, we merely want to share in your good fortune. Believe me, a commission will pay dividends in future good will. Besides, what else are you going to do with the stuff?'

'There's been a demand for it from the Czechs.'

'I heard all about that. The Petscheks tried to make a toothpaste called Urania. They even had a slogan: "For a radioactive smile!'' It's stupid. How many people want a toothpaste that glows in the dark? No, no, you and I both know the facts. We'll buy your uranium, the general has told us to. Who knows, it may even turn out to be a secret weapon, though I personally doubt it. But in the meantime, ten per cent of your profit comes back to us, or we don't have a deal.'

'Five per cent,' Matthew said mechanically. He had calculated his prices on ten.

'Ten. Göring would never accept less.'

'He knows about it?'

'He will if it's less than ten.'

Matthew looked at Steven, who gave his brother a brief nod. 'It's a deal,' he said.

Rademacher raised his glass in a toast, with a sharp, ironic smile. 'You won't regret it,' he said.

But as Steven raised his own glass, he rather doubted that.

A formal dinner at the Grünwalds' was always an impressive occasion. Even Rademacher, who was clearly determined not to be impressed, was unable to conceal his admiration for the gold dinner service, the antique china and the plunging décolleté of Betsy de Grünwald — an admiration that he noted was shared by her brother-in-law, Matthew, whose eyes remained fixed on Betsy's bosom throughout the meal.

Though Matthew had said that they would dine en famille, they had been joined by another guest, who had arrived at the last minute, his robes fluttering from his long spare body, and who spent the early part of the dinner engaging Rademacher in a penetrating and well informed discussion of German politics. Imperious, cunning, handsome and well-connected, Monsignor de Montenuovo was, as Rademacher had discovered in a whispered conversation with Betsy, private secretary to the Cardinal Primate of Hungary, a prince of the Hapsburg blood and the brother of one of Hungary's largest landowners. He was fluent in every European language, knew everybody who mattered and was highly regarded in the Vatican, where Cardinal Pacelli had praised him as 'God's subtle man of affairs' after Montenuovo carried out a particularly delicate mission regarding some letters

His Eminence had carelessly left behind in Berlin when he was Apostolic Nuncio there.

'Of course there's nothing *wrong* with anti-Semitism as such,' Montenuovo said, delicately playing with the food on his plate, 'but as His Holiness himself told me, "It isn't necessary to make a big song and dance of it." Eat your food, my child,' he said to Louise, who was staring at her plate, 'there are millions who go hungry.'

'Unfortunately,' Rademacher said, 'it's not the nature of the Führer to do things quietly.'

'One understands that. Still, soup is never eaten as hot as it's cooked, that's what I told His Holiness. Take Hungary. We are blessed with a stable government, in the person of our dear Regent, Admiral Horthy. We have almost four hundred thousand Jews — say, six per cent of our national population. To keep the nationalists happy, we pass anti-Semitic laws. To keep the Jews happy, we don't enforce them.'

'They are barred from being officers,' Steven pointed out, despite a warning glance from Betsy.

Montenuovo nodded. 'True,' he said, 'but how many of them *want* to be officers? What's the harm in barring them from something they don't want to do? And what kind of officers would they make, anyway? Once they've converted, they can become priests, civil servants, even officers, I suppose. The point is, *our* anti-Semitism is religious, not racial. That's the big difference between ourselves and the Germans, with all due respect to our honored guest.'

Rademacher bowed slightly in his chair at the reference to himself. '*Bei uns*,' he said, 'things are a little different. The religious aspect is less important, particularly since the Führer is an *Ungottgläubige*. Still, in the end it's a question of business, isn't it? Where the Jews are needed, they will remain.'

Steven was about to launch into an argument, but Betsy shot him a warning look, reinforced by a frown in his direction from Matthew. Betsy, like most women of her class, did not concern herself with politics, and in Hungary all political discussions eventually came back to the Jewish question. She assumed politics was a pastime for men like her father or her husband, of no more or less interest and importance than horse racing, or going to the club or the coffee-houses. She had the born aristocrat's faith in the established order of things. Men read newspapers, involved themselves in politics, smoked cigars, and in the end nothing much changed. It was a game, like most of the things men took seriously.

'All this is depressing to discuss at dinner,' she said. 'Also, the children are getting restless. Off you go to play upstairs, all of you, and don't fight. Say goodbye to the monsignor.'

Louise, Paul and Nicholas lined up to kiss Monsignor de Montenuovo's hand. He gave each of them a chocolate mint from the silver-gilt bowl on the table, with the same precise ceremony with which he might have offered them the Host.

'*Des enfants adorables*,' he said mechanically, with a bow toward Betsy and Cosima as the children left the room. 'You must be very proud.'

Cosima nodded. 'Mind you,' she said. 'Niki is not an easy boy to control. Nor my nephew Pali. Also, the boys are very competitive.'

'That's natural in a family of great achievement,' Montenuovo said. 'Their great-grandfather Hirsch was a man of remarkable intelligence and ambition, though unfortunately obstinate in matters of faith. Do you know, my grandfather, old Prince de Montenuovo, once threatened to fight a duel with the baron? The prince got into an argument with Hirsch de Grünwald because he discovered they were sharing the same mistress. He said it was an insult to an Austrian nobleman to sleep with a woman after she had just slept with a Jew, so he challenged Hirsch on the steps of the Opera.'

Betsy put her head back and gave a long, deep laugh that scratched on Matthew's nerves like chalk on a blackboard. Cosima seldom laughed, and Betsy's laughter had a rich, sensual promise to it. He looked at her bosom and drank his glass of wine in a gulp, banging his ring against the rim to signal the butler to refill it.

'How did he know Hirsch had slept with her first?' Betsy asked, her eyes wide open like a knowing child's.

'Well, it was arranged that way. Hirsch visited her at lunchtime, my grandfather at teatime, and neither one knew about the other, though everybody else in Vienna did. Hirsch looked at my grandfather, doffed his *Zylinder* and said, "I don't have to fight Your Excellency; I'll simply bankrupt you." My grandfather backed down right away.'

'What happened to the woman?'

'Oh, they continued to share her. They were men of the world, after all. Eventually she married one of the de Feketes, and made his life hell. Good mistresses make bad wives. They become strict moralists once they're married, to make up for the past.'

Over the champagne and dessert, Montenuovo offered a graceful toast to the two ladies, then deftly moved the conversation back to business. To Rademacher's surprise, the monsignor was well informed about the Hermann Göring Werke — so well informed, in fact, that Rademacher made a mental note to have a little chat with Sturmführer Becker, the Gestapo security man at the HGW — the Göring factories — about possible leaks in the administration.

'The Bohemian coal mines, this I can understand,' Montenuovo said. 'A nice acquisition, even if you did have to put poor old Julius Petschek in a camp until he signed.'

'He got first-class treatment,' Rademacher said with some embarrassment. 'And we didn't touch Frau Petschek.'

'No doubt. I hear the Petschek's are in Lisbon now, on their way to New York. They won't make good propaganda for the Reich, you know.'

'They got paid for the shares.'

'In reichsmarks! You know as well as I do that the reichsmark isn't worth the paper it's printed on. You paid the Bechsteins in Swiss francs for the Österreichische Pulverfabrik.'

'Well, they transferred it first to British ownership. A clever move . . . Anyway, a munitions factory is worth more to us than a coal mine.'

'Yes, I can see that,' Montenuovo said judiciously. 'Gunpowder, coal, chemicals, all that I understand. But what's this about rare earth?'

'It's a matter of no importance,' Matthew said swiftly. 'A minor import-export deal.'

'My father never discussed business at the table,' Cosima interrupted primly.

'No, and nothing else either. He and your mother never

said a word to each other for forty years . . .'

'This uranium,' Montenuovo went on, pronouncing each syllable carefully and separately, 'I gather it has a certain strategic importance?'

'Not yet,' Steven interjected, 'but it's possible. I had some very interesting discussions about it in England. They hope to unleash the power of the atom itself eventually, to put the forces of creation to work . . .'

'É vero?' Montenuovo sipped his champagne thoughtfully. 'I've heard a little about it, of course. Is there money in it?'

'We shouldn't talk about money in front of the ladies,' Matthew said, giving Cosima a quick signal to withdraw with Betsy while the gentlemen smoked their cigars.

Monsignor de Montenuovo walked to the door with Betsy and Cosima, and courteously kissed their hands. Some priests preferred to leave with the ladies so as to allow the men to tell dirty jokes and talk about their mistresses, but Montenuovo was not one of them. He was a gentleman first and a priest afterward. He accepted a cigar from the humidor, chose a Cognac, and sat down next to Matthew while Steven took Rademacher around the room to look at the pictures.

'You should be careful,' Montenuovo said in a confidential whisper, leaning over toward Matthew as if they were in a confessional booth.

'Of what?'

'First of all, of the Germans. But also of our own beloved Regent. Difficult times are coming. You can't afford not to do business with the Germans, I understand that, and they're allies — of a sort. But what if there's a dispute between Hungary and Germany? You'll be caught in between. Not a good position to be in, particularly for a family like yours.'

Matthew eyed Monsignor de Montenuovo carefully through the cigar smoke. 'What exactly do you mean by that?'

'People still remember Hirsch de Grünwald.'

'Hirsch wasn't a *practicing* Jew. He may have had a little Jewish blood — all right, a *lot* of Jewish blood — but he never went to a synagogue in his life, and he was ennobled by the Emperor.'

'True, but he began as a horse trader in Szeged, and *his*

131

father's name was Isaac Grünzspan. In the eyes of people like Putzi de Fekete, one drop of Jewish blood makes you a Jew. Remember what he said in Parliament the other day: "It matters not to whom the Jew prays, the rotten mess is in the race!" '

'This isn't the Dark Ages! It's 1936. Besides, Putzi is a professional anti-Semite.'

'Unfortunately, he's not the only one. His Eminence is deeply concerned, this I can tell you for a fact. The Hungarian Church has always taken the view that the Jew should have no place in Hungarian national life — but once he's converted, in our eyes he's no longer a Jew. The extremists don't accept that. Cardinal Serédy is under considerable pressure to modify his position.'

'The extremists are a minority — totally discredited.'

'They won't be in a minority if war comes, dear friend. And your new partners in Germany are financing them secretly. You see how it is. The extremists of the left receive Moscow's gold, the extremists of the right receive Berlin's . . . Only the Church receives nothing. The Church needs your help, my son.'

'What kind of help?'

'Perhaps a modest share in your new undertaking?' Montenuovo suggested quietly, studying the ash on his cigar. 'The Church is a discreet partner, with much to offer.'

'Such as?'

'Silence, to begin with. I hear you're making the financial arrangements through your Swiss corporation, yes?'

Matthew put his finger to his mouth to warn Montenuovo to keep his voice down. He looked as calm as ever, but there was a noticeable ring of sweat on his brow, and his smile had the fixed quality of a wax dummy's.

'Exactly,' Montenuovo continued. 'If His Serene Highness knew you were not only selling strategic material to the Germans without consulting the government but *also* doing it through a Swiss company to avoid taxes and currency control . . .'

'May one ask where you heard these rumors, Monsignor? Which, I assure you, have no basis in truth.'

'Don't worry. We have a mutual friend on the Bahnhofstrasse in Zurich — Dr. Zengli. He's a director of your company — Corvina Ores, isn't it? He also handles some of the Vatican's more discreet investments. Have you seen his collection of Flemish Primitives, by the way? Quite exceptional . . .'

Matthew waved his cigar impatiently, dismissing Dr. Zengli's Primitives. 'Zengli talked to you?'

'I talked to Zengli. There's a difference. I think you'll find that with the Vatican as your partner — let us say, for a fourth of the profits — you'll have no problems with the Hungarian government. And there's a bonus, my dear friend.'

Matthew raised an eyebrow. 'What's that?' he asked.

'Our protection, when the time comes,' Montenuovo said. 'You couldn't ask for a fairer deal than that!'

7

Nineteen thirty-eight was the year of Baron Anton von Schiller's seventieth birthday, an occasion that naturally called for a family gathering, much as the Grünwalds hated the old man. Matthew's dislike of his father-in-law was so strong that even he was unable to conceal it altogether, and the rest of the family liked Schiller even less, with the exception of Cosima, who adored her father to a degree that was positively Oedipal — or, to be more accurate, Electral.

It was not the most convenient time for a visit to Austria, in fact. The discoverer of the Oedipus theory himself, Dr. Sigmund Freud, had just fled the country, along with several thousand other Jews — and *they*, as Monsignor de Montenuovo pointed out, were the lucky ones.

The *Anschluss* between Austria and Germany had been blessed by old Cardinal Innitzer of Vienna (in Montenuovo's opinion somewhat prematurely), and the smaller countries to the east hastened to pay their respects to the triumphant Führer. In Hungary, new and harsher anti-Semitic laws were passed; in Poland the quotas for Jews in the professions and the universities were halved; in Rumania, where people always went too far, a ghastly wave of pogroms swept the country. Only the Czechs held out, optimistically counting on the support of France and England. This holier-than-thou attitude so provoked their neighbors that Regent Horthy actually challenged the amazed Czech Foreign Minister to a duel.

Still, you couldn't complain about business, Matthew de Grünwald thought, as he walked beside his father-in-law along the lakeside path. The Germans were buying everything in sight, everybody was rearming and profits had never been higher. He looked at his father-in-law and sighed. The old baron, like so many Austrians, affected the trappings of the Alps as if they were a patriotic symbol. With his thin legs, his small potbelly and his furtive face, he cut a ridiculous figure in lederhosen, worn with a green mountaineer's hat, stout climbing boots and knee-high white wool stockings. He carried an alpenstock instead of his usual gold-handled cane and wore dark skiing glasses in place of a monocle.

' "Strength through Joy," ' Schiller said in his nasal voice, taking a deep breath. 'Man is part of nature. We only discover our true selves in communion with the mountains, the trees. The Germanic soul was born in the forests. On this subject the Führer is one hundred per cent right! When do you go to Berchtesgaden?'

'Tomorrow. I've been invited to lunch by Field Marshal Göring.'

'Ah? They've made him a Generalfeldmarschall, have they? How the generals must hate that! They'll just have to smile and take their medicine, though, like the rest of us. One has to compromise . . .'

'True,' Matthew said, pausing to wipe his face with a silk handkerchief. He looked behind, to see the rest of the family trooping up the path, the children in front, Cosima, Betsy and Steven following them. 'Do you think it was wise to join the party, however?' he asked.

Schiller leaned on his alpenstock, wheezing somewhat from his exertions. 'Wise? Of course it's wise. It's good for business. Everybody is doing it. Since the Germans took over Austria, the requests for membership in the Nazi Party have been so great that the secretaries can't cope with the applications. Dr. Weberein joined, and they only found out he was Jewish after they'd given him his party card and a lapel pin.'

'What did they do?'

'They made him an honorary Aryan, of course. It was less embarrassing than admitting they'd made a mistake. At least I joined before the Gadarene swine. I have even been appointed an honorary colonel in the Allgemeine SS. I forget what they call the rank, Standartenführer or some damn silly thing. You should see the uniform! Silver dagger, black riding breeches, a death's-head cap badge like the old Hussars — an outfit for a comic opera!'

'Have you worn it?'

135

'Only once, when I was presented to Hitler at the Opera. He told me my belt buckle was on upside down. I'll tell you this: the tailors in Vienna are making a fortune. Everybody is ordering breeches, greatcoats, tunics — there's no end to it. The bootmakers can't promise delivery in anything under six months. It's ironic, really, since all the tailors are Jewish. Gustav Cohn, my own tailor, told me business has never been better. Still, it can't last.'

'The business?'

'No, the Jews. The first few days were brutal, you know. All the amateur anti-Semites were out in the street, breaking shop windows and cutting off rabbis' beards. The scum of the gutters, and the police stood by and laughed — even joined in. Now things are more orderly. The professional "race experts" have taken over.'

Cosima and Betsy were making their way around the lake, the children running in front of them, the baron's dogs barking excitedly as they followed. Both women wore white summer dresses and broad-brimmed straw hats trimmed with ribbons and flowers. Louise wore a dirndl with a flowered bodice, while Niki and Paul wore lederhosen with long socks and white shirts.

'In times like this,' Schiller said, swinging his cane, 'the ony thing that matters is domestic happiness.' He gave Matthew a shrewd stare through his dark glasses, as if to indicate that his son-in-law's domestic situation was a matter of common knowledge.

'Surely,' Matthew said, 'what matters now is politics.'

'Not at all, my dear fellow. Politics has ceased to be of any interest at all. The gutter has risen to power. There's nothing to do but wait until it's over and try to survive in the meantime. There's going to be a war, any idiot can see that, and the only hope is that Hitler loses it quickly. Last time it took us nearly five years to lose, and look what happened — everything came to pieces. People lost fortunes! Cosima tells me that you're thinking of sending Niki to school in Switzerland.'

'Possibly.'

'I'll tell you frankly: it's a wise move.'

'Cosima doesn't think so.'

Schiller snorted. His opinion of his daughter's mental capacities was well known. Not that it was the poor girl's fault, in Schiller's opinion. It was merely a question of genetics. The girl took after her mother, who came from a family of such strict aristocratic inbreeding that half its members were either lunatics or objects of medical curiosity.

Given the baroness's genetic history, nobody was surprised when Cardinal Innitzer examined Cosima's hands and feet with particular care before the baptism and gave loud thanks to God that she appeared to have been born with all her faculties intact and the conventional number of toes and fingers. Intelligence, under the circumstances, would have been too much to expect in the child.

'I'll talk to her,' Schiller said. 'All the children should go to Switzerland.'

'I don't think Steven will let Paul and Louise go. Betsy would be heartbroken.'

'Then he's an even greater fool than poor Cosima,' Schiller said with a snort of impatience, and resumed his way up the mountain. At the top, they would pause for a family photograph.

It was a photograph they would treasure forever, Schiller thought.

Matthew watched the Schiller sailboat as Steven pushed it away from the dock. He could see Betsy, dressed in white, her long blond hair glistening even at a distance, and felt a spasm of desire, irritating at this hour of the morning when he had other, more important things on his mind, or ought to have . . .

He looked at the quiet, flat, blue expanse of the lake, shadowless under the bright morning sun. Nothing moved on it except the boat, which appeared to have been painted on a mirror, the reflections from the surrounding mountains etched darkly on its surface.

The sight irritated him further. Matthew enjoyed the prestige of his position as head of the Grünwald family, but still he envied Steven his lesser responsibilities and his happy family life — not to speak of his wife.

Brusquely, he dismissed the chauffeur and took the wheel of Schiller's Hotchkiss — one couldn't rely on the discretion of other people's servants, it was bad enough having to rely on one's own. After a brief struggle with the electromagnetic gearshift — could the damn French never build anything the same way as the rest of the world? — he circled the lake and set off for his rendez-vous at Berchtesgaden.

Matthew was used to having his own way — he recognized the same signs in Niki, and he was not altogether displeased, whatever other people thought. It annoyed him more and more that the one thing he wanted was Betsy. There was never a shortage of women for a man like Matthew de Grünwald, and Cosima had long since ceased to object to his mistresses, or simply no longer cared, but the one person he wanted most, he couldn't have. More and more, Matthew found himself looking for faults in Steven, who was showing signs of an inconvenient liberalism. Steven had always been the more intellectual of the two brothers. He was interested in books (had even acquired a small publishing house), he kept up with literature and art, his friends in Germany included people like Ullstein, Rowohlt, Salomon — names that were certainly on the Gestapo's list of undesirables. Sooner or later, there would be trouble. That kind of thing was bad for business. He made a mental note to have a talk with Steven.

Matthew turned off the main road to Berchtesgaden, followed a sign that read 'Reich Forest and Game Preserve' and was stopped after a few minutes by two guards in the green uniform of Reich Forest wardens, in front of a striped pole across the road.

'Grünwald,' Matthew said, using the terse, barking tone he knew was the only language these people understood.

The senior NCO unfastened the second button of his tunic and pulled out a piece of paper. He compared the photograph pasted on it with Matthew's face, stepped back, raised the pole and saluted.

In the woods behind him, Matthew could see the evidence of a more serious concern for security — he glimpsed an armored car, a couple of tanks and several 88 mm flak guns, heavily covered with camouflage nets. An occasional flash of binoculars made clear that he was being watched.

The road climbed through the thick forest, leveled out to cross a large meadow, on which two European bison were grazing, and then abruptly swerved between concrete tank traps to bring the visitor to the door of a bizarre chalet, an elaborate confection of carved wood, tiny leaded windows, ornate balconies and painted plaster, like the house on a Swiss cuckoo clock blown up to the size of a castle. The walls were covered with antlers — in fact, the entire front porch was constructed of joined and intertwined antlers — and though the windows were decorated with flowers, they had the oily blue cast of bullet-proof glass.

On the lawn in front of the house, in the distance, a cheerful group of people were watching Generalfeldmarschall Göring as he practiced archery, with a bow of truly heroic, indeed Wagnerian, proportions. He wore a vast pair of embroidered green lederhosen, a ribboned hat of theatrical appearance, like that of William Tell, and a short loden jacket that exposed, rather unfortunately, an enormous behind clad in suede leather. Beside the butts, a forester in the costume of a Renaissance page blew on a silver trumpet every time the field marshal scored a hit.

Grünwald stepped out of his car to be greeted by the major-domo. Behind him, an ironic grin on his face, stood Rademacher, dressed in the dove-gray dress uniform of a Luftwaffe colonel. 'Come in,' he said, giving a vaguely military salute. 'The Generalfeldmarschall will join us shortly.'

'From the sound of it, he's a good shot with a bow and arrow.'

'Splendid! Of course, the bull's eye on his target is twice the normal size, but nobody's told him that, so he's perfectly happy . . . What do you think of the uniform?'

'I liked you better *en civil*, frankly.'

'So did I, but these days in Germany, a man without a uniform is nothing. I was hoping to be made a general, but the boss told me the only ranks that count for anything are sergeant and colonel. Have a seat.'

The living room was enormous and so full of objects that it resembled an epic junk shop. At one end of the room a huge stone fireplace occupied most of one wall, chandeliers made of antlers hung from the hand-carved beams, the walls were covered with spears, tusks, helmets, shields, bearskins and the snarling heads of every variety of European game, and the floors were spread with pelts, fur rugs and hides. Above the fireplace was a life-size painting of the Führer, wearing a full suit of armour and carrying a lance, his eyes fixed in a prayerful expression as he contemplated the future of Germany.

'This is just a *pied-à-terre*, of course,' Rademacher said. 'We're building a larger chalet close to the Führer's, higher up the mountain. Karinhall makes this look like a suburban villa — but, of course, you've been there.'

'Yes. Though it's always changing.'

'You should see the latest — a special room with toy trains, miles of them, and airplanes that fly down on invisible wires to drop miniature bombs at the push of a button.'

'Ingenious,' Matthew said, sipping his coffee.

Rademacher smiled, displaying perfect small white teeth. 'It's the kind of thing that makes one proud to be a German,' he said.

Matthew considered this remark carefully. One found surreptitious anti-Nazis everywhere, even in the most surprising places, but of course a good many of them were *agents provocateurs* or Gestapo informers. It seemed unlikely that Rademacher was either, but one never knew.

'Have you given up your business career?' Matthew asked, settling down in a grotesque chair fashioned of antlers.

'Not at all. I'm still very much involved in the field marshal's business affairs. Which, by the way, is one of the reasons for this luncheon. To put it bluntly: you're doing so well that we'd like to go into partnership with you on a more equitable basis.'

'You already get ten per cent, let me remind you.'

Rademacher gave a thin smile. 'I don't need reminding. We're thinking of a *real* partnership now. Say, fifty-fifty.'

Matthew stared at him. 'You're joking,' he said.

'Not at all. Your trade with Germany has increased tremendously. Why? Because of us . . . Here comes the boss. Be tactful when he brings up the subject. Believe me, it's in your own best interests. Given your family background, you understand . . .'

Before Rademacher could expand upon this remark, there was a crash as Göring slammed the door shut and dropped heavily into an oversize armchair. Grünwald and Rademacher rose to their feet.

'At ease,' the field marshal said, 'or rather, sit down.'

'You're looking well, sir.'

'Yes. I'm one hundred per cent fit. This is a time when every German owes it to his country to be in fighting trim.' Göring shifted his vast stomach to rest more comfortably on his knees and helped himself to a piece of Turkish delight from the silver tray beside him. 'You know Rademacher, of course?' he said, dusting his fingers on a handkerchief, and struggling to suck the spaces between his teeth clean as he talked.

'Why, yes. We've just been chatting.'

'He's the new Nazi. The first generation were fistfighters, frontline soldiers, like me. The new generation has brains. You're a professor, aren't you, Rademacher?'

'A doctor of law, actually. I even studied at Harvard.'

'Doctor, professor, it's all the same to me. I'm just a simple soldier. The point is, Grünwald, Rademacher here understands business. He's as smart as a Jew.'

'Thank you, Field Marshal,' Rademacher said, in a voice that conveyed both sarcasm and a detached, cool irony.

Göring ignored him. To one side of his chair was a bowl full of uncut gemstones, which he played with as he talked, running them through his fingers lovingly, as if to calm his nerves. 'Rademacher talked to you?' he asked, his eyes fixed on the portrait of the Führer as if he had never seen it before.'

'Yes, Excellency, but with due respect —'

'No, no, I know what you're going to say. But look at the matter from *our* point of view. We've steered a lot of business your way, and we're not getting anything back in return. That's not the worst of it. *Certain* people are asking why we're doing business with a Jewish company. That puts me in an embarrassing position.'

'The Grünwald family is not Jewish.'

'*Na*, what about the old grandfather — what's his name, Hirsch? Listen, I'm a realist, man. When they came to me and said General Milch, my second-in-command of the Luftwaffe, was a half-Jew, I told the Gestapo to bugger off. If he works for *me*, he's Aryan, that's what I told Himmler, and that was that! I'd do the same for you, Grünwald, but there has to be a little —'

'Give-and-take,' Rademacher suggested.

'Exactly! And another thing. These damn uranium shipments have got to stop. We've got tons of the stuff already — and at what a price! I can't afford a scandal.'

'I was told the research was going very well, Excellency,' Matthew said, happy to change the subject.

Göring shook his head. 'No, no, it's all nonsense, just as I predicted. We've got a team looking into it — what's it called, Rademacher?

'The Wotan Project.'

'Everything in Germany now has a code name,' Göring grumbled. 'You can't shit without giving it a name from the *Nibelungenlied*. Anyway, Wotan is a waste of time and money. The army has a man who's building rockets, and all we can produce is a goddamn test tube that glows in the dark! It will have to stop.'

'We have a considerable investment in mining equipment.'

'Details. I don't care about that. You write it off, or whatever you call it, damn it. And, finally, this professor of yours, the expert on nuclear physics you sent us — what's his name?'

'Meyerman.'

'Exactly. I can't have a man called Meyerman working for us.'

Rademacher gave Göring one of his most ingratiating smiles. 'Field Marshal,' he said, 'Baron de Grünwald went to great trouble to make him available to us. So many of our best nuclear physicists have left Germany . . .'

'It's out of the question. That, at any rate, is final.'

Göring's decisive mood seemed to have passed, as if he had suddenly deflated like a balloon. His attention span was remarkably short, and although he was no longer addicted to morphine, he still had the addict's quick changes of mood and sudden depressions, which he fought by eating and by admiring his own possessions. He rose to his feet with a creak of leather, snorted and stumped around the room restlessly, running his pudgy fingers over the tapestries and bronze sculptures, as if to assure himself they were still there. He paused in front of a table covered with bottles and decanters, poured himself a sweet vermouth and returned to his armchair with the crystal goblet. The antique glass, it seemed, interested him more than the liquor.

'Help yourself,' he said, waving toward the bar. 'Soon we'll eat.' He crinkled his nose in anticipation, as if he could smell the food already, although the kichens were too far away for that. At the thought of food, however, his face became flushed and reanimated and something of his good spirits returned. 'We have,' he said with a gross chuckle, 'a good lunch before us, gentlemen. Fresh pâté de foie gras with white truffles, *truites au bleu* from the lake, veal Hohenzollern, and a tart made with strawberries from the gardens here. A simple meal, but in the country we rough it. Also, the Führer has ordered that the German meal should only consist of three courses, and that the leadership should set an example to the nation of Spartan simplicity.'

Rademacher raised an eyebrow. 'Surely, Field Marshal, that's four?'

'I don't count dessert as a course!' Göring snapped impatiently. 'We're not having soup. Surely that's Spartan enough? We're not at war yet.'

'You think there'll be a war, then? Grünwald asked.

Göring sighed. 'Only the Führer knows. He blows hot and cold, you know. A diplomatic triumph might satisfy him, but of course with Ribbentrop as Foreign Minister, that's not likely. On the other hand, if the Czechs give us Bohemia and the Poles give us back Danzig and Silesia, I don't see that there's much left to go to war over. The main thing is to have steady nerves.'

Rademacher glanced at the field marshal, whose own nervousness was clearly visible as he tapped his feet on the floor and played with his glass, and gave Matthew de Grünwald a brief wink of complicity, which Grünwald studiously ignored.

The door opened and the butler entered, dressed in the costume of a medieval servant, with pointed shoes, a gold winetaster's chain around his neck and a multicolored doublet rising to his chin. Göring got to his feet, eager for lunch, but the butler, whose face betrayed every sign of panic, clasped his hands in front of him, and announced, '*Herr Generalfeldmarschall*! An unbelievable thing! The Führer himself is on his way!'

'Oh, my God!' Göring's cheeks turned white under the layer of rouge. 'Cancel lunch! No, instead quickly cook some vegetables! And pastries! Have we pastries?

Perhaps he'll stay . . .'

Cool as a cucumber, Rademacher put out his cigarette
and signaled the butler to remove the ashtrays from the
room. Outside, they could hear the servants gathering on
the front steps. Göring drew himself up to attention while
Matthew and Rademacher stood behind him, almost
hidden from view by his vast bulk.

There was a pause, a dead silence, then the sound of
someone blowing his nose. 'Mein Führer!' Göring shouted,
raising hs right hand in salute as the familiar figure,
dressed incongruously in baggy lederhosen shorts and a
brown shirt, entered the room, his hat clasped protectively in front of his crotch.

The famous eyes, which were reputed to have such a
hypnotic effect, were dull, red-rimmed and watery.
Apparently the Führer was suffering from a mild spell of
hay fever, and indeed his voice had a nasal pitch as he
greeted Göring.

Behind him, a tall SS aide carried a bunch of field flowers, which the Führer had apparently gathered on his
walk as a present for Göring. He put down his hat, took the
bouquet of flowers, sneezed and passed them quickly to
Göring, who clutched them with both hands in an ecstasy
of gratitude.

'You will forgive me for dropping in, dear Göring,' the
Führer said unctuously, picking up his hat again as if he
didn't know what to do with his hands. He went on to
explain, at considerable length, about his daily walk, the
importance of fresh air for health, the need for speeding
up the circulation and the beneficial effects on his
digestion, which the Führer described in unwelcome
detail — a description made more telling by a sudden,
strong odor which suggested that he had just broken wind.

'Flatulence,' he said, 'can only be prevented by regular
exercise and a sensible diet. I used to suffer from it badly,'
he continued. 'Now, no more!'

A new wave of odor, causing Rademacher to bring his
handkerchief to his lips, seemed to indicate that the
Führer's optimism was premature.

'Wonderful!' Göring cried enthusiastically, apparently
unaware of the malodor. 'It's another example of the
Führer's well-known self-discipline. An example to us all!
You'll stay for lunch, mein Führer?'

But no — the Führer presented his lengthy excuses. He had dropped in at an inopportune time, he himself seldom ate lunch, he did not wish to interrupt the field marshal's luncheon or his no doubt important discussion of weighty matters with his distinguished guests . . .

Still clutching his flowers, Göring hastily assumed his responsibility as a host. He presented Rademacher — rather curtly — as a Luftwaffe officer, thus setting the Führer off on a long monologue about air warfare, a subject on which Rademacher was as ignorant as any civilian, while Göring shifted from foot to foot, waiting patiently for the Führer to draw breath.

'. . . Thus we see that the function of the air is always to act in support of the ground forces,' Hitler droned on, pausing at last to sniff, and giving Göring a chance to introduce Baron Matthew de Grünwald.

'We've met before,' Hitler said. 'I never forget a face. The Hungarian banker, yes?'

'Exactly, *mein Führer*.'

Matthew bowed to the Führer, who gave a short, jerky bow back, and broke wind again, this time more loudly.

'I'm a great admirer of your Regent,' Hitler said, a moment too late to cover the noise. 'Though I have to say that I'm not happy about Hungary at the moment . . . I asked the Regent for his support against the Czechs, and he sent me a long list of his needs for the Hungarian army. Artillery, rifles, machine guns, even *boots*, can you imagine? Surely the Hungarians could make their own boots?'

'If they march on Prague they can have all the boots they want,' Göring said with a high-pitched giggle. 'They can take them off the damn Czechs!'

'Just what I told His Serene Highness. *He* wants to march, I could feel it, he's an old war-horse, but the country is run by a clique of reactionary cowards and decaying aristocrats. The Jews are behind everything there, I'm afraid.' He remembered Matthew's presence and waved his hat as a sign of apology. 'No offense, I hope,' he said. 'Allies should be frank with each other. You do business in Germany, Herr Grünwald?'

Matthew nodded. 'We export industrial machinery, chemicals, coal, minerals, rare earths, and so on, Herr Reichskanzler. Through my father-in-law, Baron von

Schiller, we have connections with the biggest German banks.'

The Führer's eyes fixed on Matthew's, regaining something of their legendary brilliance. 'Rare earths?' he asked, snuffling slightly.

'Manganese, wolfram, uranium . . .'

'Uranium!' Hitler's face took on an ecstatic expression, his cheeks flushed against the pallor of his skin. He put his hat down and clapped his hands together. 'What a coincidence! Only this morning Speer — you have to meet him, he's a delightful chap, with such a head on him — was talking to me about uranium. Apparently there's a process for making it into a bomb.'

'Not yet, *mein Führer*,' Rademacher said, 'but we're working on it.'

'Speer says with a piece of uranium the size of a melon one could blow up a city like London. Totally devastated, destroyed, annihilated, smashed to rubble so hot one couldn't live in it for a thousand years!' The Führer paused for breath, momentarily overcome by the excitement of the prospect. 'A glass of water, please,' he said. He sipped it then turned back to Rademacher. 'Is this so?'

'It's possible, yes.'

'And we are pursuing it?'

'Absolutely, *mein Führer*!' Göring boomed. 'Years ago I took steps to acquire sufficient uranium. Baron de Grünwald has supplied us with carloads.'

'We can supply carloads more,' Matthew added, beaming.

'Of *course* more,' Hitler agreed; 'all you can! Does the project have a name yet?'

'Wotan,' Göring replied.

Hitler's eyes lit up. He gave a little snort of pleasure. 'The god of destruction,' he said with a smile, bobbing his head. 'Perhaps I'll stay to lunch.'

'I'd forgotten how prissy his table manners are,' Matthew said to Steven. 'And, my God, his view of the world is like a journalist's — all clichés and prejudice. He told me King Carol of Rumania was a pimp, and that all Rumanians are whores.'

'Well, that's true enough.'

'Yes, but you don't expect a head of state to talk that way. I think he underestimates the British, too. Apparently, when the Duke of Windsor visited Hitler he gave the Führer as a present a needlepoint pillow he'd made himself. It had a profound effect on Hitler — he's convinced the British are weak and degenerate . . .'

'It's a popular assumption.'

'But hardly a fact. Did the children have a good time?'

Matthew and Steven sat on the lawn, in the dark, looking over the lake and the mountains, which were faintly visible in the moonlight, the tips of their cigars glowing red in the night.

'Wonderful,' Steven said. 'Cosima was a little seasick, however.'

'She *would* be. She is allergic to pleasure — of any kind.'

'Niki was a little sad not to be with you, Mati. He cheered up later, they went swimming, and so on, we had a picnic on the island, but the boy is very attached to you. I wonder if it's a good idea to send him away to school.'

'It's for his own good. And safety, too, I might add. When he's older, he will understand and be grateful.'

'I'm not so sure.'

'He has to be toughened up, educated, prepared for life. You're too soft with Pali, I've always said so. I admit, Pali is smart, so perhaps he'll be all right, but Niki needs — shaping up.'

'He's your son, Mati, but I don't agree with you. All right, the boy's mother spoils him, but you can't correct that by treating him like a recruit or sending him away. The problem is that he wants to be like you, and it isn't in his nature.'

'He'll be like me. He's my son.'

Steven sighed and changed the subject. 'The discussion with Göring was satisfactory?'

'Yes and no. The Germans are going to put the squeeze on us.'

'That was to be expected.'

'Surely. Well, it's still good business, even if we have to give away a little of the profit.'

'But dangerous.'

'Everything is dangerous. It's a dangerous time to live in. So was the World War, but Father did well then. So

147

was the Franco–Prussian War, but Hirsch made his first millions because of it. Anyway, what's the alternative? Should we run away to New York and leave everything behind so the wolves can come in and pick up the pieces at bargain prices? We're not talking about a tailor's shop, we're talking about hundreds of millions. If we tried to dispose of ur assets, who would buy them? And at what price? And would Horthy let us take the money out of the country? No. You know that! Look at what happened to the Gebhardts! They panicked and tried to sell off their assets, and they ended up disposing of a *Geschäft* worth maybe three hundred and fifty million dollars for less than a hundred million — most of which they won't be able to get out of Europe. Idiots!'

'Well, that was in Austria.'

'Precisely. We're much better off. Hungary is an independent country, we can do business with the Germans quite handsomely, provided we're safe at home.'

'For how long?'

'I don't see any reason to worry. If war comes —'

'When it comes.'

'I repeat, *if* it comes, the Regent will steer a cautious course. If the Germans win, he'll come in on their side at the last minute, just in time to get a seat at the peace conference on the winning side.'

'And if they lose?'

'If they lose, he'll choose the right moment to change sides — as we will. We can't look after the interest of our shareholders — and ourselves — by running away, particularly when business has never been better. You've seen the figures! The Germans are buying everything in sight; I only kick myself that we didn't increase our plant capacity five years ago. And sooner or later Horthy is going to have to rearm; he'll need steel, chemicals, cloth, cement, loans, just like everybody else. No, no, there's good business to be done. It's just a question of knowing how to play one's hand, that's all.'

'And knowing when to fold.'

'Yes. Though for people in our position, safety lies in doing business. Remember what happened to those steel mills Grandpapa bought with the Rothschilds before the war, in Belgium? As it turned out, the front line went right past them, but for four years they were never shelled by either side. Grandpapa went to the Kaiser and asked him to protect the mills, Rothschild went to the French, and everybody on both sides agreed that a steel mill was too important to destroy — although they blew up the cathedral at Rheims, which wasn't that far away! Now, perhaps we should rejoin the ladies?'

'Yes. Though, to be perfectly frank, Mati, it's a pleasure to be away from your father-in-law for a moment.'

Matthew puffed on his cigar, his face momentarily illuminated by the glow. His eyes were closed, and he nodded his agreement. 'For an Austrian anti-Semite, he has all the worst characteristics of a Jew,' he said. 'I admit it. I'm grateful you came. Look at it this way: I'm worse off. I not only have Schiller's daughter instead of a real flesh-and-blood woman like your Betsy, but I have Schiller as a father-in-law. He's treacherous and suspicious, and he despises me. I can't divorce Cosima because we're Catholic, and I can't get rid of her father because of our German banking interests. I'd hoped the old fool would be arrested by the Nazis after all the things he's said about them before the *Anschluss*, but he joined the Nazi Party just in time to protect his damn skin. He's a sly fox! With any luck he'd be in Dachau by now, but instead he went straight off to Himmler with a list of Austrian Jews who had left assets behind in his bank, and the Reichsführer congratulated him on showing a truly German sense of duty. You can't trust anyone,' Matthew added bitterly.

'The connection with Himmler might be useful . . .'

'Perhaps. But since Göring is the number two man in Germany, we shouldn't have much to worry about. Still, you're right. Odious as he is, we need to keep old Schiller happy, now that he's a friend of Himmler's. Though I don't suppose he'd want to harm his own son-in-law.'

'Not as long as you're married to Cosima, no. And so long as there's no scandal . . .'

Matthew snorted. 'She's a loyal wife, I have no worries there. And she loves Niki. Still, you're right. A marriage of convenience is now becoming a marriage of necessity, I'm afraid.'

'Take care that she doesn't turn against you, Mati. A little more discretion might be in order.'

'Oh, I'm nothing if not discreet, don't worry. Once a

week I even perform my marital duties. She doesn't enjoy
it, you understand, but she expects it. It's strange:
domestic peace has become a hidden asset after all these
years.'

'Who knows? You might end up by enjoying it.'

'Your sense of irony is your least attractive quality, my
dear brother. Let's go in before Schiller or Cosima sends
one of the servants to look for us. We have an evening of
cards and fruit brandy ahead of us, God help us . . . Try
to lose a few hands to Schiller, for the sake of family
harmony.'

'And, Steven — be careful of Rademacher! He's no
longer a messenger boy. He's becoming ambitious.'

Part Five

Acts of faith

8

Diana slept most of the way across the Atlantic while Paul made his telephone calls in a variety of languages. As he had promised, everything was taken care of with smooth efficiency once they landed. A security official from the DST met them and took them through customs, nobody asked for their papers and the policemen merely stood at attention and saluted. 'It's so nice to be in France,' he said as they stepped into the limousine. 'Here there is no complicated class system — just a simple, healthy respect for money!' The limousine was smaller than the one he used in New York, though it, too, had the rear windows blacked out. A swarthy man with burly shoulders sat up front with the chauffeur, clearly a bodyguard.

'Are you always guarded, even on holiday?' Diana asked.

Paul looked embarrassed, perhaps because he was so used to the daily presence of an armed guard that he no longer noticed the man's presence. It was something he took for granted, like the car waiting outside the customs office so he could avoid the crowds of ordinary passengers in the terminal, the leather portfolio waiting for him on the back seat with urgent messages, the newspapers in three languages neatly placed on the folding desk.

'It's more important here than in New York,' he explained. 'In Europe, businessmen are kidnapped. In America, so far, they are merely insulted by the press and persecuted by the SEC. I have no intention of being kept tied to a chair for a month or so by the Red Brigades or the remnants of the Baader-Meinhoff gang. I had enough of that kind of thing in the war.'

It did not seem to Diana a sensible moment to ask Paul exactly what had happened during the war. She was, for the moment, happy enough to be towed along in Foster's wake, especially since his high spirits seemed inexhaustible. He was having a good time, and showed it. No sooner had the manager of the Ritz taken them personally to the suite than Paul was busy making plans. Diana had no clothes? They would buy some before lunch! In ten minutes they were back in the car, the bodyguard again sitting up front with the chauffeur, while Paul, humming with pleasure, sat beside Diana holding her hand like a schoolboy on his first date.

'Most men hate shopping,' she said to him.

'Not me. I love spending money. For a man, of course, it's a dull business. What can one buy? Another shirt? A pair of cuff links, except that I don't wear them ... That's the wonderful thing about being with a beautiful woman. There's so much more choice. *Arrêtez ici*,' he said, and took Diana on a blitz tour of the rue du Faubourg St. Honoré, apparently happy to wait while she shopped. He paid for everything in cash, from an envelope that the bodyguard carried, explaining to Diana with a laugh that he was too rich to bother with credit cards and checks. When she was finished, he stopped the car at Cartier's and bought her a gold necklace with lapis lazuli beads and a diamond clasp.

'It's not an important piece,' he said apologetically, 'but no woman as beautiful as you should be seen at lunch in Paris without jewelry.'

Promptly at one o'clock, the car deposited them at Taillevent, on the rue Lamennais, where Paul was treated with the quiet respect restaurateurs reserve for the rich.

Diana congratulated Paul on his choice. She liked the quiet elegance and luxury of Taillevent, though it had never been one of Niki's favorite restaurants. 'I can imagine,' Paul said. 'In the end, for all his money, Niki always wants to to go to the kind of places rich South Americans like. Or Arabs these days, I suppose. He can't help it. That's what happens when you go to Le Rosey for five years with the Shah, the Aga Kahn and the second-generation *nouveaux riches* of the world ...'

'Isn't that a rather snobbish remark for Paul Foster to make?'

'Probably. But there's nothing wrong with snobbery. Everybody is a snob about *something*, you know. Niki was

154

vulgar even as a child.'

'And you?'

'I was merely pretentious and superior. The truth is that we were doomed to become enemies by family tradition. Only one person could have control of the family fortune, and as the son of the older brother, it was bound to be Niki, not me. Well, I suppose he can't be all bad, since you loved him.'

'Nobody is all bad, Paul.'

He shook his head. 'One sees you are American,' he said. 'As a European who grew up during the Second World War, I would have to disagree with you. . . . Talk to me about yourself. I'm tired of talking about my family.'

Paul seemed happy to sit and listen. He asked about her childhood and listened quietly while she talked about her father, who drank himself to death from some secret sorrow buried so deeply in his reticent WASP soul that it was never revealed.

He seemed to be fascinated by her family, perhaps because his own was a secret. He roared with laughter when Diana described how she had met the young Earl of Windermere when he walked into the ladies' room at Wheeler's on Compton Street by mistake. With the easy grace of a true aristocrat he had introduced himself while standing in front of her, his fly unbuttoned and his penis in one hand, as she sat on the toilet with her skirt pulled up to her hips and her panties around her ankles. Afterward the earl used to say he had married Diana because there was no possibility of disappointment — with most blondes, you never discovered whether they were genuine or not until it was too late, but in Diana's case he had seen the pubic hair first, and knew she was the real thing. 'Besides,' he later told her, 'you weren't wearing those damn panty hose, and I was delighted by that — they've put an end to finger-fucking in taxis.'

Paul laughed easily as he picked at his food. He told her a little about his early years in New York, when he had worked as a messenger in a Wall Street brokerage house, and by keeping his ears open, had parlayed his $20,000 'stake' into $200,000 and used this as the leverage that enabled him, in a series of astute moves and by interesting big investors, to acquire for himself the controlling interest in a bankrupt Connecticut arms factory, just in time for the Korean War to turn it into a bonanza. It was there that he had met Savage, then the assistant treasurer of the company, whom Foster had wined, dined and won over in Hartford.

'You must trust him completely,' Diana said.

'Not at all,' Paul replied, sipping his wine. 'I've made him a rich man; naturally, he resents it.' Paul was, she noticed, reticent on the subject of how he had acquired his first $20,000, or what role Meyerman had played in his good fortune. He always held something back.

After lunch they returned to the Ritz — a hotel Niki had always avoided in favor of the George V. They made love for the rest of the afternoon, with slow, unhurried, growing passion. 'It's the Ritz Hotel that does it,' Paul explained as they lay on the bed in the elegant gray room, watching the shadows deepen. 'I think the column outside the windows in the Place Vendôme serves as a kind of phallic inspiration. When Sacha Guitry lived at the Meurice, he used to keep a suite here for his rendezvous with women. He said that he wasn't nearly as potent in other hotels . . .'

In the evening they had a drink at the hotel bar, where Georges, the elderly barman, seemed to know exactly what Paul wanted and made sure they had a quiet table, then later dined on the Left Bank. When they returned to the hotel, the suite was full of packages — lingerie, perfume, make-up, white silk trousers, maillot tops, even a dozen bikinis in different colors. 'Why the bikinis?' Diana asked, though in fact she was astonished by the whole display, as well as by the careful thought and planning that had gone into choosing exactly the right sizes — Paul had clearly kept the staff of his Paris office busy.

'Ah,' Paul said, with a guilty smile. 'It's a little surprise. There's somebody I have to see in the South of France. I thought we might fly to Nice early tomorrow morning, and stay at the Hotel du Cap, at Antibes.'

For a moment Diana felt a sharp combination of anger and disappointment. It was like being back with Nicholas again, who never discussed his plans and expected her to fall in with them, even at the last minute. Niki, in fact,

156

prided himself on just such surprises, which were designed less to please than to test his power, and her willingness to give in.

In the beginning she had given in almost always, even sacrificing her own child, and that had been a mistake, since her growing determination to resist had been taken by Niki as a sign that she no longer loved him. He was unable to understand that it was possible to love him and yet disagree with his choice of a restaurant or his decision to fly to St. Moritz for a week of skiing without giving Diana enough warning to shop, pack and cancel her appointments. Now, it seemed, Foster was doing the same thing.

'Don't you ever discuss you plans beforehand, Paul?' she asked.

He looked at her, then sighed. Unlike Niki, she thought, he was sensitive enough to know what the problem was instantly. This was not a man you could fool easily. He would always be a step ahead of you. Despite her anger, she rather liked that.

'An error of judgment,' Paul admitted. 'It's what comes from playing my public role in private, I suppose. I should have known better. Dawn, by the way, always complained about the same thing. I'm used to deciding quickly and then keeping things to myself until the last minute, then springing them on people by surprise.'

'It's demeaning, you know. I'm a grown-up woman. And I'm used to wealth. I'm not a would-be starlet who's going to fall into your bed for a trip to Nice and a few bikinis. I don't come that cheap.'

Paul held his hands up, like a boxer fending off blows. 'You win,' he said. 'I can't stand quarrels, and anyway, you're one hundred per cent right. Ninety per cent, anyway. I wasn't trying to buy you.'

'Please don't. Niki tried to buy me. Clothes, jewelry, fur coats, he was willing to give me anything except what I wanted. He always thought an Hermès crocodile bag would do the trick, or a diamond ring if necessary. It was his way of solving problems, you see . . .

'He'd behave badly, we'd quarrel, he'd buy an expensive present as an apology, then he expected to get laid, to prove I'd forgiven him. If I took the present and let him fuck me, then the incident was closed so far as he was concerned, and he could go on and behave badly again. If I *didn't* accept it, then of course he behaved even worse. I don't want that kind of relationship, so if that's what you've got in mind, let's stop now. I don't like surprises.'

'Oddly enough, I understand. I'm not fond of surprises myself. You're a woman of strong convictions, my dear. I like that.'

Diana thought for a moment. Actually, she wasn't at all sure that she had strong convictions. 'No,' she said, 'I simply don't like being taken for granted or bought off. I'd rather be cared *about* than cared *for*. Niki would have given me anything I asked for, but all I really wanted was gentleness, sympathy, feeling. We had those things, and he took them away, so the rest didn't matter. I suppose I was stupid to think I'd ever get them back, and to wait so long.'

'Not stupid. Optimistic, maybe. And perhaps loyal. Not bad characteristics, I would say. The truth is that I didn't hear about this piece of business until a few hours ago. I should have told you about it earlier. I won't make that kind of mistake again. Happiness is hard to get used to, you see. One has to break old habits.'

'You're forgiven,' Diana said, kissing him, for he did seem to be sorry, and for a moment she felt she might have gone too far. There was, she recognized, a certain pleasure in abandoning herself to Paul's plans. In the last couple of years, as Niki spent more time away from her, she had grown used to making her own decisions about life, usually over his violent objections. It was something of a relief to let Paul take over; like being on an ocean cruise — one basked in luxury while the captain made the itinerary without consulting the passengers. Then, too, there was a certain amount of curiosity, she couldn't deny it ... Bit by bit, Paul was taking her into his world, teasing her, perhaps unintentionally, with fragments of the truth, playing out a seduction that had nothing to do with sex but that involved his secrets and his own life.

'Is your business important?' she whispered as they kissed.

'A loose end to be tied up. I don't suppose it will be profitable, but it might be interesting. We'll have lunch tomorrow at the Colombe d'Or, I think. You should have time for a swim before, if we take off early enough.'

'And you?'

'Ah, no,' he sighed, as he gently unfastened her bra and bent over to kiss her breasts,' but I'll watch you . . .'

It did not occur to Diana until later that perhaps the scars on his back had something to do with Paul's reluctance to be seen in public without his usual suit. 'I think you'll like the Colombe d'Or,' he said as he undressed.

'I've never been so happy,' Diana said as Paul led her by the arm into the Colombe d'Or restaurant in St. Paul de Vence.

And indeed, she thought, it was true. He was one of those rare men who genuinely seemed to like women.

With other men, he was defensive, suspicious and withdrawn, and it was easy to see why few of them liked or trusted him. Women did not threaten him — in part, Diana surmised, because he had a curious, old-fashioned innocence about them. Much of the modern world seemed unknown to him. The women's liberation movement had had no impact on him — he was looked after by devoted secretaries, whose aspirations, if any, were not communicated to him. Insulated by money, power and his own need for privacy, Paul remained untouched by the demands of women and the changes in their lives. Somewhere, below Savage, there were people in the organization who dealt with guidelines, social policy, minorities. It was no concern of Foster's; he was only interested in 'the big picture.'

Paul was reticent about the women in his life, though it was instantly apparent to Diana that he was a man of wide sexual experience. He was silent on the subject. Unlike most men who have lived through a divorce, he had nothing bad to say about his ex. On the rare occasions when Dawn Safire's name came up, he talked about his marriage with the detached calm of a man describing an investment that has not worked out. When Diana asked him if he still saw her, Paul had to think for a moment. 'Sometimes,' he replied. 'I financed her last two movies.'

'Then you must still be quite close?'

Paul looked puzzled and shook his head. 'Not at all,' he said. 'She's simply bankable.'

She guessed that for someone as busy and secretive as Paul, a *grand amour* was problematic. It would require a major investment of time. A man like Paul would find intimacy hard to bear — unless the woman fitted into his plans. Diana wondered if she had allowed herself to fit into his plans too easily, but suppressed, the thought.

She was already aware that Paul's reputation for asceticism was exaggerated. He was used to having the best of everything, and like many rich men was simply under the impression that his comforts, even his pleasures, were necessary to his business. A man who thought in billions could hardly be expected to worry about details. The cut flowers, the private jet, the limousines were deductible expenses, and therefore not luxuries, He could buy anything, but there was nothing he needed to buy. Antique furniture, clothes, meals, his computers, telephones and airplanes were all bought by the corporation, artfully hidden away in the overhead by an army of accountants. No doubt a way had been found to put his girls down as a corporate expense. Paul would not even bother to think about that kind of thing; it would be done for him. His well-being and that of the corporation were inseparable.

Twice he had stepped out of character — when he married Dawn Safire and when he put together his collection of art. Both initiatives had apparently exposed him to more publicity than he wanted, and he retreated from them. Dawn had divorced him, and the pictures had been hidden away. Diana wondered just how far he would take *this* experiment, and whether he would retreat from her at the first sign of publicity.

She hoped not. Paul Foster was a complicated man, but he had appeared in her life at exactly the right time. She wanted him, even if it meant playing a part in his game against Matthew Greenwood. Besides, there was a certain excitement to being *part* of something instead of sitting on the sidelines, where Niki had placed her in deference to his father's wishes. In any case, it was difficult to worry about anything in the South of France, where Paul seemed to be at home and at ease. Here, he was not a foreigner — to be rich was to belong.

Some hint of the fact that Paul managed to fit at least *some* of the normal pleasures of the rich into his schedule was recognizable as they entered the restaurant. He was greeted with deference, as a valued client. In his grave, courteous way, he greeted the staff in flawless French, inquiring after the health of wives, children and aged parents. Much admiration was expressed for Diana, whom Paul introduced as his '*chère amie*.' Old Madame Roux herself, the *patronne*, actually waddled out of the kitchen to embrace Paul and scrutinize Diana, giving a nod of approval as she conducted them to a secluded table in the back of the garden, hidden from view by a corner of the wall and an olive tree.

'*Ici vous êtes bien tranquilles*,' Madame Roux said, snapping her fingers at the staff.

'Do you come here often?' Diana asked Paul as he accepted a glass of champagne from Madame and lifted it toward her in a silent toast.

'One can eat here without attracting a lot of attention — no tourists, no reporters, no paparazzi. Onassis often ate here with Callas — this used to be his table — and nobody paid any attention to them. Even when he came with Jackie, later, there was no fuss . . . though Madame Roux preferred Callas.'

'Why?'

'Callas ate more. Also, she treated Onassis better than Jackie did. She used to cut his radishes in half, salt them and pop them into his mouth. My father came here before the war. He loved France, and my mother loved food . . . In those days, it was just the village bar. St. Paul de Vence was a place for artists then, and when they couldn't pay their bills, they gave old Roux paintings instead. Fortunately for him, they included Picasso, Derain, Matisse, Braque . . . Now, of course, it's chic, but I don't mind.'

'Is Monsieur Roux still alive?'

'No, no. Madame has been mourning him for many, many years — in fact, I think she started to wear black even before he died, just to get into practice.'

'You didn't come here alone, did you, Paul?'

He smiled and signaled the waiter to refill their glasses. 'You're already starting to ask questions about my past — that's a sure sign you're in love! Women in love always want to know who their predecessors were. Men, on the other hand, don't want to hear about it. They want to believe they're the first!'

'No woman wants to repeat her predecessors' mistakes.'

He put his hands over hers gently. 'There's no danger of that,' he said.

'It's a wonderful place to be with someone you love. Not just the restaurant, but the South of France.'

'Yes . . . It's also a good place to be when you're not in love. I used to come here a lot with Dawn.'

'You weren't in love with Dawn?'

Paul stared out to sea for a moment. 'A Freudian slip,' he said. 'Looking back on it, Dawn coincided with a period when I wanted to lead a less — severe, perhaps — life. I had bought a movie studio, so it seemed perfectly normal to marry a star.'

'You can't have thought of it that coldly!'

'No, no, I didn't think of it coldly at all! I'm talking in retrospect, you understand. I've been here with a great many women, that's true, but never with one I loved. Until now. As a matter of fact, if you don't count Dawn, for whom I have a certain amount of affectionate respect, to be precise about my feelings, you are only the second woman I have really loved in my life.'

Diana looked at him and lifted an eyebrow. 'That's refreshingly frank,' she said. 'Most men say, "You're the only woman I've ever loved." I'm not sure I like being second.'

'Two in fifty years is not so many.'

'Who was the first, Paul?'

Paul hesitated a moment. He wasn't used to talking about himself, and it was perhaps for that reason that Diana believed him. He was offering her a glimpse of the truth, not much, but it was probably the most valuable thing he had to offer her. Anything else would merely be a question of money, and money, for a man like Paul was meaningless.

It was obvious to Diana that he had never talked to anyone about all this before. Most men talk about their former loves, their ex-wives, with practised ease, she knew. They had been asked the same questions over and over again by so many women that their answers were polished to perfection. They knew how to suggest that no previous love had been as good, as true, as real as the

162

present one — which was what women always wanted to hear — and they had usually long since turned their past marriages and love affairs into a carefully rehearsed little *répertoire* of anecdotes.

After all, why not? Women seldom told men that their previous lovers had been handsomer, richer, better in bed. Everybody tailored his or her past to suit the needs of the present, except perhaps Foster, for whom it was apparently a new experience to talk about it at all.

'It was a long time ago,' he said.

'During the war?'

'No, no, I was too young then. It was after the war, in London. I was very poor, very much in love. Meyer always made fun of me. He used to say, "Women make far less fuss about going to bed with a man they don't love, Pali, because he doesn't *count* for them." ' Paul laughed. 'Even then, Meyer was always the realist. I must say he was right. Meyer never had any trouble finding girls.'

'I can't believe you did.'

'Oh, I was shy then. Anyway, I was in love.'

'Who was she?'

'An English girl,' Paul said with a sigh. 'She was very young too. Her parents didn't approve at all. I was a refugee, a foreigner, with no prospects ... Oddly enough, she looked very much like you. It struck me the first time I saw your photograph, and even more when I met you. Now I can see that there are differences.'

'I hope so. One doesn't like to be loved as the image of someone else.'

'Don't worry. It was an impression only. You stirred up a few old memories, but perhaps that was to the good. We would never have met otherwise.'

'What happened to her, Paul?'

Foster shrugged, as if the end of the story were of no importance. 'She died,' he said, his voice carefully neutral. 'In childbirth.'

'And the baby?'

'The baby too.'

He clapped his hands together, dismissing the whole thing. 'Enough!' he said. 'For a long time all that haunted me, but it's over now. No more nightmares ...'

'I hope so. You have me.'

He nodded. 'I know. We'll drink to that. We'll even kiss on it. But quickly, please, because we have a guest for lunch.'

'A guest? Who?'

'Let's just say he's a voice from the past. You'll find him quite fascinating, I think ... I haven't seen him in years myself.'

Before she could ask who was going to join them, Madame Roux summoned up a platoon of waiters, with trays of crudités, pâtés, olives and breads, and discussed in detail with Paul the preparation of the lobsters she was determined he would eat, and to which he acquiesced, throwing his hands in the air to indicate that he would leave everything to her.

'Why do restaurant owners love you so much,' Diana asked, 'since you eat out so seldom?'

'That's simple. In the first place, I'm rich. In the second place, I'm loyal. Finally, I always eat with beautiful women. The two things a restaurant owner hates most are poor men and ugly women. If there are no beautiful women in a restaurant, it looks dowdy.' Picking the word with care, Paul gave a small smile of triumph at having found le mot juste in English. 'When Meyerman was still nobody — before he was even Sir Meyer — he used to eat at the best restaurants with no money at all. He signed the check, and the owners knew it would be years before he could pay, but they didn't mind, because he always brought the most stunning women with him. If he'd been alone, they would have thrown him out or sued him! Of course, even then people recognized that Meyer was going to rise very fast — Ah, here's our guest.'

Diana looked up to see a tall, exceptionally good-looking man who appeared to be in his late sixties making his way across the garden to join them. He was deeply tanned, his thick hair was silvery-white, he wore spotless canvas espadrilles, white duck trousers and a silk shirt, unbuttoned to show a muscular, tanned chest. Even from a distance, he seemed pleased with himself, walking with the erect posture of an army officer, his white teeth fixed in a gleaming smile. Around his neck he wore several thin gold chains, and on his right wrist hung a heavy identification bracelet in solid gold, on which several diamonds sparkled in the afternoon sun.

He clicked his heels noiselessly in his rope-soled shoes and bowed when he reached the table. 'Herr Foster?' he inquired.

Paul rose, and they shook hands. '*Bitte, setzen Sie sich, Herr Oberst*,' he said. As they both sat down, he inclined his head toward Diana, and said, 'Mademoiselle Diana Beaumont.'

His guest rose to his feet once more, took Diana's hand, kissed it, and switching to French, said '*Enchanté!*' in a voice that suggested he was anything but enchanted by her presence. His eyes took a calculating inventory of her assets but did not reflect any admiration or interest. They seemed instead to convey a disturbing combination of fear and hostility, in contrast to the smile.

'Allow me to present myself,' he said, in very presentable English — though with an accent that was strangely hard to place, a mixture of German and a faint trace of the broad vowels and clipped speech of Harvard — 'Colonel' Günther Manfred von Rademacher, at your service.'

'You know,' Rademacher said affably as he spread pâté on a piece of bread, 'France is the only decent place to live. In Germany. when we want to describe true bliss, we say "Happy as God in France." I have a deep love for this country.'

'Have you lived here long?' Diana asked.

Another flashing smile — the colonel clearly patronized a good dentist. 'For years,' he said. 'It was always my dream. I had lunch here for the first time in 1942.'

'During the occupation?'

'*Aber natürlich*. My duties took me to France often. The Ritz in Paris, the Hotel du Cap . . . Of course it was cheaper then. One paid in occupation currency, black-market ration stamps. Ten liters of *Benzin* would buy you a three-star meal. One liter, a woman,' he added unpleasantly, with a quick glance in Diana's direction.

'You seem to be living quite well still, Colonel,' Paul said. 'Didn't you find it difficult to get a *permis de séjour* here after the Nuremberg trials?'

Rademacher shrugged and sipped his champagne. 'Not at all. The French are realists. I had a list of French assets taken over by the Hermann Göring Werke during

165

the occupation. The arrangement has been enough to meet my simple needs: sun, a little wine, some good food, companionship — though at my age I don't require much,' he added ambiguously, with a smile in Diana's direction as if she had just offered to service him.

'So you don't live alone?'

'Most of the time I do, yes. But one makes friends so quickly on the Côte d'Azur — particularly in the summer, with all the young people on the beaches . . . Ah, here are *les langoustes*!'

The colonel carefully tucked his napkin into the neck of his shirt, placing his gold chains on top of it, and tasted his lobster. 'Ah', he said, inhaling the aroma, 'in Germany we have a saying, "The best *Hummer*" — what is it in English?'

'Lobster,' Paul said.

'Of course. So long since I spoke English. I forget some words. "The best lobster is the hardest to cut open." '

'Yet there's always a way to open it.'

Rademacher shrugged. 'That depends.'

It was apparent to Diana that Rademacher was there unwillingly, despite his transparent show of geniality, and she wondered just what pressure Paul had managed to exert on the colonel to bring him to lunch. Perhaps he had merely trailed an interesting piece of bait, for Rademacher had the expectant look of a man who knows he is about to be offered a deal of some kind.

'I suppose Irving Kane has tried to reach you?' Paul asked.

'Who is Kane?'

'Come, come, *Herr Oberst*. Let's not waste each other's time. Kane spent a lot of time tracking you down. So have I. I assume I'm here ahead of him?'

After a moment Rademacher nodded. 'By a couple of days, yes.'

'I presume he wants to interview you for his book?'

'May I ask why that concerns you?'

'Let's just say that I have a special interest in that period of the war. A rich man's hobby, like stamp collecting.'

'*So?*' Rademacher turned this over in his mind, and dismissed it. 'I have nothing to say to you,' he said. 'Or to this Kane.'

'I imagine Kane would make it worth your while, Colonel. As a matter of fact, so would I, for my own reasons. And I can make you a better offer than Kane.'

Rademacher examined his lobster with the care of a surgeon. He did not seem impressed. 'I don't know your reasons,' he said. 'I don't *want* to know. I have my own reasons for keeping silent. The past is better buried, anyway.'

'Matthew Greenwood would certainly agree with that. I imagine he told you to keep your mouth shut if Kane turned up, didn't he?'

The colonel sipped his champagne reflectively. His eyes were narrowed and cheerless. 'What makes you think so?'

'You must have known him well in the old days?'

Rademacher dissected his lobster with delicacy, holding each leg up and sucking it, then rinsing his carefully manicured fingers. 'Not well at all,' he said firmly.

'But he *did* buy you your villa, didn't he?'

Rademacher smiled at Diana, waving his lobster fork. 'The legs are the tenderest parts, mademoiselle. *Il faut les sucer.* You have to suck them. But it's worth it. The roe is also excellent, if you have the luck to get a female. At home, I like to remove the roe and sauté it in a little butter and Cognac, then I add cream and make a sauce.' He turned his attention back to Paul. 'What makes you think that?'

'I had somebody go back and look up all the deed transfers for Cap d'Antibes since the war. Greenwood bought the house on the Boulevard de la Garoupe in 1949, and it was transferred to you in 1950 for an undisclosed sum.'

Diana thought Rademacher seemed unconcerned by this revelation. He made a final stab at his lobster, then removed the napkin from his neck. 'It was a generous gift,' he said, 'to a fellow European in distress.'

'With all due respect, you were a Nazi and a war criminal, Colonel. If you hadn't given evidence for the prosecution, you'd have been hanged. What did you have on Greenwood to make him buy you a villa?'

With a sigh Rademacher turned his attention to the big straw platter of cheeses the waiter had brought to the table. He took Diana's hand and squeezed it gently, describing the various cheeses knowledgeably, and approving her selection of a chalky-white goat cheese. He himself declined the cheese and asked for a *café filtre*, a cigar and Cognac. '*La ligne*,' he said sadly, 'how do you say it in English? My figure? Yes? At my age, one has to eat carefully or one gets fat ... Tell me, Herr Foster, what do you have on *me* that makes you think I'll talk?'

'The Wotan Project.'

Rademacher waited politely until Diana had finished her cheese, then he carefully lit his cigar. 'Wotan is old stuff,' he said, puffing happily. 'The Allies examined the file and took away the papers and the scientists. They were ahead of us, anyway. In the field of rockets, we were in front, but with the bomb, years away ... All of that is moldering in your National Archives.'

'Not all of it, Rademacher. There were the slave laborers who worked on the site. The Wotan *Kommando*. They were working outside Magdeburg in the winter of 1945, weren't they?'

Rademacher looked wary for the first time. He sniffed his brandy with the gesture of a connoisseur but then drank it down in one gulp, bringing tears to his eyes and an expression of haughty disgust from the sommelier, who was watching from the distance.

'It's hard to remember,' Rademacher said, coughing slightly. 'Such a long time ago.' He smiled at Diana. 'You understand, mademoiselle, many unfortunate things happened toward the end of the war. People were starving and so on. There were epidemics. Nobody counted the dead.'

'That's not true,' Paul said implacably. 'The dead were counted. A mistake was made, that's all.'

'There were no survivors of the Wotan *Kommando*, Foster. None! *Das war der Befehl*! It was ordered so.'

'Ah, but what is ordered is not always accomplished, even in the Third Reich. There were survivors, my friend. I know.' Paul tasted his own brandy, nodded his approval toward the sommelier, passed the glass to Diana for her to taste, and gave Rademacher a thin-lipped smile, his pale-blue eyes fixed hard and unblinkingly on the colonel's face. 'You see, *mein lieber Herr Standartenführer*, I was one of them!'

Rademacher signaled for another brandy, and contemplated the tip of his cigar. 'I see,' he said glumly. 'And were there others?'

Paul nodded. 'Over to the left of the clearing, about a hundred meters from where you were standing. Stumpff didn't finish everybody off. He was drinking heavily.'

'Stumpff was an idiot. He shouldn't have been promoted to Sturmscharführer in the first place. I should have had him shot or sent to the Russian front, the drunken swine.'

'I imagine he had something on you, or you would have. In any event, I'm not the only survivor. I have signed depositions, some of them from German citizens still living in Germany, others from Israel. It shouldn't be difficult to find the mass grave and dig it up. I think there's quite enough to get you extradited to the *Vaterland*, even for the most reluctant of prosecutors. Of course there's no death sentence now, and you're right, it was a long time ago. With any luck, you won't have to do more than five years. No sun or lobsters. Not much for several hundred deaths.'

'Six hundred and twenty-three, if that idiot Stumpff had counted right.' He seemed pleased by his precise, bureaucratic memory. Rademacher closed his eyes for a moment, then made his decision. 'All right,' he said. 'I had a copy of Greenwood's agreement with the Hermann Göring Werke and the SS for the division of his assets — and all the files on Wotan.'

'What did you do with them?'

'What do you think? I took them to Greenwood and he bought them from me.'

'Weren't you afraid he'd have you killed?'

'After what I'd lived through? Don't be a fool Foster. I deposited notarized copies with a lawyer in Zurich. Dr. Zengli. He has explicit instructions to open them only in the event of my death by unnatural cause, in which case he is to send them to the United States Justice Department. So long as I'm alive, he can't open them, even if I asked him to. And if I die naturally, of a happy old age, he burns them. A very fair arrangement, for old Grünwald — forgive me, *Greenwood* — and myself. I assure you, he has a touching concern for my safety.'

'An ingenious arrangement.'

'Yes,' Rademacher said with satisfaction. 'It's based

on mutual distrust. What could be more reliable?'

Diana sipped her coffee and looked at the two men. Now that he had played his hand, Paul relaxed. 'I hope we're not boring you, Diana,' he said.

'Not at all. But what in God's name were you doing in a work camp in 1945?'

'Oh, it was a very common experience, I assure you. All part of a European education.'

'Not that common,' Rademacher said with what seemed to be professional judgment. 'The Auschwitz staff had standing orders to send us able-bodied men only. We had the highest priority with Kommandant Höss — first-class goods, no walking skeletons or children! Of course yours was a special case.'

'A special case! My father died, and I would have been buried in your mass grave if Stumpff hadn't been such a bad shot.'

'He was a first-rate shot when he was sober, poor chap. I remember you well — the Grünwald brat! Though your face is different now. One wouldn't recognize you easily . . . Well, I did my best for you, but at the end there was nothing more I could do. There were strict orders to dispose of everyone — *Nacht und Nebel*. You were supposed to vanish into the night and fog, as the saying used to go. Of course, by that time we were far behind with our paperwork . . .'

'You were in Budapest at the end too.'

'The end of what?'

'When Matthew left.'

Rademacher nodded. 'I brought him back from Vienna in my car, after the meeting with Schiller. We stopped in Raab for a drink. He was talking about Darwin on the way, and I remember his saying that it was just a question of the survival of the fittest — one had to look at life from a scientific point of view.'

'You were present when he and my father split the Grünwald assets between them?'

'What makes you think so, Foster?'

'My father told me, just before he died.'

Rademacher sighed. 'So many unfortunate things happened . . . Yes, I was present. Your father was worried about having to stay behind while Matthew went to Switzerland, so Matthew agreed to the split as a gesture of good faith. Your mother came in with a pot of coffee at one point, it was very late at night. My God, she was a beautiful woman! Such a pity what happened . . .'

'Was it a complicated document?'

'No, there was no time for that. It was just a letter. Matthew wrote it out in his handwriting, he and your father signed it and I witnessed it, then the two brothers fell into each other's arms and embraced. It was a moving scene. Of course, you would have been upstairs asleep at the time.'

'What did my father do with the letter? He said he put it away for safekeeping while you were there.'

'The answer to that question is worth quite a lot, isn't it? You can't expect me to tell you that for nothing.'

'You're right,' Paul said, pulling a thick envelope from his pocket and putting it on the table. 'These are the originals of the depositions against you. They're yours. You can burn them, send them into *Nacht und Nebel* and forget about them.'

'I was hoping for something more generous.'

'What could be more generous, Rademacher? I'm offering you peace of mind.'

'There could be copies,' Rademacher said cautiously.

'The copies are in the envelope, too. You know as well as I do that a German court would insist on seeing the signed originals in a warcrime case involving a German citizen. Think of the sun, the wine, the good food — all those handsome young men on the beaches . . . You're buying safety and comfort, Herr Standartenführer. You couldn't make a better bargain.'

Rademacher took the envelope, ripped it open with a knife and glanced through the papers. 'Very well,' he said. 'Your father put the paper in the bust.'

Paul leaned forward, puzzled. 'The bust?'

'Have I said it wrong? *Die Büste*. The bust? When your uncle Matthew left the room, your father looked around and decided to put the paper somewhere safe. He didn't want to carry it around with him, but he wanted to be able to get at it quickly. You know the big bronze bust of Göring your uncle had? Your father tipped it over and stuck the letter inside, then put it back firmly on its marble stand.'

'And he left it there?'

'I would suppose so. When things turned out so badly, it can't have seemed all that important to him. It wouldn't have kept him alive in Auschwitz.'

'One last question, Rademacher. What happened to the bust?'

Rademacher laughed. 'A bust of Hermann Göring! Poor fat Göring! He thought there'd be one in every town in Germany!'

He stood up, bowed, kissed Diana's hand and turned toward Paul, with a nod of his head, regaining something of his composure.

'Having gone so far,' he said, 'I suppose there's no reason to stop. I thank you for a delicious lunch, and a delightful opportunity to chew the fat over old times — the good old days, eh? As for the bust, it's not hard to find. When I saw it last, it was on Matthew Greenwood's yacht, along with the rest of his memorabilia. All you have to do is drive over to the port of Cannes, go on board and tip it off its base! And how pleased your uncle will be to discover that his dear nephew survived! *Au revoir,* mademoiselle. *Auf Wiedersehen — Herr Grünwald!*'

He gave a knowing leer and vanished behind the olive trees with the springy, athletic walk of an old soldier.

9

'It's quite a sight,' Diana said, as they sat on the terrace of the Voile au Vent, on the Quai St. Pierre, overlooking the port of Cannes. Paul nodded glumly, staring at Matthew Greenwood's yacht, moored to the quay like a giant among pygmies. A converted World War II Coast Guard vessel, it was easily the largest yacht in the port with its graceful green funnel, surmounted by a tall, sweeping mast bristling with antennas. A helicopter sat on the pad at the stern. There was even a swimming pool on the aft deck for those who didn't like a dip in the sea.

At the top of the gangway was a locked steel gate, and beyond it stood a security guard and a crew member. At night the gangway was guarded and floodlit. A signboard on the steel gate read:

STRICTEMENT DEFENDU D'APPROCHER
SANS PERMISSION — 24 HRES SURVEILLANCE
STRICTLY FORBIDDEN TO BOARD WITHOUT
PERMISSION — DAY AND NIGHT SECURITY
IN EFFECT

The message was thoughtfully repeated in German, Italian, Arabic and Spanish, and reinforced by an enameled plaque bearing the picture of a snarling guard dog, presumably for the benefit of those prospective trespassers who couldn't read.

Paul nodded. Reaching behind him, he took a pair of binoculars from the bodyguard who was sitting behind them and examined the ship. 'Impressive,' he said, putting down the binoculars. 'There's even barbed wire around the top of the hawsers. Were you ever on board?'

'Never. I was hardly the old man's favorite. He didn't want to see me and I was afraid of him. For years Niki wouldn't visit his father because the old man wouldn't

173

accept me, so we didn't get many invitations to spend time on the *Cosima*. Do you plan on taking up cat burglary?'

'No. I *did* briefly contemplate a small intrusion, but the ship is a hard nut to crack. Greenwood has had very good advice on security. I know people who could get on board, but they would have to know exactly where to find the bust, and there's a time element involved — they couldn't prowl around the ship looking for it. It's really a commando operation that would be needed, rather than a break-in. But that kind of thing attracts too much attention. I have a few other plans . . . Come, I think we've seen enough.'

Paul put his arm around Diana and took her back to the car, followed by the bodyguard. He was silent as they inched their way down the Boulevard de la Croisette and through Juan-les-Pins, then took the winding, narrow Boulevard du Littoral up toward the Hotel du Cap. As the car took the last hairpin turn, he pointed to the roof of a huge white villa below, screened from the road by pine trees and a high stone wall.

'That's his house,' Paul said. 'Within easy reach of Eden Roc by speedboat. I don't suppose he does that anymore, but sometimes they bring *Cosima* around to the Cap when the weather is calm, and anchor it off Eden Roc so he can sit in his wheelchair and look at the girls. Of course, you can't see much of Villa Azur from the road, it's only possible to get some idea of its size from the water. It has big terraces in front that run down to the sea, and an elevator that takes you down the cliff for bathing. You press the button, descend a hundred meters in a glass booth and step directly into the Mediterranean! The villa used to belong to the old Aga Khan — he had the elevator built when he became too fat to use the steps.'

Paul leaned forward and told the driver to take the entrance for Eden Roc.

'It's late afternoon,' he said to Diana, 'the best time for a swim. I'll make some calls, then we can have a drink and chat.'

'You're sure you won't swim?'

Paul seemed almost tempted as the doorman of Eden Roc opened the car door and they stepped out into the hot evening sun, but he shook his head. 'I'd rather watch you,' he said. 'I am quite happy to be a voyeur in this case.'

There are very few places, Diana thought to herself, where it would be so easy to feel ashamed of one's body as in the ladies' dressing room at Eden Roc. On some of the topless beaches at St. Tropez, where Niki Greenwood had loved to spend time in the summer, away from what he thought of as the stuffy atmosphere of Antibes and the reach of his father, it was certainly possible to feel one was over the hill at thirty, lying there on the sand surrounded by endless rows of young girls in their late teens with breasts as firm as little buds, narrow waists and small, muscular bottoms with hardly more than a string running decorously down the cleft, but at Eden Roc you stood naked in front of the mirrors, thigh-to-thigh with some of the most beautiful women in the world, wriggling into their bikini bottoms, examining their tans or, in the case of a famous French actress standing next to Diana, combing out her pubic hair, which had been shaped and trimmed to resemble a heart, and tinted an improbable platinum blond.

Diana had no qualms about nudity — she knew she had a good body — though here good bodies, even great bodies, were commonplace. It was said that the elderly Marquis de Montauban had offered the management $250,000 to install a two-way mirror in the changing room at Eden Roc so he could watch the spectacle. There were even rumors that his life's ambition had been fulfilled.

She emerged from the changing room in one of the bikinis Paul had provided her with, descended the steps and walked out onto the most expensive rocks in Europe, a quarter acre of stone and concrete covered with the bodies of men and women tanning themselves in the late-afternoon sun.

It was not so much the flesh that caught one's eye here — one could see more of that on the beaches at St. Tropez — but the blinding glitter of gold against tanned skin. Everyone seemed to be covered in jewelry. Gold watches, gold bracelets, gold rings, gold-framed sunglasses on the men; women wore gold chains around their necks or waists or ankles, or all three, bracelets, earrings, even toe rings. In the rays of the setting sun, Eden Roc basked in a steady, golden glow.

Diana pulled her hair back, conscious of the fact that several men turned discreetly to give her an appraising glance as she raised her arms, then plunged into the warm, transparent sea and swam steadily out to the raft. In the distance, to her right, she could see part of Greenwood's property, but there was no sign of life at the Villa Azur, except for the French flag flying from a mast on the rocks. In front of her, on the upper terrace of Eden Roc, she could distinguish the incongruous figure of Paul Foster standing in his dark suit among the bronzed bodies, looking out in the direction of Greenwood's villa. She felt a tremor of emotion for him, though she was not quite sure whether it was sympathy or love, and waved. He turned around and waved back, almost boyishly, and she dived off the raft, swam back to the ladder, climbed up the rocks, accepting a towel from one of the attendants, and joined Paul on the terrace.

He gave her a kiss, his lips hot and dry against her cold, wet cheek. 'You swim as beautifully as I had imagined,' he said.

'You should have joined me.'

'Yes. But I had a few calls to make.'

'To New York? It's so easy to forget it exists from here.'

'You're right, it's easy to forget the real world here — that's the point, of course. Why don't we stay over the weekend? We can be back in New York Sunday night, so you'll be in your office Monday morning. A couple of days in the sun won't do you any harm, I think.'

'I would love to — if you want to, Paul.'

'Good. Then that's settled. I want to very much. Tonight we'll have a quiet dinner.'

A gravelly voice interrupted Paul. It was Aaron Diamond shouting, 'Great to see you guys!' Diamond was on his way to an afternoon swim, startling in a brightly flowered ankle-length silk dressing gown, with a towel around his neck and another draped over his balding head to protect it from the sun. He carried a rubber bathing cap, swimming goggles, a shoulder bag and a copy of the *Hollywood Reporter*, which he generously offered to

Paul, who declined.

'Guy who doesn't want to read the trades has to be having a great time,' Diamond said, his mirrored sunglasses reflecting Diana's face back to her. 'You're looking beautiful, darling.'

'You're not looking too bad yourself, Aaron.'

'I feel like a million dollars. Listen, Kane is here, we're both at the Carlton. Let's have dinner tonight.'

Before Paul could say no, Diamond gave Diana a hug and said, 'Great, it's a date. Eight o'clock, my suite, we'll have a drink, go on from there . . .' He took off his towels, and put on his bathing cap and his swimming goggles. He produced from his pockets a pair of earplugs and a small rubber clip to fit on his nostrils, then he stripped off his dressing gown, revealing a shiny purple bikini that was hardly more than a jockstrap, and began to flap his way down the stairs to the sea in his rubber beach slippers.

From all over the rocks, men and women waved to him, tried to catch his eye. After all, at least half the people there had been, were or one day would be his clients. On the way down, he stopped and turned back, staring at Paul through his swimmer's goggles. 'Hey,' he shouted, 'I almost forgot, Foster. I've been buying silver like crazy. Made a fucking fortune so far. When should I unload?'

Paul leaned over the terrace — he liked Diamond. Putting his mouth as close to Diamond's ear as he could get, Paul whispered, 'Hold on for a month or so, then take your profits and run.'

Diamond nodded. He put on his nose clips, so that his voice took on a strange nasal pitch, like a Chinese speaking English. 'I hear Nick Greenwood is puying. Pig numpers.'

Paul looked puzzled for a moment. 'Ah, big numbers. Yes, I hear that, too. He likes big risks on commodities. He's been lucky, too. More than once the company would have been in trouble if he hadn't guessed right about wheat or sugar.'

'Plice of silver is going up like a fucking locket.'

'Yes, and it will come *down* like a rocket one day, too, Aaron. Very fast, then *bang*! Dump in a month. It's all right to graze with the bulls, but don't follow them when they stampede.'

'Play the pear market?'

Paul's face was expressionless — he had apparently given Diamond as much of a warning as he could. 'In the long run,' he said distantly, as if he were talking about some historical process, like Toynbee's curves, 'the bears always win.'

'I'm sorry about our quiet little dinner,' Diana said as they watched Aaron Diamond descend into the sea, performing a stately breaststroke on his way to the raft. 'Still, I'm fond of him. He and Meyer were very kind to me when my marriage broke up.'

'Oh, I don't mind. I'm fond of him too. Besides, it might be good for me. I don't see people much, as a rule. Besides, I have to confess that I'm delighted we're being seen together. I'm tired of secret romances.'

Diana laughed. 'I thought you loved secrecy!'

'No, no, sometimes it's necessary, but secret love affairs seldom work. Where there's something to hide, there's nearly always a problem. Believe me, I know.'

'Is Niki in above his head?'

Paul looked serious. 'Not yet,' he said. 'Let's go up to the hotel and make love.'

'Ah,' Diana said, leaning over to kiss him. 'I thought you'd never ask.'

Diana took a look at herself in the mirror of the lobby at the Carlton Hotel in Cannes. Despite her makeshift wardrobe, she looked chic enough for anything. You never knew with Aaron Diamond. He might take them to a dim, smoky bar-café or to an elegant restaurant, depending on his whim and on the latest discovery of his fellow celebrities.

They took the ornate elevator up to his floor, in the company of Foster's bodyguard, and knocked on the door of Diamond's suite. There was no answer. Paul knocked again, frowned and tried the door handle. It opened and the bodyguard, with a murmured apology, went in before him.

'Personne,' he reported, and, indeed, when they entered the big room was empty.

'Aaron!' Diana called out. 'Do you suppose something happened to him?' she asked Paul. 'A heart attack? He's not young —'

'I doubt it. Perhaps he forgot. Though that's not like him . . .'

The bedroom door opened, causing the guard to reach into his pocket, and Aaron Diamond appeared, holding a towel in front of him with both hands, like Venus emerging from the bath. 'Jesus,' he said, 'is it already eight o'clock? I must have overslept.'

Paul stared at him. 'Do you always take a nap with one sock on, Aaron?'

'I didn't notice. Listen, Kane's waiting downstairs in the lobby. I gotta shower, dress. I'm really sorry. I must have missed the alarm or something. We're eating at La Bonne Auberge, take Kane, go on ahead, I'll join you there.'

'Is he sober?' Paul asked.

Diamond was indignant. He threw both hands in the air, forgetting the towel, cursed and grabbed it again. 'Of course he's sober, for Chrissake. He went on the wagon two weeks ago to get ready for this trip. The son of a bitch drank Perrier water all the way across the Atlantic, he had to get up and piss so many times I finally gave him my aisle seat . . . Listen, don't wait for me. The table's in my name.'

He opened the bedroom door and vanished.

'He's not in bad shape for a man his age,' Diana said. 'Do you think he had a girl in there?'

Paul nodded. He was, improbably, giggling, then he burst into full-throated laughter as they stepped inside the elevator, to the scandal of the hotel servant.

He was still in high spirits as they searched the lobby for Irving Kane, who was nowhere to be found. There was no answer in his room, a bellboy found no trace of him on the terrace and the concierge denied all knowledge of his whereabouts.

'We'll have another look, then the hell with it,' Paul said and stepped into the bar just in time to hear a familiar, slurred voice shout, 'Don't you tell me I've had enough, you frog bastard.'

In the far corner of the room, slumped against a banquette, one arm draped over the shoulder of a blank-looking young girl in jeans and a yellow Paris *Herald Tribune* T-shirt, Irving Kane was attempting to hold on to the wrist of an indignant waiter.

179

'You have no respect for the arts!' he shouted. '*Je suis écrivain*! A writer, *savez*, like Balzac, Hugo, Ernest-fucking-Hemingway! Get me another double Dewar's, no rocks.'

In front of Kane, the table was littered with empty glasses and overflowing ashtrays. He wore a suit in which he appeared to have slept, and a shirt unbuttoned to the navel. His face was flushed.

'Give Monsieur Kane one more,' Paul said to the waiter, in his usual tone of quiet authority.

Kane released the waiter and waved to Foster and Diana, who sat down at the table.

'I thought you were on the wagon, Irving,' Paul said.

'I am. I just got off to stretch my legs. Where's Aaron? I've been waiting for him since six o'clock.'

'We were supposed to meet at eight.'

'Damn. I couldn't read his note too well. I lost my glasses somewhere. Say hello to Paul and Diana, honey,' Kane said to his companion, squeezing the nipple nearest to his hand to bring her back to life.

She gave a small cry, opened her eyes and said, 'My name is Sherri.'

'She gives great head,' Kane said, looking at her proudly.

'How do you do, Sherri,' Paul said, but she had closed her eyes again. Kane gave her a none-too-gentle punch in the ribs, and she came to life again.

'I have some great grass here,' she said, rummaging in the big yellow canvas bag beside her, which contained several dozen unsold copies of the *International Herald Tribune*.

'Not here, I think,' Diana said kindly. Sherri nodded wearily and lit a cigarette from one of several packs on the table.

'Kids love my work,' Kane explained. 'Sherri's read all my books.'

'I think we ought to be getting to the restaurant,' Diana said. 'Aaron will meet us there.'

Kane lifted his glass, signaling for a refill, to the consternation of the barman. 'I'm not hungry. You hungry, Sherri?'

She shrugged.

'You see? No point in eating until we're hungry. Relax,

180

loosen up, have a few drinks. You know what your trouble is, Foster? You live to schedule, like a fucking machine. That's why I get along so well with kids, they don't have hang-ups about time, schedules, all that crap. Somebody once wrote that the first act of the anarchist revolution should be to abolish all clocks ... Prudhomme, I think.'

Foster corrected Kane impatiently: 'It was Viscasz, from the preface to *The Meaning of Nothing*. It was a book that had a great influence on Sartre.'

'What makes you think so?'

'Sartre told me so himself,' Foster said simply.

Kane grunted. 'The trouble with you,' he said, giving Foster a look of frank hostility, 'is that you're too fucking *smart* to be rich. If there's one thing I can't stand, it's a smart-assed billionaire.'

'How is the book coming?' Paul asked, politely ignoring Kane's truculence. He was, Diana noted, always willing to suppress his feelings when it came to fishing for a piece of information, and she realized that Paul's ordering the waiter to give Kane his drink was not by any means a disinterested gesture. Kane drunk would talk more openly than Kane sober.

'Great. I came here to see a Kraut who has terrific material.'

'You told me about him at Diana's party. Have you seen him?'

'He's playing hard to get, the cocksucker. Luckily I dug up some stuff on him that didn't even come out at Nuremberg, so the son of a bitch is going to have dinner with me tomorrow night. He'll talk.'

'What have you got on him?'

'Slave labor. The German atomic bomb. Enough. I'll tell you who won't see me — old man Greenwood. I can't get through to him at all. I spoke to some fag secretary a couple of dozen times, but no dice. So I told him, tell *Mister* Greenwood I don't need him. I'll get the story from *Colonel* Rademacher.'

Paul closed his eyes for a moment thoughtfully. 'I see,' he said. 'I hope you know what you're doing.'

'Of course I do,' Kane said, then he froze. 'My God,' he shouted. 'I think I've pissed myself!'

Sherri reached down and patted Kane's crotch. 'It's

181

okay,' she said, producing an ice cube, 'you just spilled some of your drink, honey.'

'Irving,' Paul said. 'Listen to me. A word of advice. Lay off. You're stirring up trouble.'

Kane focused his eyes with some difficulty on Foster. 'For whom?' he asked.

'For yourself. For a lot of other people.'

'The hell with that. You and Meyerman have something on Greenwood. What is it? What are you going to do with it?'

'You're imagining things, Irving.'

'The hell I am! You've been after Nick's company for years, Foster, but you can't fool me. It's *personal* — it goes beyond business. Is that why you've got his girl?'

For a moment Diana was afraid Paul would hit Kane. The muscles in his jaw stood out, and his neck was red with anger. However, Foster managed to hold his temper in check.

'I need a refill,' Kane said. He waved his empty glass in the air, sending ice cubes flying in all directions.

The waiter and the bartender exchanged dark, Mediterranean glances, shaking their heads at each other mournfully, like a couple of doctors consulting over a terminal patient. Slowly, with great reluctance, the waiter approached the table, shielding himself with his tray.

'Monsieur?'

'Another double. And no rocks. You put ice in it last time. No *glace, comprenez?*'

'*Je regrette, mais Monsieur a bu assez. Je ne peux plus lui servir.*'

'What did he say?' Kane resembled an angry water buffalo, preparing to defend his right to drink at a water hole.

'He said you've had enough,' Foster said.

Kane snorted. 'I've been thrown out of better bars than this,' he said, with some pride. 'Listen, Foster, I'm going to squeeze the story out of this guy Rademacher, and when I do, I'll know where you fit in all this. You won't be able to bullshit me then.'

Paul took Diana by the arm, rose from the table and gave Kane a warm smile. 'Good luck,' he said.

Outside, as they waited for the car, Kane's girl

appeared on the steps, lighting a joint with evident relief.

'I think he's going to start a fight with the waiter,' she said through a pungent haze of smoke. 'I figured I'd split.'

'An excellent idea,' Paul said. 'Do you have some place to go?'

'Just Mr. Kane's room.'

'I would strongly suggest somewhere else. Do you have any money?'

'No.'

Foster clicked his fingers, took the roll of bills his bodyguard offered him and peeled off a few. He handed them to Sherri. 'Go find a place to stay. Do you have a ticket home?'

'No.'

'Do you *want* to go home?'

'I guess so . . .'

'There will be an open ticket waiting for you at the American Express office tomorrow morning. Now run before the police get here.'

'Are you always kind to strangers?' Diana asked.

Paul nodded, though his mind seemed to be on something else. 'Oh yes,' he said, 'it's one of the few pleasures of being rich. Organized charities bore me. I prefer sudden gestures.' He looked out at the long line of cars in front of the hotel. His driver flashed the car's headlights to signal that he had seen Foster on the steps. 'It's a pity that idiot Kane tried to talk to Greenwood,' he said. 'He shouldn't have mentioned he was trying to see Rademacher.'

'What a *loathsome* man Rademacher is! Smooth and slimy, like a snake. I've never met a Nazi before, now that I think of it.'

'You're the wrong age, my love, luckily for you. There used to be plenty of them, believe me. And Rademacher was by no means among the worst. If you'd known Becker, for example . . . Well, never mind, here is the car. We'll go to the casino and have a bite to eat there. I'm feeling lucky tonight, so perhaps we'll play a little roulette.'

'I would have thought baccarat was more your game.'

Paul sat back in the limousine. 'No,' he said. 'It's too complicated, like my business affairs. When I gamble I like to relax. Roulette has the great advantage of being mindless.'

'Paul,' Diana said, holding his hand, 'are you worried about something? You seem a little — distant. Are you afraid Rademacher is going to tell Kane everything he knows?'

Paul shook his head, then leaned over and kissed her. 'No, no,' he said firmly, 'Rademacher won't talk to Kane. I'm sure of *that*. But now that Kane has opened his big mouth, the question is whether he'll talk to *me* now . . . I was thinking about something else . . . Ah, here we are.'

He helped her out of the car. They walked arm in arm into the casino, where Diana paused for a moment to go to the ladies' room. As she opened the door she noticed out of the corner of her eye that Paul was talking to someone who had been waiting for him. He was leaning forward, his face grim, one hand grasping the other man's lapel. He seemed to be giving him orders. The other man looked vaguely familiar, but since Paul was standing in front of him Diana couldn't be certain who he was. It was, she thought, surely someone she had seen in New York . . . Then the door swung closed behind her.

When she rejoined Paul he was alone. He kissed her hand and led her toward the *salon*, where the maître d'hôtel and his assistants waited in line, smiling with the deep sincerity that is reserved for the very rich. 'Who was the man you were talking to?' Diana asked. 'I thought it was someone I knew.'

Paul sat down beside her on the banquette and examined his butter knife, like a man looking for stains. 'A business acquaintance,' he said easily. 'Let's have some caviar first, shall we? It's the only food I know that's like sex. No matter how much you have of it, you always want more . . .'

He seemed, if anything, more distracted than before. And in his own charming way, Diana knew, he was going to field any further questions she might have about his 'business acquaintance.'

After dinner Diana noticed that Paul gambled, as he did everything else, with cold precision, but she could also see that his mind was not on the game. He placed a few chips on the double zero, lost and stood up. 'Losing is boring,' he said. 'It's even worse than winning. Let's go

184

outside on the terrace a moment. I was wrong about my luck.'

With his arm around her shoulder, Paul took her to the end of the long terrace. Below them, in the port, they could see the lights of Matthew Greenwood's yacht. Paul looked at it for a few minutes, then turned to Diana. His face was serious. 'Do you love me?' he asked.

She nodded.

He sighed, and was silent for a moment. 'Then there's something I want you to do for me,' he said.

'Allô. Villa Azur? Je voudrais parler à Monsieur Green-wood.'

'Un moment, madame, s'il vous plaît.'

There was a moment of silence on the telephone and a new voice, obviously not that of a servant, came on the line.

'Bitte?'

Diana tried English. 'I'd like to speak to Mr. Green-wood.'

'This is not possible,' the voice said, speaking in English with a heavy German-Swiss accent.

'Then could you give him a message?'

'He is not here. I not can do.'

'Let me give you the message anyway. Mademoiselle Diana Beaumont wants to see him on personal business. It's about his grandson. I can be reached at the Hotel du Cap.'

'So?' the voice said in German, and the phone went dead.

'That doesn't sound promising,' Diana said to Foster, who had been listening to the conversation on the extension.

Foster shrugged. 'We'll see. I think it may produce results rather quickly.'

A moment later the telephone rang. Diana picked it up.

'Miss Beaumont?' This time the accent was English, the rich, somewhat contemptuous tone of somebody used to giving commands.

'Speaking.'

'You wished to speak with Mr. Greenwood?'

'Yes.'

'Perhaps you could just, ah, tell me what it's all about?

185

I'm Mr. Greenwood's personal assistant.'

'It's about his grandson. I'd very much like to see Mr. Greenwood, if it's convenient.'

'I see. Would you mind waiting just one moment, please.'

There was a murmur in the background, then the Englishman came back on the line. 'Mr. Greenwood will see you tomorrow morning. Please be at the steps of Eden Roc at eleven, and a boat will pick you up. Nobody is to accompany you.'

'Thank you.'

'Not at all,' the voice said smoothly. 'Mr. Greenwood will be most, ah, *interested* to hear what you have to say.' The line clicked and went dead.

'I'm afraid,' Diana said to Paul.

'There's no danger. I wouldn't send you if there were. Listen, you don't have to go.'

'No, I'll go. I said I would.'

'I want you to know that I shall always be grateful. Always. It's the only way to find out what I need to know. I didn't want to involve you, but I can't think of another way.'

'Oh,' Diana said, 'I'm involved. It's too late to worry about that, isn't it?'

He nodded.

'I still don't see how I'm going to find what you're looking for.'

'Instinct. Luck. The fact that you're a beautiful woman. At some point, even the best-laid plans depend on chance. Express curiosity. Rich men love to show women their yachts — that's why they buy them in the first place. Also, they love to talk about themselves.'

Paul seemed buoyant about the adventure, but as Diana took off her clothes and got ready for bed, she could not help wondering if Paul hadn't planned this all along. Was he improvising, or was she merely another element in a carefully drawn plan? She did not sleep well or look forward to the morning.

Standing beside the steps to the water in the morning, she felt a leaden apprehension. Surrounded by the early-morning sunbathers — eleven o'clock was the equivalent of dawn, at Eden Roc — she felt slightly out of place

186

in her dark body stocking and white trousers, waiting for the launch like somebody at a bus stop.

About half a mile out to sea the *Cosima* lay at anchor. There was no activity on board, except for a couple of sailors lowering a speedboat into the water from the davits. An occasional puff of wind caught the flag, revealing the yacht's Panamanian registry.

Once the yacht would have attracted attention, as boats rushed back and forth. Greenwood's luncheon parties were celebrated; the guests had often included Onassis and Callas, Aaron Diamond, Brigitte Bardot, King Hussein, the Shah, Darryl F. Zanuck, Carlo Ponti and Sophia Loren, famous art dealers like Rudi von Seydlitz, innumerable millionaires, stars, starlets and fashion models.

Paparazzi risked their lives to take photographs, hanging from the cliffs by ropes with their telescopic lenses, swimming out to the yacht with cameras held above their heads, circling it in chartered speedboats, Nikons and Leicas clicking.

Here, Dawn Safire had been photographed sunbathing in the nude, Onassis had been caught quarreling bitterly with Callas, Irving Kane had been captured in a memorable shot as he fell into the sea, the Countess Grefühl had revealed to the world that she didn't wear panties when she was photographed climbing the companionway from below in a stiff breeze . . . So many parties, so many girls, so many scandals, all of it now buried in the files of free-lance photographers and magazines, while the yacht lay silent in the water, apparently deserted.

From across the water, there came the roar of a powerful motor, and one of the *Cosima*'s speedboats appeared from behind the stern, its bow up as the boat planed, leaving a foaming white wake behind it in the flat blue water.

The boat slowed down and the bow dropped as it approached the rocks, but the helmsman deftly brought it up to the stairs in one smooth turn, calculating his speed exactly so that he came to a stop right below Diana. A young sailor in the back grabbed the steps to hold the boat steady and helped her in, pointing forward. She sat down beside the man at the wheel, a heavyset officer in his fifties, wearing starched naval whites and

187

a peaked cap with a single row of gold oak leaves on the peak.

'*Setzen Sie sich, bitte,*' he said, pushing the throttles forward as he cleared the bathing area, so that the boat accelerated in the water like an airplane leaving a catapult. Diana obediently sat down — it would have been almost impossible to stand up in any event — and said good morning. There was no reply. The officer merely stared ahead at the yacht, and skilfully brought the boat alongside. The sailor leaped onto the companionway platform and secured the boat, signaling Diana to follow him. The officer nodded as she stepped onto the platform. He pointed up. 'Herr Greenwood is above,' he said. '*Im Salon.*'

At the top of the companionway was a kind of gate; as Diana passed through it she realized that it was a metal detector, like those at the security points of airports. It clicked as she passed through, and a small green light lit up. Herr Greenwood was taking no chances, however close to death he might be.

To her right was an open door. In it stood a big, bald man in the white hospital uniform of a male nurse.

'Mademoiselle Beaumont?' he asked, in the Swiss-German voice she had heard on the telephone. 'By here, please. He waits for you. Please don't smoke.'

She stepped into the dark salon — the windows were heavily tinted, giving the interior the green translucence of an aquarium — and waited for a moment while her eyes adjusted to the dimness. In the center of a beautifully furnished room she distinguished a wheelchair, with a bulky figure seated in it, its legs covered with a tartan blanket. It was hard to connect this palsied old man with the powerful and energetic father who had journeyed to England to confront Nicholas over her in a stormy scene.

She had forgotten how big Greenwood was. Even in the wheelchair he was a giant of a man, though now he had lost most of his fat and muscle. His big hands were pale, thin and trembling, the skin of his face was drawn close to the bones, accentuating the imperious nose and the prominent cheekbones; his mustache was a white, ragged strip, his eyes hidden by dark glasses with black sidepieces. Perhaps out of vanity, to conceal his baldness, he wore a Panama hat, the brim pulled low over his glasses. He had on several cardigans and a cashmere scarf, despite the warmth, and his cheeks and lips had a faint blue tone that told the entire story of his condition.

'You haven't lost your beauty yet,' he said slowly, appraising her invisibly from behind the dark glasses.

'Thank you.'

Greenwood waved one hand wearily, either to indicate that no thanks were called for or that he had no time for amenities.

'The worst thing' — he pronounced it 'ting' — 'about old age is that one doesn't lose desire. It's like the torture of Tantalus. But you haven't come here to hear my problems. What do you want?' Greenwood still pronounced his *w*'s as *v*'s. At one time he had tried to improve his accent, but now it was no longer worth the effort. His English, like his French, his Spanish, his Portuguese and his Italian, was fluent but distinctly foreign.

'What can I do for you?' he asked, with as much of a leer as his face muscles could manage.

'I hear Niki is getting married.'

'Yes. The little Biedermeyer girl. Pretty. Rich. He's a lucky boy.'

'I'm surprised he got an annulment.'

'These things can be arranged. You're a woman of the world. You know that.'

'Not for me, they couldn't.'

'You were a divorcée. And Protestant, too. Even in the Vatican they would find it hard to swallow *that*. The Biedermeyers, however, are Catholic. Augustus Biedermeyer is a Knight of Malta and God knows what else . . . Every time he goes to mass he writes out a check for some charity or other. For him, they'd annul his own mother's marriage if he asked them to. And of course I have some influence there myself, from the old days . . .'

'You must be very pleased.'

'Yes. I'll be more pleased if there's a son.'

'There already *is* a son.'

Greenwood nodded, as if he had expected the conversation to take this turn. 'Is there?' he asked with an expression of innocence.

'You *know* there is. Steven.'

'He's illegitimate. That doesn't count.'

'That's a matter of opinion.'

'Nonsense! Illegitimate children don't inherit. Besides,' Greenwood added, 'the boy is a cripple.' He looked down at his own lifeless legs, hidden beneath the blanket. He had on cheap carpet slippers.

Diana felt a spasm of anger but suppressed it. 'He's still Niki's son.'

'*Und*? These things happen, even in the best families.'

'Not in the Biedermeyer family they don't. As a devoted Catholic layman, Augustus Biedermeyer would not enjoy a paternity suit, all the publicity . . . His friends in South Salem wouldn't like it at all.'

'Biedermeyer is an ass. His grandfather made a living selling forged steamship tickets to greenhorns on the Danzig docks. He had to emigrate to America himself — his customers threatened to lynch him. Now Biedermeyer behaves as if his ancestors had all been papal knights, and spends his time *fressing* with cardinals. Still, he's a good businessman. Hoeffler! Get me a glass of tea. Anything for you, my dear?'

The Swiss male nurse appeared and Diana asked for a Campari-soda. Hoeffler made a small pantomime of pointing at his wristwatch, but Greenwood shook his head. 'I'm only allowed ten minutes to talk to people by my fool of a doctor,' he explained, 'but it's been a long time since I talked to a pretty woman, and there are worse ways to die. Better, too, of course,' he added.

'I'm not going to let Niki — or you — get away with this,' Diana said.

'Jealousy is a waste of time, my dear. As for blackmail, it's a dangerous business. Believe me, I know.'

'It's not a question of blackmail. It's a question of justice.'

'That's what blackmailers always say. Please don't take offense. I'm an old man, I haven't time to make pretty phrases. Blackmail doesn't shock a man like me. I have often found it — what is the word? — expedient, yes? *So*: expedient to buy certain things. If the price is right and the thing is worth buying, I'm willing to talk business. I'm a practical man. I don't have time to take a high moral view. In the end it never pays.'

Hoeffler returned with a silver tray, followed by a tall,

thin middle-aged man, with the figure and bearing of a well-bred stork. His thinning hair was neatly combed into two small wings above each ear, his nose was sharp, bony and aristocratic, and he wore a well-cut beige linen suit, a white shirt and an Old Etonian tie.

'You mustn't overstrain yourself, Mr. Greenwood,' he said, in the English voice that had spoken to Diana the night before. 'Doctor's, ah, orders . . .'

'The hell with the doctors, Boyce. This is Miss Beaumont. My son's ex-mistress. The boy always had good taste!' Greenwood gave a crackling laugh, coughed once or twice and took a sip of tea.

'Weren't you married to poor Robin Windermere?' Boyce asked.

Diana nodded.

Boyce beamed insincerely, putting on an unconvincing display of geniality. 'I went to Eton with him,' he said. 'We were both in Pop. Such a pity that he's, ah . . .'

'Some people' — Greenwood pronounced it 'bee-pull' — 'think he's living in Australia under a different name. I doubt it. I think his associates killed him. It would have been the sensible thing to do.'

Boyce smiled cheerfully. 'Oh, quite,' he said. 'He was a damn good cricketer at school.'

Diana glanced around the room and was disappointed to see that it was unexceptional — certainly it contained nothing in the way of personal mementos or curiosa. The furniture was slipcovered in white linen, piped in pale blue, there were a great many expensive gifts from guests, and the walls were hung with the usual rich man's collection of Impressionists.

Greenwood leaned forward and patted her knee, giving her a lopsided smile. He had a kind of ferocious charm, and it was easy to understand why he had been so successful with women, even until quite recently.

'Miss Beaumont and I were talking about blackmail when you came in,' Greenwood said to Boyce, who raised one elegant eyebrow.

'Oh, I say, that's surely absurd. Nobody would believe that you could still, ah . . .'

Greenwood picked up the cane that hung from one side of his wheelchair and deftly prodded Boyce with it. '*Dummkopf!*' he exclaimed, jabbing the rubber tip as

191

hard as he could into Boyce's navel. 'But unfortunately you're right. I'm past the age of sexual scandals, alas. If there were something I could be blackmailed about by a beautiful woman, it would be like a miracle at Lourdes. No, it's really poor Niki's problem ... Tell me, Miss Beaumont, or rather, *Diana*, do you smoke cigars?'

Diana shook her head. 'It's not one of my habits, no.'

'*So*? A pity. In my youth, it was considered an acceptable thing for a woman to do. The Empress Elizabeth of Austria always smoked a cigar after dinner. I can no longer smoke them myself, but I'd be grateful if you would do so, as a favor to me. I can at least enjoy the smell. You see, I've reached the age of vicarious pleasure, the ersatz of the senses ...'

Over the guttural objections of Hoeffler, a steward was summoned, who brought Diana a humidor. Greenwood nodded approvingly as she selected a small Davidoff, deftly pierced it and lit it by holding the flame below the cigar until it started to glow from the heat instead of the flame.

She blew a puff of smoke in his direction, and he nodded happily.

'Excellent,' he said. 'I still have boxes and boxes of them on the yacht. I suppose I should leave them to somebody in my will.'

'I'd love to see the rest of the yacht,' Diana said hopefully.

'*So*? There's no reason why you shouldn't, I suppose. However, you can't have come here for the tour. What exactly are you threatening me with?'

'A paternity suit against Niki, a claim against him on behalf of his own child ... It's all in the hands of Marvin Blumenthal. You know how he loves splashy cases.'

'Yes. I know Marvin. I imagine that he'd launch all this *Dreck* just a few days before Niki's wedding, *nicht wahr*?'

'That was Marvin's suggestion, certainly. He felt that the Biedermeyers would react very strongly to the news that their daughter was marrying a man who had a child by his mistress while his wife was in an institution — and neglected to mention it. Marvin felt it might have an effect on the merger negotiations between Niki and the Biedermeyers as well.'

192

Greenwood shrugged. 'He's not wrong about *that*,' he said. 'Biedermeyer's an old woman.'

Boyce pursed his lips in thought or disapproval. 'It won't wash,' he said to Diana. 'I don't think there's a chance you'd win in court.'

'She doesn't have to win in court to hurt us, Boyce. It will be front-page scandal. Papa Biedermeyer will shit in his pants when he sees it. Never mind the fucking marriage, we can kiss goodbye to Biedermeyer's financing! Two years of negotiations down the drain! No, no, this lovely lady has us by the balls, I'm sorry to say. Niki should have taken care of all this a long time ago. Still, what's a father for, if not to handle these problems? How much?'

'One hundred thousand a year for the rest of his life.'

Greenwood laughed. 'Ridiculous! Even a cripple doesn't need so much. Twenty-five thousand a year, or a lump sum of five hundred thousand, which you invest as you please on his behalf.'

'I'd take fifty thousand a year with a cost-of-living increase. Anything less, and I instruct Marvin to sue — and to get on the phone to Rupert Murdoch.'

Greenwood nodded happily. 'Somebody has briefed you very well my dear. If you'd asked for a couple of million dollars, it might have been worth having you taken care of, an accident, a suicide' — he gave a wolfish smile — 'it's been done, frankly. On the other hand, if you'd asked for much less, I wouldn't have taken you seriously. You're intelligent, as well as beautiful. We have a deal. Tell Marvin to talk to my lawyer, Dr. Zengli, Bahnhofstrasse, Zurich. A charming man. He has a wonderful collection of Flemish Primitives. Of course, you understand, you have to guarantee on behalf of your son that there'll be no further claims against Niki or myself at all, and no contact. *Fertig!* Finished! Yes? No lawsuits, no claims, above all, no magazine articles, no memoirs, and so forth. *Nacht und Nebel*, that's what I'm buying from you. You agree?'

'Yes. I agree. Funny, somebody was talking about *Nacht und Nebel* only a few days ago . . .'

'It used to be quite common,' Greenwood said, 'but that was a long time ago. Who put you up to all this?'

'Nobody. When I heard that Niki was marrying the

193

Biedermeyer girl, I knew I had to get something for our son. It was a question of now or never.'

'Somehow I find that hard to believe. Boyce tells me that you're staying at the Hotel du Cap with Paul Foster?'

'Yes.'

'Tell him not to meddle in my business, please. You find him attractive?'

'I wouldn't be with him in the hotel if I didn't. That's obvious.'

'Ah? It's not so obvious at all. Women will do a great deal for money. And Foster, my dear, will do almost anything to get at *me*. He's elegant, charming, persuasive, isn't he? You wait and see. He's a killer.'

'He says much the same about you, frankly.'

Greenwood laughed, wheezed, coughed, spat up a bit of phlegm into his handkerchief, then breathed deeply. 'Oh, he's right about that, the swine,' he said with a throaty chuckle. 'We're well matched. Take my advice: Don't trust a word he says. He's talked to you about his family?'

'A little.'

'All nonsense, of course. My poor brother and his son died in Auschwitz. This Foster may have met them there. After the war, he came to me pretending to be my nephew, but it was a transparent fraud. I must say he's done well for himself since, but he's a psychopathic liar. A very sad case . . . You were fond of Niki, no?'

Greenwood's expression conveyed sadness, but Diana saw, in the steady gaze of his eyes on her, that the old man knew the truth about Paul's identity.

'Yes. I was.'

He sighed. 'He's a good boy. A little soft. When he was small, I made things too hard for him. Then after the war, when he was grown up, I made things too easy. With children, it's like business – what counts is steadiness . . . Do you believe in God, Diana?'

Diana looked at him in baffled astonishment. 'I don't think so.'

Greenwood nodded. 'No,' he replied, as if he had anticipated the answer, 'when you're young you don't, but when you get old, it's something you begin to think about. I think a lot about God these days. Soon I will find out if He exists, after all. One hopes for mercy, compassion . . .

194

It's only natural.'

'And justice?'

Greenwood closed his fists for a moment, as if in a spasm of pain. 'I hope not,' he said.

Hoeffler returned to the room and cleared his throat.

'Nap time,' Boyce said cheerfully.

'*Verdammt!* Old age is a time of constant humiliation. Hoeffler, wheel me up to the top deck, and I'll sit under the awning for my siesta. There's a telescope there, I can see the girls at Eden Roc as they go for a swim . . . I shan't see you again, Diana. *Adieu.* You've been lucky. Don't try it twice.'

Diana stood up. 'I'd still like to have a look over the yacht. I've heard so much about it from Niki. Also I need – '

'Quite,' Boyce said. 'Downstairs to the left, next to the study.'

Diana walked down a spiral staircase, looked in the bathroom, which was mirrored on all four walls, the ceiling and the floor, tried a couple of doors that opened on a dressing room and a large bedroom, then went farther forward and tried another door. It swung open to reveal what was clearly Greenwood's library, a dark paneled room with two portholes and heavy leather furniture of the type found in gentlemen's clubs.

In a glass cabinet between the portholes were an ornate gilt hunting spear, sword and shield, obviously of great value. The bookshelves contained leather-bound books that did not have the look of being moved — or read — for years. On an ormolu desk, bolted to the floor, stood the bronze bust of a heavy-jowled man, a decoration of some kind where his tie ought to have been. The bust was large, but partly concealed by the rest of the bric-a-brac on the desk — a bowl of flowers, framed photographs, a Maillol bronze, an erotic Indian temple carving, a Fabergé desk set, a spotless blotter.

Diana examined the bust, concluded from the eyes and chin that it represented Göring, tipped it over and quickly felt inside. There was nothing. She shook it, to make sure, then placed it back on its socket, and left the room, carefully closing the door behind her. She stepped into the bathroom, flushed the toilet and ran the taps.

Upstairs, Greenwood and his wheelchair were gone,

but Boyce stood in the *salon*, managing to combine patrician indolence and servility in a mix that only an upper-class Englishman with no money of his own can achieve.

'Find what you were looking for?' he asked with a wink, or perhaps merely an involuntary nervous tic.

'Thank you. Can I see the rest of the ship?'

'There isn't much to see, but I'll give you the quick shilling tour. After all, you've got what you came for,' Boyce said with a sneer. He pushed a button, and the wall went back, revealing an ornate dining *salon*, with a table that could seat twenty-six, at the end of which a Picasso bronze was illuminated by spotlights. They walked through the dining room, Boyce opened another room, touched a button and waited as the lights dimmed and a movie screen descended from the ceiling.

'Below there's the old man's suite,' he went on, 'and aft there are guest staterooms, baths, etc. Below that there's a gymnasium, a steam bath, that sort of thing. All the comforts. Not that he can enjoy them anymore, poor sod. We took down the mirror above his bed because he got tired of waking up in the morning and seeing his own face. Sad, really. Had enough?'

'Yes, thank you. I was just curious to see it. Niki talked a lot about the yacht. I thought it would be bigger.'

'Oh, it's big enough. One of the biggest, in fact. But without the guests, the glamour, it's just another ship. You're a very lucky woman, Miss, ah, Beaumont.'

'Am I?'

'Oh, yes. The old man loves Niki. He'd pay almost anything to save him from, ah, embarrassment. Or difficulty. Up to a point, of course ... He wants an orderly succession, you know. The Greenwood empire passing from father to son, generation after generation, that sort of thing ... He wouldn't want it to die out, like Robin's earldom, or pass into, ah, other hands.'

A buzzer sounded and Boyce ushered her to the deck.

'The boat is ready to take you back.' He took her by the arm and led her to the companionway. His hand was unpleasantly moist against her skin, and she moved away from the unwelcome gesture of intimacy. 'Get Blumenthal to telephone old Zengli, sign the papers. Don't come back. Remember what happened to poor Robin. It doesn't pay to be greedy.'

'I don't think it was *greed* that did my husband in, Mr. Boyce. He was under the illusion that aristocrats are beyond the law.'

'Only the rich are beyond the law. Breeding has nothing to do with it. Ah, here is the dashing Helmuth waiting to take you back to Eden Roc, like Lohengrin in the swan boat . . . Such a tease!'

Boyce waved at Helmuth, who ignored him.

'The cold Germanic type,' Boyce said sadly. 'Unfortunately, *just* what one yearns for . . .'

As she stepped onto the companionway, Boyce gave her a hard, knowing stare. '*Do* be careful,' he said, with a thin smile that made it evident to Diana he was not referring to the steps. 'And give my good wishes to Paul Foster. Look out for yourself — so many of his friends pay *dearly* for the experience of knowing him!'

Diana pondered this remark as she waited beside Paul under the wing of his airplane. He seemed tense, though when she had appeared at La Bouée to meet him for lunch, he had expressed no more than mild disappointment that she had been unable to find the letter. The news that old Greenwood had been willing to pay up for her silence pleased him. 'They're on the ropes,' he had said, toasting her in a glass of Château de Selle — he believed in drinking the wines of people he knew whenever possible. 'They must be desperate for Biedermeyer's help. All we need now is a little revenge — and luck, of course. One always needs that.'

'Where do you think the letter went?'

'I don't know. It would have been useful.'

'Do you suppose Rademacher was lying?'

'No. But I think he may have double-crossed me. Never mind. These things happen in business. Rademacher, however, should have known better, poor fellow.' Foster gave a small smile, as if dismissing Rademacher altogether.

'The old man had some harsh words to say about blackmail. He didn't mention Rademacher's name, but I thought there might be a connection.'

'No doubt. Greenwood would certainly be knowledgeable on the subject of blackmail. It's a risky profession,' Paul said, with the air of a man who knew plenty about it himself.

Now that they were on the runway, Foster seemed reluctant to get into his plane. He was preoccupied, silent, and it occurred to Diana that he was perhaps eager to get back to his telephones and computers. The pilot had a sheaf of messages and cables for him, and Paul stood by the wing, leafing through them with grim determination. At intervals, he looked up and held his hand above his eyes to shade them, obviously waiting for something or someone, until a gray Mercedes appeared, and he walked forward to stand beside it. In the back was his New York bodyguard, Luther. Suddenly Diana realized that it was Luther she had seen with Paul at the casino, the 'business acquaintance' to whom Paul had been speaking with such vehemence.

Diana waited by the boarding stairs, and watched Luther as he stepped forward to talk to Foster. The setting sun, reflecting off Luther's mirrored aviator glasses, turned the lenses blood red as he whispered to Paul. They stood together for a few moments, then Paul nodded, said a few words to Luther, and walked up to the ramp to join Diana.

'Is Luther flying back with us?' she asked.

Paul shook his head. 'I have business for him in Zurich. He can fly commercial, then I'll send the plane back from New York for him.' He took Diana's arm, and helped her into the dark interior of the plane, as the door slowly closed behind them and the starter motors whirred.

'Any problem?' she asked.

Foster shrugged. His face seemed a little paler than usual, as if he were suddenly tired. 'There are always problems.'

Paul sat down on the big leather sofa-chair beside her, pressed a button to indicate that he was ready to take off, and put is feet up.

'We must see what cassettes they have brought with them,' he said. 'We can watch a movie on the way home. By the way, it seems Kane won't be seeing Rademacher tonight.'

'Somebody changed Rademacher's mind?'

'In a manner of speaking. He was shot this afternoon, in the garden of his villa.'

Part Six

Errors in judgment 1943–1944

In Hungary live more Jews than in all of Western Europe
. . . It is self-explanatory that we must attempt to solve this
problem, but where are they to go?

PRIME MINISTER MIKLÓS, KÁLLAY, 1943

10

'To victory!' Colonel von Rademacher said, lifting his glass.

'To peace,' Steven de Grünwald replied pointedly.

Matthew de Grünwald emptied his glass and gave Steven a warning glance. 'In Switzerland,' Matthew said, 'there's talk of a negotiated peace.'

'Unlikely,' Rademacher said. 'The Führer still believes in victory.'

'In Budapest nobody does,' Steven said.

'That's because you Hungarians are a pessimistic race. Look what happened after Kursk. Your troops threw away their weapons and ran from the Russians!'

Steven nodded — it was undeniably true. 'Yes,' he said, 'but so did yours before, at Moscow. And at least yours had tanks!'

'You're right,' Rademacher admitted. 'In fact, some of our staff officers ran so fast they had not only abandoned their weapons but even their loot. That's how bad it is out there. What we need is a miracle. Or at least a miracle weapon.'

'What about Wotan?'

'I think we may have left it until too late. We're making progress, but it's slow. Professor Meyerman and his Aryan colleagues don't seem any closer than they were a year ago . . . It's very dispiriting.'

'He's a first-rate scientist,' Matthew insisted.

'Yes? I hope so. The Americans got Einstein. I think we may have the wrong Jew. How was Switzerland?'

'Most agreeable. The Dolder Hotel is as good as ever.'

'So I hear. It's amazing how many people are making a quick trip to Zurich these days — those who *can*, of course.'

In the winter of the fourth year of the war, the Swiss

hotels and banks had never been busier. The Germans were beaten in North Africa, where Rommel's panzers sat stranded in the desert from lack of fuel; they were losing in Russia, where half a million men had been trapped at Stalingrad — only against the Jews were they victorious, though even in that area there were many Germans who doubted there would be time enough to get rid of them all . . .

The Hungarians, reluctant latecomers to the war, had been obliged to send an army to Russia, on the understanding that it would be used to guard the lines of communications so as to free more German divisions for the front. Instead, the German High Command had pushed the ill-equipped Hungarian troops into the thick of the fighting, then failed to supply them with rations, ammunition, winter clothing, even boots.

In Budapest, the members of the English Club were no longer optimistic either. An atmosphere of gloom had settled in the ornate rooms of that august institution. English marmalade was unobtainable, many of the servants had been called up and were doubtless even now dying of frostbite on the Russian front, decent Scotch was hard to find, though the Argentinean chargé d'affaires was making a tidy fortune by importing it from Buenos Aires in the diplomatic pouch. Prince Bardossy had been at the station when a careless porter dropped the legation's pouch on the platform, producing a crash of broken glass and the strong smell of spirits. The chargé d'affaires had cried, tears running down his fat cheeks, as he watched the precious liquid running out to form a muddy puddle on the tracks, but then, a lot of people were crying in those days.

Putzi de Fekete's cousin had returned from Washington after fulfilling the unenviable task of declaring war on the United States. It had taken him a week to get an appointment with Cordell Hull, the Secretary of State, who had opened the conversation by asking if Hungary had any claims or grievances against America.

'None,' Fekete replied.

Hull lifted an eyebrow. Against whom, then, did Hungary have claims and grievances?

'Only Rumania.'

'And is Hungary declaring war against Rumania, too?'

Fekete smiled sadly. 'No,' he said, 'the Rumanians are

our allies, unfortunately.'

At least in Hungary, it was still possible to eat well — for a price. In fact, since his arrival in Budapest, Rademacher seemed to Matthew de Grünwald to have put on weight. He had also become a frequent, if unwelcome, visitor. He regarded himself as a family friend, a feeling that Matthew was hesitant to discourage, despite Steven's objections.

Rademacher was not so greedy as to cause trouble, but he required an endless succession of small favors — a Bechstein grand piano for his hotel suite, a Mercedes limousine to replace his Wehrmacht Volkswagen, access to a Swiss bank account, hard currency . . .

It was not just Rademacher's personal demands that plagued Matthew de Grünwald — that, after all, was to be accepted in commerce — but Rademacher's stance as a hard bargainer and difficult customer. Any concessions he made were in the form of offers of slave labor, which were no use to the Grünwalds, since the Hungarian government took the position that there were already plenty of Jews in Hungary without importing more of them in labor gangs. 'Absolutely not,' the Regent said when he was informed. 'Tell them to use our own Jews first — God knows we have enough of them!'

Of course, in Hungary, an independent country and a German ally (however reluctant), it was hardly possible as yet for Rademacher to apply the methods that had proved so successful in Austria or France. Here it was still necessary to negotiate — and also to overcome the niggling objections of the Hungarian government, which on the one hand wanted to see the Jews divested of their wealth, but on the other was anything but pleased at its passing into German hands.

Rademacher discussed his problems and his successes, his 'life sorrows and joys,' as he called them, openly at the Grünwald dinner table, much to the irritation of Betsy, who found him 'as distasteful as a rotten fish,' and to the boredom of Cosima, who hated business talk at meals. Rademacher exerted his considerable charm on the two ladies to very little effect, but he did not appear to notice. He *liked* Hungary, he never tired of explaining. In the occupied countries he had to compete with the SS and even the Wehrmacht for spoils, but here he had no such problem. Rademacher, with his sardonic charm and his Vuitton trunk full of tailored uniforms, had the field to himself for the moment. He even provided himself with an art expert, Oberleutnant Graf Rudolph von Seydlitz, whose mission was to acquire masterworks for Reichsmarschall Göring's growing collection in exchange for transit visas for those Jews whose paintings came up to his standards.

Now, as the two Grünwald brothers joined Rademacher in the drawing room — Rademacher having chosen to remain with the ladies over an after-dinner liqueur — he was describing his subaltern's latest 'triumph.'

'Imagine,' he was telling Betsy, sitting beside her on the sofa, in front of the fire, a glass of kümmel in his manicured hand, 'an altarpiece, almost certainly a Cranach!' He put his thumb and forefinger together in a circle, to indicate the quality of the piece, a gesture he had picked up in France. 'Superb!' he said. 'This old Jew — Fülöp Rosenwald, I think — came to see Seydlitz at the hotel with a nice Renaissance bronze by de Keyser, and Seydlitz told him, "Mein lieber Herr, this will get you from Sopron to Vienna, but for the rest of the way to Switzerland I need something better."'

'So Rosenwald takes him home, and there is this beauty. You could have knocked Seydlitz over with a feather! "Can you imagine," he asked me, "a Jew with an altarpiece! It doesn't seem right somehow!"'

'Of course,' Rademacher added apologetically, 'I realize in Hungary things are different. Still, it's remarkable what these people have put away!'

His eyes shifted to the walls of Matthew de Grünwald's drawing room, paused at Caravaggio's Boy Bitten by a Lizard, and passed on to the rows of other paintings acquired by grandfather Hirsch.

'A sensual painting,' he said, pointing to the epicene young man crowned with flowers in the Caravaggio.

'Caravaggio is reputed to have had a feel for the subject,' Steven remarked, with an ironic edge to his voice.

'So they say. La bella Italia . . .' Rademacher sighed. 'Kennst du das Land, wo die Zitronen blühn,' he quoted dreamily. 'Goethe, too, yearned for the sun! It's in the German blood. One day I would like to live by the sea,

204

surrounded by groves of olive trees. The sun, the warmth, good wine, the smell of lemons . . . In the meantime, how are your own families? I understand Nicholas is in Switzerland?'

'At Le Rosey,' Matthew said, his eyes fixed on Betsy's bosom as she leaned forward to refill Rademacher's glass from a cut-glass decanter.

'A good choice. These days Switzerland is the only place to be!'

'We miss him,' Cosima said lugubriously, as if he were lost at sea.

'This is the natural instinct of a mother,' Rademacher said pontifically, bending forward to squeeze her hand in a gesture of sympathy that was not mirrored in his eyes. 'Believe me, Baroness, it's the best thing.' He turned toward Steven. 'Your children are still here, I understand.'

Steven nodded.

'So. Well, of course, a family wants to stay together. This I understand. All the same, it's a dangerous time and place.'

'I have no real fears,' Matthew said. 'If the Russian front collapses completely, that's another story . . .'

Rademacher laughed. 'The Russians? I wasn't thinking about *them*! It's the SS you have to worry about, my dear friend!'

'*Do* we have anything to fear from the Germans?' Betsy asked.

Steven shrugged, as they sat close together in the back seat of the Packard on the way home. 'I doubt it,' he said. 'You're a Magyar aristocrat, thoroughbred breeding all the way back to Attila the Hun. As for me, I was born a Catholic. Even by the Germans' own idiotic definition, I'd only be one-quarter Jewish. There are plenty of people on the General Staff who have more Jewish blood than that. And look at Heydrich — he was a *Mischling*, as they call it. They say that Field Marshal Kesselring's mother was the daughter of a rabbi — even Göring's mother had a Jewish lover, and there are rumors that her husband wasn't Hermann's father, in which case —'

'I see. Is Mati worried? He looked at me very strangely tonight. Also, he seems tired, nervous . . .'

'There's a lot of pressure, as you can imagine. The Germans are threatening to march into Hungary and take the country over, particularly if the Regent won't take strong measures against the Jews. Still, so long as the Regent remains in control, I don't think anything bad can happen. And our relationship with the Germans has been very close, as you know, for better or for worse. We have friends there — powerful ones! In any case —'

'In any case what?'

'In any case, my darling, I don't think the Regent or the Germans would *let* us leave. The Regent can't permit an exodus of the rich; it would sap confidence in the regime. As for the Germans, our services are too useful to them, particularly in the matter of the Wotan Project. I could possibly get you and the children out, then join you later. In fact, that might be the best solution.'

Betsy took her husband's hand, then leaned over to kiss him. 'I won't hear of it,' she said. 'Never!'

'*Sois sérieuse, chérie.* It would be safer to go. Montenuovo could take you out — he has a Vatican diplomatic passport. Schiller can see to the German transit visas.'

'I couldn't be more serious. If there's no danger, there's no reason for me to go. And if there *is* danger, then I want to be with you. That's final.'

The car stopped outside their front door. Steven nodded. 'When you say "final" in that tone of voice . . . All right, I agree, but at the first sign of real trouble, you go — no arguments! In the meantime, let's hope the Germans crack quickly. They're retreating in Russia, the German cities are being bombed every night, the moment the Allies land in France — and that can't be far off — it will all be over. As long as Germany collapses before the Russians reach our doorsteps, we should be all right.'

But the Germans obstinately failed to collapse. When the Allies at last stirred themselves to leave North Africa, the long-awaited second front was in Sicily, not France, to Steven's consternation, and by the end of the year the Americans seemed to have lost all hope of reaching Rome, let alone Budapest.

Regent Horthy had paid a visit to the Führer's headquarters at Rastenburg, and was treated to a lunch of barley soup, vegetables and fruit compote, as well as a stupefying *tour d'horizon* of the world situation, though he noted to his displeasure that Gauleiter Arthur Seyss-Inquart failed to greet him at the railroad station when he stopped in Vienna — a small but calculated insult intended to convey German displeasure. There was, as everybody predicted, worse to come.

Inevitably, it came. In the first days of 1944 a German telegraph patrol wanted to string wires from a pole just inside the Hungarian border near Wiener-Neustadt. When the Hungarian frontier guards objected, the German *Unteroffizier* in charge shouted across the border, 'You swine are still talking big now, but in a little while you'll be shitting in your pants!'

Amid rumors of German troop concentrations on the border, the Hungarian government was busy with plans for a gala performance at the opera house to commemorate the national holiday — an event that was interrupted by an urgent message calling the Regent to yet another conference with Hitler in Germany.

Unwisely, but with a certain gloomy courage, the Regent entered the lion's den again, was shouted at and detained, and was therefore absent when General-feldmarschall Maximilian von Weichs led the German Balkan Army Group across the frontier to occupy Hungary, marching through the streets of Budapest with its bands playing the 'Radetzky March' while the Hungarians stood silent and horrified in the cold, under a sky smudged by the smoke from the Hungarian government ministries, which were busy burning their files.

In the confusion, the presence of two Gestapo officers, the lean, dyspeptic Obersturmbannführer Adolf Eichmann and his elegant companion, Standartenführer Dr. Kurt Becker, passed unnoticed, particularly since they were part of the numerous entourage of Dr. Edmund Veesenmayer, the new German minister and Reich plenipotentiary.

In his expensive, brand-new briefcase, Eichmann carried a cardboard pattern for the six-pointed yellow star Hungarian Jews would henceforth have to wear, sewn firmly on the right breast of their outer garment.

'They certainly march better than our troops.'

'They have better boots.'

'*Sois sérieux*. They frighten me.'

'They're supposed to. That's the point.'

Louise and Paul de Grünwald stood in the crowd as the troops of the German army marched down the Kiraly Utca, their boots crashing on the cobblestones as they goose-stepped toward the hastily erected reviewing stand opposite Parliament. There was no applause from the onlookers, nobody waved handkerchiefs or flags, though during the night pro-German fanatics had put up posters bearing the simple warning: 'Now the Jews will get what's coming to them.'

Louise was a young woman of arresting beauty. She was not pretty, as her mother was; instead she had her father's elegant features, high cheekbones and strong nose. It was a face with character.

Paul de Grünwald so exactly resembled her that they were instantly recognizable as brother and sister, and often mistaken for twins.

'It's so upsetting,' Louise said. 'All these changes . . .'

'According to Meyer Meyerman, it's only the beginning.'

Louise shook her head in annoyance. '*Le jeune* Meyerman is one of the changes. Oh, I know *you* like him, but he's always staring at me.'

'He admires you. Besides —'

'Admiration! In some ways you're still very young, Pali. However, you have to admit he's not at all the kind of person Papa or Uncle Mati would normally hire as an assistant. Or have around the house.'

'You know perfectly well they did it as a favor to old Professor Meyerman. If the boy didn't have a job with us, he'd be sent off to the Russian front to dig antitank ditches in a Jewish labor commando. You surely don't want that?'

'No, no. God forbid. Although why it should concern me, I don't know. I'm not interested in politics. Or German soldiers. Or even Jews. Let's go. I've had enough of the damn war.'

Paul led Louise down a side street, away from the noise and crowd, stifling a sigh. Louise's aristocratic disdain for reality — an inheritance from her grandfather, Prince Bardossy — was familiar to him, but hard for him to accept.

Two years younger than Louise, Paul took everything seriously, like his father. Although still at school, he read every newspaper, took a passionate interest in politics and preferred the city to the country.

'For us, the war hasn't even begun yet,' he said to Louise.

'Nonsense. Everybody says it will be over by the end of the year. You're an alarmist.'

'I'm a realist. You're so busy with your horses that you don't see what's happening around you. Even in school the Jewish boys are being persecuted, beaten up or simply ostracized. Tibor de Fekete called me a "Jewboy" only yesterday.'

'He's a lout. His father is déclassé and a professional anti-Semite. What did you do?'

'I hit him.'

Louise gave her brother a glance of surprise and admiration. 'Good,' she said.

Paul shrugged. 'Not really. Hitting people doesn't solve anything. Anyway, which side are we on? Why should I be angry because somebody calls me a Jew? It's nothing to be ashamed of. Great-grandfather Hirsch was Jewish.'

'Pali, dear, that was generations ago! You worry too much.'

'Papa is worried too. Surely you can tell that.'

'Papa is always worried about something. Did you tell him what happened at school?'

'Of course.'

'And?'

'He dodged the question.'

'What question? You hit Tibor. That's not a question, that's a blow for good taste.'

'The question of what side we're on. You don't seem to understand that it's a moral dilemma. Did I hit Tibor because I was angry at being called a Jew, or because I was standing up for the Jews? In the first case, I should be ashamed of myself; in the second case, I should be proud of myself. The problem is, I don't know what I felt when I did it.'

'What did Papa say?'

'He said he wished we'd all gone to Switzerland.'

Louise sighed. 'Don't we all?'

'Meyer tells me that the most incredible things are happening. People are paying fortunes to have their genealogical charts drawn up. Apparently, for the right price you can buy forged baptismal certificates — they're steeped in tea to age them. All over Hungary, researchers are poring over gravestones and village birth registers. It's a whole new industry!'

'It won't do poor Meyerman much good — one has only to look at his face! But I'm sure a lot of this is exaggerated.'

'Everybody is talking about new regulations . . . ghettos, round-ups, the yellow star. They say the Germans have death camps in Poland.'

'Rumors. As if things weren't depressing enough already.'

'I'm not so sure. Papa told Montenuovo that in Germany people discuss it openly. When he was in Berlin there was a gas failure at the Adlon Hotel, and they had to close down the kitchen for a few hours. One of the porters said to him, "I'm sorry, Baron, but you see what we poor Germans have to suffer while we waste all that good gas on the Jews." '

Louise shook her head. 'Even if it's so, which I doubt, it won't happen here. The Regent wouldn't allow it, neither would the cardinal. What's going on over there?'

They turned the corner and approached the Grünwald Bank, a massive structure originally built by Hirsch de Grünwald after the pattern of the Rothschild mansion in Paris, which he had greatly admired, and transformed with plate glass and a new interior by Matthew, so that it presented an uneasy combination of Beaux-Arts and Bauhaus. Outside the entrance to the bank a small group of people was apparently engaged in some form of violent, meaningless athletic activity.

Paul drew Louise closer, then shouted, 'Damn!' He dropped her arm and ran toward the bank. From a distance, it was possible to distinguish the rotund figure of Meyer Meyerman on his knees, swinging his briefcase wildly back and forth to protect himself while four or five muscular youths beat and kicked him. The policemen standing at intervals along the pavement studiously ignored the scene, staring into space.

Breathlessly, Paul ran up, grabbed the nearest youth from behind and knocked him down with a single blow.

The last words he heard as he began to fight for his life were 'Jew-lover!'

Across the street, in a gray Opel sedan, a German officer, in the tunic of the Waffen SS, a death's-head cap cocked jauntily to one side of his head and the silver-embroidered badge of the Sicherheitsdienst sewn on his left cuff, stared at the confusion, smoking a cigarette in a gold holder.

Next to him sat a major of the Hungarian Gendarmerie, bolt upright and reeking of eau de Cologne, his dyed mustache waxed into two stiff spikes like those of the late Kaiser Wilhelm II. His nose was covered in a veritable minefield of broken capillaries and his eyes bore a star-tling resemblance to two soft-boiled eggs.

Major Voster had been deputized, much against his will and better judgment, to serve as liaison to the Gestapo, and while there was nothing the Germans might do which would shock him, or with which he was likely to disagree on moral grounds, he felt a patriotic indignation at being required to take orders from a foreigner. True, he did not like Jews. He also did not like Germans, and though he had never met a Frenchman, he would have been prepared to dislike one if the occasion arose. He was an ethnic Magyar, and had prepared for his unwelcome role by drinking half a bottle of Baracs peach brandy. All the same, he was a policeman. Disorder offended him almost as much as the presence beside him of this tall, super-cilious German.

'A disturbance of the peace,' he said in German, with the Hungarian accent that Germans found so comic.

Standartenführer Dr. Becker smiled and patted the major gently on the knee. 'Not at all, my good fellow. What disturbance? These brave young men are beating up a Jew. It's going on all over the city. Why do you think we distributed leaflets last night? Why do you think we're having a gala opening of *Jew Süss*? What we want is indig-nant, spontaneous acts of violence. First of all, it demon-strates the deep feeling of the Hungarian people against the Jews; second, it makes the Jews afraid, so they'll come to us for protection. *Alles in Ordnung*! It's all normal, part of the plan.'

Major Voster focused his watery eyes on the scene, which all his natural instincts as a policeman called on him to bring to a halt. 'It's not just a Jew they're beating up,' he pointed out. 'There seems to be another young man, a tall blond fellow. He's putting up a good fight too.'

Becker leaned forward. There was indeed a tall blond young man apparently being knocked to his knees. 'That's not normal,' he said.

'Also not normal is the young lady,' Voster remarked, as Louise ran up to the car, shouting for help. Voster, with the instinctive gallantry of a Hungarian confronted by a damsel in distress, opened the car door, got out and clicked his heels, raising one white-gloved hand to his cap. 'At your service,' he snapped, recognizing in Louise the features and effortless arrogance of an aristocrat.

'Do something!' she shouted in the commanding tone that her grandfather Bardossy used to his huntsmen. 'That's my brother they're beating up!'

'I have the honor to —' Voster paused as Becker took up a position on his flank, staring hard at Louise. He began again. 'What's your name?' he asked, anxious to put on a show of authority for the German.

'Louise de Grünwald, for God's sake! I'm the daughter of Baron Steven de Grünwald, the banker. My uncle, Baron Matthew de Grünwald, is a friend of His Serene Highness. My grandfather is Prince Béla Bardossy. Now do something!'

The list of names brought the major stiffly to attention, his eyes bulging and his mustache quivering.

Becker, however, showed no signs of being impressed. 'Grünwald?' he said. 'The banker? *Sehr interessant.* And what is your esteemed young brother doing defending a Jew, Fräulein?'

'He's defending one of our employees! Now stop it, quickly, before they kill him!'

'First a few questions,' Becker started to say, but Voster waved him aside, drew a whistle from his breast pocket, blew it sharply and waved at his men, who leaped from the doorways where they had been lounging and ran toward the fight. He silenced Becker's protests with an even louder whistle blast. 'This is a different matter,' the major said stolidly. 'We can't let them beat up the grandson of a prince.'

Swinging their batons, the policemen quickly subdued Meyerman's tormentors and solicitously leaned over to help Paul and Meyer to their feet.

'An unfortunate incident,' the major said to Louise.

Becker gave her a disarming smile. 'Most unfortunate,' he agreed, 'but may I ask, my dear lady, why your brother apparently felt compelled to come to the aid of a Jew?'

'He's a friend,' Louise replied curtly.

'Ah, *Freundschaft*! A noble instinct. This is something we Germans understand. Still, a *Jewish* friend?'

'Yes. What of it?'

'Unusual. In Germany, I don't think it would happen. Does your brother propose to make a habit of intervening in these little demonstrations of public feeling on racial matters?'

'I have no idea. Why?'

'Because, if so, he's going to be kept very busy. Ah, here comes the young hero now. They're carrying him over here, together with his Hebraic friend. They don't look too badly hurt.'

The policemen put Paul down on the pavement while Louise and the major leaned over to see if he was badly injured. He opened one bloodshot eye, smiled gamely and then groaned. Becker gave Meyerman a chilly smile, and turning to Louise, said, 'May I have the honor of taking you all home in my car?'

For a moment Louise hesitated. The tall German officer's manner was at once courteous and insolent, and his eyes seemed to focus at a point just over her shoulder, as if he was trying to avoid looking at her. However, a car was a car. What she most wanted was to get off the street. 'Thank you,' she said shortly, and stepped in as Meyer and the major lifted Paul up to prop him in the back seat.

'You must tell me more about the Grünwalds,' Becker whispered to the major as they squeezed in front beside the driver. 'It's exactly the kind of family that interests me!'

'We should complain to somebody!' Betsy de Grünwald shouted, just on the edge of hysteria, while the doctor finished bandaging Paul's cuts. Meyer Meyerman, apologetic and grateful, had already been carried upstairs to a spare bedroom, his pain somewhat relieved by the pleasure of being a guest in the Grünwalds' house.

Steven de Grünwald saw the doctor out, wondering

briefly what on earth they would do if the idiot Germans took poor Weissberger. Surely nobody would place a seventy-year-old family doctor in a camp or a labor battalion? The government must realize that without Jews, Hungary would have no doctors, no lawyers, no shopkeepers and no commerce. Even Monsignor de Montenuovo had remarked that at the first sign of prostate trouble the Regent would rescind the new anti-Semitic decrees.

'Who are we to complain to?' he asked, sitting down beside Paul while Betsy glared at them both. 'And what for? This kind of thing is going on all over Hungary. After all, if Paul hadn't played the Good Samaritan, this wouldn't have happened.'

'You put ideas into his head, Steven. First he hit Tibor de Fekete. Now he brawls in the streets!'

'It's not his fault. This poor Meyerman boy was being assaulted and Paul went to help him.'

'And came back in the car of a Gestapo officer, half dead!'

'*N' exagérons pas.* He's very much alive.'

'He could have been killed. You're his father. Make it clear to him: No more heroics!'

'Betsy, please! All right, no more heroics, *je m'en charge*, but also no more hysterics. Go bring us a cup of coffee.'

'The two of you are alike,' Betsy said. 'You make trouble for yourselves. And to involve Louise in all this . . .' Betsy looked with exasperation at her husband, concluded from his expression that further discussion was useless, walked out and slammed the door.

Steven sighed. 'Is it necessary to frighten your mother?' he asked.

'I didn't do it to frighten her.'

'No, I suppose not. Why *did* you do it, then?'

'I like Meyerman. Nobody else would help him. The police were standing around doing nothing — even looking the other way.'

'Yes. He's a good boy. I must telephone Berlin to have a word with the professor, by the way . . . Well, but your mother is not entirely wrong — it was foolish.'

Paul, for the first time, looked as if he might be on the

214

verge of tears. 'Foolish ... Yes, but one has to choose sides!'

'Not at all. We're Hungarians. Just because Tibor de Fekete insulted you, you don't have to make a martyr of yourself.'

'It's not a question of being a martyr. Why should I be insulted when I'm called a Jew? That's like saying that Tibor was right, that it *is* an insult. You don't believe that, do you?'

Steven lit a cigarette and examined the smoke as if looking for an answer. 'No,' he said after a moment. 'No, I don't believe that. One can be proud of being Jewish. One *should* be, in fact. But we're not Jewish.'

'Aren't we? You yourself have always admitted —'

'— that we're *part* Jewish? Yes. It would be stupid to deny it. And even more stupid to make a point of it. Perhaps we should have discussed all this more frankly before, but who could imagine ... Listen, terrible things are going to happen — your mother has no idea what it's going to be like. We won't be affected, you understand, there's no question of that, but it's important to remain calm. You have a little Jewish blood. So what? That's not a reason to get yourself killed. Don't make a problem where there isn't one.'

'There *is* a problem, Papa. We're going to be made to choose sides.'

'In the schoolyard, possibly, but not in real life. We go to Mass — why should we not? We're Catholic. We do business with the Germans — all right, I'm not happy about that, but it's necessary. If there are difficulties — and I don't see why there should be, frankly — we have friends, contacts, influence, even money. All we have to do is keep our heads until this damn war is over and the Germans have gone home.'

Steven leaned over, put his hands on his son's face and kissed him. 'You'll see,' he said, 'things will sort themselves out. Trust me.'

But looking into Paul's eyes, he saw with sad, terrible clarity that the boy no longer did.

'Trust me,' Matthew said.

'I trust you. But I'm still not happy about the situation.'

'Happiness is not the issue.'

Steven and Matthew sat in the study of the mansion, the heavy drapes pulled tight as a precaution against air raids, though air raids, as they both realized, were the least of the dangers before them.

'Can we rely on Rademacher?'

Matthew closed his eyes and thought for a moment. He didn't have to think for long. 'Only up to a point,' he said. 'We may have to make a deal with the Germans, frankly. The problem is that Göring is no longer the fair-haired boy. He's in disgrace with the Führer, because of the Luftwaffe's failure.'

'The problem is to get out alive!'

'No, no, things aren't as bad as that. Rademacher has talked to me about a deal — the Germans take half our assets. Absolutely incredible!'

'I'm not so sure. How much would they give us?'

'Steven, they'd pay in reichsmarks! No thank you! We still have a few cards to play, you know. They still need the uranium for Wotan, and we're still citizens of an allied country. The important thing is not to panic.'

'Panic? Look at what's happening? A blizzard of new laws! Jews have to wear the yellow star. Jewish businesses are being seized. Jews can't own cars or use telephones. Friediger told me that he was called to the Hotel Majestic, along with half a dozen of the leading Jewish figures, and kept waiting for two hours. They thought they were going to be arrested, so they each brought along a suitcase. Instead, a Colonel Eichmann told them to set up a committee and start a Jewish newspaper.'

'That doesn't sound so serious. Also, I can't see how it affects us.'

'It's a first step in a bad direction, Mati. As for us, the right-wing papers have been carrying some unpleasant stories about the Grünwald family. There have been questions in Parliament about why the government has allowed a Jewish family to control the largest banking and industrial consortium in the country. Only last night somebody painted a Jewish star on the bank and, believe me, it wasn't the work of amateurs — it's two meters in diameter!'

'Childishness! That kind of thing doesn't worry me. At the moment, Horthy is virtually a prisoner, but once he can speak freely again, who knows which way things will turn? As for the Germans, there's no point in talking to them so long as things are left in the hands of junior officers like this — what's his name? — Eichmann. I met Rochefaucon, from the French embassy, at the station in Vienna, and he told me that when the Germans occupied France it was the same story. At first a lot of nobodies stirring things up, making trouble, then the more serious people take charge and business returns to normal. He has a lot of common sense, Rochefaucon.'

'He'll need it once the Allies invade France and the Gaullists take over the government.'

'Believe me, he's aware of that. He's already put a few discreet feelers out to London, made a few useful Resistance contacts. I think we might learn from Rochefaucon's example. It's time for us to make a few contacts with the other side, a kind of insurance policy for the future. We'll see if Montenuovo can have a chat with the American ambassador to the Vatican, next time he's in Rome . . . And there's a very useful man in Berne with Allen Dulles, his name is Tyler, I think. He was in the American legation in Budapest before the war. He'd be a good man to see.'

'Mati, I don't think you understand the gravity of the situation. There's no question of getting an exit visa now. Hungary is sealed tight. Nobody is getting out.'

Matthew laughed. 'We'll see about that,' he said. 'After dinner, I'll make a few calls.'

But as Matthew sat in his study after dinner, making his calls, he quickly recognized that Steven was by no means exaggerating. The new Prime Minister, Döme Sztójay, who had also assumed the portfolio of Foreign Affairs, was effusively, even nauseatingly polite, but evasive about practical matters. He was honored that a man as busy as Matthew de Grünwald should have taken the time to call him and offer congratulations. On the other hand, an exit visa was a matter of some difficulty, the Prime Minister continued with embarrassment, though whether real or feigned was difficult to say. *Temporarily* (and Sztójay stressed the word) the Hungarian Foreign Minister could not issue an exit visa for a person of Matthew de Grünwald's importance without the prior approval of the German Reich plenipotentiary. Perhaps the highly esteemed Baron de Grünwald would therefore be good enough to call His Excellency Dr. Veesenmayer, who would undoubtedly take into account the well-known connections between the Grünwalds and the highest circles in the Reich.

Dr. Veesenmayer, unfortunately, was in conference, even at this late hour, though his aide suggested it might be useful to first obtain the authorization of Obergruppenführer Dr. Winkelmann, the newly appointed Higher SS and Police Leader in Hungary, or his deputy, the *Befehlshaber des Sicherheitsdienstes*, Geschke — a mere formality that should present no significant problem for a man of such importance as the baron.

Obergruppenführer Dr. Winkelmann's secretary regretted that the Higher SS and Police Leader was unavailable — he was a guest of honor at a gala screening of *Jew Süss*. Oberführer Geschke, who sounded drunk, expressed his heartfelt, if somewhat incoherent, regrets that he could do nothing about an exit visa without first discussing the matter with State Secretary Baky of the Hungarian Gendarmerie, a formality that could doubtless be dispensed with by a word from Prime Minister Sztójay . . . In short, Matthew concluded, the run-around!

A call to Cardinal Serédy's residence was equally unproductive. Monsignor de Montenuovo explained that His Eminence was deep in prayer and therefore unable to come to the telephone. The monsignor suggested that a call to Nicholas Horthy might produce results, but Nicholas, when Matthew reached him, sounded preoccupied and deeply depressed. His father, the Regent, was unwell, unable to sleep. Perhaps in a few days he could see Matthew, but just at the moment, with things as they were, an audience would be difficult to arrange.

Matthew put down the telephone, poured himself a brandy and sat down to think. He was not a man given to panic; he prided himself on being a realist. It might be necessary to make a few sacrifices, he told himself.

There was a knock on the door and Cosima stuck her head in. She was wearing a French negligee underneath her robe.

'Are you coming to bed soon, Mati?' she asked.

'In a moment, *mein Schatz*,' Matthew said, finishing his

brandy with a sigh. He had hoped to sneak into bed after she was asleep, but the thought crossed his mind that he might need *Hofrat* Schiller's help in the near future, now that his father-in-law was so close to Himmler, and he rose to his feet slowly to follow his wife upstairs. It was, he reflected without pleasure, a prudent moment to fulfill his marital duty — in times of danger a man will even go to bed with his own wife to save his skin!

Not far away from the Grünwald mansion in an expensive suite at the Majestic Hotel, Standartenführer Becker, still wearing his tunic despite the late hour, was sitting behind a desk at the telephone, listening to Oberführer Geschke, whom he despised. He nodded impatiently as the Oberführer droned on, said, 'I'll pass it on,' and hung up with a sigh of relief.

'He's drunk, the rotten swine,' Becker said.

'Naturally. But what did he say?' Eichmann was seated by the fireplace, laboriously going through the index-card files of prominent Jews, which he had removed from the Hungarian Ministry of the Interior. Eichmann had on his reading glasses, which gave him the appearance of an ill-tempered schoolteacher. On the table beside him was a bottle of French brandy.

'Grünwald is trying to get an exit visa.'

'That's to be expected,' Eichmann said, nodding with satisfaction. He was a professional; he knew what to expect. He had won his commission by handling the resettlement of the Viennese Jews in 1938 and no stage of the process could surprise him.

The suite was already crowded with booty, including a grand piano. During the first visit of the new Jewish Council, Eichmann had mentioned soulfully how much he missed playing the piano, and within an hour eight pianos were delivered to the hotel. He kept only one — a magnificent Steinway from Friediger's mansion — and at the next visit of the council he jokingly remarked, 'Dear gentlemen, I only wanted to play the piano, I didn't say I wanted to open a piano shop!'

Requests for women's lingerie, liquor, perfume, silverware, antique furniture and porcelain had been met with equal speed and generosity. Becker had asked the president of the council, Dr. Samuel Stern, for an original

Watteau landscape to cheer up his hotel suite, and the painting had been delivered the same day, with a charming personal note from Dr. Stern, expressing the hope that the Standartenführer would derive as much enjoyment from it as Dr. Stern and his family had . . .

It was all routine. Greed and corruption as such had nothing to do with the process. The Jew's willingness to cough up their valuables was merely an index of their spirit of cooperation. They had to be softened up by small stages, trained to comply with the smallest suggestion, lulled into thinking they could buy their way to safety . . . There must be no panic or disorder. Things had to take place in a businesslike way.

The Jews, after all, Eichmann reflected, were a commodity like everything else. There was a supply and a demand, for the death camps, for forced labor, as a means of squeezing out foreign exchange. Eichmann dealt in people, Becker dealt in their businesses.

'I assume Geschke will make sure that none of them gets out?' Eichmann asked, shuffling through his cards, already feeling a headache coming on.

'Naturally.'

'Shall I put them down on the list?'

'Not yet. They're a special case.'

'A Jew is a Jew.'

Becker stared over Eichmann's shoulder into the middle distance. 'Here there's more at stake,' he said. 'These people are friends of Göring's.'

Eichmann stared at his cards and took a sip of brandy. 'I don't want to know about it,' he said. He closed his eyes, in which fireworks seemed to be going off as the migraine pain increased. Ever since 1938, he had suffered from headaches. He opened his eyes and looked at another card. 'What about the Friedigers?' he asked.

'You can have them.'

Eichmann wrote the name on his list. He felt better already.

11

'It's enough to give one a headache, all this,' Betsy de
Grünwald complained. She was standing on the terrace of
the Bardossy palace with Cosima, Paul and Louise, while
Matthew, Steven, Montenuovo and Prince Bardossy sat
under the awning, smoking their post-prandial cigars and
continuing the argument that had made lunch so hellish.
In the distance the Bardossy lands stretched to the far
horizon — grain fields, fruit orchards, grassland for the
cattle and horses, whole villages to which the prince
represented an authority far more compelling and absolute than that of the Regent himself.

As with so much else in Hungary, there was a great gap
between form and substance. The peasants did not much
like Prince Bardossy — in fact, they hated him and longed
for land of their own. On the other hand, unlike the
government, he didn't take their sons away to serve in the
army, raise their taxes or confiscate their livestock. It
suited them, as it suited the prince, to pretend to a feudal-
ism that no longer existed. When the government sent
inspectors, the peasants could shrug and direct them to
the prince, their feudal magnate. The prince, in turn,
could put the blame for whatever had not been done
squarely back in the government's lap. How could he be
expected to rule 'his' people with an iron hand when
successive governments had systematically reduced the
powers and the privileges of the feudal aristocracy? The
prince and the peasants, however much they disliked one
another, had evolved a system that effectively discour-
aged any interference in their affairs from the ministries
of agriculture and finance, as a result of which the peasants were perfectly willing to doff their hats in the presence of Prince Bardossy as part of the bargain.

The Bardossy 'palace' was by no means on the grand

scale its name implied. Until the middle of the nineteenth century, it had merely been a large, comfortable country house, in the style of the region, barely distinguishable from the stable that faced it across a muddy courtyard full of manure, dogs and chickens. A brief period of prosperity had made it possible for Bardossy's grandfather to rebuild the family seat in the style of a French château, with towers, Gothic arches, ramparts and a working drawbridge, a choice inspired by a love of France and the aristocrat's natural fear of peasant revolt. The small windows — ideally suited for defending the house with crossbows and boiling oil — made the interior seem even more medieval and dark than it already was.

It was a family tradition to greet the prince on his birthday, and the presence of a German army corps could not be allowed to affect a Bardossy tradition. In previous years, there would have been dancing, singing, a ball for the local gentry, a whole ox roasted on a spit made from a tree trunk, its horns and hooves decorated with gold leaf, and hundreds of knives stuck like arrows in its charred back and flanks so that everyone could carve off what they liked and keep the knife as a souvenir.

In the present circumstances, it seemed prudent to celebrate with more modest festivities — a quiet luncheon, en famille, with a few old friends like Monsignor de Montenuovo, a little Gypsy music at the beginning of the meal, a glass of champagne. The moment the Gypsies had finished playing and the family had offered a toast to Bardossy, the discussion turned to the 'situation' in Budapest (as Montenuovo delicately referred to it), and despite the presence of the young people (for they were no longer children, though they were still treated as if they were), Matthew and Steven fell into a heated argument. Under the pressure of events they had switched roles — Matthew, usually the optimist, was depressed and pessimistic, while Steven now took a less extreme view of events.

'You don't know what it's like,' Matthew said irritably, sipping a large whiskey, which he continued to drink throughout luncheon to the evident disapproval of Prince Bardossy, who had arranged for each course of the meal to be accompanied by a different wine from his own vineyards.

'There are problems, agreed. But you can't judge the situation from the first forty-eight hours. It's a question of patience, surely?'

'Patience? You're the one who told me I couldn't get an exit visa, and you were right! I paid a call on the Regent, and there was nothing even he could do. He's aged ten years in the past week. "You'll see," he told me, "when all this is over, the Allies will blame the whole *Schweinerei* on me — if we live until it's over." And the decrees! Businesses are being confiscated. People are being thrown out of their houses. There's even talk of a ghetto. They've dismissed seventeen members of the Royal Opera House orchestra!'

'It's madness,' Montenuovo interjected. 'More than half the doctors in Budapest are Jewish! What's going to happen when they are forbidden to practice?'

'All this could have been foreseen,' Bardossy said, resigning himself to the fact that events had overshadowed his birthday. 'The Jews acquired too much power in Hungary. Now comes the reaction.'

'Papa,' Steven protested, 'how can you say they had too much power? In shopkeeping, medicine, law, even the Royal Opera orchestra, yes, there are lots of Jews, but in the Cabinet? None! In the civil service? Very few.'

'And in the banks?' Bardossy asked angrily, a question that was followed by an embarrassed silence, which Bardossy himself ended by saying, 'Of course, I'm talking about a certain *kind* of Jew, you understand . . .'

Cosima sniffed. She had always resented being dragged off to attend these celebrations — it was quite bad enough, in her view, to have to visit Prince Hatványi, without having to pay her respects to Prince Bardossy as well. As the granddaughter of an Austrian nobleman, she felt a certain contempt for the Hungarian aristocracy.

'I can't see what any of this has to do with us, Mati, or why you're so upset,' she said. 'If the Jews get what's coming to them, it's none of our business, surely?'

Matthew and Steven exchanged glances. Cosima was as aware of old Hirsch de Grünwald's origins as anyone else in the family, but like most people she assumed it was past history and had no bearing on the present. Every family — even the Hapsburgs! — had something to hide: ancestors who were mad, or deformed, or who become pederasts, or worse yet, Protestants — God only knew what unthinkable lapses of good taste! She thought of Hirsch de Grünwald as just such an unfortunate event in the family history, as if he had converted to Judaism in much the same spirit that her great-grandfather Alois had become a Freemason and an enthusiast for the ideas of Voltaire. The notion that Hirsch was a Jew, married to a Jew, and the descendent of an unbroken line of Jews, was something Cosima had never faced, though she was not alone in this, since even Hirsch's grandsons, Matthew and Steven, had spent a lifetime overlooking this inconvenient fact.

'Is Hirsch de Grünwald going to be a problem?' Betsy asked. As usual, she had shrewdly grasped the situation, and brought it out into the open, where the family could now consider it in silence, as the prince's butler bustled in cheerfully with the roast goose.

Steven shrugged, watching without appetite as Prince Bardossy carved. 'I don't think so,' he said. 'The laws are of course very complicated. I believe a family that has been resident in Hungary since 1849 and converted to Catholicism before 1900 doesn't count as Jewish at all . . .'

'No, no,' Matthew said angrily, 'that's the old decree. The new one merely says three or more Jewish grandparents.'

'I thought it was *two*,' Montenuovo said.

'Not if the person was baptized before his seventh birthday.'

'All this is ridiculous,' Cosima said with a sniff. 'You aren't Jewish, and that's that. The whole idea is unthinkable, and in any event shouldn't be discussed *devant les enfants*. Thank heaven Niki is in Switzerland!'

'What is the Church's position?' Bardossy wanted to know.

Montenuovo gave a sigh. 'It's difficult. We have members of the clergy, bishops even, who are defined as Jews under the new decree. His Eminence has been obliged to intercede vehemently with the authorities on their behalf.'

'And?'

'The government has suggested that in such cases the people affected by the decrees might be allowed to wear a white cross next to the yellow star on their clothes. Of course, that's hardly acceptable.'

'Can nothing be done for the Jews?' Paul asked. 'What happens to someone like Meyerman, for example?'

'We'll protect Meyerman somehow,' his father replied impatiently.

Matthew looked doubtful. 'It all depends on how far things go,' he said, staring at the plate in front of him. 'The main thing is to save ourselves. When we reach that point, it's *sauve qui peut* — every man for himself.' He thought about this for an instant, took a drink of whiskey and looked around the table. 'Every family for itself, I should say,' he added quickly.

Betsy did not feel that the rest of the lunch had been an improvement; in fact, it had become increasingly unpleasant, to the point that even her father had left his plate untouched. Over the goose, the Grünwald brothers had argued about the wisdom of having worked with the Germans ('Water under the bridge,' the prince declared gruffly), while Montenuovo made an inventory of their ancestors, helpfully trying to find a Christian grandparent.

While the salad was being served, Montenuovo made a tentative suggestion that it might be wise to put a portion of the Grünwald assets in the hands of the Church, for 'temporary safekeeping,' which Matthew dismissed angrily, reminding the monsignor that the Church had already made a fortune from its shares in Corvina Ores, and that if the Wotan Project ever succeeded, the Church would have to answer for the consequences of investing in the German war effort.

Over dessert — a magnificent iced cake, which was ignored, to the distress of the Bardossy cook — Betsy decribed what had happened to Paul in the streets of Budapest, to Paul's embarrassment and Bardossy's rage that any scum should attack his grandson. And over candied fruit, chocolate mints from Grabner's in Vienna and the prince's best Tokay, Cosima burst into tears. Louise sat with an ashen face throughout the meal, and as they rose to leave the gentlemen to their coffee on the terrace, Betsy heard her father say, 'Well, the main thing is that nothing should happen to the children . . .'

'Why should anything happen to the children?' Cosima

225

asked Betsy, glaring at the men. 'It's preposterous. My father says there's nothing to worry about. After all, the Germans are still a law-abiding people.'

'Yes, but what law!'

'A little drop of Jewish blood isn't such a terrible thing. I can understand that a Rabbi Goldstein or a Mr. Cohen may have something to worry about, but the Grünwalds are one of the richest families in Europe. They aren't any more Jewish than Field Marshal Milch — less, if anything.' Cosima snuffled into her lace handkerchief. 'Where there's money, there's always a solution. The Germans respect wealth; it's the Hungarians who are troublemakers.'

Betsy stifled a sigh. As a Hungarian she was irritated by the contempt Cosima — like most Austrians and Germans — showed for her country, but there was no point in starting another argument. And Cosima's nerves, in any case, seemed stretched to the breaking point — she began to sob, incoherently cursing the fate that had taken her to this barbarous country to live among strangers, where breeding and correct behaviour were unknown.

Betsy and Louise attempted to comfort her, but she was hysterical. The sight of Matthew, who had come over to see what the matter was, did nothing to comfort her. She accused him of being a bad father and a worse husband, and brushed aside his hand. Indeed, for a moment it almost seemed that she was about to slap him. His face red with repressed anger and embarrassment, his hands shaking from the whiskey, he finally managed to get her upstairs, where she took two sedatives and finally agreed to lie down.

Steven and the prince tactfully took the children for a walk, while Monsignor de Montenuovo, his face fixed in a mask of professional care, prepared to offer such spiritual comforts as were necessary to Cosima. Outside the bedroom door, Matthew and Betsy stood for a moment in silence as Montenuovo closed it behind them.

'A regrettable scene. She will have to go to Vienna for a while and stay with her father,' Matthew said.

'Will that help? The poor woman is very upset. You haven't been the perfect husband, you know.'

'Possibly not. It hasn't been the perfect marriage.'

'You haven't tried. Poor Cosima has —'

'Not in bed she hasn't.' Matthew moved closer to Betsy and took her hand.

'I don't want to know the details, Mati. It's degrading.'

Matthew shrugged. 'A good marriage is made in bed,' he said with a glance in the direction of Betsy's breasts. 'Mine was unfortunately made in the boardroom. Cosima, frankly, suffers from — a certain lack of response.'

'That's not an excuse for sleeping with other women, Mati — and for being so obvious about it.'

'In a different marriage I might have been faithful. No man likes to go out at night for what he can get at home. Steven, for example, in that respect is a happy man!'

'That's hardly the point.'

'Oh, but it *is*. I don't have to tell you that you're a very attractive woman. If Steven weren't my brother . . .'

'Well, he *is*. And kindly take your hand off my arm.'

'You know, my dear Betsy, brothers are not necessarily alike. With all due respect to my beloved brother, I think I am — how shall I put it? — more of a man. He's always been something of a *boy*, charming, I grant you, but charm doesn't always go far in bed . . . Whereas you and I, we understand each other. We're the kind of people who don't have false shame or guilt about pleasure. I've seen that in your face. There is no need to hurt anybody, neither Steven nor Cosima. A certain discretion is called for, but we could certainly reach an arrangement . . .'

Matthew moved closer to her in the dark hallway, his eyes gleaming, his teeth bared in what he must have hoped was a winning smile. She could smell his eau de Cologne, a subtle, bitter aroma that she suddenly found nauseating, as he reached out to embrace her. It was as if the strain of the past few days had finally brought his feelings out into the open, as if he no longer had the patience to hide them. She took one step back and slapped him as hard as she could in the face.

Matthew gave a grunt of rage, but apparently chose to regard the slap as a gesture of modesty on Betsy's part rather than a rejection. He put his arms around her, kissed her harshly, his breath reeking of whiskey, his mustache rubbing against her face, and tried to force his tongue into her mouth. 'At last, at last, at last,' he

227

muttered as he held her, one massive hand grasping her neck, the other arm around her waist, his fingers digging into her.

For a moment it occurred to her that fear and over-work had driven Matthew mad. She was a woman of the world — what Hungarian woman was not? — and it had not escaped her attention that Matthew admired her, to put it as politely as possible, but she had not imag-ined the possibility of this scene of Biblical passion between brother and sister-in-law, and had therefore been caught off her guard.

With one arm still around her, Matthew fumbled at his crotch, trying to unfasten the buttons, and she took the opportunity to kick him as hard as she could in the groin, a blow that dropped him to his knees with a sharp, stifled scream.

Even on his knees, even in pain, he continued to hold her, his arms now around her hips, his head pressed hard against her lower belly. She could feel the wetness of his tears and saliva through her skirt as he tried to force his face between her thighs, moaning from desire or agony — she could not tell which. With one hand he grabbed the top of her skirt and pulled it with all his strength, but still Betsy did not scream or shout, con-scious of the fact that a scandal would do no good at all, that there were too many ways in which the situation might be misunderstood or misinterpreted, that Steven's feelings for his brother might make it impossible for him to accept the truth. Desperately, she lunged for a heavy lamp from the hall table, and in one swift movement, using all her strength, she brough it down as hard as she could on the back of Matthew's neck.

He looked up in surprise, his eyes rolled until only the whites showed, then he groaned and fell to the floor, his feet in their handmade English brogues twitching involuntarily on the hall carpet.

For a moment she thought she had killed him, but he opened his eyes, which seemed as glazed as china egg cups, though mottled with red veins at the corners. Sensing the need for a tactful resolution to the scene, Betsy dabbed Matthew's silk pocket square in water from a flower vase and wiped it over his face.

'It's a question of too much whiskey at lunch, I think,'

she suggested. 'And on an empty stomach . . .'

Matthew nodded feebly. He seemed grateful for the lead. 'Quite so,' he muttered as his strength began to return. 'Alcohol, strain . . . Most profound apologies.' Slowly he rose to his feet, supporting himself by leaning against the wall. He brushed himself off, straightened his tie, flicked the ends of his mustache. He looked apprehensive rather than apologetic, and Betsy wondered what would have happened had she not fought back. He eyed her warily.

She pulled her skirt back up — the buttons were missing and she would have to find some safety pins. 'We must forget it happened,' she said, then added, 'and it must never happen again!'

'That's understood. Things must return to normal.'

But Betsy doubted that things would ever be 'normal' again and felt, in the aftermath of shock, the first real feelings of fear for the future.

In the car on the way home Cosima slept, apparently comforted by Montenuovo's prayers, or perhaps simply exhausted. Matthew was grateful for her silence. He felt no guilt. It was a *bêtise*, a stupidity. The whiskey had led him into a dangerous error of judgment.

After all these years of lusting after Betsy, he should have chosen a different time, a different place, used a more gradual approach. All the same, you could never tell with women. Many of them fought back hardest when what they wanted to do was give in, and most of them respected a man who came after what he wanted, even if they didn't open their legs on the first attempt. A strong approach often paid dividends in the long run. In the meantime Cosima, with her hysterics, would be on the first train to Vienna tomorrow, he decided. If there was one thing he didn't need at this delicate moment, it was a case of nerves from the bloody woman!

The car passed a checkpoint, and Matthew forced himself to think about other things. The scene with Betsy was a portent, he thought. He was losing control, allowing himself to become the servant of events instead of mastering them. There was nothing to be gained by giving way to panic, and a great deal to be lost — everything, in fact.

One had to face facts, even if it took a near rape to bring them home. The Germans had lost the war, that was the first fact. Well, that was their problem, of course, but the time was ripe to get out to the West before the Russians turned up in Budapest and Vienna.

The fact that the Germans *knew* they had lost made them all the more anxious to kill as many Jews as they could before they were beaten. The Hungarian Jews had survived more or less untouched by events until 1944, long after the Polish and German and Czech Jews had been forced out of house and home, but now they would be the last to go, stripped of their valuables so people like Winkelmann and Geschke could buy forged papers and diamonds to make a last minute run for safety in South America, and so the Führer could have the satisfaction of knowing he had killed as many Jews as possible before he died himself.

It's the next-to-last act of *die Götterdämmerung*, Matthew thought to himself, shivering slightly. It was vital to get out — and to emerge with as much of one's capital as possible. There was still time left to present oneself as a victim of circumstances, but later on there would be inquiries about those who had cooperated profitably with the Germans. The Wotan Project would surely come up — there was always the possibility of being treated as a war criminal by the Allies if one left it too late. There would be investigations, indictments, trials, probably even executions, for those who were foolish enough to sit around waiting for the Allies to arrive. The moment to switch sides was *now*, while one still had something to offer them and could claim to be fleeing from Nazi persecution.

But to get out one had to bargain with the Germans. There was no question of escape — they were too clever to allow that, and in any case, Matthew had no intention of crawling through the Alps by night. That was romantic, schoolboy-adventure nonsense, and anyway, the Alpine guides were no doubt all Gestapo informers, who made their living by betraying their clients. There was only one way to go: first-class, with one's money safely waiting in Switzerland.

It would take some hard bargaining to get there, but he was an experienced businessman, a skilled negotiator.

Perhaps one couldn't take everything. It was not the moment to be too greedy. If one got out with half, all right. Perhaps also one couldn't take *everybody*. One had to be realistic about that, too. The main thing was to save one's own skin.

Matthew deposited Cosima into the care of her maid and sat down in his study. The first order of business, he decided, was to get out, and there was only one person who could guarantee *that*.

He removed a painting from the wall, exposing a wall safe, turned the tumblers and opened it. Underneath several small suede bags with diamonds — always useful as a last resort in emergencies — he found a pocket address book. He returned to his desk, poured himself a large tumbler of whiskey, thought for a moment, then poured it back into the decanter. Drink had caused enough trouble today.

He looked up a number, placed the call with the Budapest operator and heard two faint clicks as the competing wiretappers of the Gestapo and the Hungarian Gendarmerie turned their machines on. There was a hollow sound, then a soft ring at the other end.

'*OKL Zentral*,' a voice said gruffly.

Matthew sighed. Göring would want nothing less than half of the Grünwald assets. This one telephone call would cost hundreds of millions! Then he thought about the future, and how much better it would be to spend the rest of the war in Lisbon than in a concentration camp.

'A personal call to the Reichsmarschall,' he said. 'It's from an old hunting companion.'

'The swine!' Eichmann said, taking off his headset while his subordinate rewound the spool on the wire recorder. 'So Grünwald is selling out to Göring. When there's enough money involved, racial purity goes out the window! Even at the highest level of the Reich ... Disgusting!'

'Shouldn't we pass this on to somebody all the same?'

'Of course. It's revolting that one can't get on with one's job without all this interference, but that's the way it is, my friend. Everybody wants to make exceptions, deals, bargains, then they come to *us* and ask why Europe isn't Jew-free yet. Call Becker, let him deal with it. I wash my hands of the whole filthy business.'

At eight in the morning in Berlin on the following day, Obergruppenführer Oswald Pohl knocked gently on the door of an office on the fourth floor of Gestapo headquarters on the Prinz Albrecht Strasse and waited until a quiet voice asked him to enter.

Pohl was a businessman and an administrator. He had put together an SS empire that included heavy industry, textiles, insurance, publishing, mining, shoemaking, housing, clothing, even monuments and brewing, not to speak of the concentration camps themselves, which Pohl ran at a profit — for the Jew's labor, gold teeth and belongings financed their own deaths.

From behind his big glass-topped desk Heinrich Himmler, Reichsführer of the SS, Reich Minister of the Interior, chief of the German Police Forces, looked up and favored Pohl with an expression of grim determination and devotion to duty, his prissy mouth set as if he had just bitten a lemon.

Briefly, for the Reichsführer was a busy man who prized brevity in his subordinates, Pohl outlined the report he had received during the night from Becker. There was no reaction from Himmler, who stared into space from behind his glittering pince-nez, his hands clasped in front of him on the blotter, exposing small, neatly lacquered fingernails.

When Pohl had finished, the Reichsführer displayed no discernible reaction, as if he were in a trance, or seeking communion with some distant Aryan spirit. Pohl had come to understand over the years that what appeared to be meditation or careful thought on the part of Himmler was merely innate caution. The Reichsführer's mental capacity was modest, and he knew it. Faced with a problem, he preferred to wait in silence until somebody offered a solution, which he could then adopt as his own. He waited now, his eyes fixed on the far wall.

Pohl cleared his throat, watching the movement of Himmler's Adam's apple, since it was the only sign that his chief was, in fact, alive. 'With respect,' he said, 'it's too rich a prize to let slip into the Reichsmarschall's paws. Whoever controls the Grünwald assets controls

232

the lion's share of Hungarian industry. It's a first-class acquisition.'

Himmler nodded reluctantly.

'The fact that the Grünwald family is Jewish also gives us a special interest, I would say.'

Himmler blinked, usually a sign of agreement.

'With the Reichsführer's permission, I suggest we arrest Matthew de Grünwald, ship the rest of the family off to the Theresienstadt concentration camp, then sweat him until he signs. The moment we have our hands on him, there's nothing Göring can do. After all, Grünwald is a Jew — more or less.'

Himmler took off his glasses and wiped them with his handkerchief, a gesture that he made several times every hour. It was a sure sign that he was hesitating, that Pohl had failed to come up with a solution that pleased him.

'No,' he said. He put his glasses back on and folded his hands in front of him again. 'Out of the question. You know my opinion about the Reichsmarschall — he's guilty of the most sybaritic self-indulgence and criminal neglect, but the Führer still has a certain fondness for him, from the old days ... Well, you know what the Führer's like. He's too soft, too gentle. People like Göring take advantage of him.'

'Then we should let it go, Herr Reichsführer?'

'I didn't say *that*. Find a compromise solution. Who's negotiating on behalf of Göring?'

'Baron Günther Manfred von Rademacher, Herr Reichsführer.'

'What do we have on him?'

Pohl glanced through his file. 'He seems to spend a lot of his time at expensive resorts in France. He has a Swiss bank account ...'

Himmler shook his head. 'The same could be said for most of the General Staff. Nothing more?'

'There is one thing. He would appear to be, ah — a homosexual.'

'Disgusting!' Himmler said primly. He took off his pince-nez and polished it again. 'I thought we had eliminated all those people from the Reich.'

Pohl raised one eyebrow in astonishment. The Reichsführer never failed to surprise him, even after all these years. Did he truly suppose that the Gestapo had eliminated homosexuality from German life? Some of Himmler's own personal staff were among the most obvious offenders, swishing around in their tightly tailored back uniforms and gleaming boots, giving every soldier a hard, cold stare of sexual appraisal as he saluted back. Sturmbannführer Dr. Spengler's Department II-K (Culture) of SD-Inland was known throughout the SS as the 'Fairy Kingdom,' and there were even those who regarded the Reichsführer's own plump, feminine hips, narrow shoulders and soft hands with some skepticism.

'We could certainly arrest Rademacher,' Pohl suggested. 'There's enough here to send him to Dachau with a pink triangle on his uniform, maybe even hang him. Though a lot of these people prefer to shoot themselves, particularly if they're officers.'

Himmler looked pained. 'That's not at *all* what we should do, my dear Pohl. That's the kind of suggestion I would expect to receive from somebody like poor Geschke. No, no, talk to Becker in Budapest. Tell him to show Rademacher the file you have there. Since Rademacher likes dancing, he can dance to our tune. Besides, homosexuality is a sickness. We don't shoot people because they have a heart condition or tuberculosis. We try to *cure* them. Especially when they're useful.'

'*Jawohl, Herr Reichsführer.*'

'Oh, and Pohl, these rumors that we're making soap from the inmates . . . I have a complaint here from Dr. Goebbels. Apparently people make the most gruesome remarks in the shops . . . That kind of thing gives the SS a bad reputation. Is it true?'

Pohl shrugged. 'Not exactly. Dr. Becker told me that Brigadeführer Dirlewanger tried in Lublin on a small scale, but it wasn't a success. There's no serious commercial potential.'

The Reichsführer nodded to indicate the discussion was over. He picked up a document and concentrated on it until Pohl had closed the door behind him, then he shut his eyes for a moment, and tried the deep breathing exercises dear Dr. Kersten had taught him. No matter how hard he tried, he was unable to control the pain in his head and neck, the searing spots that floated across his vision, the agony in his lower back and stomach.

Sometimes it took heroic efforts to prevent himself from moaning or screaming, but one had to be as hard as steel, as cold as ice, there was no other way ... There was so much to do, so many reports to read, such a constant need to clean out the filth and corruption. No matter how many homosexuals you sent to the camps to die in the work gangs, there were still more, like this Rademacher fellow. Even after five million Jews had been killed, here was this swine Grünwald, still making his dirty Jewish deals with no less a person than the Reichsmarschall himself!'

The whole world needed to be burned clean, the way farmers prepared a field by setting fire to the stubble! But where was the fire to come from? Himmler wondered, as he made a mental note to see if there had been any further progress on the Wotan Project.

Part Seven

The sins of the fathers 1944

The arrival of so many Jewish millionaires in Lisbon from Hungary is causing a sensation about our anti-Jewish measures here.

— GERMAN DIPLOMATIC REPORT FROM LISBON, 1944

12

Train service between Budapest and Vienna was appalling. Even the express was delayed for hours, first by a bombing raid on Vienna, then by military transports, finally by several trains of cattle cars under heavy SS guard, which everyone pointedly ignored. There was not even a dining car, but Matthew de Grünwald didn't bother to complain. It was the least of his problems.

Göring had agreed quickly enough to a deal — half the Grünwald assets for the right to leave — but the actual negotiations were time-consuming and difficult. Day after day Matthew, his Swiss lawyer, Dr. Zengli, and several assistants sat in a hotel suite in Vienna, going over the complex network of Grünwald holdings until even Matthew was bored with the proceedings. Occasionally he roused himself to explain some of the more complex transactions — for example, the Grünwalds owned 100 percent of the Bruxer Kohlen-Bergbau Gesellschaft, which in turn had a 25 percent minority interest in the Niederlausitzer Kohlenwerke A.G., which in turn gave them 'a position' in the Bohemian Mineral Consortium by virtue of a letter agreement between the Grünwald Bank, the German Lignite Syndicate, I.G. Farben and the Dresdner Bank. At tedious length, they went back into every step of these complicated transactions, like tourists trying to find their way out of a maze.

They argued interminably about price per share, about the value of the reichsmark, about what percentage of the compensation, if any, would be in foreign exchange, yet Matthew de Grünwald seemed almost indifferent to the outcome.

'He's lost his balls,' Rademacher said to Schiller when they took a breather during the discussions.

Schiller looked skeptical.

'He's trapped,' Rademacher continued. 'He can't get out until he's signed. He's got no choice, man.'

Schiller shook his head. He knew his son-in-law better than that. 'He's got something up his sleeve,' he said. 'You'll see.'

Whatever that surprise might be, it was postponed by the arrival of a new negotiator. When they assembled for the fifth day, after breakfast, Rademacher was missing. For nearly half an hour everybody sat around the green baize table, staring at the bowl of flowers in the center. In front of each man was a glass, a bottle of mineral water, a pad of paper and a freshly sharpened pencil. Rademacher's chair at the head of the table, opposite Matthew's, was empty.

There was a noise in the hall, then the door opened and Rademacher came in. He seemed tired, almost disheveled; there were lines of fear on his face, which was almost unnaturally pale.

Behind him, tall, stiff and elegantly uniformed in black, came a Standartenführer, his black death's-head cap pulled low over his eyes. 'Heil Hitler!' the SS colonel said, raising his right arm in the Nazi greeting. Then the Standartenführer took off his cap, revealing a silver-gray crew cut and a pair of deep-set unfocused eyes that seemed to have been placed too close together, like those of Hess or the late Reinhard Heydrich, then placed the cap and his black leather gloves on the table and sat down stiffly in Rademacher's place, leaving Rademacher to pull up another chair.

'Allow me to introduce myself,' he said. 'Standartenführer Dr. Becker. I am now in charge of these negotiations.'

Matthew leaned forward, as if he was trying to examine Becker more closely. 'I had understood that Rademacher was in charge — as Reichsmarschall Göring's representative.'

Becker bared his teeth in what might have been described as a smile — perhaps he hoped it was one. 'As of this morning,' he said, 'the SS is involved. It was decided at the very highest level. In view of the importance of the assets . . .'

'Perhaps we should fill the Standartenführer in on the negotiations to date?' Rademacher suggested, a new timidity apparent in his voice.

'What for?' Becker asked. 'For me it's simple. The Jew Grünwald and his family leave the Reich, and we take half their assets, including the foreign ones. The moment he's signed the document, he can leave. Until then, he stays. It shouldn't take five minutes.'

Matthew de Grünwald lit a fresh cigar and stared at Becker. It was time to play his surprise card. 'There's only one problem,' he began slowly.

When he was finished, Becker's reaction was predictable. 'Switzerland!' he screamed. 'We can't let you go to Switzerland!'

Matthew puffed happily on his cigar. 'You don't have a choice,' he said. 'Let me explain again. All our foreign assets are held by a Swiss company. According to the company's bylaws, no transfer of assets can take place without a directors meeting, which means that I have to appear in Zurich — *in person*.'

'We can't allow that!' Becker said. 'Listen to me. I can put you in Theresienstadt to think things over. A few days in a work *Kommando* hauling rocks with your bare hands on the double and you'll be a different man!'

'Possibly. But you still won't have access to our foreign assets. If you want to do business, I have to go to Switzerland. It's as simple as that.'

'What guarantee do we have that you'll come back?'

Rademacher studied the ceiling. 'If he doesn't come back, we'll seize his assets in Hungary and Germany.'

Becker frowned and shook his head. 'That's all right as far as it goes,' he said, 'but we need more than that. If Herr Grünwald is going to leave the Reich, then the rest of his family will have to be placed in protective custody. They'll be treated with every respect, you understand, it's a mere formality, but if there's any problem, they'll go to Auschwitz — *Nacht und Nebel*.'

'It will be difficult to get my brother to accept that,' Matthew said.

'That's your problem.' Becker stood up and put his cap back on. He opened the door for Matthew, and they walked down the hall together, pausing for a moment outside a door marked '*Herren*.' Apparently both thinking of the same thing, they entered and stood beside each other in silence at adjoining urinals.

'How long do you need in Switzerland?' Becker asked as he washed his hands.

'Twenty-four hours would be plenty, once all the papers are prepared. Zengli can hurry things along.'

Becker nodded, drying his hands. He picked up a piece of soap and held it between his thumb and forefinger, close to Matthew's face. 'Don't do anything foolish,' he said, 'once you're in Switzerland. You see this bar of soap? I promise you we'll be washing our hands with the rest of your family if you try to fuck us! Have a safe journey.'

'It's a formality. A gentleman's agreement, nothing more,' Matthew said, sitting down in a big leather club chair. His trip to Vienna and back showed in his face and clothes: he was unshaven, his trousers were wrinkled, there were specks of mud and dust on his shoes, he seemed not to have changed his shirt. Steven, by contrast, was as elegant as ever, which rather weakened his position, since whatever Matthew had been through, he had not. For the fact that Matthew had undergone a difficult experience was impossible to deny; Steven could tell that by the stubble on his brother's cheeks, the deep dark circles under his eyes, the way his hands trembled — though the two brandies he had drunk since he entered the house perhaps contributed somewhat to *that*.

'A gentleman's agreement? With Becker and Rademacher?'

'All right, they're not gentlemen. So what? We have to take a few risks here and there.'

'Yes, yes, that's all very well for you to say, but your family isn't going to be sitting here in "protective custody." What if something goes wrong?'

'What can go wrong? The Reichsmarschall's private railway car is waiting to take me to the Swiss frontier. I'll be gone a day or so, then we all fly to Lisbon. I fail to see any problem.'

'My dear Mati, you're asking me to put my family's lives at risk. Niki is in Switzerland already. Cosima is a Reich citizen, and anyway, her father is a Nazi. For myself, I don't mind, in principle, but you can't seriously expect me to ask Betsy and the children to place themselves in the care of this man Becker.'

'Steven,' Matthew said emotionally, leaning forward to put his hand on his brother's knee, 'it wasn't my idea. I beg you to believe that. If I thought there was the slightest element of risk involved, I wouldn't ask you to do it. But also, there's no choice. It's this or nothing. If we tried to sell out to the Hungarian government, we'd get paid in currency we can't use. They'd make our business a state enterprise so we couldn't get it back after the war, and we'd still have no guarantee of getting out because the Germans would never allow it. The only people who can get us to safety are the Germans, and we're going to have to do what they want. Trust me.'

'With the lives of my children?'

'Even with the lives of your children. You have to trust me. Listen, I will do something for you that has never been done before in the entire history of the Grünwald family. We'll split the assets before I go. Down the middle.'

Steven stared at Matthew in amazement. From Hirsch's time, from before Hirsch's time, from generation to generation, the assets of the Grünwald family were held inviolate by tradition. Control passed to the eldest son of the eldest son, but in a broader sense it was understood that he held the assets in trust for the family itself.

The assets were an object in themselves, with an independent existence of their own that transcended the lives and the interests of any one person or generation in the family. Hirsch de Grünwald had willed it so, it was his monument, its growth gave him a kind of immortality.

Steven rose to his feet and walked around the study. He tapped his fingers nervously on the bust of Hermann Göring, lit a cigarette, threw it into the fireplace after one puff, gave a deep sigh. The idea of dividing the Grünwald assets (or 'interests,' as they were usually called) was so radical a step that he was left momentarily speechless.

He did not mind playing a subordinate role to Matthew — they were brothers, after all — but Nicholas and Paul were merely cousins, and not all that fond of each other to begin with. If the family tradition was followed, one day the whole thing would pass intact to Nicholas, and while Paul's share of the income would make him a rich man, he would have to depend on his cousin for access to power, for a place in the management of the fortune. And, in turn,

Paul would have nothing to leave to *his* son but money — hardly the same thing as control over assets, industries and banking interests of one's own.

A half interest would give Steven a position of independent power to leave his son; at the very worst, Paul would be equal to Nicholas.

'Possibly,' Steven said slowly, '*possibly* such an arrangement might make sense. In the circumstances. We'd be breaking a family tradition . . .'

Matthew's eyes gleamed with relief. Who knows a brother, he thought, better than his brother?

'Yes,' he said. 'But these are extraordinary times. Who knows what a man has to do to survive? Grandfather Hirsch or our father — neither of them could have imagined that we would one day be threatened in our own country, caught in a trap. If we can get out with half the fortune, and a good chance of getting the other half back after these idiot Germans have finally lost the war, we shall have done very well. Far better than the Weinmann-Levys or the Petscheks, for instance. They negotiated and negotiated until the Germans finally took all their assets and didn't even let everybody go. Rademacher told me old Erwin Weinmann ended up in Dachau, out of his mind with grief. He thought he was in the Hotel du Cap, and addressed all the SS guards as '*garçon.*' Naturally, they made fun of the old man, but I suppose he was better off insane, when you come right down to it.'

'What happened to him?'

'One day they got bored with the joke, so they shot him.'

'Poor old Weinmann. He must have been close to eighty.'

'Eighty-one, I believe. A giant of German industry and banking, married to a Christian woman for sixty years, financial adviser to the Kaiser, a close friend of old Krupp . . . Believe me, we're doing the right thing. We'll give them what they want, and go. This, Hirsch would have understood better than anyone.'

'We'd better tell the family.'

'Without unduly alarming them, yes. It might be wise to spare them some of the details — the children particularly.'

'Of course. When do you leave?'

'Rademacher is coming over later tonight to pick me up. He's been appointed my watchdog as far as the border. I don't know what they have on *him*, but I can tell you he's scared out of his wits! Anyway, we are supposed to go at eleven tonight, though the Germans are so eager to get me to Zurich they would hold the train for me if they had to. You understand, they're frightened that the Hungarian government might put a stop to the whole thing. That's why speed is so essential. If we're caught between Sztójay and Himmler, we'll not only lose our assets but our skins. Sztójay would arrest us for making a deal with the Germans, Himmler would arrest us for being Jews, we'd have nowhere to turn.'

'So far nobody has even *attempted* to treat us as Jews. The regulations don't even begin to apply to us . . .'

'Steven, the regulations can be changed. They change every day, and not for the better, either. Besides, when there's half a billion dollars at stake, who is going to pay attention to the regulations? We have just enough Jewish blood to put us in danger. Let's hope we also have enough to show us how to survive! In any event, let's shake hands.'

The two brothers stood and shook hands solemnly, then they fell into each other's arms and kissed each other, moved by the gravity of the moment, the importance of the decision and the difficulties ahead. To his surprise, Matthew found himself crying and wondered if it was from guilt or love.

'It's madness!' Betsy said. 'What if something goes wrong?'

'What can go wrong? He's my brother.'

Betsy stared at her husband, started to speak, then realized that this was hardly the moment to tell Steven what had happened between herself and Matthew.

'So our lives depend on Matthew?'

'That's being a little overdramatic. But, yes, in principle.'

'Why not go to the Regent? Or Sztójay? I don't trust the Germans.'

'If the Hungarian government knew we were negotiating directly with the Germans, they'd arrest us. Anyway, what could they do for us? Give us exit visas, maybe. But the Germans, not our government, control the way out, so they wouldn't do us any good. Only the Germans can get us to Lisbon. It's as simple as that.'

'And if Matthew doesn't come back?'

Steven shook his head. He was tired and irritated. 'Of *course* he'll come back,' he said. 'Quite apart from us, there's Cosima. He's not going to abandon his own wife, you know.'

But to his surprise this piece of logic did not console Betsy. Instead she stared at him for a moment and started to cry.

Steven quietly left the room and ran into Paul in the hallway.

'Why is Mother crying?' Paul asked.

'Never ask that kind of question, Pali. Women cry for all sorts of reasons. It's one of life's mysteries, and better so.'

'I don't want to go to Lisbon. Neither does Louise.'

'Would you both prefer to be put in a labor battalion? Listen: this is a serious business. Your mother is upset because we have to stay here while your Uncle Mati goes to Switzerland to finish some business. About leaving Hungary, she's not crying. Believe me — the sooner, the better, for all of us.'

'What will the Germans do to us?

'Nothing. We'll be watched, that's all. After we get to Lisbon, things will be different. Perhaps we'll go to America, why not? Europe is kaput, frankly. I ought to add that your uncle and I have agreed to divide the family assets, in these extraordinary circumstances. From now on, we are equal partners. Ultimately, you'll have half, to do with what you want. Niki won't get it all, the way Matthew did.'

Paul stared at his father, understanding for the first time the gravity of the crisis. 'I don't want it,' he said.

Steven rubbed his eyes wearily. 'You may not want it now, Palikam,' he answered softly, 'but one day you will.'

The doorbell rang, and Paul, walking through the hallway thinking about what his father had said, unbolted the huge ornate front door.

Standing before him was a tall man in the black SS uniform, his death's-head cap on his head.

'*Bitte*?' Paul said.

The officer giggled. 'You don't recognize me?'

Paul squinted at the face under the polished visor. 'Baron von Rademacher!' he exclaimed.

'Standartenführer von Rademacher, if you please.' He looked up as Betsy came down the staircase, took off his cap and gave a courtly bow in her direction.

'Baron von Rademacher,' she said, 'what is the meaning of this sinister masquerade?'

Rademacher looked embarrassed. At a closer glance it was possible to see that his uniform was neither new nor up to his usual standard of cut and fit.

'A temporary reassignment,' he explained. 'I am now on the staff of the *BdS Ungarn*, the esteemed Oberführer Geschke. I come even now from a meeting with him. When I left he was lying on the floor drunk. The uniform I had to borrow from Becker.'

'Are we to take it that you have joined the SS now?'

'*Gnädige Frau*, when it's a choice between this and the tunic of a second lieutenant in a reserve infantry regiment on the Russian front, the decision is easy to make. In any case, I bring you good news. The train is waiting. We have a car to sneak Baron Matthew past the Hungarian control points to the railway station. Dr. Zengli has all the papers ready for his signature in Zurich. *Alles in Ordnung* — everything is in apple-pie order. Forty-eight hours from now you'll be in sunny Portugal! Where are your husband and his brother?'

Betsy gestured toward the study. 'I suppose we should think about packing,' she said.

'Absolutely,' Rademacher said. 'Take as much as you like. Baroness Weiss even took her dogs with her.' Rademacher bowed again, less formally, knocked on the door of the study, then turned back to look at Betsy and Paul for a moment. 'Don't be sad,' he said. 'If I could, I'd go with you . . .'

Both Matthew and Steven found Rademacher's new uniform disconcerting; in fact, when Matthew opened the door he stood frozen in horror for a moment, assuming that Becker had appeared to say the deal was off.

'What will Göring say?' he asked when Rademacher had made his explanation.

'What *can* he say? The Reichsmarschall's influence is on the decline, frankly. There was a telegram waiting for me at the Majestic Hotel, with orders to transfer to

Geschke's staff. I hear that the SS is taking over the Wotan Project, too, so it appears the Reichsmarschall hasn't been able to hold on to his chips. In any case, this particular chip prefers to be on the winning side.'

'You think the SS is the winning side?'

'For the moment, absolutely! Later on, we'll see.'

'What are the conditions of our "protective custody"?' Steven asked, putting heavy, ironic stress on the euphemism.

Rademacher flicked an imaginary speck of dust off his uniform. 'Garish, isn't it? Black is such a depressing color . . . Look, don't worry. It will all be very gentlemanly. The main thing is: no telephone calls to the Hungarian government. We don't want them interfering at the last moment. And, naturally, no silly attempts to make a run for a neutral embassy. I understand your former Prime Minister, Kállay, is still a guest of the Turks. Imagine having to eat pilaf and stuffed dolma for the rest of the war!'

'Very well.'

'Let's get on with this damn letter,' Matthew said, sitting down behind his big desk as Betsy came in with a tray of coffee, giving her husband a kiss on the cheek as she put the tray down in front of the fireplace.

Matthew took a sheet of plain writing paper from one of the drawers and quickly began to write, muttering aloud as he went along, 'This letter will signify the decision on behalf of the undersigned, Baron Matthew de Grünwald and Baron Steven de Grünwald, to split — should we say "share equally"? — the assets and *Interessen*, domestic and international, for the Grünwald Bank —'

Betsy put down her coffee cup and quickly walked out of the study, slamming the door behind her.

Matthew gave a start of annoyance, finished the letter, signed it boldly and passed it on to Steven, who added his own signature.

'It ought to be witnessed,' Matthew said.

Rademacher smiled. 'My pleasure.' He witnessed the document and handed it over to Steven, while Matthew went off to make his farewells. Rademacher turned to the bar in the corner of the study, his back to Steven, and busied himself with a cocktail shaker.

Standing in front of the fireplace, Steven hesitated. First he put the piece of paper in his pocket, then he thought better of it and took it out. It was the kind of document that ought to be kept in a safe or a bank vault, but this was Matthew's house, so Steven didn't know the combination to the wall safe, and it seemed unlikely the Gestapo would let him visit a bank vault. Like most people, Steven had a basic fear of carrying valuable papers on his person. He put the letter in one of the desk drawers, took it out again, looked around the room quickly and turned to the bookshelves, tilted the bust of Hermann Göring off its marble base and pushed the document inside. He was satisfied. It was hidden where only he could find it.

Steven walked across the room to pour himself a brandy, listening to the sound of Rademacher's cocktail shaker. He did not notice that Rademacher's cold eyes were reflected in the mirror above the bar, much less that they were focused on the bronze bust.

Matthew and Betsy looked at each other for a moment in the hallway as he struggled into his coat. They were alone. Steven had gone into the courtyard with Rademacher, to wait for Matthew by the car, and the children were upstairs.

Matthew cleared his throat. 'I wish you were coming with me,' he said huskily.

'I wish we were *all* going with you.'

'That's not what I meant. Once all this is over, there's a chance for a whole new life. Believe me, you married the wrong brother!'

'Shut up! When we're safely out of this mess I'm going to tell Steven what happened between us. He should know about it, I think.'

'Forget about Steven. I'm twice the man he is!'

Betsy raised her hand to slap him, then dropped it to her side. This was not the moment to create a scandal or stage a noisy scene. 'Go,' she said. 'If anything goes wrong —'

'Nothing will go wrong. Trust me. I love you.'

'I don't want to hear it. I won't listen.'

'I'll come back for you.'

'Come back because it's your duty as a brother and as a man.'

Matthew gave a short laugh, put on his homburg, picked up his briefcase and walked out into the rain. Reaching the steps, he turned back and looked at Betsy for a moment. 'I would do anything for you,' he said.

But there was no reply. Betsy turned her back and walked away while in the courtyard below a car door slammed and the motor started.

'*Na, los,*' Matthew muttered and walked down the steps to begin his journey.

13

'Gin,' Paul said, spreading his cards on the table.

'Again!' Steven said. 'You're a born gambler, my boy.'

'Your heart isn't in the game, that's all,' Betsy said. 'One can see from your face what your hand is like . . . I must say, this waiting is tedious.'

'I'd expected to hear from Mati before now. Or Rademacher. Listen — there's someone coming now.'

Outside, there was the noise of a car. A door slammed and the big front door was noisily unbolted.

'Thank God,' Betsy said, putting down her teacup with a crash that went unnoticed.

Steven walked across the study to greet his brother, and holding out his arms as the door opened, he almost found himself embracing Standartenführer Becker, who stood there grimly, still wearing his black leather trench coat, gloves and cap, and carrying a briefcase under his left arm. His eyes seemed even more lifeless than usual under the peak of his cap, and the muscles of his jaw were clenched.

Steven stared at this unwelcome apparition. 'Oh, my God,' he said, 'something has happened to Mati!'

Betsy looked at Becker's face and shook her head. 'No,' she said, 'I think something has happened to us.'

Becker did not bother with amenities. He walked over to the desk and sat down behind it, like a man about to open a meeting. He took off his cap, removed his gloves and placed them neatly beside his briefcase, then leaned forward with his hands clasped in front of them as if he were about to give a lecture.

'Please be seated,' he said in a low, flat voice. There was nothing menacing in the way he spoke. He had long ago learned that his presence was enough to frighten most people and that it was therefore a waste of effort to shout.

Many of the younger SS officers followed Heydrich's more traditional 'barking' technique, screaming at their victims, using their voices to inspire fear and obedience. Becker was lucky. His eyes did it all for him; he needed nothing more.

'There is a problem,' Becker continued. 'It seems Matthew de Grünwald has given that ass Rademacher the slip.'

'You mean he's abandoned us?' Betsy asked, afraid to look at her husband's face, knowing with cold certainty that she was right and that she should have warned him.

'I can't jump to that conclusion, but it seems likely. An embarrassing miscalculation on our part. Who could imagine he would do such a thing? Apparently he went to Dr. Zengli's office, but instead of signing the papers, he held a quick meeting and separated the foreign assets entirely from the Grünwald Bank, so we can't lay any claim to them. He abandoned the bank — and all of you, I might add.'

'I must talk to Matthew,' Steven said. 'There's some misunderstanding —'

'Just at the moment we'd all like to talk to him. The trouble is, he's vanished. I imagine he's probably had a hideaway set up for some time now. He isn't a man to leave things to chance. In any event, we'll search and try to persuade him to come back. In the meantime, your situation has changed. You're now in my hands.'

'With what immediate consequences?' Steven asked.

'Well,' Becker said, opening up his briefcase, 'we might start with these — which are to be firmly sewed on, by the way, not pinned.' And he drew out four yellow stars of regulation size, dropped them on his desk and pushed them toward Steven with his fingertips, as if they were contaminated.

Within the next few hours the Grünwalds' 'situation' was swiftly transformed, leaving them dazed and confused. In most cases of this kind the process of applying regulations was slow, an endless chain of small humiliations and defeats. At every stage there were loopholes, evasions, exceptions, glimmers of false hope, since the process was above all designed to weaken resistance. The poor, the foreign-born, the sick went before the rich and successful, so the rich and successful were kept malleable by the belief they might not have to go at all. The Grünwalds had been spared that experience, but now they were taken through its steps with dizzying speed as Becker read dispassionately from the list he had drawn up.

'The star, that's obvious. Sew it on with double stitching. If you go out in the street, the police will try to tear it off, and if they succeed, you'll be in a lot of trouble. For the moment I'm going to allow you a certain amount of latitude, but I can't be responsible for any trouble you provoke by yourselves. I don't have any control over the Hungarian Gendarmerie, and for the most part they behave like undisciplined beasts. Until we've had a talk with Herr Matthew, I'm not going to subject you to every regulation, but unless he comes back — which I hope for your sakes you can persuade him to do — we'll give you the full treatment.'

'Which is?'

'It changes every day.'

'Standartenführer, this is impossible,' Betsy said, holding out the cloth star. 'I can't be expected to wear one of these!'

Becker looked at her impassively. 'If you have any complaints, give them to your brother-in-law. If he'd come back as he was supposed to, I wouldn't be here and you'd be safely in Lisbon. For that matter, the only reason I'm allowing you any freedom of movement and communication at present is because I hope he'll try to get in touch with you. Or that you know how to get in touch with *him*. Persuade him to sign the papers and return. It's the best advice I can give you! As for you, Baroness de Grünwald, you can write on your star "Married to a Jew" if you like. And if you want to sew a cross next to the star as well, for the children, I won't object. I'm a reasonable man. If I have to hand you over to Oberführer Geschke or to Eichmann, you'll experience quite a different treatment, that I can promise you! You have a little time — how much I can't say. Put it to good use. Get me Matthew de Grünwald!'

Getting Matthew, however, seemed an impossible task. Steven telephoned Dr. Zengli, who denied any knowledge of his client's whereabouts, then he visited the Swiss legation, where the staff was courteous but unhelpful. He took Paul with him everywhere, relying on his son for moral support, as if the boy had replaced Matthew in his mind.

Forcing himself to think clearly, Steven realized that Matthew's flight (he found it difficult to think of it as a 'betrayal') exposed them to danger in more ways than one. The Hungarian government was now fully aware of the German deal with the Grünwalds, and the reaction in the Sztójay cabinet was explosive. There were stiff confrontations between the Hungarian Premier and Dr. Veesenmayer, who bounced what he called 'the hot potato' back to Berlin, where Himmler and Göring, despite their dislike for each other, met to discuss how to break the news to the Führer. Luckily, the Führer had developed a personal dislike of Sztójay in particular and the Hungarians in general, and endorsed the acquisition of the Grünwald *Interessen*, over the objections of Ribbentrop.

The Sztójay government was therefore forced to retreat from its position that the deal was illegal, and expressed willingness to accept an apology and a share in the spoils, neither of which was forthcoming.

Since the Hungarian government was in no position to threaten the Germans, who had managed to walk off with the richest prize in Hungarian industry and commerce, Sztójay set out to punish the Grünwalds, but here, too, the Germans intervened. The Grünwalds were to be handled by the Sicherheitsdienst, not by the Hungarians. Jews they might be, at any rate until negotiations could be resumed with Baron Matthew de Grünwald, but they were under German 'protection.'

These larger political considerations weighed heavily on Becker, who was being criticized now for his 'clumsy' handling of the situation. They also concerned Steven, who was looking desperately for some way out of the situation. Every morning he discussed the various possibilities that came to his mind with Paul, whose brains and quick instinct he came to trust. The two of them went off every day to call on anybody who might be in a position to help.

They paid a call on Nicholas Horthy, who politely refused to comment on the yellow star and promised to do everything he could for the Grünwalds. They visited

Cardinal Serédy, and met frequently with Monsignor de Montenuovo. They called on former business associates and friends. Nowhere was there news of Matthew de Grünwald, nor did anybody have much to suggest in the way of solutions to Steven's problems. Montenuovo, in fact, was uncharacteristically pessimistic. Taking Steven to one side, he whispered to him, 'Save the children.'

Steven looked annoyed. 'I hope to save everyone,' he said stiffly.

Montenuovo nodded impatiently. 'I understand, but you have to be realistic. Start with the children. Would Louise consider becoming a nun, for example?'

'I doubt it. Would it help?'

'I don't know. Maybe. It would have to be done quickly, but I could perhaps arrange that. Alternatively, get her married.'

'She's only seventeen!'

'A perfectly good age for marriage . . . I'll think of a few names. Do you have access to money?'

'At present, no. That's one of the problems. The Germans have the Grünwald assets and the Hungarian government has sealed all our personal accounts.'

Montenuovo leaned over until his lips were almost touching Steven's ear and whispered, 'The wall safe!' then made the sign of the cross.

'I should have thought of the wall safe,' Steven said to Paul as they walked home, followed by their guard.

'You can't be expected to think of everything, Papa.'

'The only problem is that I don't know the combination. After all, it's Matthew's safe.'

Paul thought for a moment. 'Try his birthday,' he said.

And indeed, when they got home and removed the painting in Matthew's study, the safe swung open at the first try.

'How did you guess?' Steven asked his son.

Paul stared down at the small leather sacks of dia-monds, the bundles of foreign currency, and the small leather address book on top of them. He shrugged. 'It's always sensible to start with the obvious.'

Dieudonné de Rochefaucon did his best to ignore the obvious as he chatted with Steven in his office at the French embassy. As a diplomat and a duke, his capacity

255

for failing to notice what it did not pay dividends to see was legendary. The yellow star on Steven's coat might as well have been invisible, judging from the duke's easy, good-natured conversation. All the same, his eyes betrayed a certain interest and curiosity. Steven de Grünwald's delicate position was well known, and it seemed unlikely that he had come merely to pay a social call or talk about old times.

Rochefaucon was by no means an anti-Semite except where the Dreyfus case was involved, which was merely a question of family tradition. Anybody who could not see that Baron Philippe de Rothschild, for example, was a more attractive and intelligent personality than Himmler, or for that matter, Laval, had to be insane.

Like the Rothschilds, the Grünwalds were rich, and therefore worth saving, if they could be saved without risk or trouble, neither of which appeared to be the case. If they could *not* be saved, then at least they had a right to dignity and sympathy, and Rochefaucon therefore treated Steven as if nothing had changed and as if the yellow star did not exist.

Delicately, Rochefaucon offered Steven a cigarette to put him at ease. They discussed the people they knew, parties they had been to, the gossip of Budapest society, carefully avoiding political realities. Rochefaucon was in no hurry — his duties were hardly time-consuming to begin with, and at this stage of the war, when it was obvious that the Allies would soon put an end to the Pétain government, they were virtually nonexistent. Rochefaucon had already arranged to pass on copies of everything that crossed his desk to British intelligence so that he could claim to have been working secretly for the Allied cause, and had discreetly helped several high-ranking Allied prisoners of war to find their way to Switzerland. A prudent man, he thought, should always know when to change sides.

Despite his prudence, Rochefaucon was poor — a ridiculous position for a duke. He doubted that Steven's presence in his office presented any kind of opportunity to rectify this situation, but he had nothing to lose by listening, which he did with all the graceful attention of a true aristocrat.

'Have you contemplated flight yourself?' he said.

Steven shook his head. 'If it were just me, perhaps I might make a run for it. But it's hopeless for all of us to try it, and anyway, the Gestapo follows us everywhere.'

'That's your son, waiting outside?'

'Yes, You've met his sister, I think.'

'The beautiful equestrienne? Of course. A wonderful seat.'

'Quite so. I was wondering if there might be some way to get her out.'

Rochefaucon raised an eyebrow. 'I frankly don't see how. If it was in my power to give her a French passport, I would be honored to, but even so, she wouldn't get far with it.'

'An ordinary passport, yes. But if she had a *diplomatic* passport?'

'Ah, that's a different story. But I don't think we can make her into a French diplomat, can we, however well she rides? Not that she isn't more *charmante* than my colleagues, but one can hardly make her a diplomat on the strength of that.'

'No, of course not. But if she were to *marry* a diplomat . . .'

Rochefaucon gave a low sigh and stared at his hands. He wore no wedding ring and it was well known that he was a bachelor, partly out of his love of pleasure, partly because a domestic life without money held no attractions for him.

'Most of the corps diplomatique is married,' he said. 'I believe the ambassador from Spain is a widower, but he's well over eighty years old and devout. It would be difficult to persuade him to undertake matrimony, I think. The chargé d'affaires of Paraguay is a bachelor, but he's a Rumanian in his sixties, so I hardly think Mademoiselle would consider him —'

'— suitable? No, though since it's a question of life and death, it might be worthwhile my talking to —'

'Señor Álvarez Gúzman y Popescu. Mind you, I don't think Popescu would do it for nothing. He's been selling Paraguayan passports for ten thousand dollars apiece, on the condition that the bearer never visit Paraguay, though who would want to . . . What his fee for marrying Louise would be I don't know. How much are you prepared to pay? I should warn you that everybody knows your bank

257

accounts have been frozen. Popescu will expect cash in advance.'

Steven drew a suede leather bag out of his pocket, and dropped it on the desk.

Rochefaucon looked at it for a few moments, picked it up and held it upside down over the blotter. Half a dozen magnificent diamonds fell out and lay there glistening in the light from the overhead ceiling fixture. Rochefaucon touched them cautiously with his index finger, affecting aristocratic indifference toward a display that would certainly be valued at half a million dollars or more in Asunción — or Paris, for that matter.

'I've no doubt these would stimulate Popescu's ardor. Though , as a father, you'd probably want some kind of guarantee that the young lady will reach Asunción — intact.'

'I would prefer it,' Steven said dryly. 'I would even *insist on it*.'

'Popescu's tastes run to women of a certain *ampleur*' — Rochefaucon sketched an enormous bosom with his hands — 'so perhaps that wouldn't be a problem. Is that your best offer?'

Steven looked into Rochefaucon's eyes without blinking. 'For Asunción, yes,' he said.

'Ah.' Rochefaucon stroked his mustache reflectively and formed the diamonds in front of him into a neat circle. 'I'm told Asunción is charming,' he said. 'A little provincial, perhaps, and the climate is not stimulating, from what one hears. Then, too, one has a natural reluctance to see one's daughter become Madame Popescu, even when it's a question of life and death . . .'

Steven drew a second bag out of his pocket and placed it on the desk top. Rochefaucon raised his eyebrows, shrugged and opened it up.

'You understand,' he said, 'I am not a gemologist. What do you estimate is the value of these stones?' He rolled a dozen large brilliant round-cut diamonds onto the blotter.

'About one and a half million dollars. The two lots together ought to fetch two million, perhaps more. In Paris, I'm told, they prefer the round-cut stones.'

Rochefaucon sighed, looked at the stones and closed his eyes for a moment.

He opened them, examined the stones again and then

smiled. Rising from behind his desk, he walked around to embrace Steven, and in a voice that cracked with emotion, asked, 'May I call you Father?'

'It's an act of insanity!' Betsy shouted. 'What makes you think she'll agree?'

'She will if we both explain it to her rationally, Betsy. There is no other way. Listen to me. Would you prefer it if I tried to smuggle her across the border, with an excellent chance of being arrested or shot? This way she gets on the train as the wife of a French diplomat. Himmler himself couldn't stop her from leaving.'

'As the wife of a French diplomat she's also going to have to share a bed with a notorious womanizer at least twenty years older than she is.'

'Rochefaucon knows my feelings about that. I don't think he'll touch her. We can always get her an annulment later on, it's just a question of money. In any event, if worst comes to worst, she's better off losing her virginity than her life.'

Betsy sat down and began to cry, great heaving sobs that were beyond her control. For the first time she was truly afraid because the hard cold logic of the situation was now clear to her. If Steven was willing to marry his daughter to a man like Rochefaucon to save her, then he must already consider himself doomed.

She had assumed that at least there was some hope. She realized at last that there was none.

There were no tears from Louise. She was not the kind of girl who cried. She simply sat in her bedroom in Matthew de Grünwald's detestable house and wondered whether it was worth killing herself. Paul sat beside her, his hand over hers.

'Please don't try to cheer me up,' she said.

'I wasn't intending to. But there's no point in being angry with Papa, Louise. He was shattered when we came back from Rochefaucon's office at the embassy. Do you know what he did? He put his arms around me and said, "Will she forgive me? Can I even forgive myself?" '

'That's touching. It's certainly nice to hear all this first-hand. I sit here at home with Maman and the Gestapo officers while you and Papa go off to give me away to a total stranger without even *discussing* the matter in front of me. A horse or a dog would get more consideration!'

'It isn't a real marriage, Louise, you know that. It's a ruse.'

'So Papa said. On the other hand, Monsignor is going to perform a marriage ceremony, so it's not exactly a *total* sham, is it? What happens later on? You and Papa aren't going to have to share a bedroom with Rochefaucon.'

'I don't suppose you'll have to, either. Anyway, be reasonable. Do you want to stay here with the Gestapo officers downstairs?' Paul looked weary. His face suddenly resembled his father's, as if he had aged by several decades in the past few days — which was true in a way, for he had had an education while accompanying Steven de Grünwald on his visits to all the old family friends and acquaintances who were now powerless to help or simply didn't want to take the risk.

One by one the relatives and friends of the Grünwalds washed their hands of the family's problems. Now that the Hungarian government had at last unleashed the passions it had tried for so long to contain, now that armed mobs were out in the streets hunting down the Jews, urged on by the Germans, now that the Germans themselves were in control, the only way to survive was to pretend that nothing was happening. The Grünwalds were an embarrassment, since their very presence proved that even the very rich were no longer safe, and their friends turned away from them when they did not, in fact, turn against them.

For Paul this had been a painful experience, but for his father it was an excruciating one, and seeing this made it even worse for Paul. He had sat with his father at countless humiliating meetings while Steven fought to control his rage, to be charming, reasonable, good-natured in the face of impotence, indifference and occasional downright hostility, all of it from people he had wined and dined for years, who had shot on his estates, danced with his wife, sat in his box at the racecourse, done business with him at the bank . . . Now they stared at the yellow star on his jacket and hoped he would leave as soon as possible.

Paul sighed and looked at Louise, whose beauty seemed suddenly to have become fragile and transparent. There was no point, he decided, in telling her that she was, in fact, lucky, or that she might in the end be the only one to escape. Recent experience had taught him a great deal, but it had also opened his eyes to the gulf yawning beneath them. Everybody talked about 'the treatment of the Jews' as if it were a social problem, but Paul, who was too young to console himself with hopeful illusions, had seen in Becker's eyes the indifference of a man who knew that to be Jewish was, in this time and place, to be dead. If they could save Louise, even by marrying her off to Rochefaucon, so much the better. In the end everybody would have to work out his own means of survival.

There was nobody you could trust. There never would be.

The doorbell rang, and Paul went downstairs to see who it was. Not that he expected good news. With his father and mother asleep upstairs, exhausted, he was already beginning to feel that he could no longer depend on his parents to deal with things for him.

He opened the lock and nodded to Rademacher, who stood in the doorway in his hateful black uniform, looking weary and defeated.

'Where's you father?' he asked, taking off his cap and gloves.

'Asleep. What is the news from Switzerland?'

Rademacher seemed momentarily surprised that Paul had asked him a question as one adult to another, but he was too tired to object, and by no means anxious to talk to Steven.

'We've found your uncle.'

'That's surely good news?'

'Not for me. Not for you, for that matter. He's taken refuge in the American legation, of all places. He went straight to Berne from Zengli's office to see Tyler. One look at the files and they'll probably make him an American citizen!'

'Tyler is a diplomat?'

'Yes and no. He's a diplomat in theory, but in fact he's looking after American financial interests. The job of the American generals is to win the war; Tyler's job is to make sure America dominates our banking and industry after it's been won. Tyler probably has one direct line to the White House and another to the Morgans or Kuhn, Loeb.'

'Did you speak to Uncle Matthew?'

261

'I spoke to him.'

'What did he say about us?'

'He said it was a question of business logic. He hoped the American government would take a reasonable view of your position, but frankly he didn't seem to me to care much. I asked him if he didn't want to talk to his wife and he told me, "Above all, not that — she's the one thing I don't regret leaving behind." '

Rademacher took off his coat. 'I need a drink,' he said. 'Frankly, my own future isn't all that bright at the moment. I was tempted to stay in Switzerland myself, but I had a couple of Becker's men on either side of me, with pistols in their pockets. Better go and wake up your father. He may as well hear the bad news.'

Rademacher and Steven talked until late into the night while Paul sat in a corner of the study and listened. Twice they were interrupted by Betsy, who brought them coffee, but their conversation was notably restrained. Rademacher could think of no solution to the Grünwalds' problem — or to his own, for that matter. The sight of Matthew de Grünwald standing in the courtyard of the American legation in Berne seemed to have shaken his self-confidence. He had always admired Matthew's cunning, business judgment and inherited wealth, and there Matthew was, wearing a suit that seemed to have been chosen for its transatlantic simplicity, puffing his cigar beneath the Stars and Stripes. He was even wearing a blue button-down shirt. Rademacher took one look at Matthew de Grünwald and knew the war was over, that Germany — and probably Europe, too — was finished.

'Finished,' he moaned as he described the scene to Steven. 'He's smarter than all of us put together. Tyler calls him "Matt", and says he's "a great guy." The baron will be chewing gum before the end of the week.'

Steven poured himself a whisky — he was drinking more heavily than was good for him, though perhaps it no longer mattered to him — and shrugged. He knew about Tyler, and he knew enough about America to understand that Matthew would find it easy to persuade his new friends that he was a victim of Nazi persecution.

'What do you think we should do, now that we've been left in the soup?' Steven asked.

'Well, there's one ray of hope,' Rademacher said. 'He wants to talk to your wife.'

14

Monsignor de Montenuovo was nervous — not that he was afraid of any personal consequences, he had simply never performed a marriage ceremony before. His life in the Church had been directed toward diplomacy and finance, and he had been obliged to send for a priest to coach him during the course of the night. Nor were the circumstances made easier by the fact that the bride, poor girl, seemed to be in a daze, while the bridegroom's eyes wandered around the room as he appraised the paintings on the walls, one of which was missing.

The Grünwald family stood behind the unhappy couple in attitudes that suggested they were about to be shot — Steven and Paul staring into space, Betsy crying into her handkerchief.

Rademacher had reluctantly consented to act as witness, having negotiated Matthew de Grünwald's Caravaggio as the price for his services. The duke's wedding present to his young bride, which was, after all, the purpose of the whole affair, was a dark-blue French diplomatic passport, made out to 'Mme. la duchesse de Rochefaucon, née Grünwald, baronne Louise de,' and bearing an old photograph of Louise taken in happier days. It was not an auspicious beginning to married life, but Montenuovo consoled himself with the thought that an annulment would certainly be possible after the war, unless of course the duke and duchess fell in love with each other. It was improbable, but it sometimes happened, even in the most cynically arranged marriages.

In any event, Montenuovo thought, the quicker it was over and done with, the better. Despite his own coveted diplomatic passport — a small white booklet bearing a gold stamping of the arms of the Holy See and the inscription of the Vatican — Montenuovo had no wish to be present when SS Colonel Becker arrived to find one of his victims gone, or at least safely beyond his reach. The monsignor rushed through what he could remember of the ceremony like a sprinter, pausing only to ask whether Louise and the duke accepted each other as man and wife. When the question was put to Louise, it broke through the wall of reserve around her and made her burst into tears.

'This won't do, *ma fille*,' Montenuovo said sternly. 'It is necessary to say "yes." '

Louise closed her eyes, tears running down her cheeks. 'I won't,' she said. The duke looked up to the ornate ceiling in obvious embarrassment, like a man who has just seen somebody make a faux pas at a party and is determined to ignore it.

'Say it, please, Louise,' Betsy implored, putting her arms around her daughter.

'I can't.'

'You have to.'

Louise gave a final sob, bowed her head like Mary, Queen of Scots, on the scaffold and whispered, 'Yes,' as her mother held her tightly.

'Yes,' the duke echoed loudly. He turned to kiss his bride, but after one look at her he thought better of it. There was no point in provoking a further scene.

'The rings,' Montenuovo said.

There was a moment of consternation. It had not occurred to anyone to provide wedding rings, least of all to the duke, whose responsibility it was.

Sadly, Steven removed his wedding ring and handed it to Louise, while Betsy, beyond tears, gave hers to the duke.

Montenuovo nodded, the couple exchanged rings and he declared them man and wife.

As Rademacher leaned over to sign the marriage certificate, Steven said to Monsignor de Montenuovo, 'I hope God will forgive us for this.'

Montenuovo was anxious to be on his way. 'Oh, don't worry about God,' he said, 'He will forgive you, I think, long before Louise does.' He took off the surplice and packed it away in his briefcase along with the rest of the paraphernalia he had borrowed from the cardinal's chaplain.

Although two bottles of champagne had been placed on

264

ice, they remained unopened, bobbing quietly in the water from the melted ice.

'Wait until Becker hears about this,' Rademacher said gloomily.

Becker, however, showed no emotion when he arrived, too late to stop Louise from leaving. 'Very clever!' he said to Steven, with a short bow.

His business, as it turned out, was with Betsy, whose presence he requested for a short time. When Steven started to protest, Becker raised his hand. 'I have a few questions to ask the baroness,' he said, 'nothing more. There is no cause for alarm.'

'I would prefer to accompany my wife.'

'No doubt. But you're not going to. Drink the champagne, why don't you? It's not every day that one marries one's daughter to a duke!'

Becker helped Betsy with her coat and took her into the courtyard, where his driver was waiting with the car door open.

'We're going for a little ride, Stumpff,' Becker said and rolled up the glass partition separating him from the driver.

'Where are you taking me?' Betsy asked, trying to avoid looking at Becker. It seemed to her unlikely that a full colonel of the SS would attempt to rape her — or even to seduce her — in the back of a Mercedes limousine in broad daylight, but one never knew. These days, the unthinkable was commonplace, and she could think of no other reason for Becker's insisting on a tête-à-tête.

He stayed away from her at a proper distance, however, and lit a cigarette, his eyes fixed on the back of Stumpff's fat neck.

'There's something I want you to see. And something I want you to do. I didn't want to talk about it in front of your husband.'

'Really, Colonel Becker, this is going too far . . . There's no shortage of women in Budapest, you know!'

Becker waved his hand. 'You misunderstand me,' he said. 'I'm interested in business, not sex. Besides, I have a certain amount of honor, you know. You have a low opinion of the SS if you think an officer would take advantage of his position in that manner.'

'My apologies. I had heard it was rather frequent.'

'Not at my level. Let me be quite frank with you, Baroness. Your charms are considerable, but they don't concern me, much as I admire them. Our problem is that they apparently obsess someone else.'

'I don't care and I don't want to know.'

'I'm afraid you *have* to know. Matthew de Grünwald has been in touch with us. He'll sign the papers and complete the deal if you join him in Switzerland.'

'You can't be serious.'

'Perfectly, I assure you! All we have to do is produce you in Switzerland and the deal goes through. It's not every woman who is worth two hundred and fifty million dollars to the Reich, Baroness.'

'I won't do it. He's mad.'

'Very possibly. That kind of sexual fixation is often a sign of severe disorder. However, there it is. If I were you, my dear lady, I would agree.'

'And my husband? And my son? Quite apart from the fact that this is all a shameful *Schweinerei*, what happens to them? Do they go to Switzerland too?'

Becker shrugged. 'Naturally not. In the first place, your brother-in-law wants *you*, not them. In the second place, we'd prefer to keep them on ice for a while, just to make sure we don't get cheated a second time.'

'Then it's out of the question.'

'Look, be reasonable, dear lady. I can hold them on ice in Theresienstadt — that's the camp for *Prominenten*. They'll be safe there.'

'Why can't you just release them?'

'That's not the deal. Matthew de Grünwald wants us to release you and hold on to them for a while . . .'

'I won't go.'

Becker sighed and rapped on the glass partition. The big car drew to a stop by a roadblock. Beyond it stretched a maze of narrow streets and leprous tenements. A few huddled figures moved from doorway to doorway, their eyes never leaving the filthy pavement, as if they were searching for scraps of food. Everywhere there were armed guards, some of them Hungarian civilians with rifles and armbands, rolls of barbed wire, crude, make-shift signposts marked with a skull and crossbones warning people to keep away. Becker lowered his window. There was a stench of garbage and human ordure, and a deadly silence. In a doorway a few yards away an old man lay dead on the steps in a torn overcoat, his eyes fixed on the gray sky. Somebody had stolen his shoes, and his toes stuck out through his torn socks.

'The ghetto,' Becker said. 'That's where you're going if you don't agree. Would you like to see it more closely?'

Betsy shook her head and closed her eyes.

'No, it's all pretty much the same. They say it's worse inside. That's natural, of course. Overcrowding, disease, starvation. Sanitary conditions are primitive, unfortunately. Ten or twenty people in a single room, perhaps with one tap . . . You'll think it over, yes?' Becker rapped on the partition again. '*Los!*' he shouted to Stumpff. 'We'll take the baroness home.'

'I didn't even realize you were interested in Zionism,' Paul said to Meyer Meyerman.

'Until recently, I wasn't. But not all of us can marry a duke. The Zionists are getting people out.'

'Many?'

'Not too many. But some. There's a man called Kastner, a doctor, who's been negotiating with the Germans to get exit visas for Zionist youths. The Germans don't mind sending a few Jews in the direction of Palestine so the British can turn them back at the border. That way they can say the British don't want the Jews any more than the Germans do — which is true enough, I suppose. So I've been reading up on Herzl. Interesting stuff.'

'And that's enough to get you on a train?'

'No, of course not. One has to bribe somebody to put down one's name as an old *chalutz*.'

'You've picked up the vocabulary!'

'Naturally. Then, it's necessary to bribe the Germans. Even so, it's dangerous. A few weeks ago Kastner got permission for a thousand carefully selected Zionists to leave, and at the last minute the Germans switched trains. Kastner's Zionists went to Auschwitz, and a thousand old people of no importance to anyone arrived in Istanbul. Nobody knows whether it was a mistake or if the Germans just wanted to teach Kastner a lesson . . . Anyway, the long and short of it, Paul, is that I need money.'

'How much?'

'A lot. Survival doesn't come cheaply. Listen: Come with

me. You get the money, I'll take care of the rest.'

'I can't. What am I going to do? Abandon my father and mother?'

Meyerman shrugged. 'In the end,' he said, 'it's every man for himself. If you won't come, will you lend me the money?'

'I don't have it.'

'You can get it.'

Paul nodded. He had never thought much about money, having been born rich, nor had he ever been called upon to perform an act of dishonesty. But he liked Meyerman. He went into the study, opened up Matthew's safe, removed an envelope full of currency, weighed it in his hand and returned to the living room.

'How much do you need?' he asked.

Meyerman thought for a moment. 'Five thousand dollars for Kastner's people, ten for the Germans,' he said. 'Perhaps a couple of thousand for expenses along the way.'

Paul counted out the money and handed it to his friend.

'You're sure you won't come with me?'

'Quite sure.'

Meyerman's dark eyes sparkled with gratitude. 'One day I'll pay you back,' he said. 'You can count on it.'

But Paul counted on nothing. He never expected to see Meyerman again.

Betsy took one look at Steven and knew he was drunk. He was lying on the sofa, an empty champagne bottle beside him, and a decanter of whiskey on the table. Before she could say anything he opened one eye and sat up painfully.

'So,' he said, his voice badly slurred. 'What did Becker have to say?'

'Nothing. The usual threats.'

'Ah? Rademacher tells me that my dear brother made you an offer.'

Betsy sighed and sat down. 'It's true,' she said.

'How thoughtful of him. Since when has he had this unlikely — or should I say *unseemly?* — passion for you?'

'He's always felt that way. I've told you countless times, but you wouldn't believe me. But it's madness. I never

268

encouraged it. On the contrary —'

'Oh, come now! He would hardly give up half the family assets for you if there weren't already something between you. You can't expect me to believe that.'

'There has been *nothing* between us. I have always found him perfectly loathsome. He tried to rape me after that awful birthday luncheon, and I told him to pay more attention to his wife.'

'Why didn't you tell me before?'

'I didn't want to worry you.'

Steven closed his eyes. 'A likely story,' he said. 'My God, what a dreadful day! Louise married to that pimp of a duke, now all this . . . Do you know that someone stole nearly twenty thousand dollars out of the safe?'

'Who has the combination to it?'

'Only myself and Paul, I thought. But I can't imagine Pali would do such a thing. Anyway, I don't care. Go to Matthew, at least you'll be safe with him.'

'I can't do that.'

'I'm *telling* you to. I may be able to get Paul out somehow. In the meantime, you have a way to escape. Use it.'

'I won't go without you,' Betsy said, but Steven had already slumped back, asleep in a drunken stupor.

Betsy sat and cried for some time, then realized that tears would do no good. They were, in any case, inappropriate. She was not so much sad as angry — angry at Steven for drinking himself into oblivion, angry at Matthew for his single-minded greed and betrayal, angry at herself because she was helpless. She went upstairs to her room and realized to her horror that Steven had been arranging his things, apparently aware that he would very soon have to leave, one way or the other, and that it would be sensible to keep a suitcase packed and ready to go.

On the bed was a pile of his personal belongings — his father's cigar cutter, his mother's photograph in a Fabergé frame, cuff links, a few first editions of books he had published, a small cloth-wrapped bundle. She unwrapped the bundle and realized with a sense of shock that it was the long-barreled pistol Göring had presented to Steven the day of the boar hunt, so long ago.

Betsy was no stranger to firearms. The Bardossys grew up around guns, and her father had taught her to shoot, both as a sport and because he believed they would one day have to defend themselves against a jacquerie of insolent, bloodthirsty peasants.

She picked up the gun. On the stock the small silver escutcheon with Göring's personal monogram and the *Parteiabzeichen* was tarnished. She absent-mindedly polished it with her handkerchief. Her father, she remembered, had nothing but contempt for the 7.65 mm Luger. The fact that the Kaiser used it for deer hunting, because of his crippled left arm, was yet another example of His Imperial Majesty's lack of sporting instincts. The small-caliber, high-velocity bullet went right through game, crippling the animals or piercing their lungs, without killing them. The prince was a sportsman. He believed in weapons that killed instantly.

There was a knock. Betsy put the pistol on the bed and opened the door. A frightened maid curtsied and announced that Standartenführer Becker wanted to see the baroness.

Betsy nodded. 'Show him up,' she said.

She heard his boots clicking on the stairs, then the creak of his leather belt. He knocked and came in, his narrow eyes as lifeless and evasive as ever.

'I'm sorry to disturb you,' he said.

'What do you want?'

'An answer. I'm under considerable pressure from my people in Berlin. Your brother-in-law is ready to sign if we let you go.'

'I'm not going.'

Becker stood in the doorway. He seemed embarrassed at being on the threshold of a bedroom. 'Perhaps there is someplace we could talk downstairs,' he suggested, blinking rapidly.

'My husband is drunk downstairs. Anyway, there's nothing to talk about. I'm a Bardossy. I'm not going to lose my honor.'

'Dear lady, this is 1944. Honor is only a word.'

'Then put *me* in the ghetto and let my husband and my son go!'

'That's not possible. Listen to me, please. You *have* to go. I have my orders from Berlin. You can walk to the train on your own two feet, like a sensible woman, or I can hand your husband — and if necessary your son — over to

Geschke's men. I promise you, after an hour or two in the cellars of the Majestic Hotel, your nearest and dearest will be *begging* you to leave for Switzerland and to dishonor yourself.'

'Get out of here!'

'Not before you have agreed, Baroness,' Becker said, stepping into the room and reaching toward Betsy to grab her by the arm, an expression of irritable determination on his pale face.

When his hand touched her sleeve, Betsy pulled away and screamed as if all her fear and rage were suddenly centered on Becker, and before he could move or even decide whether to calm her or hit her, she picked up the Luger and fired at him.

The pistol recoiled in her hand, and she realized with a start that she had been aiming at Matthew. His face had been there, for an instant, clearly in front of her — the red mustache, the hooded eyes, the full lips, the self-satisfied expression — then the vision dissolved, and it was merely Becker she saw before her, his mouth open and his eyes turned up to the ceiling, so that only the whites showed.

He gave a startled grunt, like that of the wild boar Göring had stabbed, and swayed back and forth for a moment, proving that her father had been right — you couldn't depend on a Luger to drop a man or a beast in its tracks at the first shot. She could hear the sound of someone screaming, a long moan of pain and rage, but it was her voice, not Becker's, for he seemed incapable of making any meaningful noise, either from shock or surprise. His eyes were wide open, his hands patted his chest searching for the bullet wound, the fingers twitching like the legs of a frog in an electrical experiment. A dark stain appeared on the front of his trousers as he wet himself. Then, in a quiet voice like that of a small child, he said, 'Mother!' and fell on his face with a crash, like a man who has just tripped over something.

Betsy stared at him in horror, unable to move. She was still standing there with the gun in her hand when Stumpff came crashing up the stairs in his heavy boots, breathing in gasps. He took in the situation with one astonished glance, drew his pistol and shot Betsy right between the eyes.

A more imaginative man might have stood for a moment in shock, but Stumpff had seen plenty of corpses in his lifetime, and a couple more didn't interest him a bit. He put his Walther back in its holster, gave Baroness de Grünwald a small kick in the ribs to make sure she was dead, did a quick inspection of the room and stuffed Steven's cuff links in his pocket. He carefully pried the stones out of the Fabergé frame on the bed, slipped them in his boots and leaned over to pull the rings off Betsy's fingers. Then he stood up, straightened his tunic and walked over to examine the Standartenführer.

As Stumpff leaned over, whistling between his teeth, Becker opened one eye and moaned, a froth of blood appearing on his thin lips. 'A doctor,' he whispered.

'*Zu Befehl!*' Stumpff shouted and rushed downstairs to phone headquarters.

No doubt there would be hell to pay, Stumpff thought, but *his* skirts were clean!

'There'll be hell to pay,' Rademacher said, cracking his knuckles in the back seat of the Mercedes, but neither Steven nor Paul seemed to be listening to him. Steven, in fact, seemed half dead from shock and grief, while Paul simply stared ahead, looking through the windows at the gray, wet streets as the big car skidded over the trolley tracks in the rain.

Eichmann, who was driving, grunted in agreement. The Hungarians were already making trouble. Well, you couldn't blame them, after all. The rumor was already out that the baroness had died defending herself against a Gestapo officer.

'How is Becker?' he asked, looking at Rademacher in the rear-view mirror.

'He seems likely to survive. In fact, we may even have to give him a medal. We're arguing that the woman was a resistance terrorist. Becker was going to interrogate her, and she shot him . . .'

Eichmann raised an eyebrow. 'Will anybody believe that?'

'Probably not, but it's the best anyone can come up with on short notice.'

'So Becker becomes a hero!'

'Oh, perhaps not that far. An Iron Cross First Class

272

should be enough, just to show that *we* believe the story. The only people who know better are Stumpff and our friends here. Stumpff is already on his way home, with orders to keep his mouth shut, and once we've dealt with these two —'

The car drew up to the station, but it did not stop. Eichmann took it past the platforms, waved on by the security guards, and then followed a bumpy cinder path out into the freight yards.

In the dark, with the light rain, it was difficult to see anything out of the windows, but a flashlight blinked in front of them and Eichmann braked. Paul wiped the condensation off the window in front of him, but all he could see was a freight train and the shadowy forms of a few guards huddled in their rainsheets and hastily trying to dispose of their cigarettes at the sight of an officer's car. For a moment Paul wondered if they were about to be taken out and shot, but Rademacher patted him on the shoulder, with a gesture of reassurance.

'This is it,' he said. 'End of the line!'

Eichmann opened his door, fastidiously circumnavigated a puddle and shouted at the guards. Rademacher did not get out of the car, though he gave Paul a gentle push to indicate that he should do so.

'I'm really sorry about this,' Rademacher said, 'but I'm afraid you're no longer in my hands.'

'Whose hands *are* we in?' Paul asked, helping his father out of the Mercedes.

'Theirs,' Rademacher said economically, nodding toward the train, where in the light of the headlamps two enormous guards appeared, one of them carrying a rubber truncheon, the other holding a large German shepherd by a short chain. In his other hand the man carried a coiled bullwhip. Both men had the look of retired wrestlers, though even in the light from the car it was impossible not to notice a certain dead quality to their eyes, as if overexposure to violence and cruelty had drained them of any human feeling. In their creased, rain-soaked uniforms and glistening black helmets, they looked considerably less human than the dog. The impression they projected of sheer mindless menace was so intense that Eichmann himself stepped back a few paces.

They did not bother to salute him. They were beyond the

normal disciplines and courtesies, not so much an elite as the reverse of an elite, men whose trade was mass killing and who despised those who were too lily-livered or fastidious to carry out the last step of the Final Solution.

Rademacher, with his colonel's braided silver oakleaves and his handsome lawyer's profile, was of no interest to them, still less Eichmann, a desk officer who dictated letters, answered the telephone and wore eau de Cologne. Even the Reichsführer himself would not have impressed these men. In fact, on the only occasion when he had visited Auschwitz to see for himself what was going on there, he fainted when Sturmscharführer Moll called out his ritual 'Now let them chew on this!' and dropped the pellets of Zyklon B gas into the chamber. The ghastly sight Himmler viewed through the glass-covered portholes was too much for him.

Eichmann waited for a salute, decided not to force the issue, got back into the car and slowly began to reverse it.

Paul looked at Rademacher, who shrugged regretfully and rolled up his window. Then, taking his father by the arm, Paul walked slowly over to the guards. There was no point in fighting the inevitable anymore. The only thing that mattered now was to survive it.

Part Eight

The Man who had Everything

15

'Survival is a full-time occupation,' Paul Foster said, not
so much in explanation as in apology. He had no doubt
that Diana was upset by his revelation that Rademacher
had been eliminated. Even a less sensitive man would
have noticed that, and God knows he was sensitive to the
moods, the nuances, the small signals of women.

She was distant, chilly — not at all the passionate
woman he had shared a bed with only a few hours earlier.

'You're angry,' he said.

'No.'

'Rademacher's death disturbs you.' It was a statement,
not a question.'

'A little. Doesn't it upset you?'

'Not much. He was a Nazi. Also, it was to be expected.
Greenwood wasn't going to let Kane get to him, was he?'

'Would you have?'

Paul sighed. 'Perhaps not,' he admitted after a pause.
'All the same, I asked Luther to keep an eye on him . . .
Once Kane opened his mouth, Rademacher was as good as
dead.'

'Is Luther on his way to Berne to get Rademacher's
files?'

'Yes. We'll see if he gets there first. They will be more
useful in my hands than sitting on some bureaucrat' s desk
in Washington.'

'How will he get them?'

'These are details,' Paul said impatiently. 'I don't need
to know. I don't *want* to know. And frankly, I don't think
it's a good idea for you to know either.'

'I'm not one of your subordinates, Paul.'

'No, no, I'm thinking of your safety . . .'

'You're not thinking of my safety at all. You're simply
not telling me the whole truth. I won't accept that. I'm not

going to be used when you need me, and lied to when you feel like it. I wish I hadn't gone to see Greenwood in the first place, but now that you've involved me, you'll either have to level with me or say goodbye. I don't like half-truths. Or half-anythings.'

'I'll tell you how it was . . .' Paul said, and holding Diana's hand, he began to talk about his life. Occasionally the telephone console beside him lit up with an incoming call. He ignored it as he told her about Becker, about Rademacher, about his mother's death and Matthew de Grünwald's betrayal, until the sky began to lighten on the horizon, telling her the story of his youth and his family, as if every detail were as fresh in his mind as it had been thirty-odd years ago . . .

He did not mention his father's death, nor the Wotan Project, but she had no idea of what he was editing out of his memories. It was enough that he was, at last, taking her into his confidence. She was a woman who wanted to be needed. Once Niki had needed her; then he no longer did.

In the plane, high above the Atlantic, Paul said, 'I need you, Diana,' and she knew, out of some instinct for men and their feelings, that he meant it, and put her arms around him.

'He's nothing *like* the monster you paint him,' Diana said to David Star, interrupting his perusal of Lutèce's wine list.

'The Cos d'Estournel,' he said to the sommelier, who gave a small smile of approval. 'Isn't he?'

'No. Once you *understand* him, he's not at all the cold fish you think he is.'

'Speaking of cold fish, they usually have a wonderful coulibiac of salmon at lunchtime . . . In any case, Foster's cold-fishiness was never what put me off, though it's hardly an endearing quality. What scares me about him is that he's a ruthless son of a bitch. Or am I wrong about that, too?'

Diana waited while David tasted the wine. '*Pas mauvais*,' he said. He gave Diana a smile as the waiter poured her wine, raising an eyebrow to indicate that he was still waiting for an answer.

'No, you're not wrong about that. He *is* a ruthless son of

278

a bitch. But he's also capable of quite alarming generosity and kindness.'

'He's a rich man.'

'That's not what I meant. There's a side to Paul you don't know, David.'

'You're beginning to sound like Eva Braun talking about the Führer. Next you'll be telling me he likes dogs!'

'That's a cheap shot, David. There's a lot more to him than you know.'

Star nodded, sipping his wine, and pointed at Diana's glass to indicate that she should do the same. 'There's a lot about him that I'm sure you don't know,' he said. 'Do you know how your friend Foster made his first score?'

'No. Does it matter?'

'That depends on your sense of right and wrong. Kane came across some interesting material in London. He began by asking questions about Meyerman, and Foster's name kept coming up. Did you know they were buddies in London right after the war?'

'Yes. That's no secret.'

'Have you ever wondered how two Central European refugees, absolutely penniless in 1945, each managed to make a fortune? I mean, by 1950 Meyerman was a wealthy man, and Foster had already acquired his first company.'

'They were both clever.'

'For sure. But however clever they were, they still needed capital to get started, right?'

'I suppose so. Are you trying to tell me they robbed a bank?'

Star laughed as the waiter served Diana a neatly boned smoked trout. He nodded his approval at his own plate of pâtés — Star had published a book called *Cholesterol Is Good for You*, and believed in it. 'A bank would have been okay,' he said indistinctly as he chewed. 'No, they stole from their own people.'

'Which people would that be?'

'Refugees. Displaced persons. Concentration-camp survivors. Widows. Orphans. You name it. Apparently Meyerman and Foster were friends during the war. Meyerman bought his way out of Hungary somehow. He went to Palestine via Istanbul, and managed to get into England by bribing a few people on the way.'

'It's always been one of his stories. He tells it well.'

'I know. The only trouble is that he leaves out the best part. Anyway, he gets a job teaching German at a commercial school, and in the evenings he works in an organization for the relief of Austrian and Hungarian victims of Nazism, one of those charitable foundations the English love, you know the kind of thing I mean: a house converted into a club where people can meet, drink coffee, talk about the old days, try to find out who survived and who didn't, and so on. They had a relief fund, of course, to set people up on their feet again, no big sums, you understand, five or ten pounds here and there to keep body and soul together.'

'All that sounds okay.'

'It was. Perfectly straightforward. Meyerman hung around the club in the evenings so much that eventually they made him the secretary. Why not, after all? He was young, eager, had a good head for business, was willing to work hard. You need somebody like that to run things, keep accounts, look after the books.'

'Meyerman looked after the books?'

'Of course he looked after the books. He controlled the fund that way. Then Foster turns up in London — Meyerman's old friend. *He* surfaced in Germany, presumably from one of the camps, and made himself indispensable to the British War Crimes Commission, God knows how. In any case, he managed to get into England in 1946, so he looks up Meyerman and they decide to share an apartment together. By this time Meyerman has more work than he can handle. In the mornings he's out hunting for antiques because he wants to start his own business; in the afternoons he's giving German lessons on the Fulham Road; in the evenings he's running the club . . . A busy life.'

'There's nothing wrong with that.'

'No, indeed. I never said Foster and Meyerman weren't hard *workers*, Diana. Anyway, Meyerman offered Foster a job as his assistant at the club, helping him —'

'— look after the books?'

'Exactly. The two of them are hard at work every evening, dealing with requests for help, making out checks, doing the accounts. Everybody thought they were terrific. Meyerman was warm, sympathetic, a terrific hit with the ladies . . .'

'He always was that.'

'So I'm told, though it beats my why. Foster was serious — the brooding, silent type. I guess Foster was good with the girls, too. There's a rumor he had an affair with the daughter of one of the sponsors.'

'Really?'

'So Kane says. There was a lot of trouble. Her parents didn't approve of Foster, so she ran off with him.'

'What happened to her?'

'She got pregnant and died giving birth to a child. Kane thinks Foster really began to siphon money out of the fund about the time he met the girl. I guess it figures. He probably wanted to show he could support her in style. Though I think Foster and Meyerman would have stolen from it, anyway. The temptation must have been too hard to resist.'

'How much was involved?'

'Maybe a hundred thousand pounds or so, but they played around with it pretty fast. I mean, these were "go-go" boys before anybody had heard the phrase, in and out of everything. They would buy into a deal in Beirut or Lisbon, make a quick profit, bring the money back to England via Zurich. They were fast learners. The fund's money was going into arms deals in the Middle East, tanker rentals in Lisbon, drugs, cigarette smuggling in Marseilles, anything with a quick turnover. The money had to move fast, you see, or it got too hot to touch, and besides, they needed it back in London to balance the books in case anyone ever bothered to look at them.'

'That's speculation, but it's not stealing.'

'Stealing came later.'

Diana shrugged. She was a woman of the world. Commercial fraud as such did not surprise or shock her — most rich men had something to hide or took risks that would land more timid souls behind bars, which was exactly how they became rich — and why women found them interesting in the first place. She watched the waiter slice the coulibiac, thanked him and tasted it. It was excellent. Star tasted his own, beamed at the maître d' and made a small circle with his thumb and forefinger. The maître d' and the waiters beamed back, making little circles of their own, like a chorus line.

'A great restaurant is the only place on earth where people are happy because you're happy,' Star said, masticating his salmon with such suppressed passion that his jaw muscles seemed about to pop. From behind his thick glasses his glaucous, magnified eyes were fixed on Diana's cleavage.

'Then what happened?' she asked.

'What happened? They covered their tracks. They hired a fall guy, a part-time book-keeper, and fed him a whole lot of garbage.'

'Who was he?'

'Some Englishman named Boyce — Nigel Boyce. Eton and the Guards. Window dressing for Meyerman and Foster. Actually, he was a pretty good choice — he'd been court-martialed for stealing from the mess funds of his battalion, so he couldn't find a job. I guess they figured when the shit hit the fan, suspicion would naturally fall on Boyce.'

Diana put down her fork. It seemed unlikely that the Boyce she had met two days ago on Greenwood's yacht was the same person, but looking back on it, she could easily imagine him as a disgraced Guards officer.

'This Boyce. What became of him?'

'Then?'

'No, now.'

'Now, I don't know. Kane couldn't trace him. What happened then was that Meyerman and Foster walked off with about fifty thousand pounds and left this schnook Boyce holding the bag. Boyce did two years in Wormwood Scrubs after a very discreet trial. They say he was picked up in a Rolls-Royce when he came out of the slammer. I wouldn't be surprised if Meyerman and Foster made a deal with him — you know, a few thousand pounds waiting in Zurich if he kept his mouth shut and did his time like a gentleman, that sort of thing.'

'Yes. I can imagine that. What happened to the fund?'

'It went *kaputt*. Very sad for the refugees. Meyerman bought himself an antiques business, then went into the international art-book business. By the 1950s he was in magazines, books, newspapers, television, radio, you name it. He never looked back. As for Foster, he bought up surplus weapons all over Europe, then sold them to the Israelis for payment in dollars in New York — a nice way around the British currency exchange regulations! He arrived in America on the QE-One with nothing but his suitcase and the key to a safe-deposit box. Within six months he'd acquired Connecticut Eagle Industries.'

'David, everybody's rags-to-riches story has *some* dirt in it. You know that. You don't like Foster because he's richer than you are and because he's after your company, but you don't *have* to sell, after all.'

'Well, I'm not so sure about that. I don't think there's much hope for a privately owned publishing house, now that authors are getting million-dollar advances . . . But actually, the real reason I don't like Foster is that *you* like him. I don't mind his having more money; I mind his having you.'

'Oh, dear.' Diana shook her head at the desserts and stirred her coffee carefully, trying not to look at Star, who leaned across the table to hold her other hand. She valued Star as a friend, but the notion of him as a lover, or a rival for her affections, was not a role for which she had ever seriously considered him. In different circumstances, immediately after her breakup with Niki Greenwood, she might have responded to a move from Star — he was kind, intelligent, not altogether unattractive, but he lacked Foster's energy and sense of purpose. Women love men with secrets, and Diana was no exception. Star, so far as she knew, had none.

'I'd like to make an honest woman of you,' Star said with a quick laugh, to take the edge off his remark.

'I'm not sure I want to *be* one. Anyway, you're married.'

'Say the word and I'll get a divorce.'

'David, no. I'm flattered, I understand, I'm fond of you, but I *can't*.'

'One day you may change your mind.'

'I'm grateful. I wish I could say yes. Let's go now.'

Star nodded, and waved for the check. Always careful, he took off his glasses and examined it closely, his lips moving as he added up the figures, then he signed it neatly, adding a carefully calculated tip, enough to make him a welcome client, but not so much as to give him a reputation for extravagant tipping. He stood up, and held Diana's chair.

'Can you tell your friend Foster to lay off the dirty tricks?' he asked.

'What dirty tricks?'

'You name it. Some heavy tried to pass himself off as a fire inspector to get hold of Kane's manuscript. Kane's apartment was burglarized. We caught one of the cleaning ladies going through the wastepaper baskets and stealing all the scrapped copies from the Xerox room. My secretary thinks our phones are tapped. What the hell is in Kane's book that interests Foster so much?'

'Are you sure it's Foster who's so interested?'

'Who else? Anyway, tell Foster to forget it. Kane locks every page up in his safe at night, and I have the only copy in my bank vault. What's he so afraid of, anyway?'

'I don't think he's *afraid* of anything. Perhaps he's just curious.'

'I don't think curiosity is enough to explain it, even for someone as rich as Foster. No, Kane's hit a live nerve somewhere. Tell Foster he'll have to wait and buy a copy like anybody else. And, Diana, think over what I said. I don't think Foster is good for you.'

Diana gave him a kiss on the cheek as she stepped into a taxi outside the restaurant. 'Oh, David,' she said, 'don't you know by now that women *never* want what's good for them?'

But in the taxi, as she thought about Boyce and the time he spent in prison, about Rademacher shot to death in his garden, about the family nightmare Paul had calmly described to her on the plane across the Atlantic, she wasn't so sure that Star might not be right, after all.

Business Week had once described Burton Savage as having 'the coldest eyes and the sharpest brain of any major executive'. People who had done business with him often described him as a 'shark', and his smile certainly had an eerie coldness to it. Savage smiled a lot, but the sight of his big, gleaming, perfectly capped teeth failed to convey good cheer. He was a strict bottom-line man.

Savage's domestic life was said to be serene and happy, though it was noticed that Mrs. Savage seldom appeared in public, and on the rare occasions when she did, she stared at her husband in terror, like a rabbit trapped by a fox. Savage had no known weaknesses. He did not smoke, he seldom drank more than a glass of wine, he rarely entertained and he had never been known to take a vacation.

For twenty years Savage had lived in awe of Foster's dreamy *Fingerspitzengefühl*, his seemingly effortless ability to make the right move at the right time, to outguess his competitors, to know just when a company was ripe for an acquisition or a merger.

Foster's genius was bedrock faith for Savage, but lately he had been troubled by gnawing doubts, as well as by the growing realization that Foster would give him anything except his own power. Savage had always lived in Paul Foster's shadow, content to be his detail man. He knew Foster needed him, but he was beginning to question whether *he* needed Foster.

Savage told himself daily that Foster was the better man, and every night his subconscious contradicted him. He found it difficult to sleep, in the circumstances, and even Mrs. Savage, who was used to her husbands's fits of insomnia, his restlessness and his teeth-grinding, suggested that he move into the spare bedroom, which he did, with few regrets. Savage was no puritan, but sex, like golf, demanded time and attention, and he had neither to spare.

Foster had time to spare. It was one of the many things that Savage held against his mentor, now that his doubts were beginning to surface. Foster's judgment seemed increasingly erratic to Savage. That he should take up with Niki Greenwood's ex-mistress was bad enough, but that he should spend his time intriguing against the Greenwood empire for no discernible reason was worse. Either Foster was losing his grip or he was hiding something from Savage. Like a mistress who fears she is about to be discarded, Savage brooded — and dreamed of striking the first blow.

When people talked to Savage about Foster, his face took on the lifeless quality of a stone mask; his loyalty had always been absolute and instinctive. Augustus Biedermeyer had once offered him Foster's job, complete control, a major chunk of stock, if Savage would cooperate with Biedermeyer's group in a takeover. Savage had merely stared at his host as they sat in the dining room of the Metropolitan Club, replied, 'I'm not listening,' and walked out, leaving his mixed grill untouched.

Now, for the first time, Savage was listening. Much of what he heard was that Foster was erratic, Foster had peaked, Foster was off the reservation. The Street no longer trusted him, and neither did Savage. The Greenwoods were too big for Foster to swallow, and if he was determined to try, then Savage would have to think about changing sides. You have to save your own ass, he told himself; it was the first law of business. Foster was trying to bite off more than he could chew. Only amateurs did that, as Foster himself was so fond of saying.

Foster was not a man who enjoyed sitting behind a desk. He preferred to sit opposite Savage, the two of them facing each other in identical leather wing chairs, a lacquered table between them. To one side of them a wall of tinted glass provided a spectacular view of New York — had either of them bothered to look. Once when a newcomer to the corporation had commented on the view, Savage looked surprised, as if he had never noticed it. 'Anybody in this building who has time to look out of the windows shouldn't be working here,' he said. The young man had waited for Savage to laugh. He did not. He meant it seriously, as he did everything he said.

'We're in trouble,' Savage began.

Foster shrugged. He had been in trouble all his business life. It was nothing new. 'What this time?' he asked. 'The stock is up two points. We're making money.'

'People are beginning to ask why you're so interested in silver, that's one thing.'

'What for? It's going up.'

'Well, sure. Why wouldn't it? You've been buying like crazy, and Nick Greenwood is buying even crazier. That's speculation, not business.'

'Is Greenwood still buying so heavily?'

'That's the word on the street.'

'Good.'

'What's good about it, Paul? What difference does it make to you if Nick Greenwood goes out on a limb?'

'I *want* him out on a limb. He's put nearly a billion dollars into R&D on his new compact nuclear power plants. That's taking a big risk. Now he's playing the

286

silver market because he needs a quick profit. That's an even bigger risk. He's overextended. I happen to know he's counting on Biedermeyer to float a new stock issue — and Biedermeyer strikes a pretty tough bargain.'

'It's still too big for you to bite off, Paul. Even if Nick goes down the tube, his old man will move in to pick up the pieces. The big Greenwood money is overseas, not here — Nick's operation is a side-show. The old man isn't going to let his own son go under, you know that.'

Foster finished his coffee and smiled enigmatically.

'Why not?' he asked. 'Just between the two of us, he let his *brother* go under. So I'm told, anyway.'

'I didn't know he had a brother.'

'Maybe it's just a rumor,' Foster said.

'A lot of the board members are nervous about your taking on the Greenwoods, Paul. You ought to know that.'

'You've talked with them?'

'I've listened. The feeling is, it could backfire. The Greenwoods are too big for us.'

'It's amazing how much one can eat if one just nibbles away slowly,' Foster said. 'If you should *happen* to be listening to the other members of the board in the next few days, tell them to relax.'

'They're not going to relax until they know what's going on.'

'Oh, I can't do that,' Foster said, rising to bring the discussion to an end. 'That would mean telling them the truth! You keep them quiet, Bud. You know how. You've done it for me before.' He gave Savage a gentle pat on the shoulder.

Foster opened the carved double doors of his office courteously and smiled at Savage. In the anteroom Foster's two secretaries sat behind a single long desk, like panelists on a game show, visible only from the chest up. One of them pushed a button and the door of Foster's private elevator soundlessly opened, waiting to take Savage to the floor below.

'Tell me what's going on, Paul. You can trust me,' Savage said earnestly.

Foster nodded. 'Of course I can,' he replied, but as the door slid shut and the elevator dropped, Savage felt a sudden wave of nausea and fear. Foster had always

287

been open with him about his plans. Now he was clearly hiding something, and Savage wondered, as he stepped out into the anteroom of his own office, if Foster had set a trap for *him*.

'Do you want your call sheet, Mr. Savage?' his secretary asked cheerfully.

'No,' he said, crumpling the list she had handed him and dropping it on the floor. 'Get me the file on the Star acquisition. See if you can reach Augustus Biedermeyer on my private line. And tell my wife I'll be late.'

Savage went into his office and slammed the door. His secretary turned to her assistant and shrugged. 'What do you suppose got into *him*?'

'Search me. Maybe Mr. Foster reamed him out.'

'Well, there's a first time for everyone. Isn't Biedermeyer the father of that model? The one who was all over *Vogue* last month? It says in the *Post* she's marrying Nick Greenwood.'

Savage's hoarse, impatient voice crackled over the Speakerphone. 'Where's that goddamn call to Biedermeyer?' he shouted.

His secretary sighed, flipped the switch and dialed. She glanced at page six of the *Post*. 'Some people,' she said, 'have all the luck!' There was a picture of Nick Greenwood, tall, handsome, glowering, shielding Angelica Biedermeyer from a mob of photographers at a Broadway opening. His arm was around her shoulders as they stepped out of the limousine. The caption read: 'The man who has everything!'

Paul Foster's apartment came as something of a surprise to Diana when she first saw it, the day of their return from France. Not only was it furnished like an expensive hotel suite, it *was* an expensive hotel suite.

As usual, Paul had chosen privacy over display. His suite was high in the Waldorf Towers, the only one on the floor, and it had been leased in the name of one of the company's subsidiaries. Anybody who inquired at the front desk would be told there was no Mr. Foster listed as a tenant, and none of his telephones went through the hotel switchboard. Foster's manservant, a lugubrious Englishman named Crisp, arrived every morning to make Foster's coffee and lay out his clothes, leaving in the evening when he was dismissed, with a respectful bow and a quiet, mournful 'Good evening, sir,' even if it was two o'clock in the morning.

Diana had stayed with Paul that night and been surprised to see that Crisp not only had put out a new toothbrush for her (still in its cellophane wrapper) but had also squeezed exactly one half inch of toothpaste onto Foster's toothbrush before leaving for the night. And judging from the half-empty carton of new toothbrushes Diana discovered in the medicine cabinet, she was not the first woman to spend the night there, assuming each received a fresh toothbrush.

When Diana woke in the morning, she found Crisp laying out breakfast on a table tray in the living room. He showed no surprise at the fact that she had stayed the night; he merely inclined his head, and noticing that she was wearing Foster's robe, cleared his throat politely. 'If the robe is a little large, miss,' he said, 'we have a selection of smaller ones.'

Diana took the hint and went back to the bedroom to find that Crisp had already placed a new terrycloth robe on the bed for her. Crisp thought of everything and was prepared for anything.

In the living room he had placed a second copy of the *Times* on the table along with a bud vase with a single red rose.

'Where is Mr. Foster?' Diana asked.

Crisp clasped his hands together in front of him like a professional mourner — which he resembled in his manner of dress as well, since he wore a dark-black coat and striped trousers. 'Mr. Foster is performing his morning exercises on the sun porch, miss. No doubt he will join you shortly. In the meantime, he instructed me that you take tea rather than coffee. Will Earl Grey be satisfactory?'

'Perfect.'

Crisp's pale eyes, rather like those of one of the more mournful-looking breeds of dog, appraised her briefly, then he blinked and went about his business. Diana wondered if it was a challenge.

Now, two days after their return, she realized it had been nothing of the kind. Crisp was merely checking to see whether she was up to his master's standards. He had appraised her just the way he would an orange or a pair of shoes, his whole aim in life being to ensure that everything Paul Foster came into contact with was of first-class quality. No flaw or blemish was too small to escape Crisp's attention. If you used one match from a matchbook, Crisp would remove the folder and replace it with a new one. Even the cakes of soap in the bathroom were replaced daily. Small economies did not interest him or, apparently, Paul.

It occurred to Diana that Crisp was delighted to have an audience, since Paul never entertained. When she arrived at the apartment for drinks, the day of her luncheon with Star, she found that Crisp had prepared a silver tray with toast, caviar and a bottle of champagne. He looked positively festive with his white gloves and patent-leather shoes as he filled her glass.

'Madam has had a good day?' he inquired solicitously.

'Not too bad, Crisp, thank you. Of course when I got back to my office I might as well have been away a year. I've never seen so much mail.'

'Quite. Mr. Foster has often commented on the phenomenon himself.'

'He must get a tremendous amount of mail.'

'No doubt, madam, but he never reads it. The ladies in his office give him the gist of anything they think he would want to know, and answer everything for him. Ah, here he is now.'

Crisp opened the front door. Foster came into the living room, kissed Diana, accepted a glass of champagne, stood for a moment admiring her, then lifted his glass in a toast. He looked tired. 'How was the first day back at the desk?' he asked.

'Chaos. The Carson show reneged on one of my authors. Irving Kane was supposed to do an interview with the *Times* about his new book, but the reporter suddenly changed his mind and canceled. Kane thinks it's a plot against him. I had lunch with David Star, by the way.'

'Ah?' Foster sat down. He did not seem surprised by Kane's difficulties. 'You can go now,' he said to Crisp.

'Very good, sir.'

'He's certainly a devoted servant,' Diana said as the door closed quietly behind Crisp.

'Yes. It's easy to keep good servants.'

'I wouldn't have thought so. Niki never could. What's your trick?'

'I simply let Crisp run my life, that's all. That makes him happy. I exist to please him.'

'How would you live if you had a choice?'

Paul seemed taken aback by the question, as if it made him faintly uneasy. He thought for a moment, then said, 'More simply, I think. When I was married, I lived for a time on a larger scale. Crisp wasn't happy. He liked the entertaining, the houses, and so on, but there were too many other servants. He's really a gentleman's gentleman, not a butler. He didn't get along at all well with Dawn's maid or the cook — or poor Dawn herself, for that matter. He's very possessive, is Crisp. How was Star?'

'He seemed to feel you were pushing him a bit hard, frankly. He's not one of your fans.'

'No, I suppose not. When people want to sell their companies, they always end up hating the prospective purchaser. In fact, I've made him a generous offer. Too generous, my people keep telling me.'

Diana stood up and poured herself another glass of champagne, then filled his glass. She walked around the room noticing that Paul appeared to read books in at least four languages. One wall of the room was covered in floor-to-ceiling carved wooden shelves, filled with books in no particular order, except for a single spotlighted shelf in the center, which contained a row of identical small, handsomely bound volumes in a language she didn't recognize. She picked one up, and noticed that the author's name was James Joyce. The imprint on the title page read 'Grünwald Press, 29 Andrassy Utca, Budapest.' Above the imprint was an engraving of a raven holding a flaming torch in its beak.

'Do you still read Hungarian?' Diana asked.

'Hardly. Why?'

'I was just looking at these books.'

Paul stood up and glanced at the book in her hand, took it from her, examined it for a moment and put it back on the shelf. 'My father's,' he said.

'He collected them?'

'No. He published them. It was one of his businesses.

I think it interested him more than most.'

'And you brought these from Hungary?'

'Oh, no. I left Hungary with nothing. After the war, when I could afford it, I hired somebody to find them in secondhand bookshops and rare-book dealers. It's probably the only complete set, unless there is one in the Budapest library. Not that it's of much interest to anybody.'

'It must matter to *you* if you went to the trouble of doing it. Is that why you want to buy a publishing house? Because it's something you owe your father?'

Paul thought for a moment. He looked mildly annoyed, as he usually did when someone asked him questions, but he managed to smile as if he enjoyed the experience. 'It's one of the reasons,' he said. 'Don't tell anybody, though. I don't want it to get about that I'm a secret sentimentalist.'

'Why pick Star's company? If all you want is a publishing house, God knows there are plenty for sale.'

'It's small, it has a good backlist, a reputation for quality. Just because I want a publishing house doesn't mean I have to acquire Doubleday. Star's house is about the right size for a sentimental gesture.'

'Poor David seems to be under the impression you're interested in his company chiefly to do Niki out of it. A family feud. Except that he doesn't know you're family, of course. He also thinks you've been trying to stop Kane from publishing his book.'

'Does he, now? What a nasty, devious mind he has, for a publisher.'

'Well, somebody is certainly trying to get a look at the manuscript. He thinks it's you.'

'Frankly,' Paul said, 'he's right. Though I'm not the only one.'

'Wouldn't it be better to forget about it? How much harm can Kane's book do, after all? It's all gossip about something that happened thirty years ago. It will embarrass Matthew Greenwood, and Niki too, I suppose, but I should think you'd be pleased about that.'

'That's not the point. It's a question of *timing*. I don't want to stop Kane from publishing his book — that would be risky, and probably impossible. I merely want to delay him. In my hands, the truth about Matthew

Greenwood is a weapon. In Kane's, it's merely a best seller. Besides, I want to know how much he's learned about me — or guessed.'

'You don't think Kane has found out that you and Niki are cousins?'

'No. It's a possibility, of course. Kane is no fool. Look what he did to Nixon over his brother's loans from Howard Hughes. I'll admit that it's something I'd like to make sure of by reading the manuscript, but there's no way he could have found out except by talking to poor Rademacher . . .'

Paul drank a small, ironic toast to Rademacher's memory, then put down his glass. 'Only four people know that Paul de Grünwald survived: my sister, who would hardly talk to Kane, myself, Meyerman — and you!' He looked at Diana, his blue eyes taking on a curious blandness that was at once intense and remote, as if he were making a reassessment of her reliability. Then he relaxed and smiled, leaning over to kiss her hand. 'Shall I ring for Crisp and have him serve supper here or would you rather go out?'

'It's been a long day. And I had a heavy lunch. Would you mind if we had a bite to eat here?'

Paul pushed a buzzer to summon Crisp and rose to serve Diana a little more caviar. He seemed to have regained his good humor, as if he had just negotiated a difficult passage. When he sat down beside her, holding the plate, Diana looked at him and wondered just how much of the truth he had told her. She wanted to believe him, but almost by instinct she leaned close and said, 'Paul, I've been trying to remember the name of Greenwood's secretary on the yacht. Do you remember?'

'No, I'm afraid not. I wasn't there. Why?'

'No reason, except that he'd been to school with my ex-husband. Can it have been — Boyce?'

'Perhaps. Here is Crisp. Crisp — perhaps some smoked salmon, a cold salad, and so on . . . Something light. Is that all right, darling?'

'Lovely. Thank you, Crisp. I've got it! It *was* Boyce! Nigel Boyce. Do you know, it all comes back to me now. He said he used to know you in London, just after he came out of the army.'

Paul turned toward her, his eyes as untroubled as

ever. His face was relaxed, frank, open, even reflecting a certain gentle, ironic humor. 'No,' he said in his low, precise voice. 'I've never met the man or heard the name.'

He gave her a quick kiss, but out of the corner of her eye she could see that his left hand was trembling as if he had just seen — or heard of — a ghost.

16

People often mistook Augustus Biedermeyer for a brewer, which did not displease him. His grandfather had come to America in steerage, on the run from Danzig, where the outraged greenhorns to whom he had sold forged steamship tickets were searching for him with clubs and knives. He brought his profits with him, stuffed in the soles of a pair of boots that were several sizes too large for his feet, and left behind a family that had never interested him much.

In the New World he prospered, thrived and remarried well. By the time Augustus Biedermeyer inherited the family fortune it included a bank, a Wall Street brokerage house, skyscrapers, sports stadiums, shopping malls, supermarkets, amusement parks, sports teams, hotels, a natural-gas pipeline, a chain of fast-food outlets, and numerous food and beverage interests, including, of course, beer. Biedermeyer cattle ate Biedermeyer soybeans and were processed into Biedermeyer frozen hamburger patties to be sold in franchised Biedermeyer Burgerbraus across the country.

Biedermeyer was a huge man, with a heavy belly, a big, round face, a mustache, and hands like Smithfield hams. Like many fat men, he appeared jolly at first glance, though on close inspection his small dark eyes were suspicious, greedy and dangerous.

His study was a brewer's dream of Victorian splendor, with stained-glass windows, dark paneling, antlers and Bavarian beer mugs. The furniture was made of leather, tusks and horns. On the walls plaques, framed documents, photographs and letters attested to Biedermeyer's devotion to Catholic charities; in a glass-fronted display case hung his robes as a Knight of Malta and a Papal Knight, and his regalia as a Commander of the Order of the Spiritus Sanctus. Even Savage, who was usually indifferent to his surroundings, found the effect depressing.

'Have a beer,' Biedermeyer said as if no other choice was available.

Savage nodded. Years of experience in American business had taught him that you never declined the product of the man who owned the company, so Savage, who was no beer drinker, smiled with pleasure as Biedermeyer popped open two cans and poured them into glasses.

They both sipped reflectively, like wine connoisseurs. 'Your health,' Biedermeyer said, wiping his mustache with the right forefinger, a gesture he had been taught for his recent appearances on television — for he was now doing commercials for his own beer, twenty-second spots in which he looked out at the audience and said, 'Not bad — even if it is my own!' He was in the process of becoming a media celebrity.

Savage raised his glass to indicate enthusiasm, though in fact beer made him ill, and Biedermeyer's beer in particular seemed to have a peculiar chemical flavor and an unpleasant aftertaste.

Savage belched discreetly and put his glass down on the table. 'It's kind of you to see me on such short notice, Augustus.'

'I always got time for bad news about your boss. I've been looking to get even with that son of a bitch Foster ever since he beat me out of Kris Kringle Toys five, six years ago. I was planning to give the company to my son for Christmas, and you guys bought it up right under my nose. How much did you pay? Thirty?'

'I don't remember the exact figure, Augustus.'

'Bullshit! You remember and so do I!'

'Twenty-nine five. Half in stock, half in cash.'

Biedermeyer sighed. 'A steal,' he said. 'It's worth forty, easy. And it's a nice business to be in. Christmas comes, people buy toys. They have to. Foster really shafted me on that one.'

'You win some, you lose some, Augustus.'

'Not if you work for me, you don't.'

'We like to think we play hardball, too.'

'Yeah, I guess so. Frankly, Foster gives me the creeps. You should have listened to me when I asked you to help me take his company over. We'd have pulled the whole

296

goddamn thing out from under him! Hell, Bud, you're a *mensh*. You don't need Foster anymore.'

Savage cracked his knuckles and stared at Biedermeyer. 'It could still be done,' he said in a low voice.

Biedermeyer put down his beer, stood up and walked over to the big bar in the corner. He pushed his bulky form behind the bar and poured himself a Scotch on the rocks. He took a sip and turned back to Savage. 'You want one?' he asked. 'Frankly, I like this better than beer.'

Savage nodded.

'I like a man who doesn't bullshit me.' Biedermeyer poured Savage's drink, brought it over to him and sat down again. 'Now,' he said, 'what's Foster up to?'

'He's getting in over his head.'

'He's always been in over his head. You know what they say about your company on the Street? "There's less there than meets the eye." Foster has always liked to play with the big boys without having that kind of money behind him.'

'He's done pretty well at it, Augustus.'

'Sure, but there's rich and there's *rich*. Nick Greenwood, for example, is *rich*.'

'He's also a horse's ass.'

'You're speaking of my future son-in-law. I grant you, he doesn't have the old man's brains — or balls. It's hard for a guy who's born rich and good-looking to develop his full potential. Still, he's got a lot more behind him than Foster does. He's *solid*.'

'Foster doesn't seem to think so.'

'He doesn't?'

'No. In fact, I get the impression that he's planning a takeover bid against the Greenwoods. That's why I'm here. For my money, it's a kamikaze raid.'

Biedermeyer laughed, a great booming hearty laugh, in keeping with his image, though his features reflected no particular amusement. 'Bullshit, that's all that is. They're too big for Foster to take on. Why don't you talk to Nick Greenwood?'

'I'd rather talk to you. I hear Nick's got problems. He's put a lot of his eggs in the nuclear power plant basket, and now he's short on cash. That's why he's speculating in silver, which I personally don't think is such a hot idea. And I imagine that's why the marriage with Angelica —

though looking at her pictures, I guess there could be other reasons. The word is that you agreed to put up a little financing as a wedding present, Augustus. For a position, of course.'

'The two things are not necessarily connected, Savage. I got my problems with Angelica, like any other father, but with her looks and money, I don't have to buy her a husband.'

'I wouldn't think so. But the best security for money is a family connection, isn't it? You'd have a little more leverage over the Greenwoods if Nick was your son-in-law, right? You'll be joining the board, of course?'

Biedermeyer nodded. 'Of course. We'll all be one happy family. I asked Matt Greeenwood over for the wedding, but it's a long trip for a guy his age. Listen, if Foster is planning to pull something off on the Greenwoods, he's taking me on as well. He hasn't got enough money behind him for that. Right?'

'Right.'

'So he must have something else, right?'

'Right.'

'What could he have against the Greenwoods? They run a pretty clean ship, as far as I know. I haven't heard of any trouble with the Security and Exchange Commission, have you? Bribes to foreign governments? I guess they do that, but who the hell doesn't? Anti-trust? Price fixing? Illegal campaign contributions? Offshore tax evasion?'

'They probably do all of that.'

'Well, sure they do. So does Foster. So do I. What else is new? If you played the game by the government's fucking rules, you'd go bankrupt, right? It has to be something else.'

'Maybe something in the past.'

'The *past*? Who gives a shit about the past, Savage? I mean, Nick isn't even all that *old*. What kind of past could he have? He's played around a lot, and I'm not crazy about that, but these days they give you the cover of *People* magazine for it.'

'His father might have a few skeletons in the closet. That seems more likely.'

Biedermeyer whistled tunelessly for a few minutes, then took the glasses to the bar and filled them up again, the ice cubes tinkling in the otherwise silent room. He pushed a button, and the sound of Frank Sinatra singing 'I Did It My Way' floated through the room at low volume. 'Yes,' Biedermeyer said thoughtfully, returning to his place with the drinks, 'that's certainly a possibility. It would have to be something pretty bad, though ... And how would Foster know about it?'

'I don't have the answer to that one, Augustus. He doesn't talk much about the past.'

'Neither does Matt Greenwood. I know he was rich before the war, and he had to flee from the Germans because he was half-Jewish. I asked him about it once, but he started to cry. The Germans sent most of his family to Auschwitz, you know. He told me that not a day goes by that he doesn't think about them. They even killed his brother.'

'How come he and Nick got out?'

'Nick was in Switzerland, in school. The old man got out by sheer luck, I gather. He'd arranged for the whole family to escape, and something went wrong. They went by different routes, for greater safety, I guess, and somebody betrayed them, or maybe the Germans were too smart ... Anyway, he got out and none of the others made it. He told me that if it hadn't been for Nick, he'd have killed himself when he found out. Of course, he's a Catholic. He was sustained by his faith,' Biedermeyer added, with an expression of complacent piety.

'How did he get his money out?'

'He had a lot of it abroad. I suppose he must have seen what was coming — he's no fool, after all. He did tell me that the Germans seized his assets. Göring even stole his collection of paintings. A tragic story. I told him he should write a book about it, but he said it was too painful. Irving Kane wanted to write the story, but Greenwood wouldn't even *talk* to him. He said lots of people had suffered worse than he did. He's a man of great sensibility — and modesty.'

'If that's the case, what does Foster have on him?'

'I don't know. Maybe it doesn't matter. With you on board, we can cut Foster off at the knees. Hell, we got three, maybe four times the bucks he has, right? We'll let him make his pass at Greenwood, then go for his fucking throat when he's overextended. We'll need your help, of course.'

Savage nodded. He said nothing. Only an amateur would bring up the question of price.

Biedermeyer stared at Savage, waiting, then cleared his throat. 'I guess you'd want a pretty good block of stock,' he said.

Savage nodded, without showing any enthusiasm.

'Of course, if it all works and we end up merging the three companies, we'd have a giant. We'd need a first-rate chief executive officer. Nick's a nice boy, but I wouldn't want him trying to run anything that size, even if he is my son-in-law.'

'What you'll need,' Savage said quietly, 'is a real pro.'

'I'd have to talk to Greenwood,' Biedermeyer said after a pause.

'You do that. I'll be waiting to hear.'

The anomalous nature of her relationships with men sometimes annoyed Diana, with herself as much as with them.

Here she was, an attractive and successful woman of by no means advanced years, and yet she was still faced with the choice of having her lover visit her or visiting her lover. Niki Greenwood used to visit her, dropping by in his proprietorial way to spend the night, keeping a few suits in her closet — both for convenience and to symbolize his larger rights over her person and her premises. Now her situation was neatly, though unsatisfactorily, reversed. *She* visited Paul Foster, gradually leaving behind or bringing over a few necessary objects of convenience that established her presence in Paul's apartment as Niki's cuff links and razor had in hers.

In the eyes of most people — including David Star — Diana was 'having an affair' with Paul Foster, but in fact she was not at all sure of the exact nature of her relationship with him. They were lovers, but on what basis and with what hope of permanency it was hard to say. Paul's whole life seemed transient. He lived in a hotel suite, he operated out of airplanes, he had no home, and worse, his life was directed toward, as Diana had come to realize, the single-minded goal of toppling Greenwood, as if that were the whole point of his existence. After he had succeeded (if in actuality he did succeed), he had no further plans or dreams — none at any rate that he had communicated to her yet.

'I've been thinking,' he said late one night when they were in bed.

'I thought you were asleep.'

'I'm not a heavy sleeper.' It was true, Diana thought. After they made love, Paul closed his eyes and lay still, but she doubted that he slept much, if at all. Certainly, when she woke up, his side of the bed was invariably empty, and very often he was already dressed, or completing his exercises, or on the telephone. The vulnerability of sleep obviously made Foster nervous, even with her. He was not a man who enjoyed letting his guard down.

Diana turned on the light next to her. Paul propped himself up on one elbow and looked at her. 'I love you,' he said.

She kissed him. 'I know. But do you *trust* me?'

He laughed. 'I'm trying. I'm better at loving people than at trusting them. I think we should make plans.'

'What sort of plans?'

'A place to live, for a start. It's ridiculous for us to have two apartments like this. And mine is too small for any kind of life together. I'll phone Helmsley or Rudin. There are some very suitable apartments on Fifth Avenue, with a view of the Park . . . Or perhaps you'd prefer the Dakota? I find it a bit — gloomy.'

'Well . . .'

'As a matter of fact, we don't have to live in New York. After all, money is no object. We could look at estates. There's a place in Bedford Hills for sale — a hundred acres, pool, stables, tennis courts. I could commute by helicopter.'

'Paul, are you proposing marriage?'

He hesitated a moment. 'Why, yes,' he said with some surprise, 'I suppose I am.'

'Then I accept. For a moment I thought you were out-lining a real-estate deal.'

'Tomorrow I have to go to Mexico,' he said. 'We'll make the plans when I come back.'

'Can I come with you?'

Paul hesitated. A look of doubt crossed his face. Then he smiled, kissed her and nodded indulgently. 'Of course you can,' he said. 'I warn you — it's all business. Quite boring.'

'I won't be bored.'

Paul looked pensive for a moment. 'No,' he said after a pause, 'perhaps not.'

But for one second Diana thought she saw the same furtive expression on his face that she had noticed when she mentioned Boyce. Then he put his arms around her, and she persuaded herself that she was wrong.

'I hear they're going to Mexico this weekend,' Star said, trying to think of a way of persuading Irving Kane to take his feet off the desk. Star had spent a lot of money refurnishing his office in burled walnut, and it pained him to see Kane's scuffed shoes on *his* desk top. Still, there was no way you could ask a best-selling author to take his feet off your desk. Star knew that.

'Last week it was the South of France, now it's Mexico. Diana certainly lucked in. You should have been faster on your feet, Star. You had the hots for her.'

'I *don't* have the "hots" for her, Irving,' Star said, pointedly putting the word 'hots' in quotation marks. It was not the kind of phrase he liked or would have have used himself, and he liked it even less when it was applied to him.

'Come on, Star! I've seen you looking at her. You can't hustle Uncle Irving. It's nothing to be ashamed of. Diana's a good-looking broad, self-supporting, nice tits. I'd go round the track with her myself if I had the chance. You want to know what your trouble is?' Kane asked without giving Star a chance to point out that he didn't want to hear any such thing. 'You held back. You got to go straight to the point. You never get laid if you don't ask. Me, I meet a broad who interests me, I ask straight out, "Do you want to fuck?" '

Interested despite himself, Star stared at Kane, wondering what any woman could possibly find attractive in him. 'Do they often say yes, Irving?' he asked.

'Not too often, no. It's a question of percentages, Star. You ask ten, maybe one says yes. What's Foster doing in Mexico?'

'Who knows? The only time I can breathe easy is when he's out of the country. When he's here, he's on the telephone every day explaining how much better off I'd be if I took his stock for the company.'

'Don't do it, Star. Guys like Foster shouldn't own a

publishing house. Or Nick Greenwood, either.'

'Would you rather I sold to a network or a movie company, Irving?'

'Yes. They're not as smart. You could fool those guys. You can't fool Foster. Speaking of Greenwood, Mel Kashmir on the *Times* says he's in big trouble.'

'I can't believe that. He's got that nuclear power plant thing — that's going to be billions of dollars. And the last time I looked, the company was doing nicely.'

'Mel buttonholed me at the Palm, gave me a whole spiel about Greenwood being up to his ass in silver futures. Also, he says the word is out that Greenwood may run into trouble with the government on this nuclear business. It seems a few senators have been asking questions about just what it was the old man was doing during the war.'

'Christ, Irving, you haven't been leaking stories from your book, have you? My house counsel would kill me.'

Kane frowned, as if his integrity were in question. 'I don't give leaks,' he said firmly, 'I *get* leaks. But *someone* has been spreading the word about Wotan, and doing it in the right places . . . I think we ought to rush the book out, Star. What we got here is *news*. One of America's biggest corporations owned by a family that tried to build the fucking A-bomb for Hitler! And now they're trying to take over the nuclear energy business here. It's a *dynamite* story. The goddamn Fourth Reich, that's what it is. We'll get a *Time* cover, I can see it now: "From Wotan to Washington — the Greenwood Connection." It'll be number one for a year!'

'If we don't get sued for a million dollars, or shot. Frankly, I thought the last chapters I read were a little too hot, Irving.'

'Well, I had to spice it up somehow. I never spoke to Rademacher, after all. Somebody got to him first. Listen, Star, publishing is like getting laid, you need balls. This book scares you, I can walk across town to Simon & Schuster or Random House. They'll put out the red carpet for me.'

Star sighed and glanced around his office. Kane, he knew, was right. A publisher had to take certain risks. When Kane had done his Watergate book there had been taps on the telephones, the IRS had audited Star and the CIA had gone to court to suppress certain passages in the

303

manuscript for 'national security reasons' that were entirely specious. Star had been nervous then, but he emerged from it with a major best seller — fourteen weeks as number one on the *Times* list! — and something of a reputation as a gutsy liberal publisher.

'What I don't understand, Irving,' Star said, in his most conciliatory voice, 'is why Foster is so interested in the Greenwood story. Is he just looking for more ammunition to use against them? Or does it go deeper? After all, he's Central European himself; maybe old Greenwood did something to *his* family.'

Kane nodded gloomily and took his shoes off the desk, leaving a small distinct scar on the surface. 'I don't know either,' he said. 'Foster doesn't seem to *have* any family. He appeared in 1945, as an informant for the British War Crimes Commission. He discovered Becker, did you know that?'

'Who was Becker?'

'A Kraut, for Chrissake. He was with Eichmann. Becker was in Hungary in '44. He was on everybody's wanted list, but he vanished in '45. Then, lo and behold, there's Foster, working for the British as a translator in the summer of 1945, having been found half dead in some kind of labor camp, and he fingers Becker. So you can figure Foster must have known Becker back in Hungary, or he couldn't have picked him out in a bunch of German POWs.'

'What happened to Becker?'

'He had a cyanide capsule hidden in a hollow tooth. It was the big status symbol in those days.'

'And Foster?'

'Well, Foster was the hero of the hour. After all, everybody was looking for Becker, and this kid found him. The British were so pleased they let him into England as a DP. Though there's a suggestion he had to make a few payoffs. Which was normal for the time.'

'Where would he get the money for that, if he'd been found half dead in a labor camp?'

'Search me. There was a lot of loot lying around in 1945. Maybe Foster was smart enough to pick some up for himself. Maybe he knew something. Who knows? Anyway, he turned up in England, went straight to see Meyerman and never looked back.'

'How did he know Meyerman?'

Kane stood up and looked at his photograph on the wall. With his massive chest and shoulders, he looked like a ruined prizefighter contemplating the record of his past victories — and, indeed, he *thought* of himself as a fighter, going after the truth, the facts, the real story, like a boxer, jabbing, punching, feinting, outlasting his opponents. He mimicked a quick punch in the air, weaving back and forth on his feet in a way that suggested he might at any moment trip himself up and fall to the floor.

'How did he know Meyerman?' he asked, breathing heavily from the slight exertion. 'That's a good question, Star. I don't — *know*.'

Kane punctuated his sentence with a couple of jabs in Star's direction, then stopped and fixed his eyes on Star, who nodded to signify his continued attention and interest. 'But I'll tell you one thing,' he continued balefully, 'one thing nobody knows. You know who Meyerman worked for? He worked for Greenwood, that's who! How do you like *them* apples?'

Star contemplated them apples with his eyes closed, like a man wondering whether the pain in his stomach is merely gas or the onslaught of some dread disease. He opened his eyes. Kane was still there, facing them like a trial lawyer — an image that Star found distressing even as it appeared in his mind. Kane was the kind of author who *enjoyed* libel trials. He regarded litigation as a kind of blood sport, a test of his courage and manliness. The bigger and more powerful the target, the happier he was.

'It's a small world,' Star said at last. 'Diana used to work for Meyerman before she started living with Nick Greenwood, and now she's having an affair with Foster. I wonder how much *she* knows?'

'Everything. You can bet on it. Women always do. Show me a guy who doesn't talk in bed, and I'll show you a eunuch or a mute. If you'd been faster on your feet with her, we'd probably *know* by now. But I'm going to find out, don't worry.'

Star worried. It was his role in life. 'Where are you going to start, Irving?' he asked.

'Where do you think? Mexico, of course.'

17

Cuernavaca was not one of Diana's favorite cities. Its attractions, such as they were, did not lie in the town itself, or even in its climate, but in its privacy. In what has long since become known as 'Gringo Gulch,' the houses of the rich were hidden behind gray, crumbling stone walls ten or twelve feet high, topped with barbed wire, electric warning systems and a lavish sprinkling of broken glass and steel spikes.

Cuernavaca was the opposite of Bel Air — here nothing was on display. Even the ownership of the houses, if one could find them at all in the maze of streets without nameplates and numbers, was a closely guarded secret. It was 'known' that Sam Giancana, the Mafia don, had a house here; it was 'said' that Merle Oberon had lived here in a house with an artificial waterfall in the Japanese style and alabaster floors; it was 'rumored' that the Shah's sister had a dozen rare white peacocks in her garden, and a bathtub of eighteen-carat gold.

Outside in the city, the normal, noisy chaos of Mexico went on day and night — huge trucks and buses roaring through the narrow streets spewing clouds of black, oily diesel smoke, impoverished peasants crouching in the archways of the *calles* with their wares, a few dried peppers or wilting flowers spread on a cloth at their feet, dense crowds pushing, shoving and shouting at each other in the covered market, while flies and mangy, starving dogs took their pickings from the garbage.

From behind the gray walls none of this was visible or audible. Here the silence was absolute, broken only by the monotonous noise of water sprinklers, the occasional scratching sound of a gardener sweeping up flower petals after a breeze, the infrequent screech of the famous imperial peacocks in the Shah's sister's garden.

'If you like quiet,' Paul Foster said without enthusiasm, 'this is the place to be. It has always reminded me of Forest Lawn . . .'

In the dying light of the late afternoon, the garden stretched before them, so perfect as to seem almost unreal. It dipped from the terrace to an ornate marble swimming pool, five hundred yards of turf so perfect that it would have made even an English gardener jealous. Set in the lawn were sculptures — a Brancusi, a bronze by Henry Moore, a Maillol. The effect was indeed that of a California necropolis, Diana thought. It only wanted Muzak piped in through the trees playing an organ rendition of 'Over the Rainbow'. Beyond the pool with its delicate Greek columns and marble nudes was a tropical flower garden.

'For a man with simple tastes,' she said, 'you certainly go in for luxurious Shangri-Las. How often do you use this?'

Paul laughed. He sat next to her, sipping a glass of Perrier, apparently content to watch Diana brush the salt off the rim of her margarita glass. Crisp had been left behind, since the house already had, in Paul's words, 'enough servants for a maharajah,' but Luther, Foster's bodyguard, had accompanied them in the G-2 from New York, his presence somewhat dampening Diana's enthusiasm for the trip. Paul apparently had less confidence in the safety of Cuernavaca than his fellow millionaires.

'It isn't my house,' Paul said.

'Whose is it?'

'Dawn Safire's.'

'Your wife's?'

'My ex-wife's.'

For reasons that she found it difficult to explain to herself, Diana was dismayed. There was something odd about Paul's bringing her to the house of his ex-wife, though it explained the fact that the servants kept telling him how nice it was to see him back again, as if his presence there was not so much rare as unexpected.

'She doesn't mind your using her house?'

'Not at all. Why should she? We parted on reasonably amicable terms. I gave her the house when we separated — she always liked it better than I did — but now she spends most of her time in Acapulco or Beverly Hills, with her new husband, so it's often empty.'

Paul's arrangements were always admirably neat and tidy, Diana thought, as if he always did what made sense, without feelings or emotions, except when it came to the past, where he was passionate and irrational. She wanted to ask Paul how much effort it cost him to retain such rigid control over himself, or whether by now it had become a habit, but he seemed preoccupied, so she merely inquired who Dawn Safire's new husband was.

'A Mexican gentleman,' he said. 'Porfirio de Villada. She met him here. He is an associate of mine.'

'What kind of associate?'

'He looks after my business interests in Mexico, and throughout Latin America in general. He was very useful to me over a piece of business I had in Costa Rica, for example.' Paul cut himself off abruptly. 'He has first-class connections,' he continued. 'His brother is the Mexican Minister of Commerce and his father campaigned for the presidency of Mexico four times. He always made sure to lose, which made him the ideal opposition candidate.'

'You don't mind the fact that he's married to Dawn?'

Paul looked puzzled. 'Not at all,' he said, 'In fact, it has great advantages. Family ties are sacred in Latin America. Pifi might betray his employer, but never the former husband of his wife! I can trust him in matters where I wouldn't even rely on Savage. Ah, I hear his car now.'

As he emerged from the loggia and came forward to greet Foster, Pifi presented a picture of such suave elegance that he was almost a caricature. He gave the impression of a man who was so pleased with himself that the rest of the world hardly existed.

When he smiled, as he did the moment he saw Diana, he seemed to be indicating that his mere presence would give pleasure and turn a hitherto dull evening into one charged with excitement and romance.

He made such a production of kissing Diana's hand, of admiring her beauty, of congratulating Paul for having such good taste, of complimenting her for having chosen to visit Cuernavaca with Paul, that she hardly noticed that he was not alone. Two conspicuously less attractive figures had followed him, one of them short, bulky and out of breath, the tip of his cigar glowing like an airplane's beacon in the gathering dusk, the other striding ahead, tall, enormously fat and wearing a ten-gallon hat. The taller man, as he appeared in the light, was grotesquely ugly, with a round moon face, a button nose surrounded by puffy flesh and a pair of cheap, old-fashioned steel-rimmed spectacles with lenses so small and thick that the eyes behind them resembled those of a fish in an aquarium. Instead of a tie, he wore a string bolo around his thick neck, with a huge silver and turquoise eagle at his throat. His badly creased suit, made of some material resembling mattress ticking, looked as if it had been purchased off the rack at a discount store for fat men. His feet slapped across the tiles with an amphibian flapping sound — he wore a pair of well-worn health shoes, of the kind favored by octogenarian health-food faddists in Southern California.

Villada performed a small, graceful gesture of introduction, as if he were trying to supply enough charm to make up for his companion's deficiencies in that respect, for the big man's face was devoid of any expression, like that of a fat child.

'Mr. Love Potter,' Villada said. 'Of Dallas,' he added unnecessarily, for Potter swept off his broad-brimmed Stetson, revealing a thin layer of heavily greased gray hair, and in a deep voice with an unmistakable Texas accent muttered, 'Foster, hi — howdy, ma'am,' then put his hat back on and sat down, his palms on his knees, as if he were waiting stolidly for Villada — or possibly Diana — to perform a miracle.

The second man, as he emerged from the shadows, needed no introduction. 'I have never been fond of Mexico,' he said in a husky, precise English voice that was at once *echt* Mayfair and unmistakably foreign. 'It always reminds me of the Jardin Exotique in Monaco — heat, cactuses and too many bloody steps. *Servus*, Pali. Diana, what a lovely surprise! Or should one say "pleasure", since it isn't, to be frank, *totally* a surprise to one that you're here.'

Lord Meyerman removed his cigar, leaned over with some difficulty to give Diana a kiss, whispered, 'You are as divinely beautiful as ever, dear girl, if not more so,' and sat down beside her, his thigh against hers, as if the only purpose of his visit to Mexico was to see her.

Diana wondered what two such unlikely people as Meyerman and Potter were doing together. She supposed, accurately, that it had something to do with money — an obvious deduction.

'A margarita?' she asked, playing the hostess.

Villada gave her an incandescent smile, as if she had just conferred a knighthood on him; Potter glumly shook his head. 'I'm a Christian, ma'am,' he said, as if that explained everything. 'A Scotch and soda, my dear,' Meyerman said, 'without ice, please. I can't bear drinks that are named after people, or have pieces of fruit in them . . . Ah, thank you.'

'Did you all fly down together?' Diana asked.

Paul laughed. 'No, no,' he said, 'that would be putting all our eggs in one basket. Golden eggs, at that!'

'Or silver,' Meyerman said with an oily chuckle, giving Diana's knee a squeeze. Love Potter was not amused; apparently Christianity precluded laughter as well as alcohol. He asked for a Coca-Cola, and sipped at it mournfully, with a certain amount of impatience, as if he were either eager to get down to business or simply impatient for his dinner.

Perhaps sensing the latter, Paul said, 'I've ordered a Mexican meal tonight. It's what they do best here, I'm afraid. Dawn tried to make them cook French food, but after a few days they always begin to put peppers and spices in everything. They're like Hungarians. Spices are in their blood.'

Potter sat impassively, holding his glass. 'That's okay,' he said. 'I don't mind Mex food. My dad used to bring a can of chili with him to work every day for lunch. And a can of Dr Pepper.'

'What did he do, Mr. Potter?' Diana asked.

'He was a businessman,' Potter said modestly.

Paul rose, as the butler came in to announce dinner, and took Diana by the hand. 'Love's father, my dear, was Marlon Potter. He was the richest man in the world.'

'Wasn't he the man who used to fly over Dallas in a helicopter dropping copies of the Constitution?'

Potter nodded with quiet pride. 'Yes, ma'am,' he said. 'He was a great American.'

'I only met him once,' Paul said, as they walked into the dining room. 'I remember he had a pay phone in his office.'

'Yup,' Potter said. 'Dad believed you thought twice about making a telephone call if you had to put a nickel in the slot first, instead of just dialing. He had a three-minute timer, too, from the dime store. He used to say, if you couldn't make a deal on one nickel, you probably couldn't make it at all. It near to broke his heart when they raised the price of a call to a dime.'

The dining room was spectacular. A wall of glass gave a view of the garden, where hidden floodlights illuminated each of the sculptures. The ceiling was mirrored in antique glass, reflecting the lights from the two chandeliers, and the walls were hung with paintings of Foster's ex-wife, who, like so many stars, seemed to think of herself as a work of art, like the Taj Mahal. In a niche on one wall was a spotlighted life-size bronze of Dawn Safire in the nude, arms raised as if in supplication, an expression of ecstasy on her face. Love Potter did not even glance at it, though he carefully inspected each piece of silverware as if he were appraising it at an auction.

'Potter,' Paul explained to Diana, 'has a great interest in silver.'

'Antiques?'

Potter blinked, like a rabbit caught in the headlights of a car. 'Not especially, ma'am. Back home we use stainless steel at the table. I got interested in silver as a hedge against inflation.'

'I suppose that makes sense. Do you have much of it?'

'About a billion dollars' worth, I guess. Of course a billion ain't what it used to be.'

'That's a lot of silver.'

Potter nodded. 'It was my daddy's idea,' he said modestly. 'When Roosevelt passed a law against Americans owning gold, Dad saw the writing on the wall. He was ahead of his time. Since he couldn't buy gold, he bought silver. He used to have sacks of silver dollars out in a shed behind the barn when I was a kid, I remember. He knew they were going to debase the currency sooner or later. It's all in the Kremlin's master plan.'

'How much money did he have, Mr. Potter?'

'Love, please, ma'am. He never counted. He used to say people who know how much they're worth ain't worth much.'

'I have always had a pretty good idea of what I'm

311

worth,' Meyerman said. 'One likes to know, after all. It gives one a certain satisfaction. . . .'

Potter blinked and nodded in his ponderous way, his fingers clutching his knife and fork like fat sausages. He ate as if this might be his last meal for some indeterminate time, copiously and quickly, shoveling the food into his mouth like a machine. 'Yes,' he said between mouthfuls, 'but then you and Foster ain't really *rich*. I don't say you're poor, mind you, but what you've got is stock in a corporation. Stock is paper. I don't believe in paper. My dad wouldn't touch anything if he couldn't have one hundred percent of it, and I'm the same. I once met Harold Geneen, the guy who runs ITT, and he was telling me he makes eight, nine hundred thousand a year, something like that. I told him, "Salary is salary". I don't care if it's a million dollars a year or fifty bucks a week, you're still a hired hand. I never took a paycheck in my life. I'm a trader.'

'That's exactly why we wanted to talk to you, Love,' Paul said, signaling the butler to refill Potter's plate.

'I figured it might be.'

'The thing is, there's a rumor you're getting out of silver, Love.'

'There are rumors about everything.'

'Quite,' Meyerman said, 'but these are very specific. Though not, I must say, *widely* known. I gather you're planning to sink a few billion dollars into offshore drilling.'

'Where did you hear that?'

'From a chap I know at the Rothschild bank. Charming fellow, by the way.'

'I don't trust bankers.'

'Well, who does, Potter? That's not the point. A lot of people have been buying silver lately, and the price has been soaring by leaps and bounds, but very few of them have looked at the situation carefully and asked themselves where most of the silver *is*. And the answer, my dear fellow, is that *you* have it! You're sitting on the silver mountain, while the *shmucks* drive the price up for you, am I not right?'

'Maybe. So what, Meyerman? There's no law against cornering a commodity.'

'Actually, Potter, there are *numerous* laws against it,

312

but that's none of our business. You need a fortune to start a deep-sea oil drilling. If you dump a billion dollars worth of silver onto the market, what's going to happen to the price?'

'Who cares?' Potter asked, his mouth full. It occurred to Diana that Meyerman and Potter, sitting opposite each other across the table, resembled Tweedledum and Tweedledee.

'The bottom will fall out,' Meyerman said. 'The price will go from forty dollars an ounce to ten, or even less, wouldn't you say?'

Potter grunted. 'Could be,' he mumbled. 'Right now, people are buying big.'

'Nick Greenwood, for instance,' Paul said smoothly.

Potter raised an eyebrow. 'Is that so?' he asked.

'Come, come, Love. You *know* he is. You've spent a fortune heating up the market. Greenwood has been buying silver futures all over the place, playing the bull market. He's forgotten about your silver hoard, or maybe you've simply held on to it for so long that nobody takes it into account anymore. After all, you've kept pretty quiet about it.'

'My dad didn't believe in talking to strangers,' Potter said, wiping his plate with a piece of bread. 'What have you boys got in mind?'

'We've been buying short, Love — betting against Greenwood, you might say. If the price of silver were to drop in about ten days' time, we'd make quite a lot of money. And Greenwood would lose a fortune. He's been buying on margin, his brokers and the banks would call everything in, he could be wiped out.'

'Yup. That sounds likely enough.'

'It would be very helpful if you began to unload soon,' Meyerman said.

'How soon?'

'In about ten days.'

Potter waved toward the butler and pointed at his empty plate. '*Más*,' he said simply. 'This ain't bad Mex food, Foster, though I'm partial to the stuff we get in Texas, personally. I can't eat refried beans,' he complained with an unsuppressed belch, emphasizing his point.

'What's in it for ol' Love?' he asked.

313

Paul and Meyerman looked at each other, then Meyerman leaned forward, one hand on Potter's forearm, his black eyes gleaming, his voice dropping to a confidential whisper, a smile on his face that was at once ingratiating and greedy. 'Dear boy,' he said, 'if we were in a position to control Greenwood's assets, we would avail ourselves of the opportunity to *spin off* certain things.' He paused. 'Greenwood's interest in Marine Oil, for example,' he added, his expression taking on a quality of ecstasy as if he had just handed Potter the Holy Grail.

Potter stopped chewing. His moon face was immobile, a stone mask except for a drop of sauce at one corner of his mouth. He shut his eyes for a moment as if in silent prayer, then opened them. 'What makes you think I'd want it?'

'Come, come, Love. Marine has the offshore drilling rights to the north and south of yours. If you strike it rich, you're giving Marine a bonanza. Unless you *own* Marine, of course, in which case you have the whole thing sewed up tight — one hundred percent, as your father liked to say.'

Potter was at some pains to affect a lack of interest, but beads of sweat ringed his forehead like a halo, and for the first time since they had begun eating he put down his knife and fork.

Paul was better at pretending a lack of interest than Potter — in fact, he seemed indifferent to the whole discussion. 'We're offering you an attractive deal in return for what amounts to nothing more than a favor, Potter. A question of timing, that's all.'

'Ten days?'

Paul nodded, his eyes fixed on Potter's impassive face.

Potter stuck out his lower lip. 'Okay,' he said after a long pause, 'we'll shake on it. Now, what's for dessert?'

'It was a mistake to bring you here,' Paul said glumly, in Dawn's huge white bed. A cloud of depression seemed to have settled over him suddenly, and it was apparent to Diana that the bedroom, of which one wall was a collage of Dawn Safire memorabilia, did nothing to relieve his mood.

He stared at the wall in front of him for a moment, where a poster of Dawn Safire as a taxi dancer caught his attention. 'It's like a museum to Dawn,' he complained. 'I should have remembered that . . . Somehow, to bring you to this bloody house seems — *wrong*.' He picked the word with exaggerated care. 'Besides, I'm not sure it's such a good idea for you to hear all this business talk.'

'My God, Paul, I'm not a chorus girl! I'm a business-woman myself.'

'Yes, yes, I've expressed myself badly. What could be duller than three middle-aged men — four, if you include Pifi — talking business?'

'I'm used to middle-aged men discussing business, Paul. It's a lot better than middle-aged men discussing women. What happens when Potter unloads his silver?'

'Nicholas' stock will drop like a stone. We've been buying it up quietly, a bit here, a bit there. We'll buy up a lot more, at bargain prices, and take over the company.'

'And then?'

'From a business point of view, we'll have brought off a very successful coup.'

'I know that. But that's not why you're doing it, is it?'

Paul studied his fingernails carefully. 'No,' he admitted. 'It's why Meyerman is doing it, but for me there's one thing more. I'll have the pleasure of telling Matthew Greenwood that I have a controlling interest in his com-pany. I'll have what my father was supposed to have. The account will be settled.'

'And after that?'

'After that, I don't know. I might keep a few of the things that interest me and retire. Why shouldn't I make a new life, for both of us?'

'With a little less drama, I hope.'

'With *no* drama. A quiet, peaceful life. I'm getting tired of all this.'

Foster waved his hand in the general direction of the window. He thought for a moment. 'Maybe I will take up gardening,' he said.

Diana laughed. The idea of Paul gardening was not one that would have occurred to her. 'Flowers?' she asked.

'I suppose . . . Somehow I like the idea of vegetables better. There's always a market for vegetables.'

'Paul, what's Niki's father going to do when all this happens?'

'He'll be furious. That's natural. He gave Nicholas too much power, and now he's too old and ill to take it back. I don't think he knows how deeply Nicholas has plunged into speculation. Old Greenwood would be horrified.'

'If Niki goes under, he'll never be able to face the old man.'

'He'll have a *mauvais quart d'heure* — an unpleasant scene. Nothing more, I assure you. They'll still be rich.'

'I know him better than you do, Paul. In some ways he's still a child. I don't know how he'll cope with failure on that scale. He has awful mood swings — wild elation, deep depression. And he lives in fear of the old man.'

'He'll lose control of his American assets. At worst. Bad news for Nicholas, yes, but not the end of the world. The old man will pick up the pieces eventually. Believe me, this kind of thing happens every day. Nicholas tried to do it to me, in partnership with that ass Biedermeyer, and if he could, he'd try again.' In the distance a peacock screeched mournfully. 'This place has no happy memories for me,' Paul said quietly. 'I only picked it because it's secure. No journalists, you see. Anybody who asks questions about the rich here gets put on a bus back to Mexico City by the police. *If* they're lucky!'

Diana switched off the light and reached over to embrace Paul. 'Then let's try to do at least one thing we can have a happy memory about,' she said, and Paul rolled over to kiss her, his mood apparently lifting.

At breakfast, which they all took together on the terrace, like people on an economy tour, Luther appeared. He did not sit down, nor did Foster ask him to.

'Kane's in town,' he announced.

'Damn!' Meyerman said. 'Still, we can't stop him from being here. It's a free country.'

Villada smiled. 'Speaking as a citizen of Mexico, that's a debatable statement . . . What's he been up to?'

Luther shrugged. 'Asking questions. He was at the airport when Potter's plane landed. Somebody must have said Potter was going to Cuernavaca. Or maybe Kane followed him here.'

'Where's he staying?' Villada asked.

'He's at Las Mananitas. The hall porter there said he was asking where Dawn Safire's house was.'

'That's just what we *don't* need,' Foster said, glancing at Meyerman, who nodded in agreement.'

'I can take care of that,' Luther said flatly, his face so devoid of expression that Diana shivered involuntarily.

Paul noticed her shivering. His face was grim, as if he was turning over Luther's offer in his mind, but he shook his head at him after a moment. 'Perhaps not,' he said. 'There may be another way.'

He and Meyerman looked at each other, then at Diana. Meyerman placed his cigar in the ashtray and cleared his throat.

'It might not be a bad idea if you were to have a — *chat* — with your friend Kane,' he suggested, putting his pudgy hand over hers.

'A chat about what? Irving is an old friend — *and* a client — but I don't think I can tell him to lay off you. If that's what you mean.'

'Of course not,' Meyerman said smoothly, 'but you *could* steer him, ever so slightly, in the wrong direction. Nothing too elaborate, of course — elaborate lies are always risky.'

'I don't feel comfortable about lying to anyone, let alone Irving Kane.'

Meyerman's smile remained fixed, but his eyes flickered briefly in Foster's direction. 'Darling,' Paul said, leaning forward intently, 'you don't have to *lie* to him. Just find out how much he knows. For me.'

'The goddamn cranes keep me awake at night,' Kane said. 'It's their mating call or something.'

He looked terrible to Diana. His face was puffy, the pouches under his eyes sagged, and he seemed to have shaved with a dull razor blade, then attempted to repair the damage by means of small patches of toilet paper.

They sat beside the small pool, which was fed from an ornate waterfall. The cranes after which the hotel was named stalked about staring at Kane with their beady eyes, giving an occasional high-pitched screech. 'Fuck off,' Kane shouted, flapping his arms to drive them away. They flapped their wings back at him and retreated a few inches with ominous hisses. Kane morosely drained his glass of bourbon and refilled it. 'This is a hell of a place,' he said. 'How did you find me?'

'I heard you were in town.'

'From whom?'

'On the grapevine, Irving. After all, you're a celebrity.'

Kane looked at her with eyes that rather resembled the cranes'. 'Word certainly gets around fast in Cuernavaca,' he said. 'You sure you didn't hear it from Foster's gum-shoe? What's Foster doing here, anyway.'

'Nothing much. We flew down here for a little rest, that's all.'

'With Meyerman and Love Potter? That's some romantic group, Diana!'

'Meyerman is an old friend. Potter just dropped in for dinner.'

'Sure. Diana, nobody, and I mean *nobody*, sees Potter except on business. People don't invite Potter into their homes; they meet him at midnight in parked cars, like Howard Hughes. That's a creepy bunch of friends you have. What are they up to?'

'They're not up to *anything*, Irving. You know how it is with rich men — they gather together naturally.'

'Like these goddamn cranes. I don't buy it, Diana. This particular group of rich men wouldn't gather together unless they were cooking up something. Meyerman and Foster, I can see — they go back a long way. But Potter? He's a shitkicker with romantic illusions about the com-modity market. A few years ago Potter discovered cocoa futures, and before anybody knew what had hit them, he'd cornered the fucking cocoa market. Hershey had to dou-ble the price of their chocolate bars, you had to pay a quarter for a cup of hot chocolate, every *shmuck* in town was trading in cocoa like it was gold, then Potter pulled the plug out and the price fell so low you couldn't *give* the stuff away. Whole countries went bankrupt overnight. If Potter ever showed his face in Sierra Leone, they'd butcher him like a hog. Then it was soybeans, I think, or maybe bauxite . . .

'Do you know that Potter invented the macadamia nut? No, I'm not joking. Somebody told him about these nuts in Hawaii. People fed them to the animals, but they were full of oil, so Potter cornered the market. Well, it turned out that processing the nuts cost too much to make it worth doing, so Potter was stuck. He's up to his ass in these goddamn nuts, which even the hogs won't eat, so finally he says, "Hell, salt 'em and pack 'em as delicacies, what have we got to lose?" '

'At the beginning he had to pay the airlines to give them away for free to first-class customers, but he was right, the son of a bitch, they caught on and he made a fortune. Of course, his first love is silver . . .'

Kane gave Diana a searching look and helped himself to a handful of macadamia nuts from the tray in front of him. He chewed noisily for a few moments, then tossed the rest of the nuts toward the cranes, which ignored them.

'The birds aren't so dumb,' he said, 'I always thought they tasted like salted cardboard. Of course, that's part of Potter's genius. Give Americans something expensive and tasteless and you can't go wrong. Listen, your friends wouldn't be talking silver, by any chance, would they?'

'Silver?'

'You know. The stuff they make spoons out of?'

She avoided the question. 'Why would they?' she asked.

'Potter couldn't take a crap without talking about silver. Listen, have you joined the bad guys, Diana?'

'There are no bad guys. Paul Foster and I are very close friends. He doesn't talk about his business to me. Anyway, he runs a big corporation. What's wrong with that?'

'If you and I were *close* friends,' Kane said with a leer, 'I wouldn't talk about business either . . . Funny things seem to happen to people who get in Foster's way. There was some guy in the corporation who ran off to Costa Rica with a few of Foster's files. Gehtmann, I think his name was. He ended up with his throat cut. They don't teach that at Harvard Business School. That creep Villada set that one up for Foster, and got Dawn Safire as a reward! Nice people!'

'That isn't the way Paul tells the story.'

'I guess it isn't. I wouldn't tell it that way either, if I was in his shoes. Why does he hate Greenwood? What's the story?'

'I don't know, Irving. He doesn't hate him, anyway. There isn't a story.'

'Oh yes there is, and it goes back a long way. Listen, Diana, these people play for keeps, you know what I mean? Foster's not *competing* with Greenwood, for Chrissake. He's out to kill.'

'I think that's a little overdramatic, Irving.'

Kane stared moodily at his drink. 'You think these ice cubes are okay?' he asked. 'They're supposed to make

319

them out of boiled water, but who the hell knows . . . Don't kid yourself, it's a blood feud. Your old friend Nick may not know it, he's too goddamn pleased with himself to notice, but Foster's gunning for him, and Foster's loaded for bear. He means business, Kiddo, believe old Uncle Irving.'

Diana shook her head thoughtfully, as if her mind were elsewhere.

'Don't say I didn't warn you,' Kane shouted as she put on her sunglasses and stood up to leave, but whatever else Kane had to say was drowned out in an explosion of shrieks from the birds, which were doing what appeared to be a mating dance around his deck chair, apparently in love with the sound of Kane's voice.

At the villa, Meyerman was waiting for Diana in the garden, surrounded by his luggage, which seemed excessive for so short a stay. He appeared to own one of everything Vuitton has ever produced, except a steamer trunk, all of it marked with his initials and his crest stamped in gold.

'You don't believe in traveling light, do you?' she asked.

'No. It's been my experience that those who travel light travel uncomfortably. The only reason not to take a lot with one is if one has to carry one's own things, and I'm happy to say that I haven't had to do that for thirty years. I didn't want to go without saying goodbye . . . Or congratulating you.'

'Paul told you?'

'He did. I gather it's still a secret, but we're old friends. I'm *delighted*. Well, I told him you were beautiful and intelligent. I feel like a matchmaker!'

'Why don't you join us in New York for the wedding?'

'I think Paul rather wants to keep it private. Besides, I must be off.'

'You're going back to London?'

'Eventually. I have business elsewhere first. Paul has kindly put one of his planes at my disposal.'

'You don't have one of your own?'

'No, no. You know, Diana, American magnates love airplanes. I prefer to take my perks in the form of old-fashioned comfort and high living. I don't share Paul's passion for high-speed business travel.'

'Yet you've flown all this way to see him.'

'We owe each other many favors. Besides, this is an important piece of business.'

'For you?'

Meyerman made a gesture of self-deprecation. 'For many people,' he said vaguely. 'I must go, my dear.'

'Meyer, what's going to happen to Nicholas? He's not a man who'll take defeat lightly. His father will never forgive him . . .'

'Careful with that case,' Meyerman snapped at the butler, 'it's got my cigars in it. Diana, dear, I will give you a word of advice as a parting gift: Always be sure whose side you're on — *particularly* now!'

He held out his cheek for her to kiss, stepped into the waiting limousine, pulled the curtains shut and was gone.

'*Dónde está Señor Foster*?' Diana asked the butler, who pointed in the direction of the loggia. Diana skirted several reproductions of Dawn Safire in various poses and materials, and walked up the steps. There, on either side of a big glass table, Villada and Paul sat, so absorbed in their conversation that they failed to hear her approach. At the sound of her heels on the tile floor Villada paused to gather up a few papers from the table. It was only as Diana sat down next to Paul, accepting a perfunctory kiss, that she realized the two men had been looking at a passport. From a distance the face in the photograph bore a striking resemblance to Irving Kane.

The atmospherics played dazzlingly on the wings of the airplane with Wagnerian theatricality, which Paul ignored and Diana found depressing. Paul seemed sunk in thought and Diana, who responded to his mood and was in any case preoccupied with her own fears, was curled up in one of the leather armchairs with a blanket spread on top of her. From his own airborne command post, Paul was in touch with the world he had created, and that now seemed to have taken control of him again.

She heard him place a call to Savage in New York. His fingers drummed against the porthole as he listened, then he said, 'Keep them in line, for God's sake . . . I made them members of the board, I can unmake them if I have to . . .' He sat silent for a few minutes, then placed another call.

'What's Savage up to?' he asked, and paused while he listened, his fingers drumming again.

'I don't know,' he continued. 'I can't put my finger on anything in particular, but he sounded off. Perhaps a shade too obsequious. It's not his style. Sniff around. No, Luther is in Mexico, doing something for me. You'll have to do it yourself. Don't tell me your problems, you're paid to solve mine.'

Paul switched on his console, glanced at the New York stock exchange figures, grunted, then turned it off and stared out at the St. Elmo's fire playing over the wings as the aircraft bucked and danced through the storm.

'I hope it doesn't disturb you,' he said to Diana.

'No.'

'You're very quiet.'

'I'm a little tired.'

'Tired? Or upset?'

'What have I got to be upset about?'

'I don't know. But I recognize the symptoms.'

'Paul, did you use me to set Irving Kane up?'

Paul remained silent.

'You sent me off to have a little chat with him and while the two of us were sitting by the pool, Luther broke into his room, didn't he?'

'The timing was accidental. What makes you think it was Luther?'

'I thought he was the great expert on break-ins. He got my passport out of my apartment, I seem to remember.'

Paul nodded. 'In this case he would have been too conspicuous.'

'Villada recruited the local talent, and Luther provided the know-how and the burglary tools?'

'Something like that, I imagine. Of course, one doesn't need anything very sophisticated to open a hotel suite.'

'I feel used, Paul. It was a disgusting thing to do.'

'Not disgusting, Diana. That's too strong. I couldn't think of another way, frankly. It had to be done quickly. Now, at least, we have what Kane knows, and a good idea of what he doesn't know. I don't think any of us would benefit if the world were to read about our little deal with Potter in too much detail.'

'I don't see what good it does you. When Irving discovers that his papers and his passport are gone, he'll know he's on the right track.'

'Yes. But he might not notice they were missing if he had

322

other things on his mind.'

'What things?'

'Oh,' Paul said airily, 'a drug charge, for example. The Mexicans take a dim view of foreigners who are found in possession of hard drugs — cocaine, heroin and so on . . .'

'That's what you've planned?'

'To be candid,' Paul said, looking at the clock on the bulkhead, 'it's already happened by now. Would you like a cup of tea?'

'No. How *could* you do that to Irving?'

'He's in the way. That's hardly my fault. Nobody asked him to stick his nose into my business. In any case, we're not going to let him be locked up for life. A week or so of comfortable detention is enough, then Pifi will pull a few strings and get him out of Mexico. We just want Irving on ice temporarily, that's all.'

'So you set him up by planting drugs in his room.'

'Well, that was necessary. There'd have been no point in tipping off the police if there was nothing for them to find, would there?'

'I assume that's one of Villada's little numbers?'

'Quite. Pifi has contacts everywhere. He can produce a bag of heroin or *el jefe de policía*, on request. An invaluable fellow.'

'I gather he can have a throat cut, too.'

Paul raised an eyebrow. 'I wouldn't know about that,' he said. 'Probably only in Central and South America.'

'Paul, I don't think I want to be a part of this anymore. Perhaps we should separate until it's over and see how we feel about each other then.'

'What does it have to do with us? All this is just business.'

'It's not the kind of business I'm used to.'

'It will all be over in a week or so, Diana. Bear with me. I promise that the rest will be calm and quiet — no problems, nothing terrible. We had a little problem here. We solved it, perhaps a little too harshly, I admit. Now events will take their course.'

'I wish I could believe you, Paul.'

'Then believe. Please. Because it's true.'

323

'And what happens to Niki? What's in store for *him*?'

'I don't much care,' Paul said softly, after a pause. 'Do you?'

'Well, do you care?' David Star asked, peering at Diana through his thick glasses. Behind his desk was an easel, on which stood two alternative jacket sketches for Irving Kane's *The Golden Traitors*, both of which combined a lurid swastika with a dollar sign, in different color combinations.

'I don't know,' Diana said, stretching out her legs on Star's ottoman. 'Has Irving finished his book?' There were few people she could talk to, but she counted Star among her friends. If there was one thing he loved, it was a heart-to-heart chat.

'No, those are just jacket sketches, so we're ready to go when he finishes. Actually, I'm worried about him. He's in Mexico, and I haven't had a single call, not even a request for money. That's not like Irving.'

'He's still in Cuernavaca. He'll be back in about a week,' Diana said authoritatively. 'Don't you think the jackets are a little too sensational?'

'You want understatement, you go to Knopf. I still don't understand why you're worried about Nick Greenwood. Anyway, he can take care of himself.'

'I'm not so sure.'

'What does your boyfriend Foster have to say about it?'

'That's the trouble. He's reluctant to talk about it. I don't mind if Niki loses a couple of billion dollars, but I don't want to see him get *hurt*.'

'That figures. Do you still care about him?'

'Paul asked the same question. So did Meyerman. I just don't want to be used to destroy him. He's the father of my child, for what that matters.'

Star nodded sympathetically, his eyes fixed on Diana's legs. 'You have to know where your loyalties are, kiddo. Straddle a fence line and you know what you'll get?'

'No. What?'

'Barbed wire between the legs. That's a piece of folk wisdom from Love Potter.'

'I've met him.'

'You've *met* Love Potter? For God's sake, *nobody* meets Love Potter!'

'Well, I did. He and Meyerman were in Cuernavaca.'
Even as she spoke, Diana was conscious of making a slip,
but it was too late to correct it. She had intended to tell
Star about her impending marriage, but decided this was
not the time or place. Besides, Paul had decided to delay
the announcement for a few days.

'You move in high circles,' Star said. 'Do you know that
when Potter's father built his house in Dallas he had the
architect produce an exact replica of the White House,
right down to the bathrooms and the light switches?
Marlon Potter said if he ever got elected President he
didn't want to have to fuck about trying to find the
crapper, or the lights. Are you *really* worried about Nick?'

Diana back-pedaled. 'No, it's all business intrigue, I
suppose. Big fish eat little fish. Bigger fish try to eat each
other. David, you'll keep our little chat confidential, won't
you?'

Star gave her a smile of intense, heartfelt sincerity and
put his hand on his wallet, which was roughly where he
supposed his heart was. 'I've forgotten it ever happened,'
he promised and made a mental note to call Aaron Diamond. If you wanted to do business with Aaron, you had to
give him the latest news and gossip. If you held out on him,
he took his clients elsewhere.

'My lips are sealed,' he said.

Aaron Diamond was not the only person in Bel Air to have
a telephone in his Jacuzzi, but he had been the first, a
trend-setter as always. There were telephones all over his
house, in the most unlikely places. One floated on a raft in
the middle of the pool; there was another under a water-
proof bubble in the shower; many of the trees in the garden had been hollowed out to provide a niche for a
telephone; there was even a telephone in the refrigerator,
in case somebody called while Aaron was making himself
a midnight snack.

Aaron was the maestro of the telephone, he played it
like a Stradivarius, in his hands it became an instrument
of art. Two secretaries were occupied most of the day and
night placing calls for him. Aaron waved, gestured,
shouted, indicated by means of a quick thumbs up or down
which call he would take next, who should be put on hold
and who should simply be told that he'd call back.

Occasionally he became confused and pushed the wrong button, once greeting the Cardinal Archbishop of Los Angeles, who had called about getting some of Diamond's clients to appear at a Catholic charity, by cheerily shouting, 'Hey, you lucky bastard, I hear you got yourself laid last night!'

He sat at his Louis XV desk (Diamond was a collector of antiques as an investment), dressed in a lemon-yellow terrycloth bathrobe, a green towel wound around his head to ward off drafts, his feet stuck into red Arabian slippers with toes that curved up to a sharp point. The elegance of the desk was only slightly marred by the fact that the price tag was still affixed to one drawer handle.

'Put two hundred on Hustler's Choice in the second . . . I know he's twenty-to-one, for Chrissake . . . I met somebody last night who's been *shtupping* the jockey,' Diamond shouted as his secretary wrote on the pad before him, in big letters, 'David Star on three,' and put Star on the Speakerphone.

'How are you, Aaron?' Star asked. His voice was tinny and hollow.

'Great, only I got no time to give you a health bulletin, kiddo. What's up?'

'I hear Kane is still in Mexico.'

'Kane? In Mexico? What's he doing there, Chrissake?'

'He went down to do some research. Diana told me Foster was down there meeting with Love Potter and — guess who!'

'I got no time for guessing, either. Who?'

'Meyerman. What do you think of that?'

'They got to be making a move against Nick Greenwood,' Diamond said, then shouted at his secretary, 'Remind me to call my broker as soon as I hang up on Star — I got some stock to sell.'

'Kane thinks Greenwood is in big trouble. He told me so before he left.'

'Shit, Nick's got a five-billion-a-year company *and* a rich father. What kind of trouble can he be in?'

'Cash-flow trouble.'

Aaron Diamond whistled tunelessly. He wrote the number of shares he had in Greenwood's company on a piece of paper, then drew a line through it. 'Where's Kane staying?' he asked.

'He was supposed to be at Las Mananitas, but it's a funny thing — I tried him there, and he's vanished. The manager said he checked out, but the guy at the desk seemed to be saying he'd been arrested. I don't speak Spanish —'

'*Arrested*? Why would anyone arrest Kane? He's a writer, for Chrissake!'

'He may have stepped on Foster's toes too hard,' Star said. 'Listen, all this is just between us —' But before he could go any further, Diamond cut him off. He tore up the piece of paper. He wanted to know what to do with his shares, and he wanted it from the horse's mouth, not secondhand from Star.

'Get ahold of what's-his-name, the Secretary of State,' he shouted to his secretary. 'If you have trouble getting through, tell him I've got a publisher interested in his memoirs. That always brings them to the phone!'

Late that afternoon in Washington, the United States Secretary of State poured himself a martini and sat down opposite his wife.

'I had a surprising telephone call today,' he said.

'Really?' she replied, in a voice that suggested nothing in her husband's day could surprise her.

'Aaron Diamond called. You know, the agent.'

'What on earth did *he* want?'

'Apparently there are a number of publishers after my memoirs. Diamond said that David Star is hot for them. To use *his* phrase.'

'Bunny, who on earth would want your memoirs? What would you put in them?'

'*Some* people might find them interesting, dear, Not *everybody* thinks I'm a dull dog.'

'If you say so, Bunny. Is that all he had to say? No good Hollywood gossip?'

'No. One rather strange thing . . . he seemed to think Irving Kane, the writer — you know, the one who's always getting into fights — was under arrest in Cuernavaca.'

'And was he?' The Secretary's wife yawned.

'No. The police there said they'd never heard of him. And when our ambassador checked at the hotel, he'd never even been registered there. Diamond must have gotten his towns mixed up, I suppose. Ah, well, all in a day's work . . .'

'Bunny, if that's the kind of story you're going to have for your memoirs, they're going to make pretty slow reading. Pour me another martini, and this time, *try* not to make it watery.'

If Nicholas Greenwood believed in anything, it was his own luck. A large staff of executives, research specialists and lawyers worked hard to provide him with 'homework,' but he seldom made use of it. Details bored him, arguments irritated him. He liked his options listed neatly at the end of a report ('Yes; No; Delay'), and seldom, in fact, bothered to study the backup material that preceded this checklist. Like most lazy men, he preferred instinct to thought. He paid other people to do the thinking.

He was a European through and through, and had never assimilated himself to the work habits of Americans. Often he spent days at a time away from his office, skiing in St. Moritz or following the sun. It was his underlings' job to put in a daily appearance at their desks. A rich man, he felt, shouldn't have to. His friend the Aga Khan didn't. Gianni Agnelli didn't. The Vicomte de Ribes didn't. They enjoyed themselves and saved their energy for the big decisions, unlike American businessmen, who worked harder than their own subordinates, and mostly led social lives of stupefying, middle-class dullness.

Niki thought he had modeled himself after his father, the redoubtable Matthew Greenwood, but he overlooked the fact that Matthew's taste for the good life masked an unbridled ruthlessness, accompanied by single-minded, ferocious energy and a set of survival instincts as finely tuned as a bat's sonar. Even lying in the sun with a beautiful girl at his side, Matthew Greenwood's mind was hard at work, scheming, plotting, weighing the possibilities, whereas when Nike enjoyed himself, he forgot business completely.

Niki sighed, hardly even glancing out at the view of Central Park from his forty-second-floor bachelor's penthouse — owned, of course, by the company. Soon he would have to give this up. Angelica Biedermeyer had already pointed out that it was too small for married life, hardly more than a *pied-à-terre*, and old Papa Biedermeyer was on the telephone half a dozen times a day about duplex cooperatives on Fifth Avenue, townhouses in the East Sixties, property in the Hamptons.

The whole subject depressed Niki. It was not so much that he didn't *like* Angelica Biedermeyer — it would be hard to find a more beautiful young woman, or one who was more spoiled, unfortunately. Still, even the fact that she was inordinately greedy, grasping, vain and demanding was not necessarily a stumbling block, since Niki could well afford to indulge her whims. It was the thought of marriage that depressed him.

An affair with Angelica would have been an exciting prospect, but marriage was a more doubtful proposition — though the real problem was, of course, not Angelica herself, but her father, who, despite all evidence to the contrary, believed his daughter was a virgin and insisted on a wedding with all the appropriate trappings, including Cardinal de Montenuovo, who had agreed to fly over from the Vatican to perform the ceremony himself.

The truth of the matter, Niki told himself morosely, was that Diana was the only woman he had ever *wanted* to marry — though not enough to do it ... Well, perhaps that had been a mistake. There had been so many mistakes. Sometimes it seemed to Niki that the entire Greenwood family was a kind of vast historical-biological mistake from the very beginning.

He remembered the years before the war, when he had been a child. Everything seemed so simple then. Then he was sent away to Switzerland, and everything changed. His mother died. His Uncle Steven was killed in a camp, poor Aunt Betsy shot, a heroine of the resistance ... Even his loathsome, stuck-up cousin Paul died in some nameless camp, and Niki had survived, skiing happily in the Berner Oberland while the rest of the family was engulfed in tragedy. When his father escaped to Switzerland in 1944, he was no longer the same man. He had always been a little harsh and cold, as fathers go, but that had been tempered by the rest of the family, particularly by Steven. After the war the old man's

329

harshness increased, together with Niki's guilt at having survived so easily unharmed. When Niki had taken over the American side of the business, his father had given him only one piece of advice: 'Don't make a mess of things.' Well, Niki reflected, he had done pretty well for a while, nobody could deny that, but now he had made a mess of things, and there was nothing for it but this damn marriage!

Niki poured himself a drink, looked at it and doubled the strength. There was no point in dwelling on the 'ifs' of life, but he couldn't help it. If he had not invested so much money in the nuclear reactor business; if the price of zinc hadn't dropped; if he hadn't lost a fortune on a movie that had to be withdrawn the day after it opened; if his partners in the new casino hotels he was building in Atlantic City, Las Vegas and the Caribbean hadn't turned out to be fronts for an unsavory group of investors, which meant endless delays and bribery in getting the necessary permits; if he had made these decisions, and several others, in a different way, he wouldn't be obliged now to dance to Biedermeyer's tune.

Niki didn't believe that he had been wrong, or even mistaken, in making any of these deals, it was simply a question of timing, nothing more . . . The delays and the problems had seriously affected the company's cash flow, there was no denying that, but eventually it would all work out. Niki was an optimist, like most people who operate on instinct. In the meantime, undeniably, a billion-dollar infusion of capital was necessary, and Augustus Biedermeyer would provide it — for a price.

Well, Niki thought, draining his drink, there was a price for everything. The important thing was that nothing should go wrong; there should be no 'slip-ups,' as his father liked to say. Niki looked out the window and caught a glimpse of Foster's building, reflecting the light of the late afternoon. Above all, he thought, no surprises from that madman!

The telephone rang. He walked across the soft white carpet into the sunken center of the living room with its white suede furniture, sat down on one of the sofas, on which he had made love to Angelica to the point of exhaustion only a few hours earlier, and picked it up. He heard, with acute distaste, the voice of his future father-in-law.

'How's my boy?' Biedermeyer boomed.

'Just fine,' Niki said. Already Biedermeyer behaved as if Niki belonged to him. A second father was the last thing in the world he wanted.

'Listen,' Biedermeyer went on, in the confident tone of a man who knows that he will always be listened to, 'I had a funny call from Aaron Diamond today.'

'Funny? In what way?'

'Oh, he was asking after Angelica, congratulating me on the marriage and so on, all that crap. Well, you know Aaron, there had to be a reason for him to call, and there was. He'd heard that your old friend Paul Foster had a little meeting down in Mexico with Meyer Meyerman and — guess who?'

Niki remained silent. He was not about to answer a rhetorical question or show anxiety.

Biedermeyer waited a moment for a question, then plunged on irritably. 'Love Potter,' he said, 'that's who. That mean anything to you?'

It meant a lot to Niki, in fact he broke into a sudden sweat, but he was not about to discuss his fears with Biedermeyer. 'I doubt if there's anything to worry about,' he said. 'With silver taking off, they're probably trying to get in on the market. They're a little slow, but they're not wrong.'

'With Potter? I don't buy that. Listen, my boy, just how much silver are you into?'

'Augustus, it's under control. I know what I'm doing. Take my word for it. Once they start buying, the price will go even higher.'

'You'd better not be wrong, my boy.'

'I'm not wrong,' Niki said firmly, and hung up. He felt a faint, growing spasm of alarm, as he thought about Paul Foster. Foster was the enemy, God only knew from what irrational spirit of insane competition. Meyerman was known to be close to Foster. His presence meant nothing. But Love Potter? What on earth was he doing there? Of course, he was a billionaire, however eccentric, but it was not the kind of company he usually kept; in fact, his pattern was to operate alone . . .

Niki shivered slightly. Silver was the one thing he had been right about, his trump card. He had predicted silver would go through the roof and it had. A disciple of Paul Sarnoff's, Niki had for once done his homework, with a thoroughness that astonished his staff and his father, without altogether convincing them of his wisdom. The United States used 160 million ounces, he told them with missionary zeal, Mexican production was down, Peru and Canada were digging deeper for smaller ore seams, and the Soviet Union was at last becoming a net importer. Silver, like oil, was a vanishing commodity, impossible for an industrial society to do without.

The more conservative silver bulls, like Sarnoff, had predicted silver at $32 an ounce and turned out to be cautious, while Bunker Hunt confidently announced that silver would be selling for over $200 an ounce by the mid-eighties. Eastman Kodak, the world's largest user of silver, was stockpiling, then the Japanese moved in as quantity purchasers, as they had with copper in 1974, as the Russians had with lead and zinc in 1978; now the Germans, the Arab investors, the Swiss bankers had all jumped on the silver wagon and the race was on, the price surging up day by day, month by month, while all over the world people rummaged through their attics, sold off their silver trays, tennis trophies, spoons and baby pushers, cashing in on the hottest game of all — and Niki had ridden the market up. The Metals Division of his company became the place where the action was to be found. Niki himself actually appeared there, watching the flickering screens (silver was used to make them), giving his okay to future deals of unprecedented size, urging his people on to buy with the passion of a true believer — which he was, for at last he had found a way to cancel out the losses of his other mistakes.

No company had more at stake in the price of silver than Niki's, a fact that he had gone to elaborate lengths to conceal. Even now, Niki held futures and options on over ten million ounces at prices of $50 an ounce and up. Why should it stop? The silver mines in Canada were shut down by a strike. In Mexico and Peru unrest and labor problems had reduced output to a trickle; in the Soviet Union, the decision to challenge the American aerospace industry's lead in miniaturization and in-flight computerization had tripled the demand for silver . . . All the signs were right for another jump in price, Niki told himself.

But what could Potter, the biggest silver bull of them all, be talking to Foster about?

'The moment Señor Foster heard about this outrage,' Villada said, 'he told me to straighten it out. I'm afraid you've been the victim of a cynical plot — and, of course, the stupidity of the police. Alas, our country is still very backward about human rights, as you know.'

'I hear the Ambassador was looking for me, and they denied I was here,' Kane said indignantly.

'Yes, yes, of course. Well, you know, the police wouldn't pay too much attention to the ambassador here, unfortunately . . . At least you've been treated comfortably, I hope? No rough stuff?'

'I got the runs.'

'I'm sorry. It's the water. Everybody gets it. But apart from that?'

'Apart from that, I can't complain. I was in *el jefe*'s bedroom, with a guard at the door. It was a lot quieter than Las Mananitas, with those goddamn birds.'

'Birds? Ah, the cranes. I expect you'd like to get back to New York?'

'I'd like to know who had me locked up first. I figured it was your boss, Foster.'

Villada looked astonished. He seemed as much at ease in *el jefe*'s living room as if it were his own. 'Just between the two of us,' he said confidentially, 'I can assure you that it wasn't Paul Foster at all. He was shocked. The rumor is that Nick Greenwood put a lot of pressure on the Ministry of the Interior. Apparently the object was to get a look at your manuscript.'

'I only had notes with me. They were in my room at the hotel.'

'Yes. Of course, the police seized them during the search. Who knows whether they made a copy or not? One must assume that they did.'

'I want that stuff back.'

'I have it all here.' Villada removed a pile of papers, several leather-bound notebooks and a passport from his briefcase and stacked them neatly on the table. He lit a cigarette and stared at Kane through narrowed eyes. 'I took the liberty of looking at your notes,' he said quietly.

Kane grunted.

'An interesting story. The old man doing business with the Nazis . . . There is so much evil in the world.' Villada sighed deeply.

'Do you usually read other people's papers, Villada?'

'Only when it's necessary. I will tell you frankly that I had a talk with Paul Foster about your material. He was *furious* with me. He said I had no right to read it, and of course he's right. Personal curiosity got the better of me. The opportunity of studying how a great writer's mind works . . . However, he felt there were some areas in which your information was a little sketchy, so he asked me to give you this, in the strictest of confidence.' He drew a package from his briefcase.

'Does that mean I can't use it?'

'No. It means you can't say where you got it from.'

Villada pushed the bulky evelope across the table to Kane, who opened it and drew out a cardboard file. The file was old and faded, the light-blue cardboard fading to washed-out gray. Stamped across the front, in large red Gothic letters, were the words '*Streng Geheim!*' Below them was a Luftwaffe eagle holding a swastika in its talons, and the legend '*Fall Wotan.*'

Kane opened it up and glanced through the contents. Choosing at random, he withdrew a faded letter written on the stationery of Corvina Ores, Budapest, and addressed to Oberst G.M. von Rademacher. The signature was that of Matthew de Grünwald. The word 'uranium' appeared several times in the text.

'Rademacher's file?' Kane asked, looking hard at Villada.

Villada nodded.

'There must have been more than this.'

'Yes. This is only a first installment. It deals with the period when Grünwald was selling uranium ore to the Nazis. There are some interesting transcripts of conferences between Grünwald and Göring. Historical material, you might say. There's even an account of Grünwald's visit with Hitler. I wonder what people would say if they knew the man who collaborated with the Nazis to produce

334

an atomic bomb was now trying to get the United States government to back a huge nuclear energy scheme? From the Brown House to the White House, eh? People already have their fears about nuclear power plants, but nuclear power in the hands of ex-Nazis is still more frightening.'

'Nick Greenwood isn't an ex-Nazi.'

'No, but everybody knows he's just a front for the old man.'

'How come Foster is giving me this stuff?'

'Let's just say that he doesn't like Nazis. Also, he was pained to think you might suspect him of being responsible for this sordid little plot. He was planning to hand this file over to the Justice Department, but it occurred to him that a piece in the Washington *Post* or the New York *Times* might have much the same effect, and reach a larger number of people. Besides, it would be a scoop for you, wouldn't it?'

'How soon can I use it?' Kane asked suspiciously.

Villada flashed him a gleaming smile, like a man posing for a toothpaste advertisement.

'The sooner, the better,' he said. 'How about the day after tomorrow?'

Diana had supposed that Paul would buy her a ring at Cartier, or possibly Harry Winston, but instead he took her to a small, crowded room on the second floor of a building, on West Forty-seventh Street, where an elderly, bearded Orthodox Jew in a broad-brimmed fur hat greeted them brusquely.

He and Paul talked for a few minutes in Hungarian. The conversation was low-keyed, both men standing close to each other, their hands in their pockets, their eyes half-hooded. Then they shook hands, and the old man produced a crumpled handkerchief from the pocket of his worn frock coat and handed Paul a magnificent diamond ring.

Paul slipped it on Diana's finger and kissed her.

The old man nodded. '*Mazel tov!*' he said, putting his handkerchief away. 'Give my regards to Meyer Meyerman.'

They spent the afternoon hastily securing the necessary papers and blood tests, a procedure carefully organized by Foster's secretaries, then they dined quietly at the Four Seasons.

335

Paul lifted his champagne glass to toast Diana.

'Where are we going to do it?' she asked. 'City Hall?'

'I thought it would be more private in a judge's chambers,' he said. 'It's all set up — for the day after tomorrow. By then all this business will be over and we can go away somewhere.'

'Not Mexico, I hope.'

'No, the South of France, I think. Who knows? I might even go swimming this time . . .

When she woke in the morning, Paul was already up and dressed, standing in the living room with a cup of coffee in one hand and the New York Times in the other. He kissed her gently and continued reading. which was out of character for him, since he usually only glanced at the headlines — articles of interest to him were carefully clipped by his staff, placed in folders and put on his desk, with 'action memos' attached to each clipping outlining the ways in which the story might affect the company's business. Paul had no interest in news for its own sake.

'Something interesting?' Diana asked, pouring herself a cup of tea.

Paul nodded. 'An old scandal breaking to the surface,' he said. 'It seems your friend Irving Kane has got hold of the Wotan story, part of it, anyway. A long piece about old Grünwald and the Nazis. I must say he spices it up.'

Diana looked at her copy of the Times. On the front page was a photograph of a heavyset young man, obviously Matthew de Grünwald, shaking hands with Göring. Both of them were dressed in hunting clothes and smiling into the camera. Next to it was a publicity photograph of Niki Greenwood, looking handsome and serious.

A sidebar story was headlined 'Greenwood Heir Alleges "Misinterpretation of Facts." ' Nicholas Greenwood, reached by telephone, had described Kane's article as a vicious smear on his father, who was, in fact, a victim of Nazi persecution. The company's plans for nuclear reactors was vital to America's energy future, and it would be a tragic mistake if these unfounded rumors were to delay in any way the necessary approvals. The story went on to list comments from several senators who seemed to feel the allegations raised serious questions about the entire program. 'I'm for a thorough investigation,' one of them was quoted as saying, 'and if their skirts are clean, maybe they should go ahead.' Delays, it was made clear, were now inevitable.

A story datelined 'Antibes' indicated that Matthew Greenwood was unavailable for comment, due to age and ill health. His spokesman, Nigel Boyce, described the old man as 'frail,' and promised 'clarification' at the earliest moment.

'What's going to happen?' Diana asked.

'I think Nicholas will find it difficult to persuade people in Washington that he should be in the nuclear business. Eventually, if the process is good enough, it will be approved, but if he was hoping to move quickly, he will have to forget about it. He'll need capital to bridge the gap. A great deal of capital. I think you can be sure his stock will go down sharphy when the market opens this morning. That won't make Biedermeyer happy, by the way.'

Paul glanced at the paper again, then picked up the telephone and dialed a number. 'Aaron,' he said, 'I'm sorry to wake you at this hour in California, but do you remember when we were talking about silver at Cap d'Antibes?' . . . You do? Then you will recall I promised to let you know when it was time to get out?'

Paul nodded impatiently as Aaron Diamond began to talk, and quickly interrupted. 'Aaron,' he said, 'the time is now!' and hung up.

'You see,' he said, looking at Diana, 'one must always keep one's promises — good ones and bad ones, it doesn't matter.'

Augustus Biedermeyer was a man who prided himself on knowing when to write something off. 'Never reinforce failure' was one of his mottoes, and as he read the New York *Times* in his study it was apparent that a kind of failure was even now taking place in the affairs of his prospective son-in-law. Biedermeyer ate a hearty breakfast — it was part of his image — and liked to linger over the breakfast table, a habit which was made obligatory today by the presence of Cardinal de Montenuovo, who had elected to stay with the Biedermeyers during his visit to New York.

The cardinal, partly because of his age, was not a man

who enjoyed a heavy breakfast. He sipped a cup of strong black coffee, his eyes closed in meditation. 'A bad business,' he remarked.

'A disaster,' Biedermeyer agreed.

'There is worse to come, I fear,' the cardinal said mournfully. 'I spoke on the telephone to Rome. There's a rumor that enormous quantities of silver are being sold.'

'Profit taking. You have to expect that.'

'More than profit taking, I think, Somebody is unloading. Luckily, the Bank of the Holy Spirit had advance warning. The Holy Father was most anxious for us to take a strong position on silver, but when I learned Paul Foster and Meyer Meyerman were selling silver short in a raging bull market, I told His Holiness, "Let's not fall into a trap! Remember what happened to us when poor Sindona went into the commodity market." '

Montenuovo crossed himself at the thought of that unhappy relationship, which had cost the Vatican at least two billion dollars and created a major scandal.

'And His Holiness listened?'

'His Holiness always listens. He is a man of great simplicity, with the profound common sense of his peasant background. "God doesn't go for the quick profit, Montenuovo. He prefers long-term security." That's what he told me. Words of wisdom! So we got out when silver was at forty dollars an ounce. True, we could have ridden it up a few more points, but we are obliged to be careful with God's money.'

'Are you telling me the silver market is collapsing, Your Eminence?'

Montenuovo shrugged. 'Like all bubbles, it has burst. *Vanitas vanitatum.* I'm informed that Love Potter is dumping his holdings. There will be tears and lamentations in many places tonight. Not, however, in the Holy See.'

'Not here either. I figured that anything Love Potter was hoarding was bound to drop with a crash sooner or later. It will hurt Nick Greenwood.'

'A death blow, I should think. Sad. He's a charming young man. I knew him when he was a baby. God so often punishes the children for the sins of the fathers!'

'What sins? His old man sold uranium to the Nazis. Hell, that was a long time ago. Sosthenes Behn sold them electronics, but it hasn't hurt ITT. Standard Oil did a deal with Hitler on synthetic fuel — who remembers that? I'm not saying it was the right thing to do, but people have short memories.'

'Possibly, but God's memory is a long one. Matthew Greenwood was guilty of greed — and poor judgment, by the way, which is worse. After the war I helped him during the Nuremberg trials, since we had certain business dealings together. I told him then he had gone too far. Do you know what he said?'

Beidermeyer shrugged.

'He told me, "Father, the Vatican got its share of the profits, it can take care of the sin." When I told Pacelli that, the Holy Father closed his eyes and said, "God will punish him." It seems he was prophetic.'

Beidermeyer crossed himself and said, 'I'm sorry I ever agreed to the marriage.'

'Why? Niki is still a handsome, charming man. Angelica, you tell me, loves him. Adversity may bring out the best side of Niki's character. It is often so.'

'Maybe. I'm not so sure. I always had my doubts about the whole thing, to be perfectly frank. Angelica is a sweet, beautiful girl, but she's a little innocent for her age, you know what I mean?'

'*Certo*,' Montenuovo said, lifting one eyebrow in surprise, for the state of Angelica's innocence was well-known to him, both from gossip and from several conversations with her confessor.

'I wasn't too happy about her being married to a guy who's been leading a swinging bachelor's life for twenty years. I thought he might be a little too — ah, experienced — for her.'

'Oh, quite.' Montenuovo's expression was tactfully bland.

'Now there's all this. I'd like to break the whole thing off, but I don't want to hurt Angelica, you know what I mean? I can't ask her not to go through with her marriage just because our deal has gone sour.'

'No, that would be difficult, I agree. Though I think Angelica might be more realistic than you suppose. But if Niki had been married before and had a child by another woman, wouldn't that constitute a breach of faith?'

'You're not telling me —'

339

Montenuovo smiled consolingly. 'Oh, yes,' he said. 'You may set your mind at rest. There's ample reason to prevent the marriage.'

'In writing?'

'If need be.'

'How can I possibly thank you, Your Eminence?'

'By prayer. By the example of your faith. And possibly by your help with certain investments we'd like to make in the United States. The Holy Father expressed a strong interest in the American leisure-time market . . .'

'Breweries?'

'Breweries, yes. Distilling. Also television, the movie business, sports, and so on. The Church is against frivolity, you understand, but there's nothing wrong in betting her money on man's instinct for pleasure, especially in the United States. Oh, and Augustus —'

'Your Eminence?'

'If you'd like me to break the news to dear Angelica —'

'I'd be most grateful. She may be very upset. You know how it is with women.'

'Indeed. But I have no doubt she'll find consolation quickly. In prayer, of course,' he added hastily.

By nightfall Niki Greenwood could hardly bear the thought of another telephone call. For eight long hours he had sat in his office facing a series of disasters as implacable as a flood or an earthquake, and just as inescapable. At first his executives and associates had been sympathetic; then, as it became apparent that their own careers and futures were at stake, they became distant. He was president of the company, chairman of the board, a major controlling stockholder, but he had run the ship on the rocks and it was every man for himself. Some of the management might survive the disaster, but Niki certainly would not.

All over the big glass-walled building on Park Avenue, the lights burned as executives rummaged through their files looking for memos and notes that would put the responsibility for everything on his shoulders, and the telephone rang incessantly in the darkened hall-ways and outer offices, now that the secretaries and assistants had gone home.

Niki was alone. By noon he had stopped asking for the

price of silver. It had already dropped well below the level of his futures and options, as lot after lot came on the market, driving the price inexorably down. He had stopped taking calls from banks and brokerage houses by one in the afternnon. There was no point in listening to an endless series of margin calls and threats.

Biedermeyer's call, at three in the afternoon, had not surprised him. In fact, the only consolation in this catastrophe was that the marriage between himself and Angelica would not take place, after all.

Niki turned off the lights, poured himself a drink and stared out the window. Everything around him was in ruins, but he knew, by long experience, that the worst was yet to come, and it would make everything else seem bearable when it did. As if on cue, his private line buzzed. He picked up the receiver, and a crisp, familiar English voice said, 'This is Boyce. I have your father here for you.'

Niki heard a wheezing, puffing sound in the background as his father picked up the telephone. 'So,' Matthew Greenwood said, the harsh, guttural voice dragging the word out, pronouncing it in the German fashion. '*Was für eine Schweinerei!*'

From childhood Niki had been afraid of his father, afraid of disappointing him, afraid of not measuring up. The money meant nothing, but the shame, the disgrace, the endless recriminations and investigations were more than he could bear. He remembered his cousin Paul and how he had failed to warn Paul about the wild boar. Niki had never forgotten that moment of cowardice, never forgiven himself for it, never come to terms with it. All his life he had struggled to erase it by proving to the world that he was courageous, but the unspoken reproach had never been exorcised, any more than he could exorcise the feeling that his own father would have preferred to have Paul for a son.

Niki hardly even heard his father's words — the message of rage and contempt was clear enough. He summoned up his energy to interrupt, if only to gain a moment's relief.

'I was in too deep, I admit,' he said.

The old man's anger crackled over the line.

Niki tried again. 'I underestimated Paul Foster,' he said. 'I should have guessed he was behind all this. But

341

why, God knows! I've hardly even met the man . . .'

There was silence at the other end, but it was not the silence of forgiveness. Matthew's anger was out of control now, and he spoke coldly, precisely, almost spitting out the words. 'You fool,' he said. 'He's your cousin! He always did have a better head on his shoulders than you.'

Niki stared out the window, half listening to the old man's lengthy explanations. He dimly heard familiar names. Uncle Steven, Aunt Betsy, Auschwitz, Rademacher, the Grünwald fortune. A tone of self-justification and apology had crept into the old man's voice, but Niki wasn't interested. He understood now much that he had suspected all his adult lifetime. The details didn't matter — his defeat had been preordained a long time ago, and he felt weary, drained, unable to cope with further revelations.

'Niki,' the old man said, 'what I did was for you, my boy.'

It was almost as if he were demanding to be forgiven, of God knew what crimes, what overpowering greed, what cold betrayals. Niki had been spared the knowledge of them, but they had caught up with him all the same. There was a bitter taste in his mouth. His father had betrayed everyone. In the end his father had betrayed *him*.

He put the receiver down on the desk; then, quickly, as if he were afraid he might change his mind, Nicholas Greenwood put on his jacket and nerved himself for the second and final moment of cowardice in his life.

From the receiver on the desk, he could hear his father asking, 'Are you there?' Niki opened the window, took a breath of fresh air and stepped out into the night. He had always believed that if you jumped from a skyscraper, you lost consciousness before you hit the ground, but to his surprise and anguish, it turned out not to be true.

Part Nine

Twilight of the Gods 1945

From Vienna the line to Cracow runs to the East through Oświeçim (Auschwitz) junction. Country uninteresting.
— BAEDEKER'S
Austria-Hungary, 1912

18

'I am so sorry,' Steven de Grünwald said for what seemed to Paul the hundredth time since their journey had begun. His father apologized, with impeccable, if misplaced, courtesy, for stepping on other people's toes, for bumping into them, even for being knocked off his own feet. What was the point, Paul wondered, in apologizing for something that couldn't be helped? After all, with over a hundred people packed into a stinking boxcar like sardines in a can, pressed so tightly together that it was impossible to fall even if you lost your balance, you could hardly *avoid* sticking your elbow in your neighbor's stomach — or receiving his in yours. As for sanitary arrangements, in one corner of the sealed cattle car there was merely a filthy, overflowing bucket, the stench of which was almost worse than the crowding. It was impossible to push one's way through to use it, so those farthest away from it had to relieve themselves where they stood, to the indignant complaints of those next to them. Steven had held himself back as long as he could before letting nature take its course, and he was so ashamed that he not only apologized yet again but began to cry.

The quality of rage in the car was almost as pervasive as the smell and the fear, and it was mostly turned against Steven and Paul, since they had been pushed into the car after it was already loaded and locked, adding two more bodies to an already unbearable situation, like unwelcome last-minute guests at a crowded party.

Paul struggled to hold his father and himself upright, using his elbows vigorously to give Steven room to breathe. In the dark interior it was difficult to distinguish people's faces, but from what he could see, his fellow travelers were mostly old and middle-aged, still carrying or wearing the vestiges of middle-class respectability —

345

fur coats, overcoats with velvet linings, homburgs, and even, in the case of one elderly gentleman, spats. The prevailing rumor that the train was bound for a work camp seemed unlikely to Paul, in view of the age and physical condition of the travelers.

By late 1944 Auschwitz was no longer a secret. Even Reichsfürer Himmler himself was busily compiling documents to show that he had not been informed of the 'excesses' that had 'apparently' taken place there. His subordinates, he confided to the Papal Nuncio, had 'acted with too much zeal.'

Unfortunately, this Olympian view of events was not communicated to the Reichsfürer's subordinates, or indeed to the Führer himself, who believed, like the rank and file of the SS, that the gas chambers were to be kept going as long as there were Jews to fill them.

Under the circumstances, it was a tribute to human optimism that those who were 'transported' could still persuade themselves they were destined for labor camps in the Reich, particularly since the Germans no longer even bothered to elaborate on this deception. The truth was that everybody knew, but nobody *wanted* to know, least of all the victims. The only hope left was in lying. It was a last crumb of comfort no one was willing to give up, which was why the stunned terror of Paul's father enraged his unwilling traveling companions — there was no room in the boxcar for pessimists.

At dawn Paul half expected his father to be among the dead, but the faint gray light filtering through the cracks in the boxcar's sides revealed that Steven was still alive, at any rate in the sense that his eyes were open and he was breathing. Paul squeezed his father's hand, but Steven seemed to have passed into a state of shock so profound that he felt nothing or perhaps didn't wish to.

Paul kicked his father in the shins. 'Wake up!' he said.

Steven groaned. 'Leave me alone, Pali,' he mumbled. 'Let me die.'

'What are you talking about?' the man next to Steven asked indignantly. 'Nobody's going to die here!'

'People are already dying.'

'The very old and the weak, perhaps. After all, there's a

war on. Those who can work will eat.'

'Shut up,' Steven said wearily, closing his eyes, 'we're all going to die.'

'How dare you?' shouted the man beside him. His own fear turning to anger, he began to pummel Steven with as much force as he could, given the fact that he could hardly move his arms.

Paul reacted swiftly. He managed to get his hand into his trouser pocket and pull out his penknife. There was no point, he thought, in arguing or using his fists — the only way to survive was to act calmly, swiftly and, if necessary, brutally. He pulled open the little blade with his fingers, grasped the knife with a clenched fist and pushed it as hard as he could into the man's side. It did not penetrate deeply, but it was enough to end the fight. It struck Paul as ironic that the knife had been given to him by none other than Göring, but it had served the purpose.

Still, it was not the penknife jabbed into his ribs that stopped Steven's attacker. As the man turned in surprise he found himself staring into a pair of pale-blue eyes so cold and suddenly emptied of feeling that he began to shiver. The boy's face was that of a good-looking, pleasant adolescent, but the eyes were those of a hangman.

'I'll kill you if you don't leave him alone,' the boy said quietly.

And clearly, he meant it.

By the late afternoon of the next day, the train had screeched to a halt at what appeared to be its final destination. At intervals it had stood on sidings, sometimes for hours, while more important freight passed by, but these stops had been strangely silent, except for the noise of the guards walking back and forth on the cinders of the roadway, and the occasional sound of one of them relieving himself or coughing as he lit a cigarette. Now there were signs of more concentrated activity: dogs barked, men shouted out orders in hoarse, guttural voices, the air smelled of concentrated human activity, as it does on the outskirts of a city: smoke, industrial pollution, garbage, chemicals, the sweet stench of ordure.

Ahead of them, down the length of the train, could be heard the noise of doors being slid open with a crash, of shouted orders or sharp cracks that would remind those familiar with country living of cattle whips. Even the most optimistic of the deportees turned pale and rigid, staring at the black, wood-planked door of the boxcar, its edges bound in rusty tin and reinforced with heavy timbers. For nearly two days it had oppressed them, a symbol of their helplessness; now, suddenly, it seemed like a protection from the world outside and they prayed for it to remain shut.

That prayer, like most in this time and place, remained unanswered.

There was little Paul could tell from his surroundings. To the left was a dark mass of squat buildings, with high chimneys that gave off thick black smoke and occasional lugubrious bursts of flame. To the right was a muddy, potholed road leading to what looked like endless rows of small wooden huts stretching to the horizon, where the towers and stacks of a giant industrial complex rose against the darkening sky. On the far side of the train was an ornate railway station, in the fussy style of provincial Austro-Hungarian official architecture.

The station clock had been painted in trompe l'oeil fashion, with the hands fixed at one minute to twelve by some unknown humorist. Even the windows were merely paintings, complete with lace curtains and flowers, although a real timetable had been placed behind a glass door, apparently as a last-minute touch of authenticity. Whatever purpose this stage set had once served, and it was easy enough to guess, it had long since fallen into disrepair, like an old abandoned movie set left to molder on the studio back lot. The Germans no longer felt the need to pretend that Auschwitz was anything but the end of the line for the deportees.

It took no great imagination for Paul to conclude that the process toward which they were now shuffling was in the nature of a preliminary screening; for those who failed, there would be no striped uniform. He had little doubt of passing it himself, since it was evident that the young and able-bodied were at a premium, and it was in fact a relief to realize that even at this stage survival was still possible. About his father, however, he had serious misgivings. Steven looked healthy enough, but he seemed dazed and stupefied, as if he had lost the will to live. Paul

348

dragged him forward, encouraging him, urging him to look alive, but Steven merely mumbled, 'I'm sorry, I'm sorry, I can't help it,' as indeed he couldn't. His mind was fixed on Betsy's death, on Matthew's betrayal, on the past. Here the past was a dangerous thing to think about.

Like each deportee before him, Steven stood for a moment before an elegantly uniformed SS officer carrying a gold-handled walking stick. The officer held a handkerchief scented with eau de Cologne over his nose in a fastidious gesture of disgust, and his manner was at once impatient and detached. The eyes above the handkerchief were not so much cruel as cynically humorous, as if the only way he could bear the boredom of the selection process was by playing an occasional practical joke.

'Next!' the Hauptsturmführer called out impatiently. He did not turn his head. It was the prisoner's job to present himself for inspection at a convenient spot directly in front of the Hauptsturmführer's eyes, which hardly even flickered as each new arrival appeared before him.

Steven hesitated, swaying back and forth on his feet as in a trance. Impulsively, Paul took him by the hand and led him forward.

'*Na, na,*' the officer said, in a voice that was not at all unkindly, but all the more menacing for that fact, 'one at a time, please.'

'He's my father,' Paul said, holding on to Steven. 'He's very strong. He simply isn't — feeling well.'

'That's a shame, *mein Junge.*'

'He's a banker, sir.'

'We don't need too many bankers here.' The officer prodded Steven with the tip of his cane, but failed to produce any reaction. 'I'll tell you what I'll do, boy. One of you has to go to the left, one of you has to go to the right. You can choose yourself.'

Before Paul could say anything, Steven opened his eyes and spoke. He did not look at his son. His mind was elsewhere, as if he had already reached a decision — had reached it, in fact, long ago. 'Which way is the death camp?' he asked.

'Why, to the left, of course. You can see the chimneys! Make up your mind. I haven't got all day. As it is, I've missed my lunch. Roast chicken with red cabbage and noodles . . . They'll keep it hot for me, but it isn't the same.'

'I will go to the left,' Steven said slowly and firmly. 'Let the boy live.'

'Whatever you say.' The Hauptsturmführer, losing interest, pushed Paul to the right with his cane and turned his attention to the next person in line.

Paul hesitated, torn between the desire to survive and the instinctive feeling that it was his duty to sacrifice himself for his father, but once a decision had been made there was no turning back. He was shoved to the right by kicks and blows in the back, and by the time he had turned around to shout goodbye to his father, Steven was gone, lost in the straggling line making its way through the mud and debris toward the rusty barbed-wire gates.

There was no time here for mourning. That would come later, Paul guessed. If one survived to do it.

In later years Paul was to claim that the only truly international organization he had ever known was a concentration camp. Auschwitz, as he quickly discovered, was nothing if not cosmopolitan — every known European language could be heard here, as if the camp were a distorted and psychotic experiment in European unity. By late 1944 few of the guards were German, except for the SS officers themselves and the key personnel. Ukrainians, Balts and Poles, as well as Russians with vague claims to ethnic German ancestry, filled out the ranks of the guard units, most of them picked for this duty because they were in some way unsuitable as fighting material.

At first sight, in fact, many of the inmates of the Auschwitz work camp looked healthier than the guards, but of course this was an illusion, in part produced by the daily process of *Selektion*, in which the weak, the sick, those who were too exhausted to work or who seemed likely to be troublemakers were 'weeded out' and marched over to the Birkenau death camp to be disposed of. Here the Darwinian process of natural selection had at last been applied on an accelerated scale, so that every afternoon and evening, during the interminable inspections of the *Appellplatz*, only the fittest were permitted to survive.

Prisoners rouged their faces with brick dust, stuffed old rags in their cheeks to fill out the gaunt hollows, took care to stand next to someone who looked worse than they did, in the hope of appearing fit by contrast. A cough, a sprain, a minor injury, a moment's weakness brought instant death in the form of Oberscharführer Moll's attention. When he noticed a 'customer' (as he liked to call his victims), he squeezed the inmate's cheeks hard with his meaty fingers and waited to see how long it took for the flesh to fill out again. If the marks were still there on the prisoner's cheeks after a couple of seconds, he nodded to his Ukrainian Kapo and told the prisoner, 'Mensch, you've lived long enough.'

Even in the SS there were debates and misgivings about this policy — not on humanitarian grounds, of course, which would have been ridiculous, but about the practical consequences. Obergruppenführer Pohl had not found it easy to 'sell' Speer and the Wehrmacht on his concept without making at least a token promise that the camps would not only be self-sufficient but even contribute to the war effort.

Based on Pohl's grandiose estimates, I.G. Farben had been persuaded to construct the world's largest synthetic-fuel plant at Auschwitz, as well as the enormous Bunawerk, which was designed to produce ersatz rubber out of coal. Others followed in the wake of the I.G. project. The inmates were rented out on a daily basis at a considerable profit to the SS. In a country whose major shortage was labor, Pohl had access to an unlimited supply of bodies, and the Reichsführer dreamed of consolidating all German industry under the control of the SS.

Unfortunately, reality fell far short of these dreams. The rank and file of the SS had no experience in keeping Jews alive, and little enthusiasm for the task. Neither the camps nor the system was designed to provide a healthy work force, and their customers complained constantly of the low quality of the 'goods' supplied to them.

Pohl was enraged and humiliated by the vehemently expressed dissatisfaction of his customers, and worse yet, by the displeasure of the Reichsführer. He urged Kommandant Rudolf Höss to 'improve productivity.' Höss addressed himself to the problem by having a dozen inmates, chosen at random, whipped to death at the morning *Appell*, in front of their fellow prisoners. It was just a question of understanding prisoner psychology, Höss informed Prinz Albrecht Strasse proudly — a comment that brought not just a smile, which was rare enough, but an actual laugh to the lips of Obergruppenführer Pohl, in whose opinion Höss was not fit to understand the psychology of an ox.

'The ox would be smarter,' he told the Reichsführer, over a cup of medicinal tea — which the Führer himself swore by as an antidote to flatulence — but Himmler was not amused. If the industrialists didn't want his inmates, he would find a use for them himself. With any luck, there was still time for the SS to provide the Reich with the ultimate V-weapon, the bomb that Göring had ignominiously failed to build.

'Use them for Wotan.' Himmler told Pohl.

No sooner had Paul been urged into a foul, dark, drafty hut than he came to grips with the reality of life in the camp. A bulky figure emerged from the shadows, grabbed him by the arms and banged his head against the wall.

'Name?' the man shouted in German.

'Grünwald, Paul,' Paul answered as best he could, since he was being choked.

There was a pause, and he felt air coming back into his throat and lungs.

'Magyar?' his tormentor inquired.

'Jo.'

Paul was released. In the dim light he could see that his interlocutor was a heavyset, muscular man with a vaguely familiar face who spoke German with the strong Hungarian accent that the Germans called *Miklós-Deutsch*.

'You don't remember me?' he asked Paul.

Paul shook his head.

'Voster. I drove you home after you were beaten up in the streets. I remember you were with your sister. A young woman of great beauty and strong character, by the way . . .'

'What are you doing here, Voster?'

'What we're all doing here. Trying to survive.'

'No, no. I mean *why* are you here? I would have thought an officer in the Hungarian Gendarmerie would have been safe. You're not by any chance —'

'Jewish? No, not at all. I was arrested with Nicholas Horthy by the Germans. They kidnapped him to make the

352

old man toe the line. You can't trust foreigners.'

'I suppose not.'

'That was your Uncle Matthew's mistake. How is your esteemed father, by the way?'

'He was sent to the death camp.'

Major Voster crossed himself and sighed. 'The Germans have no decency,' he said sadly. 'It's one thing to gas Jews, but quite another to gas a *gentleman*. We live in a sad world.'

'*If* we live,' Paul said, looking around him at the grim interior of the hut. The rows of *Pritschen* — unfinished wooden planks nailed together as beds — were stacked three deep. The *Pritschen* had been designed to accommodate five inmates, but as many as fifteen people were wedged into each one, without blankets or pillows. Occasionally a *Pritsche* collapsed under the weight, in which case the inmates in the shelf below were crushed by the bodies and splintered timbers that fell on them.

The planks of the floor were rotted and damp, exuding a nauseating stench of human waste, for the camp authorities had never bothered to install plumbing, and in the soft, marshy ground the sewage from the open pits that served as latrines simply drained off under the huts, to rise with every rainstorm. Typhus, cholera and typhoid fever were commonplace, amoebic dysentery was endemic even among the guards, and the I.G. Farben plant managers boiled water, wore gloves and even put on surgical masks when they were obliged to approach their workers.

For years the SS had prevented inquisitive German dignitaries from visiting Auschwitz by saying there was an epidemic in the camp; now this convenient lie had been allowed to become true. Though the prisoners could not know it, Höss was deeply humiliated by these frequent epidemics. They were supposed to die according to plan, not by an act of God. He gave orders that anybody who fell sick would be shot, but even this failed to halt the epidemics, which the Kommandant regarded as an act of insubordination and revolt. A prisoner who died of disease had taken his fate in his own hands; it was a clear case of disobedience, just like suicide, which the Kommandant punished by having the suicide's body tied to a chair and shot to prove that death here remained the exclusive prerogative of the SS.

'Oh, you'll live,' Voster said. 'After all, you're Hungarian.'

In the first light of dawn, Voster's *Kommando* seemed to contradict his optimism. The inmates, thousands of them, stood in the huge, muddy *Appellplatz* in the rain, like an army of derelicts, while the German guards went through the tedious business of roll call, a process that, in bad weather, constituted a kind of punishment in itself. Everybody had to be counted — if anyone died during the night, and inevitably many did, the corpse had to be dragged out and counted before it could be disposed of. Not until the figures had been checked and rechecked to Oberscharführer Politsch's satisfaction could the work parties move off. The entire operation took hours, during which the inmates sometimes died of exposure, while the guards themselves became irritable and therefore more dangerous.

Voster's small work *Kommando* was in order, but all the same his face turned pale at the sight of Oberscharführer Moll's roly-poly figure making its way down the lines. Moll's presence meant that there was going to be a 'clean-out' — a certain percentage of inmates would be removed to make way for a new intake. Against this process of selection there was no appeal. Moll had his orders and had to produce so many bodies; it was as simple as that. Since the inmates who had died during the night didn't count against his quota, Moll ignored them — only the living were of any use to him.

When Moll arrived at Voster's *Kommando*, he consulted his clipboard for a moment without even bothering to look at the men lined up in front of him. His glass eye stared out toward the side of his face, as if something in the far distance had attracted its attention, but the good eye glared at Voster with piggish cunning.

'*Na*, Herr Major,' Moll said, 'everybody in good health?'

'Absolutely, Herr Oberscharführer!'

'No coughs? No fevers? No little complaints?'

'Nothing, Herr Oberscharführer.'

'It must be all the garlic you Magyars eat! Mind you, myself too, I'm a great believer in garlic. It opens the bowels, cleans the blood, wonderful stuff . . .'

'We're ready for work.'

Moll looked at his clipboard, moving his lips as he read. 'You're being moved,' he said.

'Moved? Moved to where?'

'I don't know. Anyway, it's none of your business. Get your men over to the transfer block, on the double.'

Moll glanced back to his clipboard, then raised his hand. 'One moment,' he said. 'You have an inmate down here for a whipping, *nicht wahr*?'

Voster nodded. 'Meyerman,' he said.

'Where is he?'

'The professor is dead. During the night.'

Moll looked irritated. 'He was supposed to be whipped.'

'What's the point? He was an old man. He died of exhaustion.'

'If a whipping is ordered, a whipping takes place. I'll take someone else.' Moll looked down the line of prisoners and nodded at Paul. His good eye focused on him while the glass eye continued to stare at Voster. 'That one will do,' he said.

'But, Herr Oberscharführer, he hasn't done anything! He just arrived.'

'Voster, I can't waste time. It's you or him. He's young, he's new, who knows — he might live. He'll do as well as anyone else.'

Voster sighed, and turned toward Paul with a shrug. 'Bad luck, kid,' he said.

When Paul was dragged out in front of the other prisoners, it briefly occurred to him that the humiliation of being stripped and whipped in front of several thousand inmates would be worse than the pain, but this was a romantic illusion that did not survive the first stroke. Moll prided himself on his ability with a bullwhip. It made for a welcome change of pace, since most of his day was spent working with corpses.

Tied to a hurdle, a gag in his mouth and his head down, Paul felt the whip cut through his flesh to the muscle at the same time that he heard the crack. The next blows, he guessed, would lay his back open to the bone and he hoped it was true that one passed out long before the last strokes. He counted the strokes, waiting for the pain that would crush the breath and the consciousness out of him, but to his surprise they seemed to lessen in strength, and he came to the conclusion that he was dying.

He heard Moll shout 'Zwanzig!' as he cracked the whip for the last time, then someone threw a pail of cold water over him and he fainted at last. When he came to, he was lying in a bunk with a blanket thrown over him. Voster was sitting on the next bed, looking at him. He did not seem pleased.

'You're alive,' he said. 'Moll wasn't up to form.'

'Where am I?'

'In the transfer block.'

'Where are we going?'

'Who knows? East, I suppose, to dig antitank trenches. Everybody gets a medical check, then a bowl of soup. Unless you don't pass the doctor's inspection, of course. In that case, you get gassed, and miss your bowl of soup. I'm sorry about what happened.'

'I understand.'

'Moll is a bastard. Still, I'm not so happy that we're leaving.'

'Surely anything is better than Auschwitz?'

Voster thought about this for a moment, then made a face. 'Believe it or not, my boy, there are worse places. The doctor here knows all about them . . .'

But the doctor who examined Paul was a familiar figure. Dressed in a physician's white coat with his name embroidered on the left side, he was the same man who had greeted Paul and his father on the railway siding, cane in hand.

With a stethoscope around his neck, Dr. Mengele might have passed for any ordinary medical man, except for the polished riding boots and a certain un-Hippocratic gleam in his eyes, which were made even more sinister by a slight twitch that he appeared unable to control.'

'Name?' he asked.

'Grünwald, Paul.'

Mengele examined his list and checked off Paul's name.

'Strip.'

Paul did so, as quickly as he could. If nothing else, Mengele's eyes conveyed authority. Paul winced in pain as the coarse prison jacket tore away the scabs that had congealed on his wounds.

'You have pain, *mein Kind*?' Mengele asked softly.

'A little.'

'Show me.' Mengele gently felt the wounds on Paul's back. He cleaned and dressed them with professional care, whistling between his teeth. 'Moll must be losing his touch,' he said cheerfully. 'You'll have some scars, but they won't show with your clothes on, and you'll find they drive women crazy, you lucky lad! I've seen you before, haven't I?'

'At the railway siding, Doctor.'

'Of course. With your father. A touching scene. Abraham and Isaac — except, of course, in reverse. Well, you can put your clothes on. You're fit enough. The Reichsführer doesn't want you bringing back any diseases. It's bad enough bringing Jews back into the Reich without bringing back their epidemics as well . . .'

Chained next to Voster in the back of the truck, Paul said, 'We're going to Germany.'

Voster stared at him. 'Surely not!' he said. 'They move prisoners east, but never back into the Reich. It's a matter of principle.'

But as the convoy of trucks turned off the bumpy roads of Poland and began to drive along the smooth surface of what was clearly a Reich *Autobahn*, Voster fell silent. He dozed for a while despite his uncomfortable position. When he woke, he sighed and said, 'We were better off there.'

'Why? I don't understand what could be worse.'

'I don't know why it didn't occur to me . . . Why would they select a convoy full of healthy inmates and take them back to Germany? There's only one answer that makes sense, my boy. Medical experiments! We're going to be guinea pigs!'

And with a strangled sob he crossed himself, his chains clanking like those of a ghost.

19

Stumpff thought of himself as a professional policeman, though in fact he had only served two years on the job in the Munich Schutz-polizei, after which he had been sacked for corruption, a matter that would have ended his career had he not been a Nazi party member.

When the party came to power in 1933, Stumpff was reinstated with honors and back pay, and quickly developed such a reputation for brutality that it was judged expedient to transfer him to the Munich headquarters of the Gestapo. There, it was rightly thought, he would fit in. Now that the end of the war was in sight, he was anxious to transfer himself back into police uniform as quickly as possible. The difficulty in this simple ambition lay in the fact that several hundred thousand other people had reached the same conclusion, anticipating correctly that the victorious Allies would pay very little attention to the local policemen they encountered, not interrupting their daily rounds.

Stumpff hated the slave laborers he guarded, he hated the Kommandant — a cunning pansy with the furtive eyes of a shopkeeper, in Stumpff's professional opinion — and he hated Project Wotan.

Not that Stumpff knew what Wotan was about, except that it was Reich top secret and had the 'V-priority' that was only assigned to the most important weapons programs. So far as Stumpff could see, it was a waste of time — several hundred Jews digging an underground bunker outside Magdeburg for a bunch of scientists who looked as if they'd spent the war playing with themselves. Even in the completed tunnels there was not much to see except what looked like an enormous brick fireplace, which was called 'the Pile,' and vast storage bins where some kind of filthy dirt gave off an eerie glow at night.

Standing under one of the few remaining trees on the site, bundled up against the chilling January winds from the east (and there was worse to come from there, he thought), Stumpff surveyed his muddy empire, hawked and spat. Before him, clad in rags and torn blankets, a group of prisoners labored at a deep trench that would eventually be lined in concrete and serve as a conduit for the main power lines. For the moment it was merely an eyesore, a huge, filthy pit in which the prisoners worked up to their knees in mud and stagnant rain water. Occasionally one of them would fall face down from exhaustion and drown, but apart from that, there was little to amuse Stumpff or his men. Stumpff was under pressure to get more work out of the prisoners, but apart from kicks, beatings and the random shooting of anybody who seemed to be losing enthusiasm for the task, there was little he could do to increase the pace. As the Kommandant complained, the material Höss was sending them from Auschwitz was human garbage.

Stumpff roused himself to slosh through the mud and watch two men trying to lever a huge boulder out of the ground. They were so covered in mud that they might have been niggers, except that the ones Stumpff had seen in films were stronger, more muscular, with big white grins. 'Put your backs into it!' Stumpff shouted. The two men — one a large fellow with the bearing of a soldier, the other hardly more than a boy — grunted, heaved, groaned and finally moved the stone out of the trench. They stood up, stretching for a moment, and the younger one wiped his face.

Stumpff stared at him for a few moments, then a ponderous look of recognition crossed his face. 'Why, it's the Grünwald brat,' he said. 'Welcome to Wotan!'

Stumpff's recognition did not have any immediate consequences for Paul. He and Voster labored twelve hours a day on the edge of physical collapse until the trench began to resemble, in Paul's mind, the pyramids, about which the workers must have had similar feelings of despair and loathing. Work and exhaustion produced a mind-numbing sense of routine, which was probably a blessing. Paul did not want to think about the past and he was unable to think about the future, if there was one. Every day brought more work, 500 grams of coarse bread and a bowl of watery soup. That was as much as you could expect and it was enough. The alternative was death at the hands of one of Stumpff's *Genickschussspezialisten*, who solved your problems by putting a bullet in the back of your neck.

There were rumors that the Russians were close to the east, that the British and the Americans were on the way, that the Third Reich was collapsing, but the prisoners were too tired to speculate. Experience had taught them that hope was dangerous — it took your mind off the immediate, day-to-day task of surviving.

Paul, more than most, had no wish to look to the future. Assuming that he survived the war, he would face the need for revenge — that could hardly be avoided. Nor was it likely that Uncle Matthew would greet him with open arms — on the contrary, Matthew's position would be secure only if Paul was silent or dead. Matthew was a desperate man. He had allowed his brother to die, among other crimes; he would hardly hesitate to have Paul silenced. There was only one way to confront him — by becoming his equal. It would require strength, time and a lot of money. And, of course, luck.

'We're out of luck,' Voster whispered as they dug in the freezing rain. 'Here's the bloody Kommandant!'

An open Opel tourer bumped over the muddy track through the gates and came to a halt. Stumpff drew himself up and saluted, while the prisoners stood at the attention and doffed their caps, their heads bowed to avoid eye contact, since they knew from long experience that looking an SS officer straight in the eyes often brought death.

'All going well?' the Kommandant asked.

Stumpff glanced at the muddy hillside, over which the prisoners labored like waterlogged ants. It was not a landscape to inspire enthusiasm.

The Kommandant plodded through the mud accompanied by Stumpff, whose face reflected a surly insubordination. They came to a halt beside Paul's trench and paused for a moment. 'It looks pretty much the same as it did last time I inspected the site,' the Kommandant complained to Stumpff. 'Progress is too slow.'

Stumpff shrugged. 'How close are the Russians?' he asked.

'That's not the point, Stumpff. The Reichsführer himself has given Wotan the highest priority! What we're making here is the weapon of victory!'

Stumpff looked sullen. 'We're digging trenches.'

'Well, dig them faster!'

'For that I need more men.'

'Nonsense! You've got able-bodied stock here. Höss's best. You're not getting the most out of them.'

'Anybody who doesn't fill his quota is shot. What more can we do?'

'*Inspire* them! This is a historic task!' The Kommandant turned to the nearest prisoner, but the inspirational appeal he had in mind died on his lips as he found himself looking at Paul de Grünwald. He coughed, then smiled. 'You've joined the family business, I see,' he said.

Paul stood at attention. He raised his eyes to find himself looking into Rademacher's face.

'It's ironic,' Rademacher said. 'Your Uncle Matthew and your father created Wotan. Now you're working on it. If it were not for your father, you wouldn't be here . . . "*Es irrt der Mensch, so lang er strebt.*" Goethe wrote that.'

'I know, Herr Standartenführer.'

'Of course. You *would*! As long as man strives, he errs. How is your father, by the way?'

'He was gassed.'

Rademacher gave a sigh. 'Yes, the selection process is pretty primitive. The most *uneducated* types make these decisions . . . A pity. It was out of my hands, I assure you. Still, work hard and you'll be all right. You have my word.'

'Thank you.'

Rademacher waved Paul back to work, turned on his heels and walked over to Stumpff. 'Keep your eyes on that one,' he said. 'He's a smart little bastard.'

'Standartenführer Rademacher?' The voice on the telephone was faint and distant, interrupted by static and strange crackling noises. The telephone system of the Third Reich was collapsing along with everything else.

Rademacher pressed the receiver against his ear. Outside the window of his quarters in Magdeburg the noise of traffic was constant. Everything from Tiger tanks to Mercedes limousines was moving south in a traffic jam that stretched from Berlin to the Bavarian Alps, and

361

Rademacher's only ambition was to join it. His rank and duties, however, made that impossible for the moment.

Below his window he could see the body of a Waffen-SS general dangling from a lamppost, with a card strung around his neck on which the Sicherheitspolizei had written; 'I am a coward who ran away.' The message was misspelled, but clear. Someone had stolen the general's boots, or perhaps one of the Feldpolizei had removed them before hanging him. A policeman with a macabre sense of humor had fastened the general's Knight's Cross to his big toe. Nobody had bothered to steal *that* — people were throwing their Iron Crosses, their decorations and especially their party badges into the river as they crossed the Old Bridge.

Rademacher fingered his own War Service Cross nervously and acknowledged the call.

'Götterdämmerung,' a familiar, nasal voice said, as if it were a greeting.'

'What?'

'The code word, for God's sake. Blow the place up.'

'What should I do with the prisoners?'

'What do you *think*? Get rid of them. Also the documents. Don't forget to burn the files. A certain person is anxious to make sure of that.'

'A certain person — in Switzerland?'

'Where else? Soon you'll need his help, *nicht wahr*? Do a favor for him, and he will do one for you . . .'

'I understand.'

'Of course you do. There's one more thing that he'd like to be sure of. The boy. For him especially — *Nacht und Nebel*! Understand?'

'Understood!' Rademacher said, but the line had already gone dead before he could complete his conversation with Standartenführer Baron von Schiller. In the end, Rademacher thought, money is thicker than blood. Matthew de Grünwald's father-in-law was a banker, and although his daughter Cosima was dead, killed in the bombing of Vienna, he was already looking to the future. The war was lost, Matthew de Grünwald had preserved his wealth, soon there would be business to do. No doubt, at this very moment, Schiller was burning his uniform, and Rademacher intended to do the same as soon as possible.

He poured himself a Cognac, drank it in a gulp, went to the safe and took out several packages. One was a large painting. He unwrapped it, gazed at Caravaggio's 'Boy Bitten by a Lizard' for a moment and recited a few phrases of Goethe — wonderful how he soothed the soul!

He carefully cut the painting out of its frame, wrapped it in a tube and put it in his briefcase. Then he removed the files from the safe, selected the ones from the Wotan Project — those that concerned Matthew de Grünwald — and placed them in his briefcase next to the painting. The files were his insurance policy — better still, an investment. He had no intention of destroying them.

Rademacher changed into a Luftwaffe uniform and slipped his black leather SS trench coat over it. He placed a Luftwaffe cap in the briefcase, drank another Cognac and called for his car.

Now for the hard part, he said to himself.

Stumpff was uncooperative. Stumpff was insubordinate. Stumpff was drunk. 'Why become a war criminal now that it's all over?' he whined.

Rademacher shrugged. '*Befehl ist Befehl.* I don't like it any better than you do, but orders are orders. Besides, there's a platoon of security police at the gate to make sure we do it. The war isn't over yet. If they can hang generals, they can hang you, Or me.'

'The prisoners will know something's up.'

'Divide them into working parties. Each guard will take a dozen or so. Once they're in the trenches, they should be easy enough to shoot.'

'Then what? We can't leave them in the trenches.'

'There's a bulldozer outside the gates. Everything will be covered over. A nice neat job.'

'If you say so.'

'I say so, Stumpff. Get cracking.'

'You're not planning to shoot a few yourself?'

'It's not an officer's job. Stumpff — carry the whole thing out in an efficient, decent way, and I'll see that you get away safely. You'll be back walking a beat in Munich taking bribes off whores and nobody will be the wiser. Just one thing . . . Make sure of the Grünwald boy.'

'I don't like it,' Stumpff said, but he didn't have a choice.

'I don't like it,' Voster said.

He and Paul had been led along the earthworks to a small clump of trees, along with ten other prisoners, while Stumpff stumped along behind them, muttering under his breath and occasionally stopping to drink from a bottle of schnapps. Paul said nothing. It was not unusual for work parties to be formed this way, and in any case, he had long since given up speculating on what the day would bring. No doubt a portion of the trench had caved in — a daily occurrence.

'I don't see what's wrong,' he whispered.

'Stumpff is drunk.'

'He's always drunk.'

Stumpff scrambled out of the trench with a curse, balanced on the edge and looked down at the men. He put the bottle back in the pocket of his greatcoat, spat and waited until the prisoners were closed up in a file, squeezed into the narrowest section of the trench.

Then, with astonishing rapidity for such a bulky man, he drew his machine pistol up to his shoulder and swung it toward them. 'Eat this, Jew bastards!' he said and pulled the trigger, while they stared at him, not so much surprised — for in this time and place being shot was more or less the normal course of events — as immobilized. However, there was only a dry click. Stumpff stared down at the machine pistol, which he had forgotten to cock, and said, 'Shit!' He braced the folding stock against his knee and fumbled for the cocking lever. His victims would wait for him. He wasn't worried.

For a terrible moment Paul stood in the trench petrified, looking up at Stumpff, until it dawned on him that in a moment they would all be dead. He gave a howl of rage and grabbed Stumpff's ankles, pulling with all his weight. The big man fell, still holding his weapon. He pulled one leg free and kicked Paul in the face as hard as he could.

Paul could not let go — once Stumpff was free to stand up he would open fire — so he hung suspended above the trench from Stumpff's ankle, while Stumpff, steadying himself in the mud with his free hand, again smashed his boot into Paul's face.

Briefly, Paul wondered if death might not be the better choice. He heard his nose break; his mouth was full of mud, saliva and blood. He was too frightened to feel any pain, but his face seemed to be disintegrating under the kicks. Stumpff was panting and sobbing with exertion, when Voster, shouting at the other prisoners to run for the trees, pulled himself out of the trench and tried to pull the gun away from Stumpff.

Stumpff rallied with a last heroic effort. He was lying on his back, his legs hanging into the trench, while Paul pulled on his ankle and Voster wrestled for the gun. Stumpff let go of his hold, cocked the gun as he slid into the trench and fired a burst into Voster's chest. Then he toppled into the mud at the bottom of the trench, too breathless to curse, landing on top of Paul.

For a fleeting moment Paul thought he had been crushed to death; then he struggled free, receiving a final feeble kick that split open his cheek to the bone, and crawled on his hands and knees away from Stumpff. He did not look back. He remembered the boar hunt and the terrifying moment when the enraged animal had charged him. All around him there was the noise of firing and the smell of cordite fumes and blood, as unseen small massacres took place in the trenches on either side of him.

Paul thought of Niki, standing there at the edge of the forest, too terrified — or hating him too much? — to shout a warning, and somehow it seemed to him, in the pain and confusion and horror, that this moment was merely an extension of the boar hunt, a delayed final act. Stumpff had done to him what the boar had tried to do, and Niki, his old enemy, probably even now skiing and drinking hot chocolate in Switzerland, was to blame. It was all clear to him at last, and Niki's face was in his mind when Stumpff, catching his breath, rose to his knees in the mud and shot Paul in the back.

But Paul was already out of the ditch and on his way to the woods. He ran until his lungs felt as if they would burst and the pain began stabbing at his shoulder. Eventually he crawled, pulling himself by the fingers under barbed wire and down drainage ditches, his ruined face covered in mud and filth, his nose so badly broken that he could only breathe through his battered mouth. He had been stripped of everything but his survival instinct and his hunger for revenge. For the first time, he felt hope.

When the firing stopped there was a moment of quiet, soon interrupted by the roar of bulldozers.

Stumpff made his way toward the gates in search of Rademacher to report Paul's death. After all, he reasoned, Rademacher wasn't the type to go searching through piles of bodies to confirm it — besides, the graves would be covered over in a few minutes.

He looked around, but Rademacher's car was nowhere to be seen.

'Where's the Standartenführer?' he asked one of the Feldpolizei.

The policeman waved toward the road. 'Gone,' he said. 'He left you this.'

Stumpff slung his machine pistol over one shoulder and opened the small brown manila envelope. In it was a thin metal box, like those in which aspirin are sold. He slid open the lid and for the first time in many years found himself crying, while his stomach lurched in a spasm of rage and fear.

Nestled on a bed of neat white cotton wool were two blue cyanide capsules.

When Paul came to, he was looking up at a thin, pale, foxy face, bisected by a ginger mustache of aggressively military appearance.

The man's uniform was recognizably not German, but Paul could not decide what it was and wondered briefly if he had fallen into the hands of partisans. The man bending over him wore a pair of corduroy trousers, a jaunty black beret, a khaki shirt, a knotted silk scarf in dark blue with white polka dots and a leather jerkin over a ribbed sweater.

'What's your name?' this strange apparition asked.

Paul pondered this question for a moment through a fog of pain, hardly even noticing that he had been spoken to in English. Instinct told him that it was probably better to lie. He dimly recognized the need for a new beginning.

He closed his eyes for a moment and thought the matter over, and then said in the clear, well-modulated

English he had been carefully taught by Nanny, so long ago, 'My name is Voster.' The poor major, he thought, wouldn't mind. He had always believed Hungarians survived.

'So nice that you speak English,' the Englishman said while a medical orderly put a field dressing on Paul's wound. There was nothing he could do for Paul's face, from which he politely averted his eyes.

'I haven't spoken much English in the last few years,' Paul mumbled.

'One wouldn't know. You speak it well. Lucky for you, actually. Our chaps have got rather tired of looking after concentration camp prisoners. Of course, a chap who speaks English is quite another matter. By the way, I haven't introduced myself. Nigel Boyce, lieutenant, Second Battalion, Coldstream Guards.'

The British army's curiosity in Paul was limited. He was 'patched up,' and wearing borrowed clothes, soon made himself useful as a translator. His face was left to heal by itself. There was not time to perform plastic surgery on DPs. He claimed to be a Hungarian Jew of good family whose parents had died in Auschwitz — a story common enough to preclude any further investigation or interest.

The British were, if anything, even less curious about the Wotan Project, which the Russians had seized while Boyce's men were less than five miles from the site. Germany was littered with underground secret-weapons factories, and for most of the troops the thrill of finding them had long since worn off.

Like his men, Boyce was looking for valuables, not scientific knowledge, and was embittered at having made his way across Western Europe with nothing to show for it. Everywhere he heard stories about hidden Nazi treasures — Rembrandts in the Moravian salt mines, gold ingots in the caves of the Harz Mountains, industrial diamonds by the sackful in the Ruhr — but Boyce had liberated nothing more valuable then a Wehrmacht clothing depot and Paul Foster.

Making the best of what little he had, he set Paul to interrogating the prisoners who were now coming in by the thousands, clogging the roads south and west from Berlin in their eagerness to find a British or American unit that would accept their surrender. The roads were full of weary men in Wehrmacht *feldgrau* uniforms, and it was remarkable that in this massive exodus there were no high-ranking officers of the SS or the party; indeed it was as if the brown shirt, the death's-head badge of the SS, the silver SD armband and the party *Abzeichen* itself had all vanished, or never even existed. It did not escape Boyce's attention that many of the prisoners seemed ill at ease in their threadbare infantry uniforms, their plump, rosy-cheeked, jowly faces contrasting strangely with the down-at-the-heels boots and battered helmets. Here at last was the way to make money out of the war: a racket.

A lesser man might simply have stolen what he could from the long files of waiting Germans and left it at that, but Boyce had initiative and he was a gentleman. Mere highway robbery was not his style. Years of cheating at cards had taught him the wisdom of leaving the loser enough to get home with. For a reasonable percentage of whatever the prisoner had on him, Boyce was willing to turn his captives loose into the prisoner-of-war compounds as ordinary soldiers, where, with any luck, they would hope to remain undiscovered. Those who were reluctant to make a deal he passed on to the Intelligence Corps for interrogation as 'suspicious persons,' where their spurious identities were unlikely to survive scrutiny.

He did not bother to cut Paul in on the proceeds. It was enough that Paul had three meals a day and a place to sleep — assets that were rare enough for a displaced person in that time and place. Boyce was thus among the first of those who made the same major mistake — he underestimated Paul Foster.

Paul was never bored questioning Boyce's 'clients.' He had a sharp eye for detail and a good ear for language, and there was a certain pleasure in trying to establish the difference, if any, between the identity on a person's military papers and the real man himself. The trick was in the eyes. Most of the prisoners who filed into the small office Boyce had appropriated were sullen, weary and defeated; their eyes were dull and downcast as they told their stories. Others had the bright, fast-moving eyes of people who had to remain alert, who were obliged to *think*, if only for a fraction of a second, before replying to a question. A man's fingernails told a great deal — a private with well-manicured hands was automatically suspicious — but the eyes told more, and Paul learned to concentrate on them.

He had not, as yet, found a way out of his own dilemma. His new identity was all right so far as it went, but at some point he would undoubtedly be cast loose from the British Army, and relegated to a DP camp. This was not a prospect that held any great appeal for Paul. The sooner he was out of Europe, the better, but the possibility of getting to England or America from a refugee camp was a remote one, nor was Boyce likely to be of much help, even had he wanted to be. Paul was thinking hard about the various ways in which he might hope to escape from his rescuer when he looked up into a pair of worried, though familiar, eyes.

Standing before him, unshaven and nervous, was a private of the reserve infantry, his grubby passbook held for Paul's inspection. The private seemed to be sweating heavily and his pale eyes flickered back and forth with alarming speed, apparently searching for something over Paul's shoulder.

Paul quickly translated Boyce's questions, staring down at the papers in front of him so that the prisoner couldn't see his face.

'What do you think?' Boyce asked. 'Anything unusual?'

'Not a thing,' Paul replied.

'He looks a little *sleek* for a private, don't you think? And shifty.'

'He was in the supply services. They're all sleek and shifty.'

Boyce nodded. 'So are ours. Stick him in the compound. There's a corporal waiting farther down who's wearing handmade riding boots, the stupid sod. A dead giveaway . . .'

In the evening Paul was free to come and go as he pleased — not that there was far to go. His armband gave him entry to the POW compound and while he did not enjoy going there — the company of several thousand Germans made him nervous — he did not find it difficult to trace his quarry, who was sitting on the

369

ground eating a plate of soup, most of which he spilled at the sight of Paul.

'Don't get up, please, Dr Becker,' Paul said softly. 'We have things to talk about.'

Becker's first instinct was to run. Since that was clearly impossible, he talked. He explained to Paul that everything had been a tragic accident — a misunderstanding, really, if one knew all the facts; he complained bitterly about the conduct of Matthew de Grünwald; he commiserated with Paul about his face, and dwelt at length on the miracles of plastic surgery; he mentioned his own desire to make a new start in life. This was a time, Becker was convinced, to bury the hatchet, to live and let live.

Paul nodded. Shorn of his authority, Becker was not so much frightening as pathetic, though his story failed to kindle any warmth in Paul. 'How much have you got with you?' he asked, interrupting Becker's flow of self-justification.

Becker looked mournful. 'Nothing,' he replied. 'I should have gone to Argentina with Eichmann while there was still time . . .'

'Don't be silly. You wouldn't schlepp all the way down here on foot with nothing. If I turn you in to Boyce, he'll hand you over to the Military Police as a war criminal. I'm doing you a favor, man.'

Becker sighed. 'Ten thousand dollars,' he said. 'I always treated your family with respect.'

'Where?'

'In my boots, of course.'

'I should have guessed that's why you were limping. You took a pair of boots a couple of sizes too large for you and stuffed them with money.'

'Precisely. And they hurt like hell.'

'You can take them off right now. You're giving me the money.'

Becker looked as if he were about to argue, then bent down to take off the boots. 'Then what?' he asked.

'Then you sit tight and hope nobody recognizes you.'

'That's not much of a deal.'

'It's the best deal you'll get,' Paul said, putting the money in his pocket while Becker struggled with his boots.

He left the compound, made his way past the red-capped guards and knocked on the door of the intelligence major, a red-faced, bristling officer whose ferocity failed to conceal a patently unscrupulous nature. The major, a former Fleet Street journalist, hated Boyce, whom he once desribed in the mess as 'a stuck-up Etonian pansy,' and on the whole disliked the DPs more than he disliked the Germans.

Paul stood patiently, waiting to be noticed.

'Well?' said the major at last.

'What would I have to do to get to England, Major?'

'We don't need any of your kind in England, Foster.'

'But if I were to produce a big fish for you? Right from your own pond, so to speak?'

'Boyce is supposed to send anyone who's suspect to me.'

'This one slipped through. He's on the most-wanted list. One of Eichmann's top men.

'Can you point him out to me?'

'That's hardly necessary. He's eating his soup in front of the water tower. A tall man with boots too big for his feet. He's posing as a reserve corporal named Schmidt — not a very original alias. In fact, he's Standartenführer Becker.'

The major rummaged through the papers on his desk, produced a thick binder and leafed through it. He whistled in amazement. 'A nasty sod, isn't he?'

'Do you think finding Becker would get me to England?'

The major looked pensive as he held the card with Becker's picture and curriculum vitae in front of him, like a man playing poker. 'It will certainly be to your credit,' he said, 'but of course it's still rather — difficult . . .'

'Often there are ways of overcoming these difficulties,' Paul said, and with a tactful, economical gesture, he slid $5,000 of Becker's money halfway across the cluttered desk. The remaining $5,000 would, with luck, pay for repairing the damage to his face once he was in England. Paul wondered who the best man was. Meyerman would know . . .

The major stared at the pile of notes, slid it under his blotter and nodded.

'That's the spirit,' he said. 'I think you're going to do

very well for yourself in England . . . Do you know anybody there?'

'I have a friend from Hungary, Meyer Meyerman. He's supposed to have gotten there.'

The major smiled. He stood up and shook Paul's hand. 'Do give Meyerman my regards,' he said.

'You *know* him?'

The major nodded. He reached under the blotter, put the money in his tunic pocket and patted it flat. 'I did a small piece of business with Meyerman in Palestine,' he explained. 'He, too, was anxious to settle down in England. He wanted to stop running.'

'Don't we all?' Paul asked sadly.

Part Ten

A Taste of Ashes

20

For the second time in his life, Paul Foster felt like running. Everywhere the press waited for him, the television reporters sticking their boom mikes toward him like the guns of the SS, the reporters lined up like the Feldpolizei, shouting and pushing. He had felt an irrational moment of terror when they found him at Teterboro Airport, as if he were back in that muddy field in Germany thirty years ago, and even now, in his own airplane with the cabin temperature set at 55 degrees, he was sweating.

He took off his jacket and felt something hard in the pocket, then sat back with a sigh. It was the diamond he had given Diana. He closed his eyes and tried not to think about her, but that was almost as hard as not thinking about Nicholas as he stepped out of his office window — perhaps even harder.

When Diana had heard the news, she simply stared at him, a single tear welling up in each eye.

'Who could have imagined . . .' Paul began, moving to comfort her.

Diana wiped her eyes. The expression on her face was enough to prevent Paul from touching her, or even from coming closer.

'Poor Nicholas,' he said in a low voice. 'This wasn't part of my plans. I am as shocked as you are.'

She stood. 'You got your revenge,' she said flatly.

'I didn't kill Nicholas. He killed himself.'

'I know. It's more efficient that way, isn't it?'

'Please, Diana . . . This will pass.'

'I'm sure it will. But without me. Understand, Paul — I didn't love Niki anymore, he destroyed that. But I can't live in your world. I don't want to play a role in the family tragedy — not even a supporting one.'

'It's over now.'

'No, it's not. You know better than that.'

He shrugged. 'Almost over.'

'That's not good enough, Paul. I'm tired of secrets. And tired of all this.' Diana waved her hand as if to indicate not just the suite, but the building, the airplane, a life lived behind a curtain of secrecy and protection. She noticed the ring on her finger, took it off and put it on the desk. 'I'm going now.'

'I love you,' Paul said.

'I know. I love you too. That's the sad part.'

'Then think it over.'

'I've thought it over.'

'You can't forgive me?'

'Oh, I can forgive you, Paul. That's easy. It's *myself* I can't forgive. You persuaded me to go on the yacht, you persuaded me to lie to Kane, and in the end you made me an accomplice to murder.'

'I didn't murder Nicholas.'

'Not with you own hands, no. You let it happen, that's all. Just the way Matthew let you father and mother die, Paul! I can't live that way. I'm sorry.'

'Try to understand,' Paul said, feeling himself crying for the first time in decades, but by the time he turned around, astonished at his own tears, she was already gone.

At least, he thought, she hadn't slammed the door, as most women would. The only woman I've ever met who has no taste for dramatics, he told himself, and now I've lost her. He wiped away his tears, but to his surprise he couldn't stop crying.

There is no logic to events, Paul thought. You can't escape them. He had spent a lifetime trying to control them, but in the end *they* control *you*.

He felt, despite himself a twinge of pity for Matthew de Grünwald. There must have been times when Matthew, too, had been tempted to stop, but by then events had gone too far — he was no longer in control ... A man with partners is never free, and Matthew's had included the Nazis and the Vatican, neither of which would have let him off the hook. So he went on until he confronted his conscience in a Swiss bank vault and chose money over family. As a result, Steven de Grünwald had walked to his death at Auschwitz, Betsy had been shot and now

Nicholas had killed himself . . . Too much money was at stake.

With a sigh Paul contemplated his own situation. Like Matthew, he had partners, obligations, money at stake. There was no stopping the machinery now that it had been set in motion. Nicholas was dead, but the situation that had killed him lived on, as planned; his company's stock was sagging, his debts were catastrophic — as the price of silver sank, Nicholas' futures would pull the whole structure down. It was time for a raid on the company. Even now, Paul's agents were buying up small packets of stock. The money he had made by selling silver short would be poured into the acquisition of Nicholas Greenwood's corporation — a very economical transaction, though not without its dangers. Still, Paul doubted that there would be any serious problems. Savage would handle the press, the SEC, the market. He always had.

A small light glowed at his elbow. He picked up the telephone quickly, happy to have his thoughts interrupted.

'Diana?' he asked, but then he realized that the voice on the other end of the line, though familiar, was that of another woman.

'I read about Niki,' the voice said.

'How are you, Louise?'

'How should I be? I read about you, but I never hear from you. And when I read about you, it's always some *Schweinerei*. After all, I'm your sister. You *could* call.'

'I know, I know. I've been very busy . . .'

'Apparently. It's probably just as well we didn't talk. I would have told you to drop this blood feud.'

'You already did. Many times.'

'And you should have listened. I have just as much reason to hate Matthew as you do . . .'

'Not quite.'

'Oh, all right. I didn't go to Auschwitz, but I had to marry that loathsome toad Rochefaucon, and it took me nearly twenty years to get an annulment.'

'Which I paid for.'

'I admit, I admit! I didn't say you're not generous, Palikam. I don't even mind if you get your revenge against Matthew. But poor Niki is another matter. Well, all right, it's happened. A tragedy, but what's new about tragedy in this family? Now, however, you should stop. Forget about the past, try to live some kind of normal life. You're a rich man. Be happy.'

'Not yet.'

'Idiot!' Louise said in the kind of harsh but affectionate tone she would have used to chastise a horse — indeed, Paul thought, she scarcely seemed to know the difference between people and horses, though she preferred the latter. 'That girl you brought down here,' Louise continued, 'what does she think of this?'

'That's over.'

'Ah. Well, I'm not surprised. Go get her back, if you can. I'm told she rides decently. And Paul: if you go ahead, and I implore you not to, be careful.'

'Of what? I've won, for what that's worth.'

Louise laughed. 'Not yet, dear brother, not yet. Matthew may still beat you.'

'You think he's smarter than I am?'

'No, no. You're smart, Palikam, and tough, too. But he's evil, you see, through and through, whereas you're only an amateur. You can do evil things, yes, but he has an evil heart. There's a difference. Take care of yourself.'

The line went dead and Paul replaced the receiver. He was fond of his sister, but the years had separated them and he was never quite sure now whether he was talking to the young girl he remembered or the leather-skinned professional horsewoman she had become. Marriage to Rochefaucon had killed whatever taste for men she might have had. Most people assumed she was a lesbian, because of her masculine voice, her physical strength and her habit of shouting orders like a cavalry sergeant-major, but in fact, the horror of living through Matthew's betrayal and her forced marriage to Rochefaucon had simply destroyed her ability to love people, whether men or women. She placed all her love in her horses, and to a lesser degree in her dogs, and Paul was perhaps the only creature on two legs of which she was fond.

Still, even if Louise was right, it was too late. Paul had planned this moment for years, faith in it had sustained him when he was young and poor, and even before that, when he was a slave laborer. He had anticipated that victory over Matthew de Grünwald would give him pleasure, but he no longer expected it to do so, and indeed felt none. Diana was right. He had built himself a prison, and now he was trapped in it. For the first time in years he felt tired. He had won the game at last and was suddenly bored and horrified by it, filled with self-disgust, aware that he was completing the last sordid move like a sleepwalker. In the end, poor Nicholas turned his triumph into ashes, Paul thought grimly.

He poured himself a cup of coffee and tried to catch a few hours' sleep before landing at Nice.

The Villa Azur was shuttered as Paul's car took him through a crowd of reporters drawn up like an unruly guard of honor in front of the gates.

At the front door of the villa, out of sight of the road, Boyce stood at the top of the steps. He was dressed in a black suit and looked like an undertaker.

'It's been a long time,' Boyce said, ushering Paul into the hallway. His manner and tone were friendly, as if he and Paul had shared some particularly happy experience together, but the halo of sweat around his forehead revealed that he still feared and hated Foster.

Paul did not look at Boyce. 'London, 1948,' he said crisply. 'How is he?'

'Very weak. He hired me not long after I came out of prison, you know.'

'I know.'

'Two years of prison! It's a long time, Foster.'

'That was the deal, Boyce. You got paid for it.'

'I saved your life, too.'

'You got paid for that as well. Where is he?'

'Resting upstairs.' Boyce led Foster up a wide marble staircase. The villa had been designed in the 1930s, when bronze gilt and mirror Art Deco was the current rage. No expense had been spared to create an interior that resembled Radio City Music Hall. A certain obsession with the unclothed female form was evident. Everywhere there were nudes, etched in mirror, carved in marble, sculptured in bronze lampstands and Lalique columns.

'I can't imagine why he agreed to see you,' Boyce said as they paused on the landing. 'He knows you were behind this. You might just as well have pushed Nicholas out the window with your own hands.' He knocked gently on a door, then pushed it open.

379

'Ah, no,' Paul said sadly, 'somebody else pushed Nicholas.'

'And who would that be? Meyerman? Or your friend Potter?'

Paul stepped into the darkened room, and as he closed the door behind him he said, 'His father, of course.'

'So it's you,' the guttural voice said. 'Stand away from the window so I can see you.'

In the dim light it was hard at first to see where the voice was coming from. Against one wall there stood a wheelchair, but it was empty, then Paul saw that there were two beds in the room, one a huge luxurious affair, the other a narrow hospital bed, of the kind that can be raised and lowered by electric motors. Matthew was in the latter, and as Paul turned toward him he pushed one of the control buttons, a motor hummed softly and he was propelled into a sitting position. 'What do you want with me?' he asked.

Paul stared at the hospital bed. Matthew seemed to have shrunk, as if there was nothing between the skin and the bones. The hand clutching the pushbutton controls for the bed was a mottled claw. Above the bed was Caravaggio's 'Boy Bitten by a Lizard,' the picture that Rademacher had once admired so much. Looking at it brought back a flood of memories, which Paul quickly repressed, though not before Matthew had noticed his change of expression.

'You know who I am,' Paul said. It was a statement, not a question.

Matthew coughed, fumbled in his bedclothes, found his glasses and carefully put them on. He stared at Paul for a moment, then removed them. 'You still look like your father,' he said. 'The eyes . . . I miss him.'

'You killed him.'

The old man paid no attention. 'I was very fond of your mother,' he said.

'That didn't save her.'

'No. I wanted to save her, but she was a woman of extraordinary virtue and courage . . . Well, you've had your revenge.'

'Why didn't you warn Nicholas?'

'Ah, poor Niki . . . He always wanted to have things his own way. Your dear father warned me about that. How could I tell him? The boy loved me. What should I have told him? That I left my brother to die? I lied to protect Niki. Is that so terrible?'

'It killed him.'

Matthew wheezed, then waved feebly. 'Don't play the moralist with me, my boy. You set out to destroy him. You succeeded. You will have to live with that, not me.'

'I hadn't intended his death.'

'I didn't intend your father's, either. Business is business. These things happen.' Matthew coughed slightly, then giggled, and it occurred to Paul that the old man might be senile. His eyes, however, seemed to have none of the bewildered, unfocused blankness so characteristic of senility — indeed, they fairly glistened with improbable good humor.

'Lately I haven't been well,' Matthew said. 'I left the business decisions to Niki — a mistake, as it turned out. One always hopes one's children . . . Ah well.'

'Nicholas was an amateur.'

'Yes, I agree. You've played your cards very well. I suppose you and your friends are going to move in for the kill now?'

Paul shrugged.

Matthew blew his nose on a piece of tissue and dropped it on the floor. 'You don't seem happy about it,' he said. 'Well a man with partners always has something to be unhappy about . . . I hear you're marrying Diana?'

'I don't think so.'

Matthew smirked. 'She was a little shocked, was she? That's the way it is with women, my boy. They don't understand business. Your mother didn't either . . . Oh, you've made your bed, soon you'll be lying in it. Like me. I lie here waiting to die, all alone except for Boyce. Take a close look, Pali. I am your future.'

'What happened to the letter you signed with my father?'

Matthew de Grünwald smiled. 'What letter?'

'You split the Grünwald interests between you before you left for Switzerland.'

'I don't remember anything about it. On top of everything else you want to be my heir as well? You know, you're just like your father. He was a romantic, too.' Matthew still pronounced 'was' with a *v*. In extreme old age his accent had thickened.

'I'm not a romantic.'

'A man who pursues revenge for thirty years has to be a romantic. That's a great mistake for a businessman. If you're always looking in the same direction, sooner or later you forget to look behind you. I was saying much the same thing to some friends of yours only a little while ago . . . In fact, they're still here.'

Matthew gave a small chuckle and pushed the button by his bed. The big double doors on the other side of the room opened, and as Paul turned his head he was able to see past Boyce that two men were standing in a light, airy room, looking like doctors who had just arrived for a consultation, their dark suits lugubrious against the white walls, the sunny windows and the Impressionist paintings.

One of them was a large man, smoking a cigar, wearing a three-piece suit with a heavy watch chain.

'Hello, Augustus,' Paul said as Biedermeyer raised his hand in an ironic greeting.

The other man came forward nervously, a curious expression on his face, like a combination of fear and triumph — and perhaps even remorse. 'Hello, Paul,' Savage said, holding out his hand, and suddenly Foster knew he had been stabbed in the back.

'He had self-control, all right,' Savage said. 'No doubt about it.'

'He bit off more than he could chew, that's all.'

'The trouble with Foster is that he's not really a businessman. There wasn't a business reason for him to go after Nick Greenwood the way he did. It was personal. He lost the confidence of his own board.'

'Well, you can't blame them. He didn't fill them in. They heard about the commodity speculations, the vendetta with Greenwood, so they worried. Foster always figured he'd bought them, but you know what directors are like — they still have to be stroked.'

Savage nodded. Undermining the board's confidence in Foster had not been difficult, since most of them were aware of his contempt and afraid of his taste for conspiracy. The two men were standing on the terrace of the Villa Azur, looking out over their host's expensive rocks, from which beautiful girls had once dived nude, in the days when old Greenwood was able to enjoy such things. 'He'll still be a rich man,' Savage said. 'All he's lost is control of the company.'

'Of course, he can't be happy about that,' Biedermeyer said.

'Who cares?' Savage said, 'He's through.'

'They handled the press nicely,' David Star said between mouthfuls. He was lunching with Irving Kane and Diana Beaumont in the Grill Room of the Four Seasons, at a semicircular banquette appropriate to his status as a man who has just escaped from a takeover. Kane was glum. A late riser, he had asked for scrambled eggs and coffee and been refused, and after a vociferous and unsuccessful protest, was persuaded, only with much difficulty, to order a chopped steak.

'They would have made eggs for Gore Vidal or Norman Mailer,' he complained, picking at his food. 'Foster got off easy.'

'Nobody wanted a scandal. Not after Nick Greenwood's death. Everybody thought Foster had gone too far.'

Kane shrugged and looked around the room to see if there was anybody worth table-hopping with. 'Foster could have fought back,' he said. 'He's got more balls than Biedermeyer or Savage, after all. No, the truth is, I think he just gave up. I don't know why, do you, Diana?'

Diana stared at her plate and shook her head. She felt sick, as she had for days.

'Well, if you don't know why, I guess nobody does,' Kane said, waving in the direction of a woman he had mistaken for Jackie Onassis.

He chewed on an ice cube thoughtfully. 'Frankly,' he said, 'Foster's board didn't have a choice. It's a question of image. Once Nick jumped out that window, the only way to keep the company was to throw Foster overboard. Guys like Foster, they go up fast, they come down quicker. The bankers pick up the pieces. What surprises me more is Nick Greenwood's killing himself. There's a lot of talk he didn't walk out that window on his own steam . . . People are saying maybe Foster had him pushed.'

Star shook his head. 'I don't believe that,' he said. 'Remember the guy at United Brands who jumped in his overcoat and hat, carrying his briefcase, too. It was still in his hand when he landed.'

'Sure,' Kane conceded, 'but that guy wasn't like Nick. He was an old guy. Nick was a healthy young man, with all the money and broads in the world . . .'

'You're not eating, Diana,' Star said. 'I know all this is difficult for you, but you've got to keep your strength up. We've got a book to sell.'

'I'm not hungry.'

'Then you won't mind if I take a bit of your salad? From what I hear on the street, Greenwood and Biedermeyer are joining forces to take over Foster's company. Savage is going to be chairman.'

'If the SEC okays it.'

'Oh, the SEC will roll over and let Biedermeyer tickle its belly. The Feds hated Foster. He was a troublemaker. But Biedermeyer's a different story. Everybody trusts a brewer. He owns a baseball team, he wears an American flag lapel pin, he plays golf at Burning Tree, his daughter is a sex symbol, there's even talk of making him Ambassador to the Court of St. James's.'

'He's a pompous fuck.'

'Yes . . . but smart.'

'What's Foster going to do now?' Kane asked Diana.

She shook her head. 'I don't know. I haven't heard from him.'

Kane nodded. 'I hear they were generous with him, on the condition he got out of the country fast. Of course, he's still a rich man. He can live like a king — if he doesn't mind doing it in Guatemala.'

'It's quite a fall,' Star said, waving for the dessert tray. 'It's hard to imagine what could make a man as rich as Foster risk it all like that. He hardly even knew poor Nick, did he, Diana?'

Diana seemed lost in thought, her plate untouched in front of her. 'No,' she said, 'he wasn't close to Niki at all. But it was bound to end the way it did.'

Before Star could ask her why, she stood up, took her handbag and was gone.

'What did she mean by that?' he asked Kane.

Kane pushed his plate away from him. 'Hell,' he said, 'you got to figure she slept with both of them. Women hate losing a guy, even when they don't want him anymore.'

'I thought she and Foster had broken up.'

'You don't understand broads, Star. They can break up but they never *give* up. Broads don't let go. Not even when a guy is dead.'

'Foster isn't dead. He's in disgrace.'

'Same thing. For a guy in his position.'

In Los Angeles, Aaron Diamond was already up and about, after the first of his ritual four showers a day. Swaddled in a bathrobe, he picked at his sliced papaya, reading the Los Angeles *Times* through a magnifying glass. 'Get me Diana Beaumont,' he said to his secretary. 'Try the Four Seasons.'

There was a pause and she looked up from her desk. 'They say she left there, Mr. Diamond.'

'Then try her at the office or at home, for Chrissake. Just *find* her, that's what I pay you for! And make a note: my goddamn papaya isn't ripe again.'

'You see the papers?' he said into the telephone a few minutes later.

'I saw them, Aaron,' Diana said.

'I'm sorry, kid. It's a lousy deal. Though it's going to be terrific publicity for Irving's book, I got to say that.'

'I just saw him at lunch.'

'Where's Foster? The Feds have a warrant out for him.'

'That can't be true, Aaron.'

'That's what I heard. He's got a lot of enemies. I was him, I'd get the hell out before they got guys looking for him at the airports. You speak to him, pass the message on, okay?'

'I don't imagine I'll be speaking to him, Aaron, but why the concern?'

'He's a man of his word, that's why. He tipped me off about the collapse of silver just in time. He promised and he delivered. You can't ask more of a guy than that.'

'He's not very popular in New York today. They're writing about him as if he were Ivar Kreuger.'

'So he took a tumble? So what? He's a young man, he'll find something else. How are *you* holding up, kid?'

'You're the first person who's asked, Aaron.'

'I figured. What are you going to do now?'

'Work. Maybe I should take David Star up on his offer.'

'Don't be a *shmuck*. You fly out here, we'll have a

weekend in Palm Springs or Vegas. In the meantime, if Foster calls, you tell him what I said.'

'He's not going to call, Aaron.'

'A hundred bucks says you're wrong,' Diamond said, switching to another line.

21

In Guatemala the temperature had already reached 90 degrees by eight in the morning and the humidity was stifling. The big villa by the sea shimmered in the heat, its white walls in stark contrast to the jungle behind it.

There were no houses nearby. The rutted, dusty road ran straight through the jungle to intersect the main highway — two lanes of dilapidated, decaying concrete, in which the potholes served as mud baths for pigs during the rainy season. A mile away, invisible from the house, a small army of laborers worked on the site of a new resort hotel. Fifty miles inland, deep in the jungle, a much larger army worked to complete the huge industrial complex that Foster had created, its towering chimneys and immense silver walls rising hundreds of feet above the trees, the country's only four-lane highways, built by Foster, connecting it to the seacoast. Flames and steam rose, lighting the jungle at night, the parrots and monkeys screeched as helicopters landed on the brightly lit landing pad — more electricity was produced here than in the rest of the country and in its neighboring republics combined.

Whatever else Paul had lost, he kept this. Guatemala had always been a personal obsession, shared neither by Savage nor by the rest of the board; in fact it had been Foster's passionate interest in his Guatemalan project that first aroused doubts about his common sense. It was far away; it was risky; it involved questions of politics, human rights, ecology; it was, as one doubter put it succinctly, 'hard to sell to Wall Street.'

Paul had gone ahead, with his usual obstinacy, and now he was stuck with it. Biedermeyer, as spokesman for the new controlling group, had been happy enough to spin off Guatemala as the price for Paul's early departure and discretion.

The house itself was handsome, even luxurious, built with an eye to the use of native materials. The rooms were so big, light and airy that it was sometimes even possible to do without the air conditioning. Designed by a student of Frank Lloyd Wright's, the house resembled, from some angles, a piece of Mayan architecture, with terraces, steps, overhanging stone balconies and gardens in unusual places, so that it was difficult from the outside to tell where the rooms were inside. A small waterfall had been built into the façade, which had been lavishly praised by architectural critics, but it kept Paul awake at night.

'I find it difficult to sleep here,' he told Pifi Villada.

'The waterfall? Yes, it makes one want to get up and piss in the middle of the night. Why not turn it off?'

'I tried that. It's an integral part of the system, unfortunately. Turn off the waterfall and you can't flush the toilets or take a bath. I should have had Philip Johnson build me a house. It would have been a glass cube, but quiet.'

The two men were sitting on an odd-shaped terrace, carved out of limestone and planted with flowering shrubs. Before them a glass-topped table was laid for breakfast. Behind them there was an impenetrable wall of jungle, alive with the screech of parrots; in front of them the sea stretched to the horizon, flat, empty and calm. The water was so warm that you could swim for hours, except for the fact that it was shark-infested.

'Colonel Perez-Bernsdorf expressed his sympathy and sent you his personal greetings. "Our land is your land," he asked me to say to you.'

'For a price.'

'Oh, of course, that goes without saying. But there's no question of extradition. The colonel made it clear that you're an honored guest — though he'd prefer you to keep a low profile for a while. He doesn't want any difficulties with the American ambassador.'

'How much does the colonel want?'

'A million Swiss francs.'

'That's not too bad.'

'No. Of course, it's only a first installment, you understand. He has quite a large family, and we'll have to find jobs for them.'

'Give them jobs, but for God's sake don't let them do anything.'

'That shouldn't be difficult. Most of them have government jobs already. I think you can live here very quietly. The press will be restrained — you can rely on Perez-Bernsdorf for that.'

Paul nodded. In his dark suit and dark glasses he seemed curiously out of place against the lush background.

'You passed through New York?' he asked Villada.

'Yes. You've seen the press?'

'It's all been sent to me. I haven't looked.'

'You should.'

'What for? I could have fought back. I should have. It wasn't Greenwood who defeated me, you know. Oh, I was outsmarted for a moment, I can't deny it, but I could have turned the situation around . . . Suddenly, I didn't care. It was a very strange feeling. I had it in the war, once, on the train to Auschwitz. I felt helpless, it seemed easier to simply let things happen. Of course those who felt that way died. That's what happened to my father. Well, I recovered my wits at Auschwitz, and I suppose I'll eventually recover my wits here. But for the moment, I'm not interested in reading about what happened.'

'All the same, it's quite a story. Front-page news. There's a House investigation, a Senate committee, an SEC inquiry, subpoenas everywhere. Though I don't suppose Perez-Bernsdorf will let them try to serve you with a subpoena here . . . Irving Kane did a long piece for *Newsweek* called "The Rise and Fall of a Billionaire." There's talk of making it into a movie for television, but I suppose you could stop that.'

'I suppose so. Though, really, I don't care. Did you see Diana?'

'No. I didn't think it was wise to stay too long.'

'I had hoped she would call.'

'It's been a difficult time for her, you know. Poor Niki's death, then all the publicity. I hear she's seeing a lot of David Star.'

'I suppose so.'

'She might appreciate a call from you, Paul.'

'It's possible. One hesitates, in my position, to sound weak. After all, I am no longer Paul Foster the

389

entrepreneur, I am merely Paul Foster the exile.'

Villada shook his head impatiently. 'You know, Paul,' he said after a pause, 'that might be an advantage.'

The shimmering heat haze burned off every day by eleven, but long before that, Diana had stretched out by the pool. She was a serious sun-worshiper and never felt that a moment was wasted so long as she was in the sun. Early in the morning, right after breakfast, she spread a towel on the marble border of the pool, took off her bikini top and lay down. Once an hour she would swim a few laps, put more oil on and start the process all over again. The servants occasionally came out to stare in amazement, since they spent most of their lives trying to escape from the sun, and the maids gathered on the terraces when they had nothing to do, giggling politely.

At the edge of the pool Paul occupied himself with his gardening. He had chosen to specialize in vegetables rather than flowers, and a radiotelephone connected him to the vast fields inland, where modern farm machinery was being used to cultivate sugar beets and where the Indians labored to install irrigation pipes. Occasionally he would fly over his fields in a helicopter, accompanied by an agronomist. In the end, he told himself, the land was the one thing you could count on.

'Why don't you relax?' Diana called to him.

He put down the documents he was reading, rose, stretched, examined the temperature of the pool. He still wore his dark suit. He was not about to become a beachcomber.

'I'm relaxed,' he said, 'now that you're here.'

'Then stop working for a few minutes.'

'There's so much to do.'

'Paul, you already seem to own most of this country.'

'It's a small country.'

'I don't care. You've got a beautiful house, more money than you can spend in a lifetime . . . What more do you want?'

'You.'

'I'm here.'

'But are you staying?'

'That depends.'

'On what?'

'On whether you're prepared to lead a normal life.'

'Normal? What is normal? I'm an exile.'

'There are plenty of countries you can go to. Besides, that's not what I mean. I came here because I missed you. But I won't stay here if you're planning a comeback. You had your revenge, Paul. It wasn't worth it and it backfired. Forget about the past. It's dead and buried.'

Paul shaded his eyes and glanced out toward the sea. It was flat, empty, shimmering with heat. Unlike the Mediterranean, it promised no relief. Bathing in it was like sitting in a hot salty bath. 'I'm not sure that I'm cut out for a life of leisure,' he said.

'Nor am I, but you could give it a try. You've done everything else in your life. You could try doing nothing for a while. You once told me happiness is a boring ambition. It isn't, you know.'

'I'll sleep on it,' Paul said. 'It doesn't sound like too bad a deal.'

'It's the best deal you've ever been offered. Would you rub some lotion on my back?'

Paul sat down in the sun and squeezed lotion onto the palm of his hand. He gently massaged Diana's back and for a moment he almost seemed relaxed. 'You know what's needed here?' he asked, staring out to sea.

'Mm?'

'A free-trade zone. What do they have here in abundance? Cheap labor. All one has to do is ship components, pieces, whatever, down here, assemble them and ship them back to be completed in the United States. There's a fortune to be made.'

'You're scheming again.'

Paul laughed, leaned over and kissed her. 'Only a little bit,' he said. 'It's in the blood.'

Biedermeyer was nervous. Biedermeyer was irritable. Everything had fallen into Biedermeyer's lap, but he itched. He and Savage stared at each other across the table in the corporate dining room, over their chef's salads and breadsticks (both were on a diet), smelling each other's fear.

'I hear Foster is getting married,' Savage said.

'I heard that too.'

'I didn't think he was the marrying kind.'

391

'Nobody is. Everybody does it, anyway. He's made quite a splash in Guatemala. People are talking big numbers.'

'We shouldn't have given him Guatemala.'

'Don't tell me what we shouldn't have done. Tell me what we do next. That's what you're paid for.'

'The stock isn't moving. The natives are restless.'

'*I'm* restless, for Chrissake! Somebody's out there buying stock. I can smell trouble. What's that son of a bitch Meyerman doing?'

'They say he's traveling.'

'I don't like it. Where are the fucking rolls, for God's sake?'

'You asked the waiter to take them away.'

'Well, tell him to bring them back!' Biedermeyer shouted, but then he saw the expression on Savage's face and rang the bell himself. If Savage could betray Foster, he could betray Biedermeyer.

It's a mistake to push a guy too hard when you need him, Biedermeyer warned himself.

The bulky figure in the dark double-breasted suit got out of the limousine, walked under the waterfall and paused for breath at the first level of the terraces.

'*Servus, Pali,*' Lord Meyerman said, as affable as ever.

From below, Crisp could be heard, seeing to Lord Meyerman's luggage in his vestigial Spanish. Crisp was the kind of servant who can master enough of any language to cope with the necessities of his master's life. Early on in his career, as a soldier-servant, he acquired a working knowledge of Swahili, Urdu and Pushtu; in Foster's service, he had picked up French and German. Spanish presented him with no difficulties.

'An admirable chap,' Meyerman said, sitting down next to Paul. Meyerman dabbed at his face with a silk handkerchief.

'Indispensable.'

'Has he adjusted to the marriage? Servants are so often jealous.'

'He adores Diana.'

'And how have *you* adjusted?'

'As you see, I am relaxed, happy — marriage suits me. Diana is just changing. She'll be down in a moment.'

'You've heard the news? Matthew Greenwood is dead.'

'I heard.'

'I hear other things, too, Paul. Poor Biedermeyer is beside himself. He controls three giant companies, but he feels *vulnerable*.'

'He should. He's not up to the job.'

'No. That's what people are beginning to say. He could be toppled, my dear. And Savage along with him.'

'It would take a lot of money.'

'My dear boy, that's not a problem! I've just come back from the Middle East. My friends in Riyadh and Abu Dhabi are *most* interested. Capital is no obstacle. It's coming out of their ears, frankly. What is needed is somebody with *credibility* to take the lead. Your name would make all the difference — Ah, Diana! As ravishing as ever!'

Meyerman rose, kissed Diana's hand, then dropped back into his chair again, saying, 'He looks well, my dear.'

'He is. But restless.'

'It's hard *not* to be restless in Guatemala,' Meyerman said, fanning himself and giving the palm trees a glance of distaste.

'There are beautiful ruins.'

'Yes, yes . . . Fascinating, I'm sure.' Meyerman stared out to sea. 'Before I forget,' he said, 'I brought you a wedding present.' He reached into his jacket pocket, pulled out an envelope, hesitated for a moment as if he couldn't decide whom to hand it to, then offered it to Diana.

She tore it open and pulled out a stained piece of writing paper. Unfolding it, she struggled for a moment to read the cramped handwriting, but it was in German. At the top it was dated October 8, 1944, and the numbers '50 percent' appeared several times in the text. At the bottom of the page were two signatures, both with the same last name, Grünwald. Below them, in precise, neat handwriting and black ink, were a few lines of witness that read:

> Zum Zeugnis dessen
> G. Manfred von Rademacher
> SS Stf. und Oberst
> bei OB. RSHA, Ungarn

The same hand had written across the top, '*Existiert nur ein Exemplar*,' which Diana assumed was a verification that no signed copy existed besides this one.

She passed it to Paul, who read it without comment.

'Half of Grünwald's assets are yours,' Meyerman said. 'That gives you a nice position for a takeover. With that letter in your pocket and my friends in the Middle East behind you, you can come back. Nobody could stand in your way!'

'Where did you get it?'

'Boyce brought it to me.'

'How much did he want for it?'

'Does it matter? You once stole twenty thousand dollars from your father's safe for me. I owe you my life. Even if the letter cost me a million dollars, it would be cheap at the price.'

Paul held the paper in his hand and looked at Diana.

'What would you like me to do?' he asked.

She looked into his eyes, her face expressionless. 'I'd like you to choose,' she said.

'A choice between the past and the future, between death and life ... That's an easy choice to make. I've made it before.'

'Surely there's some kind of compromise you can make, between the two of you,' Meyerman said. 'There's a great deal involved here. Billions of dollars!'

'I don't think there's any compromise possible here this time,' Paul said evenly as he looked at Diana, and taking a match from a silver box on the table in front of him, he lit it.

'My dear boy,' Meyerman said in a hushed voice. 'You can't do it!'

'Why not?'

'It's your claim to three or four billion dollars!'

Paul touched the match to the paper. It blackened, then burned. He held it as long as he could, then blew the fragments out to sea.

Diana stood up, came over to Paul and kissed him.

'Let the dead remain buried,' Paul said. 'The war is over.'

'It's been over for thirty years.'

'It wasn't for me. Now it is.'

In the garden below, a child walked stiffly toward them, helped by a nurse in flowing white.

Meyerman raised an eyebrow.

'It's my son,' Diana said.

'Ah,' Meyerman said with a sigh. 'Niki's boy. Another generation of Grünwalds . . .'

'No.' Paul shook his head. 'I plan to adopt him. There have been enough Grünwalds. His name will be Foster. He's entitled to a clean slate. We'll have dinner soon; you'll meet him. A very nice boy. The fish is excellent here, by the way. We have some caviar, too. Crisp had it flown down on yesterday's plane.'

'Ah,' Meyerman said, 'there's a lot to be said for money.'

'Oh, yes,' Paul agreed. 'But one has to know when to stop.'

THE END

THE MAN FROM ST PETERSBURG
by Ken Follett

AS LONDON SOCIETY WALTZED TO THE BRINK OF THE GREAT WAR, AN IRON-WILLED FANATIC RELENTLESSLY PURSUED HIS PRINCELY QUARRY . . .

In the summer of 1914, at the British government initiated Anglo-Russian talks to counter the threat of German aggression, a fanatical Russian assassin arrived in London . . .

His name was Feliks. He was an anarchist, pledged to prevent the deaths of thousands of young Russians in a futile war – prepared to kill in order to stop the treaty from being signed . . .

But as Feliks closed in on his victim, he met the woman he had loved – and lost – years ago in St Petersburg . . .

0 552 12180 0   £1.75

SOPHIE'S CHOICE
by William Styron

"The most haunting and powerful novel I've read this year." Daily Express

William Styron's narrative of artfully sustained suspense takes us back to pre-war Poland, to Auschwitz, through a past strewn with death that Sophie alone survived – until, at the core of this electrifying story, we reach the essence of Sophie's terrible secret – the choice she had to make.

"A novel of stunning audacity and imaginative range." New Statesman

0 552 11610 6   £2.50

THE BROKER
by Harold Q Masur

Mike Ryan, a hard-driving, ambitious investment banker, has fought his way up to become chief executive of Anson Gregorious' Wall Street broking company. Now he is poised to bring off the biggest coup of his career – but in order to achieve it he is forced to commit Gregorious and its entire resources to a gamble that could bring the firm – and his career-crashing about his ears.

0 552 12123 1   £1.75

PRINCESS DAISY
by Judith Krantz

She was born Princess Marguerite Alexandrovna Valensky. But everyone called her Daisy. She was a blonde beauty living in a world of aristocrats and countless wealth. Her father was a prince, a Russian nobleman. Her mother was an American movie goddess. Men desired her. Women envied her. Daisy's life was a fairytale filled with parties and balls, priceless jewels, money and love. Then, suddenly, the fairytale ended. And Princess Daisy had to start again, with nothing. Except the secret she guarded from the day she was born.

0 552 11660 2   £1.75

THE ATTORNEY
by Harold Q Masur

Dolly Wayne lay dead: strangled and mutilated. Ken Sheridan, her daughter's law-student boyfriend, stands accused of her murder . . .

Paul Slater, the lawyer for the defence, faces a vital challenge. He is defending not only a young man with his future in jeopardy, but a family with whom he is deeply involved . . .

0 552 10174 5   £1.75

A SELECTED LIST OF FINE NOVELS
AVAILABLE FROM CORGI

While every effort is made to keep prices low, it is sometimes necessary to increase prices at short notice. Corgi Books reserve the right to show new retail prices on covers which may differ from those previously advertised in the text or elsewhere.

The prices shown below were correct at the time of going to press.

ORDER FORM

All these books are available at your book shop or newsagent, or can be ordered direct from the publisher. Just tick the titles you want and fill in the form below.

CORGI BOOKS, Cash Sales Department, P.O. Box 11, Falmouth, Cornwall.

Please send cheque or postal order, no currency.

Please allow cost of book(s) plus the following for postage and packing:

U.K. Customers—Allow 45p for the first book, 20p for the second book and 14p for each additional book ordered, to a maximum charge of £1.63.

B.F.P.O. and Eire—Allow 45p for the first book, 20p for the second book plus 14p per copy for the next 7 books, thereafter 8p per book.

Overseas Customers—Allow 75p for the first book and 21p per copy for each additional book.

NAME (Block Letters) ....

ADDRESS ....

....